ISLAND TIME

NOELLE EDWARDS

ISLAND TIME

This is a first edition.

Contributions by Nina Ritter
Editing by English Proper Editing Services
Cover art and design by Nina Ritter
Map design by Noelle Edwards and Nina Ritter

ISBN 979-8-9945312-2-8

Printed in the United States of America.

For Nina -
Happy birthday.

CONTENT WARNING

Island Time is a survival thriller containing depictions of death, substance abuse, and other triggers that may be harmful to some readers. Your mental health is my top priority; that being said, please carefully look over the list of triggers below before you read.

Traumatic event (natural disaster)

Violence/Physical assault

Suicide

Dead/decomposing bodies

Drugs/drug use

Medication overdose

Alcohol consumption

Blood/gore

Sex and sexual language

"There are some things you can only learn in a storm."

- Joel Osteen

DAY ONE

10:24 A.M.

Ten minutes go by a lot faster than you'd think.

It's 10:24 when I catch sight of the analog clock hanging on the wall. It's a beautiful clock: a colorful, vibrant, stained-glass image of a lighthouse at sunset. I worry about it falling and shattering as I watch the second hand tick its way further around the circle. It's too pretty to break into pieces. Too pretty for all of us to be trusted anywhere near it.

Ocean mist sprays against the window beside the clock, drawing my eyes to the turquoise water. It looks similar to the ocean I see at home in South Carolina, but it's worlds away. It's warmer, clearer. More unwilling to be polluted by the cigarette butts and empty beer cans my friends will undoubtedly throw its way.

The boat smells like fish and stale liquor, but I don't *hate* it. It reminds me of this hibachi restaurant me and the girls went to every Friday night to get drunk on cheap mai tais before we turned twenty-one. We always sat by the sushi bar because the waiter working those tables never carded us.

Fresh air has been hard to come by today, but at least the boat is nice. I don't want to call it a *yacht* per se, but it's pretty big—big enough for all eighteen of us to fit comfortably. James claims his family doesn't use it very much, but it's all nice and furnished, like someone should be living here. James's family only really uses it when they're traveling from Miami to a little private island in the Bahamas, where they own a house. That's where we're headed today.

I'm exhausted, and the pre-mixed margarita bottle Aaron keeps handing me isn't helping. We were all up at three to make our flight from Connecticut to Miami that landed at eight this morning, where we went straight to the marina. I thought I'd get to nap on the boat, but I should've known better, given who I'm with.

“Flynn Rider!” Erin shouts, clutching Aaron's margarita bottle.

“Popeye,” Ava says with a blush.

“Okay, hear me out—Cap’n Crunch,” Leah says.

James rolls his eyes at her. “That's your daddy issues talking.”

“Maybe, but there's still something about him that really gets me—”

“No wonder you take so long in the cereal aisle,” Madison comments. Leah, her best friend, ignores her and plucks the joint from between her fingers before taking a puff. “These are shit choices. I'm going with Prince Eric.”

“Very original,” Aaron teases. “There's only one right answer for me: Daphne from *Scooby-Doo.*”

I lean in close to Nick at my left. “What's everyone talking about? I zoned out.”

“Nani from *Lilo and Stitch!*” Nick chimes in. I wince at the loudness of his voice and pull away, right as he turns to grin at me. “We're talking about the sexiest cartoon characters. Nani's a good one, don't you think?”

From his other side, his girlfriend, Danielle, throws an arm around his shoulders. “It's because she kind of looks like me,” she explains to me. “Nick's *such* a girlfriend guy, right?”

I open my mouth to reply, but someone interrupts me: “What about you, Sadie?”

I follow the sound of the voice—the snobby, disinterested tone poorly masked by fake politeness and sickening sweetness—and find Madison watching me from her seat across the room, nestled between Leah and James. She picks at her manicured nails while she raises an eyebrow at me, making it clear she couldn't care less about my response. She's only trying to make me feel like I'm a part of things, which I guess would be nice if it wasn't so damn obvious.

She knows how badly I want it. The random, late-night trips to get cheap burgers and milkshakes minutes before the restaurant closes, the trips into the city for parades and special events that nobody else seems to know about. You'll find some of them there, but not all of us. I want that type of friendship desperately, but I haven't earned my place, and Madison knows it—maybe the others do, too.

My eyes find the clock again, a momentary refuge from my discomfort. It's 10:26 now, and the second hand is ticking over the rocky shoreline along the bottom.

“If I'm being honest,” I say, “I've always had a thing for General Shang.”

“Interesting choice.” James smiles at me, making me blush, before turning to the side. His face darkens as he jumps to his feet. “Hey! What's the matter with you? Do you have any idea how expensive that is?”

Eli freezes midway through ashing a cigarette on an antique table. He wipes the ashes onto the floor, muttering an apology, and spits on the wood to try rubbing the stain away.

"You do anything like that at the house, you're sleeping outside," James tells him, then turns to the rest of us. "My grandparents were nice enough to let me bring all of you here. They've got nice shit at the house, and they'll kill me if anything is damaged. Unless you want to pay for repairs, don't do anything stupid."

I know he's serious, but I can also see how some of the others just snort and chuckle in response. He's smiling when he says it, his voice calm, and he has the same look in his eyes that he did a few months ago when we came across an abandoned asylum and decided to explore it—the look of someone who's ready for an adventure, consequences be damned.

"Don't worry, man," Brett says, setting a hulking hand on James's shoulder. "It's gonna be great. We'll all be on our best behavior."

The second James starts to respond, Zeke stands up to show Reid something on his phone. Suddenly the boat lurches, and down goes Zeke. His phone slides across the floor, and the bottle of Jameson in his other hand falls and shatters. Erin rushes to help him while he groans, half of the group starts cackling at him, and the others—notably James, Brett, and Madison—don't waste any time before they're hollering at him. Only me and Henry get up to find towels and a trashcan so we can pick up the glass and mop up the liquor.

After Zeke is settled back down, snapping at the others for yelling at him over an accident, everyone takes a second to either cool off or stop laughing. It's not long before they've all moved on: Eli asks about which of our college professors we think is the kinkiest behind closed doors, and it takes about ten seconds for the group to start hollering again, gesturing with liquor bottles and shouting over each other like it's the most important debate of their lives.

Henry meets my eyes as he tosses a few pieces of glass into the trashcan I'm holding. I don't know him well, but I presume to know what he's thinking, because I'm thinking the same thing: *At least they're not fighting.* A small laugh escapes me, making him smile, and I listen to the debate in silence while kneeling in a pool of whiskey mixed with Zeke's backwash.

By the time we sit back down, three towels are spread over the floor, soaking up whatever remains of Zeke's mishap, and it doesn't look like there's any glass left. I'm not surprised when I see Zeke open another bottle, taking a large sip before washing it down with a Coke in his other hand.

Everyone knows Zeke's a liability around anything—or anyone—of value, but I guess that's part of his charm. He's the only person here who's *mostly* unpredictable; I mean, we can always count on him to do something stupid, but what that stupid thing might be…It's anyone's guess, really. There's something of a method to the madness amongst this friend group, and Zeke's role is to keep everyone on our toes. You'd think that some of us would find his behavior annoying, especially the ones with easily breakable fake nails or Rolexes slapped on their wrists, but it's hard to stay mad at him when he's always making a fool out of himself.

I glance at the clock again. I'm right on time to watch the second hand cross the threshold, bringing us to 10:30 on the dot.

James gets up to leave, drawing my eyes from the clock, and I can't stop myself from watching him go. He smiles as he passes me, his green eyes sparkling against the sunlight peeking through the windows. He runs a hand through his wavy, dark blond hair, his toned arms bulging with the movement. He looks like a California surfer boy with his hair and that tanned skin—not my usual type, but there's something about him that makes me…curious.

I catch Aaron smirking at me from across the room. A few years ago, I would've flushed at the attention, embarrassed to be caught looking at James like that. Now I just roll my eyes. He first noticed it sophomore year at a party, and instead of teasing me as I expected, he'd pulled me aside and told me to be careful: *Don't get too caught up on James.*

It sounded more like a warning than a joke, but I'd just laughed it off at the time, blaming the tequila. I'd told him it wasn't a big deal—I wasn't looking for anything. He didn't look convinced, but he let it go.

Aaron knows James's type as well as I do. The thought of James ever looking twice at someone like me still strikes me as a little absurd. We'd laughed about it back then—the way you do when something feels safer as a joke than a possibility—and somewhere in there, we became friends; real ones. He tries to look out for me in his own messy, silly way, and I love him for it. I probably wouldn't even be on this trip without him.

James comes back, his hair tousled by the wind. "All right, guys. Listen up. We're half an hour out—" Whooping and cheering interrupts him, making him grin, "—and we have to go over some ground rules before we get there. First thing's first: the boat is heading right back to Miami after we get dropped off. My parents are flying down tomorrow, and they're taking the boat to Aruba for a wedding. They'll pick us up at the end of the week. Basically, that means make sure you leave with everything you brought onboard. If I see a single bottle, can, butt, or joint lying around—"

"—we'll be sleeping outside. Got it." Joe raises an eyebrow. "Anything else?"

"Most of you know this already, but the house is on a private section of the island," James continues. "We have a few neighbors, but they usually mind their own business. There are shops and markets and all of that on the other side of the island, but it's a hike. We have Grandpa's car, but I'm not letting any of you idiots drive that thing. You want to go and explore, I'll drive, or you can take the bikes. And for the love of God, don't bring anyone back to the house. We're already pushing it as it is. I told my grandparents there'd only be ten of us, and my parents were nice enough to lie for us, so let's not have even more people at the house."

"And don't forget we have to buddy-up for rooms." Brett's voice rings out next. I'm not surprised he's acting like this is his house, too—he's James's best friend, so he's been coming here for half of his life. "There are six rooms and eighteen of us. Some of us will have to take couches or the floor."

James nods. "Everyone got it?"

We all echo our confirmation, but while everyone's still muttering, Eli springs up from his chair and holds two six packs over his head as he rushes to the middle of the room, demanding our undivided attention.

"It's spring break, motherfuckers! Let's fucking *go!*"

Reid holds up a fifth of vodka. "Our last one!"

Everyone clinks their drinks together, laughing and whooping before taking swigs, but my hands are empty. Henry doesn't hesitate to hand me his beer after he drinks from it. I flash him a grateful smile, cheers with Nick and Dani, and take a small sip before handing it back to Henry.

As the hoppy IPA tickles my tongue, Reid's voice replays in my head: *Our last one.*

Our last spring break before everything changes—before moments like these transform into memories we'll look back on for the rest of our lives, wishing they hadn't gone by so fast.

The lighthouse tells me it's 10:34 now. If ten minutes could go by so quickly, I think I know what to expect from the next eight days: a vacation gone in the blink of an eye, days blurred together under a veil of mindless conversation fueled by a frenzy of alcohol and drugs only college kids can get away with.

11:10 A.M.

The first thing you do when you visit a tropical paradise is admire the scenery, right? Nope. Not here. We admired the island from a distance—enormous palm trees, clear water, pure white sand—while the boat inched closer. But from the second we docked, the only thing any of us have paid attention to is the house.

The dock's on the property, so all we have to do is cross the beach to get to the house. It reminds me of home in a way: a small community with beautiful, overpriced houses all along the coast. My house isn't high up on a hill like James's, but I imagine the view of the ocean and the surrounding homes isn't so different.

None of us except for James and a select few others move an inch when we get to the edge of the dock. Pictures of James's family vacation home don't do it justice. This place is massive: three stories, beige and white coloring, with countless balconies and perfect landscaping. I can see a really nice staircase that leads from the house directly onto the beach, handrails and everything—which will come in handy when we're all plastered out of our minds.

James's section of the beach is pretty empty other than a motorboat tied up at the dock. We're right on the coast at the edge of the island, so there are only neighbors on one side of the house. They're still pretty far from us, but I can see a few chairs and umbrellas down the beach, in front of houses that are nowhere near as extravagant as this one.

After taking it all in for a second, we ditch our shoes and follow James toward the house. We're all breathless by the time we climb the stairs with our luggage, but I ignore my burning muscles when I see the house up close. There's a huge deck with a firepit, tall torches, and lounge chairs. James says the shed off to the side is for the gardener, but there's another shed on the beach where the family keeps their beach gear and water sports equipment.

We follow a stone walkway to the front of the house, surrounded by tropical flowers and lizards. The front is even crazier: there's a circular driveway with a marble fountain and a small lawn in the middle of the pavement, and a winding road leads from the driveway to what I assume is the main road. It looks like a movie set—like people shouldn't be living here, because it's all too perfect.

That'll change within a day or so.

James unlocks the house using a keypad by the front door. The second we walk inside, the air conditioning whacks me in the face, soothing the sweat clinging to my skin from the humid air. We're only in the entryway, but I can already understand why James is so adamant that we're careful here: this place screams money in every way, from the crystal chandelier over our heads, to the extravagant paintings on the walls, to the furniture that looks like it spent most of its life covered in plastic.

"Christ," Reid mutters, his eyes widening. "This place is nuts."

"It didn't look like *this* on Zillow," Ava adds, snapping pictures left and right. I peer over and see she's taking the pictures directly on Instagram, immediately posting to her story.

A smug grin washes over James's lips. "Pretty sick, huh? I'm not giving you a tour, though. You have eight days to look around, and I want to relax. Let's put our shit down and change. There are three rooms on the second floor and three on the third. The rooms with open doors are up for grabs. The bedrooms with closed doors are my family's, so don't get any ideas. They're locked, anyway, but that's never stopped some of you."

Us girls are the first to race toward the staircase, which is wide enough for five of us to walk up side-by-side, and some of the guys aren't far behind. As soon as we're on the second floor, Madison and Leah take a sharp left and disappear into the first room. They've been here a few times before, so I assume that's the room they usually take. Brett and his younger brother, Spencer, take another room on the second floor, leaving the last one for Ava and Erin.

I manage to find a room on the third floor with one twin-sized bed. I leave the door open in case someone wants to stay in here with me, but everyone passes by after peeking inside, so I figure I'm on my own. I don't mind—the only girl left is Dani, and she'll be with Nick, so I'd rather be alone than with one of the guys sleeping on the floor.

James's room is on the third floor, too, but he doesn't offer to share with anyone. Eli and Aaron take one of the other spare bedrooms, and Henry and Zayn claim the last one. I don't know where the rest of them will be staying, but I can hear Dani whining to Nick about not having their own room, so I won't be surprised if someone gives up their space to save the rest of us from listening to her complaints.

We all get our own bathrooms, too—thank God. I get changed in there, because I don't trust that one of the guys won't walk into my room by accident. I'm not sure about what the others are doing, but I don't bother putting my things away. I just change into a bathing suit, grab my beach bag, and slather sunscreen over my skin so I can get to the beach as soon as possible.

When I meet up with the group downstairs, nearly everyone is gathered in the living room, which alone looks like it's worth more than my parents' entire house. I wince when I join them, Dani's shrill voice bouncing off the walls. She's pacing beside Nick as he sits on the armrest of a chair occupied by Joe. Magnus, a Swedish exchange student, is standing by the chair with Reid and Zeke, and they're all peering over Nick's shoulder while he concentrates on his phone.

“What are you doing?” Aaron asks. He's pouring a drink at the bar cart across the room, but all the liquor is in identical glass bottles, so I have no idea what he's drinking. “If you're trying to order food, don't bother. There's no Taco Bell on the island.”

“We're looking for an Airbnb,” Joe explains. “None of us wants to take a couch or the floor. We're on vacation, not in the dorms.”

Spencer rolls his eyes. “Oh, get a grip, you guys. I doubt there's even anything—”

“Not the worst idea.” James talks right over Spencer, making the latter clamp his jaw shut and lower his eyes. “Less people staying here means less of a mess, in theory.”

“Found one,” Nick mutters, squinting through his circular glasses. “It's a few houses down; looks like your neighbors rent it out. Only three bedrooms and two bathrooms, but that's fine for the six of us. Not super expensive, either. We can swing it.”

“Seriously?” Brett makes a *tsk* sound with his tongue. “You're gonna leave us? I thought we were all gonna stay together.”

“Well, the rest of you got bedrooms, and we didn't,” Dani retorts, sniffing. “Sorry, but Nick and I aren't squeezing on a couch together.”

Joe coughs to mask his scoff. “You don't have to be on top of each other every second.”

She glowers at him, and Nick ignores him. I wonder how that works—Nick and Joe are best friends, but it's clear to anyone with eyes that Joe isn't Dani's biggest fan. I don't know Dani very well since she and Nick have only been dating for a few months—she's not friends with any of us, so he's the only reason she's here—but she's definitely an acquired taste. I don't blame Joe for getting annoyed with her, especially when she clings to Nick like she'll evaporate if she moves an inch away from him.

Madison flicks a lock of dark hair over her shoulder. “Can we go already? The sun's strongest at noon, and I'm not sitting here waiting for you idiots to figure your shit out when I could be tanning.”

“Go, then,” Aaron tells her. “Nobody's saying you have to wait.”

She and the other three girls—save Dani—roll their eyes at him and set out for the back of the house. Only Leah stops and asks me if I want to come with them. I hesitate, because I'm really not sure if I want to be alone with these girls. I'm only here because I'm somewhat close to the guys, and I don't know how to chat with the girls for more than just small talk.

Luckily, some of the guys decide to come with, so I grab my things and follow. Only James stays behind with the group looking at the Airbnb, probably because he's now trying to convince them to stay here—maybe because he doesn’t trust them in someone else's house, especially one of his neighbors who his family probably knows. But honestly? It might be nice to have six less people running around here.

I pull my sunglasses down from the top of my head, pinning my bangs to my forehead, and follow the others through the deck door, soaking up the salty air and the warm breeze with every step.

12:30 P.M.

I can already feel my skin burning, but I don't mind. I'll get a nice base burn today, and I'll try to stay in the shade for the next few days. If I'm lucky, the burn will turn into a tan, and I won't spend the whole trip looking like a walking tomato.

Naturally, we were all confused when Eli brought a suitcase down to the beach. We were setting up chairs we took from the shed when he dropped it on the sand, immediately crouching down beside it to unzip it. I had to laugh when I saw nothing but liquor, beer, and seltzers inside. James assured us before we left that there's plenty of alcohol at the house, but clearly, Eli didn't think it'd be enough.

The six without a room aren't here. They went to check into the Airbnb a few houses down, and they'll meet us once they've settled in.

The rest of us are scattered around the beach, soaking up every bit of it. I'm lounging in a chair with Aaron, Eli, and Henry nearby, watching the other girls paddleboard in the water. The rest of the guys already set out with James to visit town and grab a few things for the house, like food and drink mixers.

"Look at this!" Ava rushes over from the water with something in her hands. I lean in, as do the others, to get a better look at the baby moon jellyfish cupped in her palms. "How cute is it?"

"It looks like a puddle of goo," Eli says with a snort.

She ignores him. "I think it's dead, though. Does it look dead to you?"

"I don't know how to tell if a moon jelly is dead," Henry admits.

"Me either," I add.

"Might as well throw it back," Aaron advises. "Those things sting."

Ava frowns. "Do they? I thought not all jellyfish sting."

"Those ones can sting," Henry confirms.

Ava makes a face—I can't tell if she's scared about getting stung or upset at us for ruining her fun—then quickly jogs back to the shore. She tosses the clear, gooey creature back into the water before rejoining us while accepting a seltzer from Aaron. The first thing she does when she's settled is whip out her phone, pose the seltzer in the sand, and crouch down to capture every angle while the sunlight hits the can.

"Man, this is nice." Eli has a beer can in one hand and what I assume is a concoction of various liquors in a Solo cup in the other. "It's been way too long."

Ava raises an eyebrow. "You've been here before, too?"

"Only twice."

She snorts. "'Only.'"

"This is my fourth time." Aaron readjusts his glasses—they have transition lenses, so I can barely see his eyes now—and takes a drag from a cigarette. "Brett's been here a ton, same for the girls. I think Spencer's only been once or twice, too, like Erin."

Nobody has to ask who he's referring to when he says *the girls*. It's always Madison and Leah. Everyone's good friends here, obviously, but six of them—James, Aaron, Eli, Brett, Madison, and Leah—have been inseparable since freshman year. Eli, Brett, and Spencer don't go to Saint Maren College like the rest of us, but they're James's childhood friends, so they've been hanging around our school forever. In four years, I've never partied with this group without Eli and Brett being there.

We're all here because we're friends with one or more of them. Nick and Zayn were roommates with Aaron for two years, and they eventually brought in Joe, Magnus, Zeke, Reid, Dani, and me. Madison and Leah befriended Ava and Erin, Spencer goes wherever big brother Brett goes, and James used to room with Henry.

"Jesus Christ!" Aaron guffaws, pointing toward the other end of the beach where Nick's group is trudging over to us. "Is Joe already beet-red, or am I seeing things?"

Joe is, indeed, already turning red. I don't know why he thought it was a good idea to walk here shirtless, since he's always complaining about his sensitive skin, but he'll be paying for that decision soon enough.

"It's not a bad walk!" Dani calls out. Aaron mutters something about mourning the peacefulness as they inch closer. "About fifteen minutes or so! The house is nice, too. Nick and I got the master bedroom, of course, and—"

"—and I'm stuck with the sleepwalking Swede," Zeke grumbles. He throws his backpack onto the sand next to my chair, taking a beer from the back pocket of his swim trunks and cracking it open. "I swear, man, if you start doing weird shit to me in your sleep, I'll fucking end you."

Magnus shoves him. “You aren't my type.”

“Yeah, you go for the gentle giants,” Aaron teases, wiggling his eyebrows. “Remember when we caught you rubbing Joe's back while he was sleeping? While *you* were sleeping?”

I laugh. *“You* didn't catch him.”

“Ah, yes. With Sadie as my witness,” he says, mimicking my laughter. “How did you end up there, anyway?”

“We were all passed out in the common room.” I shrug, taking a sip of my seltzer. “I woke up to Magnus fondling Joe at five in the morning, then ran into your room to tell you and Nick as soon as I processed it.”

“Thanks for giving me a reputation,” Magnus says with a grunt, but he's smiling at me. “Half of campus knows me as *the sleepwalking Swede* now.”

We chat while the new arrivals lay out their towels or rush to grab chairs from the shed, but the second poor Nick sits down on his towel, Dani pleads with him to get an umbrella. Her dark skin is already turning white from the amount of sunscreen she's rubbing onto her flesh, and when she reminds him—“For the tenth time, Nick!”—that skin cancer runs in her family, he just sighs and gets up to find an umbrella in the shed. She doesn't thank him when he walks off.

I beckon Reid over with my finger. He raises an eyebrow and tilts his head down so I can whisper in his ear: “Will this trip be the end for them, you think?”

He snorts. “Not if Hurricane Danielle has anything to say about it.”

Hurricane Danielle. It's fitting.

5:39 P.M.

"Get the fuck out of my way, Eli!"

"Calm your tits, psychopath. I'm not doing anything."

Madison glares at him, waving a knife in the air. "I'll fucking gut you. I know how to do it."

"Go for it, Little Miss Nursing Major. So high and mighty compared to the rest of us peasants, aren't you?"

James grabs Eli by the back of the shirt and yanks him away. "Go watch TV with Duke and Spencer, you idiot. She's drunk and armed—don't try her."

A foggy-eyed Eli grumbles something incomprehensible before trudging into the living room. Spencer and Zeke—who some of my friends call *Duke,* since he transferred out of Duke University freshman year—are watching some animated TV show, both too fucked up to move without puking or falling over.

I throw a salad together while Madison mutters complaints to James behind me. He usually tells people to fuck right off when they complain to him, especially when it's about someone else—he never wants to get in the middle of anything—but he *always* listens to her.

"The grillmaster says ten minutes!" Ava chirps, peeking her head in from the deck door. "Who wants cheese on their burgers?"

"Just tell Brett to put cheese on all of them," Aaron says tiredly. "Everyone likes cheese."

"I can't have cheese," Joe says with a frown, watching the rest of us cook from the kitchen island.

"Me either," Zayn adds from beside Joe. "It makes me gassy."

"Oh, for fuck's sake," Madison snaps. "You're all so high maintenance."

"Salad's done," I say, but nobody acknowledges me.

A few minutes later, Ava and Leah come bounding inside, laughing hysterically while Brett and Reid carry in trays of burgers and dogs. James yells to let everyone know that dinner is ready while Henry pulls a few trays of fries from the oven. The boys come in from the living room, Erin comes downstairs from her shower, and Nick and Dani appear from a second living room, where they went to take a nap. The only person missing is Magnus, but he's down on the beach, wooing some girl he met on the walk from the Airbnb to James's.

Half of us manage to grab seats at the dining table, but the other half is forced to stand or sit on the floor. James directs Joe and Nick, who volunteered to make the plates and hand everything out to avoid a chaotic buffet line. I immediately notice everyone who helped make dinner is served first, and everyone who didn't—including Joe and Nick—are served last.

Erin makes rounds for drinks, taking orders and delivering, and nobody denies the offer. Most of us are just buzzed now that some of the alcohol burned off after we showered and rested, but Eli and a few others are on the verge of getting sloppy. But everyone keeps drinking regardless of where we're at, ignoring the exhaustion and our burnt skin like it's second nature.

We do this every weekend, but it feels different to be here in James's island paradise instead of in a college dorm in Connecticut. I never thought I'd be here with them—drinking and soaking up the alcohol with greasy food—anywhere but at school. It's something I've always wanted, yet I can't fully process that it's my current reality. I guess it just hasn't fully sunken in yet: the fact that I'm here in person and not experiencing it vicariously through Instagram pictures and Snapchat stories.

"Thanks for cooking," Erin says to nobody in particular. "I was starving. The sun wore me out."

"Try to be careful out there," Madison replies with surprising sincerity. "Overheating makes your heart work harder. Stay hydrated and try to spend some time in the shade, okay?"

Erin just smiles and thanks Madison for looking out for her. I'm not really surprised: Madison has a habit of forcing her medical knowledge upon us all whenever she can, but especially Erin, who has a heart defect. She lives her life pretty normally now after a few surgeries and such, but she still has to be careful when it comes to certain things.

"Thanks for grabbing groceries, too," Ava tells the guys, though she's mainly just invested in her phone and taking the perfect photo of her plate to share to her social media. "We'll be running to the store every day at this rate, though."

James waves a dismissive hand. “It's right over the bridge on the way to the other side of the island. Not a far drive. We got more than enough for the next, like, two days, though.”

Magnus walks in, announcing he got the girl's number and will be meeting her on the beach tomorrow, then snatches the last two burgers and the last three hotdogs. He tries to finish the fries, too, but Madison swats his hand away when he reaches over her to take the tray.

James winces. “Maybe we don't have enough. I forgot how much you eat, dude.”

“You got two stomachs in there or something?” Reid pats Magnus's flat abdomen. “Nah. Too damn skinny for two stomachs.”

Leah sighs. “I wish I had your metabolism. It must be a European thing.”

That makes Magnus snort. “Your food in America is mostly preservatives and chemicals. I don't know how any of you can feel full when you aren't eating real food. I have to eat triple the amount I would at home so I don't starve to death.”

“Drama queen,” Eli mutters under his breath.

Magnus throws something at him—a plastic fork—and Eli retaliates by grabbing the rest of his burger, winding back to toss it. Like it's second nature, Brett seizes Eli's wrist, makes him drop the burger, and tells him to shut up and eat.

“Hey.” Reid's uneasy voice silences the group. I furrow my brows when I see him staring down at his phone, anxiety flickering in his eyes. “My mom just texted. She says there's a hurricane hitting this area soon. It's gonna sweep across Florida and make its way here.”

Dani gasps and clutches Nick's forearm. “Oh, God.”

“Don't worry about it.” James doesn't even look up from his plate. “My grandparents had this place built to withstand crazy storms. You kinda have to do that if you want a house in the middle of the ocean. My dad texted me about the storm earlier, too, and he's not worried. Him and Mom are still headed for Aruba, and they'll get more bad weather there than we will. It's gonna miss us by a few miles.”

“We'll definitely get some of it, though,” Erin says, sighing. “Maybe a few days of rain and clouds.”

“A little rain never killed anyone,” I chime in. “It'll be fine.”

7:55 P.M.

“Thanks.” I accept the bowl from Magnus, light it, and take two long drags before handing it to Ava on my right. The smoke spewing from my lips disappears instantly when it meets the smoke from the firepit in front of me. “Who brought the bowl?”

“It's mine,” James replies. “I keep it stashed in my closet here.”

“We call it *Mrs. Puff.* Get it? 'Cause it's a fish?” Eli grins as he takes the bowl from Ava and holds it up. “We came up with that senior year of high school. I can't believe the old girl's still kicking.”

“She's missing part of her fin. Aaron's fault,” James says, taking it from Eli. “He dropped it once. The fin nicked the edge of a table and broke off, but somehow, the idiot managed to catch it before it hit the floor.”

As if on cue, Aaron's laughter echoes from the beach. A second later, there's a loud pop and a whizzing sound, followed by an unimpressive burst of red and green lights flying a few feet into the air. I hear Zeke, Magnus, Joe, Reid, and Zayn laughing and shouting, too. They somehow managed to find a box of old fireworks in the back of the shed, so it didn't take long for them to rush down to the beach with the box and lighters in hand.

“Idiots.” Madison takes a hit from the bowl while James holds it for her, because—as she's said five times already—she doesn't want her fingers to smell like weed. “Aren't fireworks illegal here?”

“Yeah, but nobody actually cares. It's fine.” James takes another hit when she finishes, then passes it to Leah. When Leah tries handing it to Henry, he shakes his head and gestures for Magnus to take it. James raises an eyebrow. “What's going on with you tonight? You haven't smoked at all. You're usually the first one to hit it.”

Henry shrugs. “Headache. Drank too much.”

“Well, Spencer's in bed.” All attention shifts from Henry to Erin as she emerges from the deck door. She sits on the ground between me and Ava, her eyes bloodshot. “I left him with some water and a few Tylenol. He'll be fine in the morning.”

“Kid can't handle hard liquor,” Eli comments, snorting.

She rolls her eyes at him. “I think it was the weed that screwed him.”

“That, or the line of coke him and Brett did in the bathroom,” James quips, making everyone laugh. “Where the hell is Brett, anyway?”

Madison jabs her thumb toward the beach. “Skinny dipping. Said he wanted to do it while the fireworks go off above him.”

Leah snickers. “Fucking dork.”

“Can't blame a guy for wanting to live a little.” Eli stands up, stretches, and yanks off his shirt. “I'm gonna join him, but I'm gonna stay a respectable distance away.” When nobody replies, he raises an eyebrow. “No jokes? That's a first.”

“If you want, I'll come with,” Madison offers. “We'll see which one of us you gravitate toward.”

“There it is,” he says with a grin. “I've seen you both naked already, and no offense, but you're not my type. I like my women thick and my men skinny. We've been through this.”

“Just fucking go already,” James says, laughing. “Someone go with him so he doesn't fall down the stairs. And tell Aaron to shut the hell up—I bet they can hear him on the other side of the island.”

Erin goes with Eli, and I suddenly realize that not everyone is here. “Where are Nick and Dani?”

“Probably fucking in the house somewhere,” Ava offers. Everyone groans. “At least they aren't doing it in front of us. Remember that time they did it in Nick's room when a few of us were there visiting Aaron? Us being there didn't stop them. Didn't even slow them down.”

Leah shivers. “It was last week. I don't think any of us have forgotten it.”

Lo and behold, ten minutes later, Nick and Dani walk through the deck door to join us. They’re both flushed and slightly damp with sweat, and Nick's shirt is on inside-out.

I'd love to know where they did it so I can avoid the area at all costs, but at the same time, ignorance is bliss.

9:22 P.M.

"We're heading back to our place," Nick announces, holding both his and Dani's things in either hand. "Dani's getting tired."

"Come on, man." Aaron claps him on the back and scowls. "I know you've got a few hours left in you."

Nick shrugs. "She's tired."

"I'm staying. I'll meet you there later," Magnus says, sweeping a hand through his blond hair. "Anyone else?"

"I'm game," Zeke tells him. Reid and Joe mutter in agreement.

Nick feigns a yawn. "All right. See everyone in the morning."

We mumble goodbyes, and he disappears from the deck to find Dani inside. The rest of us are grouped around the fire now that the guys have abandoned both skinny dipping and setting off dinky fireworks. The bowl's still being passed around, but most of us have tapped out. We've turned to mostly just drinking a few bottles of chardonnay James found in the back of the fridge in the garage.

I excuse myself to use the bathroom, and Eli volunteers to save my seat after his was stolen by Reid.

I know I won't be getting my seat back.

On my way back from the bathroom, I have to pass the kitchen to get to the deck door. I hear voices whispering in the kitchen, so I stop in the hallway before passing by. It sounds like Madison and Leah, who were upstairs changing into their pajamas when Nick left. I don't want to eavesdrop, but Madison's panicked tone catches my interest. I know they won't confide in me if I ask what's wrong—and I'm too curious to just walk away.

"...fucked up," Madison says, sniffling. "I know what I said, but to make it so obvious? It's rude. He could at least try to hide it."

"Well, if you don't hide it, you can't expect him to do the same."

"I know, but—"

“Stop flirting with Adam, and he'll stop flirting with Erin. I bet it's that simple,” Leah insists. “It's not like he's getting anywhere with her, either. She's still hung up on Aaron.”

The Erin/Aaron drama is pretty well known in the group. When Erin first came along, Aaron teased her about how similar their names are, saying there could only be one in the group. Everyone knew he had a thing for her, but she rejected him to go after one of the guys on the baseball team. By the time she started catching feelings for him, he'd already moved on. There's still some lingering tension between them—they'll never be in the same room alone together—but nobody can guess where things will go. They're too messy.

Madison sniffs again. “I don't flirt with Adam.”

“You totally do.”

“I barely know him.”

“Maybe, but he's cute, and you know he is. I don't think you can help yourself.”

“Fuck off.”

“I'm serious, Mads. I'm sorry, but it's true.” Leah sighs. “Let's go back out there. I need a drink.”

I know exactly who they're talking about: Adam DeLuca, a kid in our grade on the football team, who Madison's been innocently flirting with for a little while now. I bet he's the reason I've seen her grinning at her phone while her pretty pink nails clack away on the screen at the speed of light. She'll never do anything with him; she just likes to flirt, and guys love when she gives them even an ounce of attention.

There’s been a rumor circulating about Madison and James, but nothing’s ever been confirmed. From what I've heard, there are no strings attached—though it seems like everyone involved keeps tripping over them, anyway. It’s strange to hear her so torn up about James flirting with someone else, especially knowing how easily she flirts herself. I don’t want to say it serves her right, but I can’t quite bring myself to feel bad for her, either.

I wait until I hear the back door open and close. After a minute goes by, I meet the others outside, and the first thing I see is Madison pouting in her chair next to James while Zeke fills her Solo cup with vodka and soda water. The next thing I see, much to my surprise, is Henry sitting in my chair.

He smiles and stands up when he spots me. “I stole your seat from Eli when he got up to piss in the shrubs. Figured he wouldn't actually give it back to you.”

“Such a gentleman,” Eli grumbles. “My ass hurts from sitting on the ground. Anyone wanna give up their seat?”

I thank Henry, ignore Eli, and reclaim my chair while Henry sits on the ground between me and Magnus. It's quiet for a moment, the only sounds being the crashing waves and the crackling fire. This is the most peaceful it's been since we got here.

Zeke breaks the silence: “Do you guys think President Windham is fucking Ella Carpenter?”

“Without a doubt,” Reid replies.

“It's literally all she talks about,” Leah adds.

“I don't think it's much of a secret anymore.” That’s from Erin.

“He paid for her veneers, y'know.” James.

“I thought he was fucking Naomi Bates.” Joe.

“Probably both of them. He's gonna be pissed when we graduate.” Aaron.

And that's pretty much how the rest of the night goes.

11:53 P.M.

At some point after ten o'clock, I went to the bathroom again, and somehow ended up on the couch in the living room. I wake up to someone gently shaking my shoulder, and the first thing I see when I blink my bleary eyes is the clock across the room. It's almost midnight, and the house is silent.

I expected everyone to be up until sunrise, like we usually do on weekends when we're partying on campus. I guess all the traveling and time in the sun did a number on everyone.

“Good morning, sleeping beauty.” James grins as he stands beside me, yawning and running a hand through his tousled hair. “I thought you'd wanna get to bed instead of sleeping here. Sorry for waking you up.”

“No, it's okay. Thanks.” I stand up on wobbly legs, my head pounding, and he reaches out and grasps my arms to steady me before I stumble. “Sorry. I-I have the spins a little bit.”

“You and me both,” he says with a laugh. “I'm grabbing a water before I head up. Want one?”

I nod and follow him into the kitchen. It's eerie, being in this massive house in the middle of the night when it's pitch black and silent, but I'm glad James is here. He can get around this maze in his sleep.

That, and…I like being alone with James. He’s different when it’s just the two of us—quieter, like his sharp edges soften when there’s no one else around to perform for. I first noticed it sophomore year one night when Nick and his roommates threw a party, and we ducked into his room to grab the alcohol we’d stashed. For those few minutes, James felt very unlike the version of him I’d gotten to know from hanging out with the whole group. He was…kinder. Easier. It was almost like he’d slipped out of something without realizing it.

The realization stayed with me after that night. The way he could be so present one-on-one, and then disappear back into the noise like it didn’t mean anything at all. Sometimes, I catch myself wondering if that version of him is something he gives out freely, or if it only shows up by accident—something entirely out of his control.

I don't know why the question matters. I just know I notice when he's like this, and when he's like this with *me.*

"Here." James hands me a water bottle from the fridge, then cracks open his own and takes a gulp. "So, how was your first day?"

"It was great, it's really nice here. Thanks for inviting me."

"Don't sweat it. Happy to have you here." His green eyes shimmer against the tiny nightlight beaming at him from behind me. "I know things will get crazy when we graduate and start working, but I hope we can do this again. I hope you come back, too. Even if we're not coming back *here,* I want everyone to stay close. And you should be there with us."

Butterflies flutter in my stomach, even though he's not *exactly* counting me as one of the people he wants to stay close to.

"I'd love that, James."

"Good. I would, too." He smiles. "Anything else you need before we go up?"

I bite my lower lip. There isn't, but my drunk ass wants to keep talking to him. "I'm not sure I remember where my room is."

That makes him chuckle. "You picked the one with the sea turtle wallpaper, right? That's my sister's old room. She doesn't use it anymore."

"She moved to Australia last year, didn't she?" I ask as I follow him upstairs.

"Yeah." His eyebrows furrow. "How'd you know that?"

You'd be surprised at how much you overhear when nobody realizes you're in the room, I want to say. But I don't.

"I heard you talking about it with Aaron," I reply. "She got a job offer after she studied abroad there, right?"

"Yep. She hasn't been home since except for Christmas. She loves it too much to leave."

I don't say anything as I follow him to the third floor. He opens the door for me like a proper gentleman when we reach my room, and even pulls down the covers for me, grabbing an extra blanket from the closet. He's spreading the blanket over the thin comforter before I can tell him not to worry about it.

"It gets cold in here at night, and the comforter doesn't do shit," he explains. "This should do the trick, but come and get me if you get too cold, okay? I'll switch rooms with you for the night, and I'll find a better comforter tomorrow."

My face warms. "I-I will. Thanks, James."

He winks at me. "Night, Sadie."

I can't bring myself to speak again until the door clicks shut behind him. "Night."

DAY TWO

8:12 A.M.

I wake up to a pounding sound, thinking it's my throbbing head, but when I open my eyes to the sea turtle wallpaper, I remember where I am, realizing I'm hearing the waves crashing on the beach.

Yesterday feels like a fever dream. It's hard to believe today is only the second of our eight-day-long vacation—we're just getting started. I'm not sure if I can maintain the pace from yesterday—the constant drinking and smoking—but at the very least, I can take advantage of being in the Bahamas instead of Connecticut or even Anderson, my hometown in South Carolina.

After chugging a bottle of water and swallowing a few painkillers, I get ready for another day at the beach. My stomach growls when the smell of maple and bacon wafts to my nose. I'm quick to get myself together and rush downstairs, and the second I open my door, I hear muffled arguing from downstairs.

Nothing out of the norm, but it's too early for fighting, especially after how much everyone drank and smoked last night.

When I get downstairs, I can't tell who's still asleep and who's already on the beach. Ava and Leah are sitting at the kitchen table with Aaron, Spencer, and Henry, picking at plates of eggs, bacon, and waffles. The kitchen is a disaster from whoever made breakfast, but there's still some left, so I make a plate before someone—more than likely Magnus—arrives to finish it off.

I'm so distracted by my hunger that I don't process the arguing at first. Brett and James are shouting at each other in the next room, but they're talking so quickly that I can't understand what they're saying.

“What's all that about?” I ask, pouring a cup of coffee before joining them at the table.

Aaron sighs. “Sydney showed up first thing this morning. Brett didn't tell anyone that he invited her. He's got Spence in his room, too, so clearly, he wasn't thinking about sleeping arrangements for her.”

“I'll take the floor,” a weary, half-dead Spencer mutters.

"James is pissed," Leah adds, munching on bacon. "Brett forgets this isn't his house, and he can't just do whatever he wants. We all gave James money for groceries and stuff before we got here, too, and Sydney didn't pay him. Brett's trying to say he'll pay for her share, but James—"

"—is saying that's not the point," Ava finishes. Leah glares at her. Ava's pretty well known for interrupting everyone, whether it be with her words or with her phone in someone's face. "It's not going well. Luckily, Madison and Erin took Sydney down to the beach so she doesn't have to hear James give Brett shit about it."

Spencer clenches his jaw. "Cut Brett some slack. He just forgot to mention it."

"Nick asked permission to bring Dani," Leah reminded him. "Brett should've done the same thing when Nick did. He just decided not to tell anyone."

"It was a mistake. Leave it alone."

She rolls her eyes at him. "Sure it was, Spence."

I grimace a little as I shovel eggs into my mouth. You know James is mad when he's yelling at Brett like this, of all people. I wonder how he'd react if someone else brought a guest without asking first—someone who isn't his best friend.

I've only met Sydney a handful of times. She visits school when Brett does every now and then, but she keeps to herself. She reminds me of Dani if Dani didn't mistake noise for presence. While Dani's glued to Nick because she's obsessed with the idea of him, Sydney seems glued to Brett because she's anxious about being separated from her safety person. We've exchanged a few words, but never a real conversation, so I really don't know much about her.

I hear James's voice calm, and he says something about a principle, which eases Brett's tone, too. The yelling has completely stopped by now, replaced by quiet murmuring. Within a minute or so, they're walking into the kitchen, James's arm slung over Brett's shoulders.

"Morning, Sadie," James says to me. I return the greeting while Brett walks right past the table, heading outside to the beach. James makes a face at the waffle batter glued to the countertops and the bacon grease plastered over the open microwave. "Jesus. Who do they think is cleaning this up?"

"The last ones up, probably. So, us," Ava mutters.

“Well, that's not how things are going to be this week. You make the mess, you clean the mess.” James runs a hand through his hair. “Who wants to come make a scene with me?”

“I will,” I say, ignoring the knowing look Aaron gives me. I haven't finished eating, but honestly, the food isn't mixing well with the alcohol in my gut. “Who cooked?”

“Madison, Erin, Eli, and Zayn,” Henry replies. “They booked it out of here as soon as they finished. Took their plates and cups down to the beach.”

James meets my eyes, smiling. “Ready to give 'em hell?”

I laugh a little. “I guess so.”

12:32 P.M.

It wasn't easy convincing today's cooks to leave the beach and clean up the kitchen, but eventually, they did it. They tried to fight it, saying they wanted to wait for the others at the Airbnb to come and eat, but the timing was impeccable: right as I was standing next to James while he scolded them, Nick's group walked over to us, all holding iced coffees and breakfast sandwiches wrapped in foil. They borrowed bikes at their Airbnb to explore the island, and apparently, there's a food stand not far over the bridge, selling everything from breakfast sandwiches, to fish and chips, to massive seafood boils in plastic bags.

The four who cooked were gone for half an hour after reluctantly returning to the house, but everyone's back now, gathered on the beach. It's safe to say we're all still recovering from yesterday. It's quieter today, even with the music playing from Leah's speaker, and we've all been nursing the same drink for the last two hours. Even Eli, whose only hangover remedy is to keep drinking, looked like the smell of his beer was going to make him puke when he first opened it.

At least we've managed to enjoy the island. We all went swimming when everyone reunited, and I eventually found myself on a paddleboard with James. I know he just felt bad because I was standing there alone, waist-deep in the water and hugging myself, but still, I was glad for it.

Someone found a few beach balls in the shed, so we tossed those around for a bit, but soon enough, we all just wanted to lay down. We haven't moved from our chairs or towels in over an hour. The sun is hotter today than it was yesterday and there's no breeze, so most of us are underneath umbrellas. It's nice in the shade, but the second I stick my hand out in the sun, it feels like my flesh is boiling.

That, and the sun's way too bright today to even think about taking off my sunglasses. My grey eyes are too sensitive for a UV index of 11, and I really don't want my contact lenses to melt into my eyeballs. They're the same pair I wore yesterday, too. I fell asleep wearing them, and I only recently realized I forgot to switch them out. I think I was still a little high when I woke up.

"We're so weak," Aaron mutters, eyeing his drink. "We're seniors in college, we're on spring break in the Caribbean, and we can barely rally on day two of eight. What the hell's the matter with us?"

"We're getting old," Ava jokes.

Amusement twinkles in Sydney's eyes. "I can't tell if I'm sorry I missed yesterday or if I'm glad I did."

"Be glad," James replies. Her cheeks pinken a bit as she averts her eyes from his. It's obvious she feels bad about intruding, even though it was Brett's fault, but James seems to be over it now. "Why didn't you leave with us, anyway?"

"My family's visiting my dad's parents in Orlando. I had to make an appearance." Sydney ties up her hair—blonde with faded pink highlights and dark roots—in a messy bun, letting a few pieces hang down her back. "There's a boat that takes people to the other side of the island, where the little resort is. I gave the captain some cash to drop me off here on his way back."

"There's only one resort here?" Zayn frowns. "That's odd. It's a great island."

"It's mostly private," James explains. "The resort is owned and operated by natives of the island. It's not a chain or anything like that; they try to keep big corporations out of here. It's not big enough for more hotels or resorts, so it's better to keep everything private than to have chains fighting over who gets to develop here. Land preservation and all that."

Land preservation. It's all a big scam, if you ask me. I've heard my dad say that more than once. He develops real estate on the coast, and fighting pushback for whatever reason—like land preservation, especially for maintaining wildlife habitats—has always been his biggest headache. I expected him to be furious when I declared environmental science as my major, but he was actually happy about it; he thought I'd be able to pull some strings for him using *"what I know will be a significant and trustworthy reputation in the industry."* I didn't bother telling him that I have absolutely no intention of using my professional reputation to convince conservationists to let him destroy sea turtle nests because some out-of-touch socialite wants a mansion on the water.

Zeke removes his sunglasses and squints at the water. "That's the third boat I've seen leaving the island since we got here."

We follow his gaze. It looks like a small motorboat, and it's coming from the other side of the island. I saw one before this, too, but the boat was bigger, and it left from a dock a few houses down—right around where the Airbnb is.

"People must be getting worried about the storm." Erin chews on her lower lip. "Should *we* be worried, too?"

"Nah," Eli says, taking a swig from his beer. "We've been here during storms before. It's fine. Besides, everyone who's leaving is headed for Florida, and the storm's supposed to hit Miami directly. It'll be way worse there. They're idiots for leaving."

James nods. "Exactly. Just remember to put everything back in the shed when we go in. My dad said it looks like we'll be getting some strong winds, so I don't wanna see my shit flying around the island. It'll rain a little, too, starting around dinnertime. Dad said we might be stuck inside tomorrow. Let's just enjoy it while we can, and hopefully, everything's back to normal on Tuesday. We can go jet skiing on Tuesday, and then maybe, on Wednesday, we can find something to do near the resort. I know there's ziplining somewhere over there."

We all trust that he knows what he's talking about, but I find myself doubting him when, over the next four hours, another five boats leave the island for Florida.

4:05 P.M.

The sky darkens around four o'clock, so we take that as our cue to head inside. We'd left most of the chairs and umbrellas outside yesterday, but we obey James and put them back in the shed so the storm doesn't blow them away. He doesn't even close the shed door all the way, though, so clearly, he's not that worried.

The only person who doesn't go back to the house is Magnus. He just got a text from the girl he met yesterday—Danica—asking if he wants to take a walk with her. He barely says goodbye before he grabs his things and bolts toward her house, where she's staying with her two sisters for the week. Apparently, they're not worried about the storm, either.

As we're walking up the stairs, Joe's phone rings. "Hey, babe," he says, answering it after the first ring. "What's up? Oh, really? That's awesome! Yeah, things are good here. We're heading up to the house now. It's probably gonna start raining soon, but it'll be over by tomorrow."

Next to me, Nick rolls his eyes. "Is he ever not on the phone with her?"

"Are you ever not sticking your tongue down Dani's throat?" Aaron shoots back from a few steps ahead. Nick's face darkens while the rest of us laugh. "You're no better, dude. You're way worse, actually."

Nick doesn't answer, probably because he knows Aaron's right. Luckily, Dani doesn't hear any of this. She's a few steps below Nick, talking Leah's ear off. When I glance over my shoulder, I almost want to laugh at Leah's face—she looks like it's taking everything in her power not to jump over the railing and roll down the side of the hill to get away from Dani.

As soon as we're inside, Joe drops his things in the middle of the floor and navigates to a quiet room so he can talk to his girlfriend, Cait. She was supposed to come with us, but she had a last minute change of plans. She's in California with her family now, saying goodbye to her terminally-ill grandmother.

I follow some of them into the living room when Zeke declares he's putting on a movie, but the rest of the group lingers in the kitchen to pick at snacks. It's the six close friends—plus Sydney—who disappear into the walk-in pantry, whispering and giggling like whatever they're talking about has to be kept secret from the rest of us.

I feel a lurch in my chest, like something's tugging me over to them. It's not any one of them specifically I'd like to join or be closer to, either—it's all of them. This little family they've created that feels so innately unshakable compared to other friendships.

I could easily walk in and join them, but they could just as easily cease their conversation when I approach. I think it's better to be here—adjacent to the group to some degree, but still on the sidelines—than to put myself in a position to be rejected.

Instead of following the tug, I'm sitting on the floor with Zayn and Henry, watching the TV as Zeke flips through movie selections. He eventually settles on *Cast Away*, prompting Reid to grab a beach ball from the floor and attempt drawing a face on it with a pen from his backpack. Naturally, it pops instantly. The seven from the pantry come running out to inspect the noise, each holding a bag or box of snacks with their fists buried inside.

"We'll start dinner in an hour or so," James says, munching on potato chips. "We have a few frozen pizzas for tonight. Sound good?" A chorus of affirmative replies follows. "Cool. Then we have a big thing of buffalo chicken sub rolls for tomorrow night, and a ton of pasta and sauce in the pantry. We'll be good for the next few days, but we'll definitely need another trip to the grocery store."

"What about breakfast?" Henry asks. "I think we used up all the bacon and waffle mix."

"We have a shit ton of cereal and frozen hash browns. I think I left some Jimmy Deans in the freezer when my family came here for Labor Day. They're definitely freezer-burned, but they'll be edible."

Nobody has said a word so far about lunch. Today and yesterday, it's been just breakfast and dinner. I'm not surprised nobody has asked for lunch, only relying on snacks and drinks—James told us before we left for Florida that we'll probably be sticking to two meals a day for money's sake. We spent a lot just to get here, and the cash we gave him for drinks and groceries can only go so far.

"It's gonna start raining soon," Ava says suddenly, wrapping her arms around herself. "I can smell it."

"You can *smell it?*" James raises an eyebrow, amusement flickering across his face. "That's a new one."

"It's a thing!" she insists. "My grandma always says it's an ancestral ability."

He laughs and shakes his head. "It's not gonna rain any time soon, Ava. If we get anything, it'll be a small shower tomorrow morning. Don't start spiraling."

"She's right, actually," Madison pipes up. "Some people really can smell the rain. I learned about it in one of my electives last year. I don't remember what it's called, but there's a name for the smell." *Petrichor,* I think. I was in that class, too. "I think we should trust Ava's nose on this one—plus, it's pretty gloomy out there. I'll bet rain's coming sooner than we think."

James considers that for a moment, the humor draining from his expression. "All right. Then it's good we put everything away. I wouldn't want anything we brought to get ruined," he says, glancing toward the door.

"Enough weather talk." Erin stands up from her spot on the couch between Dani and Spencer, and raises an eyebrow at everyone. "I'm gonna make some frozen margaritas. Who wants one?"

There's a resounding *me* from everyone. I see a tiny flicker of annoyance pass over her face when nobody offers to help her, so I volunteer. She flashes me a grateful smile, and the two of us venture into the kitchen, heading right for the section of countertop that holds nothing but liquor.

She doesn't have to ask James where to find the blender. She hums to herself and pulls it from a cabinet like it's second nature, then starts dumping ice, tequila, and margarita mix into the blender. She doesn't say a word to me while she does it, so I make myself busy by spreading out eighteen Solo cups and slicing limes from the fruit basket on the island. This batch only makes enough for six, so I leave her to make another while I deliver half of the drinks. Eli and Aaron have already finished theirs by the time I come back to bring the rest.

I wonder if Erin knew she'd be here at the blender for the next hour when she volunteered to make the margaritas. I think she did; she's always in this position—doing everything for everyone and very rarely complaining about it.

By the time everyone has a drink, and the two of us are finally sitting down again, Tom Hanks has befriended the volleyball, and half of the group mutters something about needing another round of drinks.

Erin gets up without a second thought. I don't.

7:29 P.M.

"I can't get through to Magnus. He must be in a bad service area," Reid mutters, staring down at his screen. "I'm sure he's eating with what's-her-name, anyway. It's his own fault if he comes back hungry at midnight and everything's gone. Serves him right for ditching us."

There's about three pieces of pizza left—one cheese and two veggie—out of about eight frozen pizzas James was storing in a chest freezer in the garage. That definitely won't be enough for Magnus, but Reid's right. It'll be his own fault if he comes back hungry.

The sky is completely dark now, but I can't tell if it's because it's late or because of the storm clouds. Probably a mix of both. It hasn't started raining yet, though, and there's still no breeze. I'm starting to believe James was right, and the storm's actually going to pass us.

"My *Godddd,* Reid." Dani rolls her eyes and takes a sip of her margarita. "Leave him alone. We all know you're just jealous because Magnus found a girl and you didn't."

He glares at her, but he doesn't retaliate. He won't—not while Nick is here, and even if Nick wasn't here, honestly. Dani would tell Nick that one of his best friends was mean to her, and it'd start more shit.

Dani's been drunk off her ass for the last hour. She's slurring everything she says. *Jealous* came out sounding more like *jealoush,* and *Magnus* sounded like *Magnish*. Some of us lock eyes whenever she speaks, trying not to laugh, because we've all been drinking the same amount, yet she's the only one teetering on the edge.

"This is boring. I've seen it a thousand times." Madison lifts her cup and points it at the TV. We've been watching old reruns of *Friends* ever since *Cast Away* ended. "Is there a game we can play or something?"

"I have an idea," Dani says, already sitting up straighter. "Spin the bottle."

Groans ripple throughout the room.

"Absolutely not," Reid retorts. "I'm not kissing anyone in this house. I know where all your filthy mouths have been."

"Not that kind of *Spin the Bottle.* I don't want Nick kissing anyone other than me," Dani snaps back, narrowing her eyes. "It's more fun this way, anyway: you have to imagine switching lives with the person the bottle lands on for a year. Careers, routines, everything. You have five minutes to convince us you'd last, and if we don't believe you, you have to take a shot."

Aaron snorts. "You'd last a week switching with anyone here."

"Oh, *please."* She tries to say it with conviction, but a light flush rises up on her cheeks. "I thrive under pressure."

"Yeah, sure," Leah cuts in. "You don't like being bad at things, either. That's a recipe for cracking under pressure."

Dani opens her mouth and closes it again. Aaron grins like he knows he's won—won what, I don't know.

"I hope I'd get to switch with someone who actually makes money," he adds. "No offense."

"Some of us don't want to hate our lives," Ava says lightly, though she tugs at the end of her braid like she's trying to convince herself.

Henry shrugs from the corner. "I don't think I'd be good at anything else."

I glance over at him, surprised. He almost looks uncomfortable, like he didn't mean to say that out loud.

"You're underselling yourself," Ava says. "You're smart."

Henry smiles, but it doesn't look very convincing. "Thanks."

James clears his throat. "Okay," he says, clapping his hands once. "Before this turns into a group therapy session, someone tell me who's making drinks."

Erin's already standing.

"I'll do it," she says, like it's a reflex.

Nobody argues, and she heads into the kitchen without another word.

"You have to be smart to be in environmental science." Ava's still talking at Henry—*at,* not to—like she knows she didn't convince him, and she can't let it go until she does. "Anything having to do with science means you have to be smart. What's it like, anyway?"

Henry shrugs. "It's interesting, I guess. Sadie's an environmental science major, too, though. She's a better student than me, so take her word for everything over mine."

I smile a little. Henry's so quiet that I sometimes forget we've been in all the same classes since freshman year. I mean, we both kind of keep to ourselves in class, anyway, but I at least have a few friends—none of them are here, unfortunately—to sit with. He's always alone in the back of the room.

"It's definitely really cool," I tell Ava. "We take a lot of field trips."

"See, I'd love that," she says. "You guys know how much I like taking pictures. I'd love to be one of those people who does science things outside, taking pictures of everything for research and shit."

From the other side of the room, Henry's honey-colored eyes land on mine, his lips curling into a smile that I quickly mirror. *Science things.* She couldn't sound more like a fashion major if she tried.

"Does nobody want to switch with me? Exercise science?" Dani demands. Nobody replies, but a few of my friends bow their heads and puff out their cheeks, trying to contain their snickers and chuckles. She waves a hand, her drink sloshing over the edge of her cup. "That's *fiiiine.* Nobody likes exercise science unless they work out."

"Careful not to spill on the rug," James says, a biting edge to his voice, "and a bunch of us work out, by the way. We just have lives outside of sports and the gym."

Her dark eyes narrow. "That's *super* presumptuous. I have plenty of—"

"Dani," Nick says tiredly, "you're starting to yell."

"I don't care. I have to yell, since nobody in this fucking house ever listens to me."

"Dude," Joe says with a laugh, "relax."

"Relax?" The wildness in her eyes almost scares me. "The fuck did you just say to me?"

Nick tries to take her cup, but she holds it out of his reach. "I think it's time to switch to water, babe."

"Don't tell me what to do."

"I'm not. I'm just trying to help."

"You're not helping. You're being a dick to me."

"And so it begins…" Reid says with an exasperated sigh. He pauses and glances out the window to his left when rain starts pattering against the glass. It's just a drizzle for now, though. "You know what? I'm gonna head back to the Airbnb. If the rain picks up, I sure as hell don't wanna be walking through it in the middle of the night."

"I'll come with you." Joe stands up with Reid, briefly eyeing a red-faced Dani and Nick before turning to the rest of us. "We'll text when we get back. Maybe we'll pick up Magnus on the way."

James laughs. "Good luck with him. He'll be feral if he hasn't eaten."

After the two of them say goodbye and collect their things, Nick says to Dani, "Maybe we should head back, too. The rain—"

"I'm not ready to leave," she protests, but her bloodshot eyes beg to differ.

Madison offers her a fake smile. "I think it's a good idea. It'll suck if the rain starts coming down harder when you leave, and it's dark out."

Nick nods and rubs Dani's back. "Come on, babe. We'll get into our PJs, and we'll get some water before bed, and—"

"You think I-I'm fucked up." She inches away from him, drops her now-empty cup on the floor, and folds her arms over her chest. "I'm fine, Nicholas. You need to stop worrying about me all the time. I'm big girl. I know how to take care of myself. You can be so fucking annoying sometimes, you know that?"

If she wasn't drunk twenty minutes ago, she definitely is now.

Nick's hazel eyes darken behind his glasses. "*I'm* annoying? Really? Look around, Dani. Everyone's uncomfortable because you're making a scene." She gasps at him and surges backward, horrified, while he massages his temples and stands. "You know what? I'm heading back. Stay here for the night if you really don't want to leave, but I'm not getting caught in the rain."

Her jaw drops. "You're *leaving me here?"*

"It's not like I'm stranding you by yourself. Get a grip." He exhales, turning his apologetic eyes to the rest of us as we watch in mortified silence. "I'll see everyone in the morning."

Then he's gone, and Dani spends the next half an hour crying in the corner while a miserable Erin and Leah try to calm her down. I feel like I should help, but I really don't want to.

“God Al-fucking-mighty.” Zeke stands up and glares at Dani while she sobs into her hands. “I need a line. Maybe a molly instead. Anyone else?”

Spencer and Eli follow him into another room after he takes a baggie out of his backpack, and just minutes later, Dani's gotten a hold of herself. She's more angry than sad now, and she keeps telling us—while standing directly in front of the TV—how much Nick is in for it, how he's gonna regret how he spoke to her when she gets to the Airbnb.

“I'm going back,” she slurs, grabbing her things from the floor. “He's in so much fucking trouble.”

Erin frowns. “Maybe you should call him and have him pick you up. Or maybe a few of us should go with you. It's dark.”

“I'm fine,” Dani snaps, stumbling while she puts on her sandals. “I want to be alone for a little.”

James looks hesitant. “I don't know. Erin's right. It's dark, and if you get lost...”

“You think I'm an idiot?”

“Of course not, but—”

“See you tomorrow.”

Then she's gone, ignoring all of us while we yell after her. Even Aaron, who can't stand her half the time, shakes his head and says, “Someone should go after her.”

“You heard her. She wants to be alone,” Madison replies. “She'll be an asshole if anyone follows, and that'll probably make things worse for Nick and the guys. It's only, like, ten minutes away, anyway. She'll be fine.”

“Yeah, she will,” Brett concedes, then grins. “At least she didn't stay the night.”

Everyone laughs, but the air is still tense because we all know we shouldn't have let her leave alone. We’re all feeling the alcohol kick in, too, and tequila makes it hard to do the right thing sometimes.

10:10 P.M.

Erin and Aaron have both tried texting everyone who left—Dani, Nick, Reid, Joe, and even Magnus—but the messages haven't gone through. Nobody's gotten texts from any of them, either, about Dani, Nick, or Magnus getting back to the Airbnb. James reminds us that service isn't great on the island sometimes, so we'll just have to be patient.

It's been a few hours since they left, and we've been doing this and that, mostly forgetting about how Dani stormed off alone. Everyone's hammered now, and though James originally told us not to smoke in the house, even he got antsy, so we've been passing the bowl and a blunt around for the last hour.

I'm in the kitchen playing King's Cup with James, Erin, Ava, Aaron, and Henry. Leah and Madison are blasting ABBA from the TV in the living room and dancing, pausing only to blow cigarette smoke out the window. Zayn's sitting on the couch with Brett and Sydney, who look like they'd rather be anywhere than trapped with Zayn while he tells them about the graphic design job he has lined up after graduation. The only people missing are Zeke, Eli, and Spencer, who haven't returned from their date with cocaine and/or molly.

James is tucking a card under the tab of a seltzer in the middle of the table, moving slowly and cautiously to avoid cracking it open and having to drink the entire thing. His Solo cup—Jack and Coke—is clenched between his teeth while his unblinking eyes focus on the task at hand. I hope he cracks it, because it's getting close and my turn is next. I don't want to be the one who has to chug it.

There's a loud bang from outside, making James fumble, and the can cracks. Aaron and Ava cackle at him, Aaron telling him to drink up while Ava orders him to wait until her camera is ready, but he—and the rest of us—are distracted by the sound. The others in the living room have stilled and quieted down, too. Leah walks over to the window and bends over to peer through it, saying, “For fuck's sake.”

James rushes over to see for himself, lets out a string of curses, and runs through the deck door. The rest of us hesitate, not wanting to face the drizzle, but when we hear him hollering, we follow him out.

The stairs are slippery, and paired with our drunkenness and the darkness, it's a miracle nobody falls while we try to catch up with James. He's already on the beach by the time we're halfway down the stairs. Madison, leading the rest of us, stops and forces us to a halt.

“Jesus Christ,” she says. “Those fucking buffoons.”

I squint through the slow yet steady rainfall, and that's when I see the movement aboard the motorboat. Zeke's bright yellow shirt gives him away immediately, and after a second, Eli's shrieking laughter gives him away, too. There are only two people on the boat, though, so I assume Spencer went to bed.

We meet James on the beach while he screams at them to get back inside. Eli yells back, telling James to ease up and let them enjoy their vacation. I can tell James wants to be angry, but a smile reluctantly forms on his lips. He folds his arms over his chest, visibly fighting the smile, while the rest of us either laugh or comment on the duo's idiocy.

“Let them be,” Leah urges. “They'll probably fall asleep out there, and we can make fun of them in the morning. Maybe if we're lucky, we'll find them naked tomorrow, and we can finally put the rumors to rest.”

I raise an eyebrow. “What rumors?”

“We think they've been kinking. Secretly, of course,” Aaron says with a grin.

“I didn't know Zeke's gay.”

“He's not,” James says quickly. “I mean, he could be, but if he is, he’s not ready to tell anyone yet. It’s not our business what he wants to do with Eli or anyone else until he’s ready to share.”

Brett laughs like James is full of shit. “You could cut the sexual tension with a fucking butter knife, man.”

“I think it's sweet,” Erin comments.

“It'll still be sweet from inside the house.” James shakes his head. “I should be more upset than I am. My family will skewer me if anything happens to that boat.”

Zayn looks up at the sky, blinking through the rain yet still puffing on his Juul. “The rain's picking up. They won't be out here much longer, anyway.”

“I don't know. Look who we're talking about.” Leah grimaces when Zeke and Eli whoop, yelling inaudible things at us. “They'll probably push it for as long as they can. We should get them inside before the waves get rough."

"How?" Aaron asks with a laugh. "They won't listen, and we can't pull them back to the dock. They're too fucking high to give a shit about the rain or the waves."

"At least they didn't find the keys or untie the boat from the dock," Henry offers. "They won't be going anywhere."

James nods. "They'll come in eventually. I'm going back inside before I get seriously drenched. Someone remind me to check on them before I go to bed, all right?"

We all promise to do so, but by the time we make it back into the house, the promise is forgotten.

11:28 P.M.

"Mmmm."

I turn the corner after leaving the bathroom to find Henry alone in the kitchen, gnawing on a chocolate bar. I have to cover my mouth to stifle my laughter when he meets my eyes and flushes, because a few of our friends are passed out in the living room a few feet away. Brett and Sydney are cuddled up on one side of the couch, Ava's on the other side, and Zayn is talking in his sleep on the floor by the fireplace, using his hoodie as a blanket and his backpack as a pillow.

Zayn was awake when I went to the bathroom, and James, Aaron, and Erin were still down here. I must've been puking for longer than I thought.

"Feel any better?" Henry asks, his voice low.

I nod and take a water bottle from the fridge. "Much. That last margarita wasn't a good idea."

"Yeah, I saw the life start to leave your eyes after the first sip," he says, making me laugh. He raises an eyebrow and holds out the chocolate bar. "Want some?"

Snorting into another laugh, I accept the offer and take a bite before handing it back. He finishes whatever's left in the wrapper before throwing it in the trash, then smiles a little when he turns back to me.

"You have a little..." He gestures to the corner of his mouth. I blush, wiping the chocolate away with my tongue, and his eyes flash. "You got it."

"Thanks." Ignoring my embarrassment, I slide onto one of the chairs at the island while he stands across from me. "Did Eli and Zeke come back in?"

"Not yet. James tried convincing them to come inside, but they insisted on sleeping in the boat. James said they sounded...flustered."

"Flustered." A smirk plays on my lips. "Interesting."

"Very."

Not knowing what more to say, I start to stand and say goodnight, but he interrupts me by asking how I did on our ecology mid-term exam. We talk about that for a little bit, because it's basically the only thing we have in common.

“I didn't expect to be thinking about school and work while I'm here, but I can't help it,” he says. “This place has a really cool water filtration system, I guess, that's really important for conservation on the island. James told me on the way here. Thought I'd find it interesting.”

“I'd like to see that, too. Maybe if we go and take some notes, Professor Brown will give us extra credit,” I joke, making his face light up. “I'm surprised you haven't seen it before.”

He shrugs. “I haven't been *here* before. On the island.”

“Really?” I blink at him, a little surprised. “You and James have been friends forever.”

“Yeah, but we've never been that close. We've always been friendly because we lived together, and we get along well enough—most days, anyway.” He grabs a water bottle from the fridge, then slides it over to me and takes another when he sees that mine is almost empty. “I wasn't even expecting to get the invite for this trip. I think he felt bad, 'cause I told him I was just planning on staying home with my family in Maine.”

“If it makes you feel any better, that's the only reason I'm here,” I admit. “I was gonna be stuck at home in South Carolina for the week. I told Aaron, and he told James to ask me if I wanted to come.” I feel my face grow hot. “Just a pity invite. Not the first, and won't be the last.”

His smile is sad now, but familiar—it's the same one I'm wearing. “At least two of us are here for the same reason.”

Maybe we have more in common than I thought. “Yeah, I guess.”

Neither of us replies when the wind howls outside, rattling against the window over the sink. Rain is pattering the window, harder than before, and I can hear the trees whistling while they sway.

“Sounds like the storm's getting closer,” Henry remarks. “James's dad said it's gonna go around us—south toward Cuba. All the islands below us will get the brunt of it.”

I shiver. “It still doesn't sound good.”

His eyebrows furrow, and he starts shrugging off his hoodie. “Are you cold? You're shivering. You can have my—”

“No, no, it's okay. Thank you, though.”

He puts his arm back through the hole. “Are you sure?”

"Positive. I should be getting to bed, anyway."

"I'll walk with you."

I offer him a grateful smile. Until now, I never realized how sweet he is—and handsome, too. He's the kind of handsome that anyone can acknowledge just by looking at him, but he gets more attractive as his personality comes through, you know? He has a different kind of charisma than the other guys, too. It's…softer, and it makes me wonder if the others have to actively think about their charm while they're dishing it out, because it just seems more natural with him.

I guess I just never really paid enough attention before to pick up on that. I wonder if the others would say the same about me if they took the time to know me better, too—that they've never given me enough attention to really know me. Somehow, though, I get the feeling that Henry already has an inkling about who I am under the surface. Call it an instinct.

Henry follows me to the stairs. We climb them side-by-side, both clutching the railing while our swaying puts us at risk of falling, as he adds, "You're lucky you got your own room. Zayn talks in his sleep."

I chuckle. "I know. At least you have the room to yourself tonight, though."

"True. Tonight's my only night of peace."

We both stop at my door when we reach the third floor. "Well, I'll see you in the morning," I say with a smile, wrapping my hand around the bronze knob. "Enjoy your single."

That makes him laugh. "Dorm humor. Cute. Lame, but cute."

My cheeks warm again. "Night."

Something twinkles in his eyes. "Night, Sadie."

I slip into my room, listening to the sound of his receding footsteps, and immediately climb into my unmade bed without bothering to change. I can hear the wind and the heavy rainfall even more from my room, but for now, it's soothing.

Before burrowing under the covers, I plug my phone in on the nightstand, wincing when I see it's at 2%. It starts charging right away, my lockscreen lighting up with a picture of my golden retriever, Thor. I hope the storm hasn't affected South Carolina, because my sweet boy can't handle thunder and lightning without whimpering—ironic, given his namesake.

Poor little guy. I miss him.

11:58 P.M.

I wake up to thunder and pounding rain. I try checking the time, but instead of Thor's face lighting up my phone, it's a dead battery symbol. The lamp doesn't turn on when I reach up to flip the switch, either.

The power's out.

DAY THREE

4:08 A.M.

I don't remember going back to sleep after I realized the power was out. I have no idea how long it's been since then, or what time it is now, but I'm woken up by a bang and the sound of something shattering—something too close for comfort.

I sit up with a start, heart pounding, and my eyes follow the sound of shrieking winds to my right. The solar-powered floodlights aren't pointed directly at my room, but they're close enough to cast a faint glow outside my window. A gasp escapes me when the floodlights reveal a baseball-sized hole in the window, shattered glass all over the floor, and a mystery chunk of debris that landed across the room. The floor by the window is soaked, and the fierceness and direction of the wind is sending streams of rain everywhere.

My heart pounds as I climb out of bed and slip on my sandals. I grab the nearest thing—the extra blanket James gave me—to plug the hole. My face is sprayed with rain as the wind pelts against my skin so roughly that it feels like tiny shards of glass are hitting me instead. I stuff the blanket into the hole as best I can, glass crunching under my shoes, and rush to grab a towel from the bathroom to dry myself off.

I hear commotion from the hallway, so I quickly tear off my drenched t-shirt and replace it with a thick sweatshirt. The second I open my door, James skids to a stop in front of me, holding a flashlight as he's rushing toward the stairs.

"Sadie." His eyes are wide with alarm. "Are you okay? Are you hurt?"

"N-No, I'm fine, but—"

When he sees me trembling, he pulls me into his embrace. I sink into his warm chest while his arm is loosely wrapped around my back, his other hand cradling the back of my head with an iron grip. The Sadie who started crushing on James a few months ago wants to believe he's holding me like this because he cares for me, because he's glad I'm okay. The Sadie who just woke up to debris flying through the window, on the other hand, feels him shaking as much as I am. I know he's just looking for comfort, and I'm the only person here right now.

"I think everyone's downstairs already," he says when he releases me, taking my hand and guiding me toward the stairs. "A tree came down on the other side of the house. Everyone's okay, but there were a few minor injuries."

Right before we descend the stairs, I look over my shoulder at the other end of the hallway. A ball of terror forms in my stomach when I see debris, glass, and fragments of trees obstructing the hall, right around where the other bedrooms are. The floodlights are peeking in from outside, illuminating the water on the floor and the torrential downfall visible through holes in the wall. If we try to put up a tarp or something, it probably won't make a difference while the wind is aimed directly at us.

The house rattles as we walk, groaning and shrieking with the wind. It gets louder as we make our way to the first floor, probably because of how many windows there are down here. I know it's not a good idea to gather on the first floor, but everyone's already here, and half of the upstairs floors are fucked.

At the bottom of the stairs, I freeze with my hand on the railing, and James keeps going, rushing over to help the others. I want to move, but my feet won't budge from the last step. I'm used to waking up to a hectic scene, my friends yelling and running around, but this is different.

Brett, Aaron, and Zayn are leaning mattresses against the tall windows and the glass deck door while Leah holds a flashlight for them. Erin's trying her best to prop up pillows against the smaller windows. Ava's stuffing towels along the bottom of the door, and there are already damp towels scattered around, soaking up whatever flooded inside from the deck or through the ceiling from the damage above. I don't know what the front of the house looks like—the foyer, the other living room, and a few other miscellaneous rooms—but I'm not sure I want to know.

Then there's Madison sitting on the ottoman with a flashlight in her mouth, a first aid kit spread out next to her, while Henry and Sydney claim spots on the couch. Madison's treating a cut on Sydney's forearm, and Henry's sitting next to Sydney, holding a bloody cloth to his forehead.

"Oh my God." I finally move when I see the blood. I stand behind the couch while a shaking, white-faced Madison tries to calm a whimpering Sydney. "What happened?"

"I woke up to go to the bathroom," Sydney manages, "and a branch came through the window. It cut my arm when I blocked my face. The whole bathroom's fucked."

I wince, remembering the pineyard forest surrounding the property, as Madison takes the flashlight out of her mouth and says, "You're gonna need stitches, and I don't have the materials in the first aid kit. We'll have to just clean it and wrap it for now."

"I don't want stitches without lidocaine, anyway," Sydney says, her face turning green.

James sets a few lit candles around the living room while Madison barks at me to hold the flashlight for her. I can't watch the blood ooze out of Sydney's arm while Madison cleans it with iodine, so I turn to Henry, who's not as pale as the girls, but still shaky and slightly gray.

"What happened to your head?" I ask him.

"A tree came down in my room. Half the wall's fucked up. It missed me in bed, thank God, but the glass went everywhere. Had a little shard lodged in my forehead before Madison pulled it out. Wasn't pleasant. I'm just trying to stop the bleeding now." He trades his grimace for a forced, lopsided smile. "So much for enjoying my single, huh?"

I shake my head. "This is crazy. I thought the hurricane was supposed to pass us."

"We all thought that," Erin says, sitting beside Sydney to hold her hand. She gives Ava a weak smile. "I guess your sense of smell was right after all."

Ava only grimaces.

"The storm probably changed course at the last second," James rationalizes. "We have no way of knowing when it first started here or when it's gonna stop, either. No power, no service, no nothing. Even the water isn't running. We have a backup generator, though." Most of us sigh in relief. "But it's outside, and it's manual. We'll have to wait for the storm to calm down a little before someone goes out there. For now, let's just try to curb the damage where we can. Sadie and Erin—wanna help me in the garage while Mads takes care of the patients?"

We nod and follow him, where he directs us toward boxes and bins of materials we need to bring inside. There are extra flashlights and candles out here, plus cases of bottled water and gallons of distilled water. We grab some extra blankets, too, and struggle to balance everything while James hefts a water vacuum. We make two trips, and during the second one, James shoves toolboxes in our arms before grabbing two large coolers, which he fills with bags of melting ice from the garage freezer.

"It's not the best solution, but we have way too many perishables in the fridge," he says as we return to the house. "The stuff in the freezers will stay cold for a while as long as we don't open the doors, but everything in the fridge will start going bad soon enough. Better to let it freeze a little than to let it all go bad."

We start helping him move everything from the fridge to the coolers, but after a few minutes, Erin freezes. "Oh, God."

"What?" Ava asks from across the room. "What's wrong?"

Erin's face is drained of color. "Zeke and Eli."

Everyone stills, and for a second, nobody speaks. With all the chaos, it seems like every last one of us forgot that the duo decided to spend the night on the motorboat. In the water. During a hurricane.

"We have to go get them," Henry says, wincing when Madison lowers the cloth from his head. "It's fucked out there. Power lines, telephone poles, and trees are down everywhere. The wind's carrying debris from all around. And the waves..."

Brett peels a mattress from one of the windows to peek outside. "The floodlights don't reach past the backyard. I can't see the beach from here. It's pitch black beyond the deck."

"They had to have gone for the shed," James rationalizes, his face blanched. "When it started getting bad, they definitely ran to the shed. They probably didn't think they'd make it back to the house, and the shed is sturdy enough. Right? That's what they did, right?"

"I don't know." Madison tries to clean Henry's forehead, but she's shaking so much that she keeps bumping him, making him flinch. "S-Someone has to go outside. We have to make sure they're okay."

"Have you seen it out there?" James asks. "We won't be able to see shit, even with our flashlights. The rain and the winds are way too strong. I'm not risking anyone else. It's too dangerous."

"But—"

"He's right," I say, as much as I hate to admit it. "We have to wait until the storm calms down a bit. If someone goes out there and gets hit in the head with flying debris..."

Silence. Then Leah whispers, "What about Nick and the others?"

"They're inside. They'll be okay," Aaron reassures her. "They're probably doing the same thing we are right now. Let's just keep doing what we're doing, and we'll wait out the storm for now. It's our only option."

Nobody likes it, but we know he's right. We can't help the others if we get ourselves killed or injured in the process.

6:55 A.M.

Not long after we realized Zeke and Eli are still outside, James disappeared into his grandfather's office near the front of the house, insisting there's an old emergency radio in there somewhere. Except it's been over two hours, and he still hasn't come back.

Everyone else went back to sleep, but I don't know how. The sounds from the storm are terrifying enough to keep me awake, but when I remember that two of our friends are outside during such a violent hurricane...I'm not even that close with Zeke or Eli, but I'm so scared for them that I can't will myself to sleep, no matter how hard I try.

Everyone's scattered around the living room, sleeping in perhaps the worst place possible. Even with the windows covered up with the mattresses and pillows, I know it's not a good idea to be in the only room in the house that's more window than wall. But nobody wants to separate, and we can all fit semi-comfortably here.

Whoever didn't manage to squeeze onto the couch or one of the chairs is wrapped up in sleeping bags on the floor. Madison is the only person sleeping while sitting up, her back pressed against the side of the couch. Henry is in a sleeping bag next to her, a large bandage on his forehead, close enough that she can check on him every now and then to make sure he's not concussed.

I've been squished on the couch between Aaron and Ava, staring at the mattresses against the windows while the candle flames slowly die out. Exhausted by this feeling of helplessness, I stand and take a flashlight from the ottoman, hoping James is awake to keep me company.

To my surprise, the front of the house doesn't look terrible. Someone closed all the doors and leaned mattresses against the windows and the door in the foyer. There's a little bit of water seeping in from the bathroom where Sydney was injured, but towels on the floor are soaking it all up, for the most part.

I knock on the office door before letting myself inside. James is sitting on the floor, two candles and a flashlight beside him, while he tinkers with the radio. Another three candles flicker on the desk in front of him. He briefly looks over his shoulder when he hears me, but he doesn't say anything when I sit next to him.

“How's it going?” I murmur.

“Not good,” he replies. “I can't figure out what the issue is. It's either the antenna, or there's interference, or this thing's just too damn old to get a good signal.”

“It's okay.” I try to reassure him, because I can see in his eyes that he feels like he's failing us. “Help will be coming soon, anyway. As soon as the storm ends, and it's safe, someone will come. I don't think there's anything more you can do to call for help.”

A bitter laugh escapes him. “I know, but I want to try. I've never felt inadequate for being a poli-sci major, and now I'm thinking my dad was right—I should've gone after something that'd be useful in everyday life. Something…applicable.”

“This isn’t an everyday life situation, James. It's unrealistic to dedicate your entire life to being prepared for something that might never happen. None of us could've known that we'd need survival skills someday.”

“Your career path is more useful now than anything else.”

I shrug. “Sometimes. It won't help us repair an emergency radio or find Eli and Zeke during a hurricane, though. And I didn’t choose it because I wanted survival skills, either. It’s a really broad area that’s always interested me.” I pause for a moment, thinking about what he said. I’ve heard him talk about his disagreements with his parents before, but never in much detail. Now’s my opportunity to learn more. “I'm sorry your parents pressure you like they do. I think it's great that you're doing what you're passionate about, even if they have a hard time believing in you.”

“Thanks.” He tears his eyes away from the radio, stands, and opens a drawer in the desk. “Want a drink?”

“Sure.”

He pours two glasses of what I assume is a very expensive liquor, then hands one to me as he sits on the floor. We don't speak for a moment, only focused on the feel of the scotch burning our throats, and both stare at the broken radio like it'll magically repair itself.

“Do your parents support your career?” he asks.

I let out a short laugh. “Depends on which parent you’re talking about. My dad doesn’t really care what I do as long as I’m not miserable. My mom cares more about whether it…adds up.”

"Adds up how?"

"Oh, you know. Stability. A solid plan. Something she doesn't have to explain when her friends ask about what I'm doing with my life."

He nods slowly. "Yeah. That makes sense."

"She means well," I say, because she does. "We just don't always agree on what's worth worrying about."

He grimaces. "Don't feel bad. That's the case for a lot of us." He hesitates, then adds, "Madison wanted to be a dancer. Her parents weren't exactly flexible about it. They wanted something safer, and she went along with it."

"Really?" I'm surprised. "I didn't know that."

"Yeah. People give up a lot more than they care to admit when support starts to feel…uncertain." James sighs and takes a large gulp. "It's not like that kind of threat holds any real substance, either. Everyone makes threats like that, and nothing ever really happens."

At my silence, he gets up from the floor to plop down on the massive leather chair behind the desk. He pours himself another drink, and when he raises an eyebrow at me, I join him behind the desk for a refill. Neither of us says a word while we sip, and he doesn't hesitate to refill his glass as he drinks. I can already feel the scotch making my brain fuzzy, but honestly, with everything that's happened this morning, I need to numb the anxiety before it gets any worse.

I lean against the edge of the desk, facing the bookshelves behind James's chair while he stares into his glass to my left. I want to say something, to keep the conversation rolling before he decides to leave, but for a minute, I don't know what to say.

"I hope Sydney and Henry are okay," I mutter. "Sydney's cut looked really deep, but I think it'll heal fine. And Henry...as long as he's not concussed, he'll be okay. I don't think it's okay to sleep if a concussion is a concern, but I don't blame everyone for wanting to get some rest. I'm sure it's fine."

James raises an eyebrow. "You worried about him?"

"I'm worried about everyone."

It's true, but either way, the question sticks. I replay it in my head, the way he asked it. Something faint and sharp underneath, easy to miss if I wasn't listening for it.

I recognize it. I've heard that note before—even used it myself once or twice, too, when I wanted something and didn't want to ask for it outright.

The memory comes back to me—uninvited, as they always do. My sister never wanted things until she saw them in my hands, and then suddenly, they mattered. Somehow, they always ended up hers—sometimes taken outright, sometimes replaced with something identical so no one had to deal with the fallout.

I learned early that wanting something quietly didn't count for much.

A jolt courses through me as I recall that memory—and the tone in James's voice. I know exactly what the jolt is: a sense of opportunity.

"Why did you say it like that?" I ask.

"Like what?"

"Like there's something else you want to say about it."

He chuckles, but it's not condescending. "It just seemed like you really cared when you were talking to him earlier. Like, really cared. I think it's just because you're a good person with a big heart, but I don't know. You two have almost all of your classes together, and..."

"And what?"

"He talks about you a lot."

That makes me furrow my brows. "Really?"

"Yeah. He's always saying how smart you are and how he thinks you're gonna go far in life." His own eyebrows furrow a little. "You really never picked up on anything? I kind of thought you two had a little thing going. He never said anything, but I got those vibes after hearing him talk about you."

I don't believe that. I've known Henry as an acquaintance since freshman year: someone who I always see in class and occasionally at parties, but not someone I'd fully consider a friend. We've never spoken enough for me to feel anything for him, and I doubt he actually feels anything for me. James is probably just mistaking Henry's kindness for affection, especially since Henry and I are the only people in the friend group following the same career path. It's easy to want to push us together when we have more in common than the others.

"I think you're just looking for something that isn't there." I sink onto the floor when the scotch makes it difficult to stay standing. "He's a nice kid, but we're just friends—and we're barely friends, for that matter."

"If you say so. Are you still hung up on that Matt guy?"

"Matt Rothschild?" I laugh. "No. We hooked up twice in the fall, but that's all it was. Wasn't even that good, either. I haven't spoken to him in months."

"I'm glad to hear it. He's a douche. You should be with someone better than him."

"I've been told."

He doesn't answer; only watches me curiously for a second before reaching over for the bottle to top off his glass. Still intent on reaching for that opportunity I sensed a few minutes ago, I scooch over to him on my knees, then rest my arm on his thigh while holding up my near-empty glass with the other. I feel him tense when our eyes meet, and I don't look away from him as he pours the last of the scotch into my glass. I finish it in one gulp, already too numb to feel it burning my throat.

Up close, I notice how still he is, like he's waiting for something.

I let my fingers toy with the hem of his shorts, tracing the seam, feeling his muscles shift beneath my palm. He inhales, slow and controlled, like this isn't a moment he wants to rush through by any means.

"You've been kinda off the radar since Michelle last year," I say casually, like the observation just occurred to me. My hand flattens against the inside of his knee, my thumb brushing his skin.

There's Madison, maybe—but even that feels more like an assumption than anything real. A name people attach to him because they like things to make sense, and James and Madison would make *perfect* sense. Nothing about him ever really settles into fact, though.

Girls throw themselves at you all the time, I almost say. But I don't. Instead, I wait, watching what he does with the space I've given him.

He clears his throat. His fingers press into my bicep—not pulling me closer, but not pushing me away, either. Just firm enough for both of us to register the choice he's made.

"I just haven't really thought about it." He says it like he's answering something larger than the question. His grip tightens when my fingertips drift higher. "About…any of it."

His eyes flick down to my hand, then back to my face. He's more focused now. Present.

"Christ, Sadie."

I tilt my head, stilling my hand where it is—just close enough to matter, to confirm.

"Do you want me to stop?" I whisper.

"Fuck, no." He sets both of our glasses down, then gently wraps a lock of my shoulder-length blonde hair around his finger. His face is already flushed. "That feels—"

He lets out a grunt of pleasure right as I pull my hand away. I don't want things to go any further right now—I just want to know if interest is all it takes for him to want me.

He surprises me when he takes my hand and presses it firmly against the bulge in his pants, guiding me and adding more pressure as gasps escape his lips. His other hand finds the back of my head as he grabs a fistful of my hair, like he needs to hold onto something to keep him steady. I watch as his face contorts, his head dangling backward, barely moving my own hand while he's doing it for me.

As weird as I feel about doing this now under the circumstances, I'm filled with something inexplainable, knowing I'm capable of having this effect on him. I made him hot and hard like this—I made him want this. He didn't turn me away. He didn't tell me it's better if we just stay friends. I'm here, showing him that I'm willing, and he can't help himself. Maybe it's a primal instinct he can't ignore, or maybe it's something else; some sort of system override in his brain telling him he has to respond, circumstances be damned.

He breaks us apart just long enough to pull me up from the floor, lift me up, and set me down on the desk. His lips are on my neck before I can process what just happened, his hands kneading my tits while his hardness pokes me between my legs.

I resist the urge to cry out when I feel his teeth nibbling on the sensitive skin below my ear. One of his hands slips beneath the waistband of my shorts, making me gasp with pleasure, but before he can get so much as a finger into my underwear, there's a bang from another room. We jerk apart, both panting, and turn to face the door.

I touch the wet spot on my neck where his mouth was. "Should I—"

"Go get cleaned up. I'll see what that was." We both stand, and when we do, my nose is practically kissing his chest. I'm stepping backward when he sets a hand on my ass, squeezes, and pulls me close to him again. I shiver when his lips tickle my ear. "If I knew you were so good with your hands, I would've come to your room a long time ago."

I chew on my lower lip. “Is that all you'd want from me?”

“Oh, fuck no.” I can feel him smiling against my ear. “We'll finish what we started later on. I promise.”

Before I can reply, he pulls away and leaves in a split second. I stand here for a minute, frozen, as my lips curl into a small smile. I don’t know how to explain how I feel. Satisfied? Maybe. Intrigued? Sure.

I hope he’s true to his word. If not, then he’s just a victim of opportunity—someone who feeds into a situation as it’s happening, but couldn’t be bothered to even think of it again. That would explain all the dirty looks he gets from girls in the hallways at school. Nobody likes to be led on, especially by a man like James who practically oozes with that *you’re lucky to be seen with me* type of energy.

I remind myself that I’m different from those girls for one big reason: I’m his friend. I may not be on the same level as his other female friends, like Madison and Leah, but the closer I get to him, the better my odds are of reaching that status. I’m already in—I just need to get a little bit closer. The others will start seeing me as a core member of the group as soon as James does, after all.

Only after I start to leave the office do I realize we never even kissed. My best friend, Taylor, always says that you can guess a man’s vibe by the way he kisses you—whether he only wants you and to keep you around because of where a kiss can lead, whether he wants to be with you, and whether he only wants you just this once, in the moment, for his own pleasure.

I guess I’ll just have to try again to decide where James fits on Taylor’s judgment scale, and whether that means he’s willing to give me a higher rank in his circle.

10:20 A.M.

As it turns out, the bang we heard was a tree falling over in the driveway. We couldn't see it until around ten in the morning, when the torrential rainfall and strong winds finally started calming down enough for us to see more than a few feet outside.

The bang woke the others, but luckily, nobody has sensed anything weird between me and James. He's acting like nothing happened, and I'm trying my hardest to do the same.

The storm is breaking up now, finally starting to settle, but that doesn't mean we're in the clear. Henry knows that because it was taught to us in one of our electives, but I doubt he's ever experienced it like I have. South Carolina is no stranger to hurricanes, especially on the coast where I live. I've seen it time and time again: storms ripping across numerous counties, then miraculously settling down long enough for us to breathe. It's just a mirage, though—that break in the storm is temporary, like the intermission at a play before the second act begins.

Any lover of theater will tell you the same thing: the second act, more often than not, is when the most action happens. With hurricanes, it's the last stretch that usually causes the most damage. I'd need more than my two hands to count how many hurricanes I've lived through that didn't seem so bad at first, only to come back stronger after a break. After they tore houses from their foundations, carried cars down flooded streets for miles, and took down trees that've held strong since the Victorian era.

That's what Henry and I are trying to tell our friends now. They don't want to hear it, though—they want to go outside to look for Zeke and Eli while we have the opportunity. I want to find the boys, too, but the wind is still strong enough to carry debris, and if the rain picks up while we're outside, we'll have a hard time getting back to the house.

"It's possible that this is the end of the storm. Right?" Brett asks, looking between me and Henry. We both reluctantly nod. "Okay. So, we can worry that it's gonna get bad again and wait until we know for sure that it's over, leaving Eli and Zeke outside for even longer. Or, we can choose to believe it's over—at the very least, taking advantage of the break—to find them. I don't know about you guys, but I'm willing to take the chance."

"It's definitely gotten better," Ava observes, peeking through the window behind a mattress. "It's still cloudy and raining, but there's still a little bit of light. If we all stick together, we'll be okay."

"Let's just go while we can," James decides. "I'd rather try than leave them out there any longer."

The rest of us agree, however reluctantly, and everyone suits up in hoodies, jackets, and even blankets to somewhat protect us from the rain. We don't bother looking for umbrellas, because the winds are still strong enough to rip them out of our hands.

Zayn asks us if we're ready as he and Brett stand on either side of the mattress blocking the deck door. After we nod, they move the mattress and open the door for us. They're the first two outside, and when they immediately stumble from the wind forcing them back toward the house, my stomach twists into knots.

Sydney and Henry are staying inside to avoid injuring themselves further, and Madison is waiting with them—mainly because she's the only one of us with first aid training, and if something happens while we're outside, we'll need her expertise.

Wordlessly, everyone joins hands after Madison closes the door behind us. My heart hammers when we start inching down the stairs. We're moving slowly, but still, the steps are slippery, and the wind and rain aren't helping us stabilize.

Everything is dark, gray, and soaked. The palm leaves are still jerked to one side while the wind forces the trees to bend. The waves remain dark and violent, too, and from what I can see, there's no sign of the boat—there's no sign of the dock, either. I hope it's just the storm and the hood of my sweatshirt obstructing my vision that's making the dock hard to see, but a part of me knows the dock is gone.

"Buddy up!" James yells as we near the bottom of the stairs. "Look everywhere you can, but don't go off alone!"

When we reach the beach, our feet sinking into the wet sand, everyone grabs someone. I inch toward James, but he and Leah are already walking away. Someone grabs my elbow, and as I blink through rainwater, I barely recognize Aaron's green jacket tugging me along.

Aaron pulls me toward the shed—or, rather, where the shed used to be. Nothing's left except for a few pieces of wood. Everything inside has been blown across the beach. Even the kayaks are now stacked sideways against the side of the hill the house sits on, having tumbled out of the shed when it broke apart. There was a lot more being stored in the shed than what I can see scattered over the beach, so it's all long gone now.

While Aaron and I look through the trees, I see a flash of bright blue nestled in a pile of debris on the ground. I bend down to pick it up, and my heart lurches when I realize it's a dinosaur plushie. I hope the kid this belonged to just left it behind before he and his family left the island. If the kid's still here...I don't want to think about what he's experiencing right now.

The plushie slips from my fingers when I hear one of the guys release a gut-churning cry. Aaron grabs my hand and tugs me along, yanking me so hard that my feet slide across the muddy sand. We both skid to a stop when we see most of our friends gathered a few yards down the beach, right in front of a neighboring house that's been almost completely demolished.

We're still a bit too far to see anything clearly, but I can make out the silhouette of a boat at the shore, lodged in between massive chunks of debris. I can't tell how many of my friends are over there, but I can easily identify one person in particular, laying on the sand, by their bright yellow Pikachu t-shirt: Zeke.

My heart sinks to my knees. He's gone. I know he's gone. I hope I'm wrong, but I know in my heart that I'm not.

Aaron and I are on the move again in the blink of an eye. As we get closer, the sound of Ava's wails replace the whistling winds in my eardrums, as does the panicked pleas of both James and Brett while they shake Zeke's body. Aaron collapses to the ground beside them, his hands hovering over Zeke's wet, pale face. All I can do is stare from my place beside Leah, who, like me, is too stunned to speak.

From what I can tell, the boat isn't completely destroyed, but I highly doubt it's still working properly. It's partially buried in the sand and lying on its side as angry, gray waves lap over the sides and fill it with water, seaweed, and debris. There's no sign of Eli in or around the boat—just Zeke.

He's gone. I knew it before, and I know it now that I'm close to him. His entire body is gray, and his lips and his hands are blue. There's no blood on or around him, and given his closeness to the boat, I have to assume he drowned when the storm ripped the boat from the docks and tossed it around in the waves. There's no way to tell how long he's been gone for, and no way to tell when or how he and Eli got separated.

The wind picks up again while we're gathered here by the angry ocean, mourning our friend, and our window of opportunity to find Eli closes as quickly as it opened.

11:09 A.M.

When we make it back inside with Zeke's body, Madison isn't alone with Henry and Sydney. Our friends at the Airbnb—Nick, Joe, Reid, and Magnus—are in the living room, too.

The guys are here, but Dani isn't.

The first thing I see is Nick pacing back and forth across the room, hands buried in his dark hair as tears stream down his cheeks. If Dani's not with them, then they must've thought she stayed the night here with us. Nick probably spent the last few hours feeling a bit of peace, knowing Dani was safe with us, only to have that peace snatched away from him when Madison and the others told him she'd left shortly after he did.

I hope Dani managed to find shelter of some sort, but if not...That leaves us with two of our friends lost on the island during a hurricane.

James, Aaron, Brett, and Zayn are the last to walk in, carrying Zeke's body. Those who weren't on the beach with us immediately break down, yelling or crying, rushing to Zeke's remains as the guys set him down on a towel on the floor. The sight of him like that, paralyzed by rigor mortis, makes me back up until I find myself standing alone in the kitchen. I've never seen a dead body before, and now that he's here in the house, illuminated by flashlights and candlelight, I'm finally processing that he's really dead, and his corpse is just lying here in the middle of the living room.

Erin had said something on the beach about not letting herself freak out until she saw his body in the light, to make sure it's really him and not another poor soul. There's no doubting it's him, and there never was. The short, scrawny body, the buzzed head, the tattoos on his fingers, the hoop in his nose, the diamonds in his ears...It's him. He's blue, bloated, and stiffer than a board, but he's still Zeke. When Erin finally lets herself believe it, she starts hyperventilating, but we're all too shocked and mortified to even try calming her down.

"This can't be happening." Reid moves like he wants to touch Zeke's arm, but retracts his hand immediately. "This...This isn't real. It's not real. Right, guys? I'm hallucinating, right?"

"I-I should've forced them to come inside." James's sopping golden hair is plastered over his eyes, concealing his tears. "I should've tried harder to make them listen. I-I should've—"

"They're two grown men. You couldn't have forced them to do anything they didn't want to." Leah's voice is barely a whisper as she wraps her arms around herself, shivering. "W-We all thought they'd come inside eventually, or..."

Madison removes her mouth from her hand. "E-Eli," she chokes out. "Did anyone—?"

"Nothing," I answer, because nobody else seems willing to admit that we couldn't find him. "Not even a piece of his shirt in the debris. W-We have to believe he got off the boat and found shelter somewhere. Maybe he jumped overboard and swam to shore, and Zeke didn't, and..."

"God." Joe hangs his head, shoulders shaking. "H-How are we gonna tell his mom? It's just the two of them. His dad left when he was ten. His mom doesn't have anyone else. Jesus Christ, you guys—how are we gonna tell her? How do we tell her that her son is dead, and he's dead because we let him sleep on a boat during a hurricane?"

"We didn't *let* him do anything. We tried to stop them, and they wouldn't have it," Brett argues, running a hand through his dark hair. "I-It'll be hard, but we'll find a way to explain it to her. Maybe we leave out the part about the booze and the coke, though."

Aaron shakes his head, his green eyes bloodshot. "Duke's gone, Dani and Eli are missing, and the hurricane's still going strong. What the fuck do we do?"

"We have to go looking for them again," Nick urges. "I-I would've been out there already if I knew she wasn't here. I can't believe I didn't think—"

"What? That she'd go off on her own?" Joe gives him a look. "Come on, dude. She shouldn't have gone. No one staying here should have let her go. The rest of us shouldn't have left without her. It was a recipe for disaster in hindsight, and we're all in the wrong, but none of us knew this would happen."

James clears his throat and kneads his fingers into his temples. "We'll go looking for them when the storm breaks again. Hopefully, that's the end of it. But...But we can't keep Duke in here. We have to move him before he starts to stink."

"What the fuck do you want us to do, then?" Aaron snaps. "We can't throw him back out there. That's messed up."

"James is right," Madison says with a sniffle. "We can't keep a corpse in the house with us. We'll have to bury him somewhere."

"We can't go back out there right now," Henry insists. "It's too dangerous, and we won't make any progress while the weather's working against us."

Ava ponders for a moment. "What about the freezer outside? It's not gonna be cold for much longer, but—"

"No." James shakes his head. "We might need the freezer for storing food—it still won't last long, but it's something. Either way, we can't get him in there. Rigor mortis already set in. It would probably feel like breaking his bones to get him to fit."

Sydney rushes by me and retches into the sink. Zayn and Leah aren't far behind. Zayn makes it to the trashcan, and Leah practically slides across the wet floor as she runs toward the pantry. Luckily, she holds in her vomit just long enough to find a garbage bag. The rest of us manage to keep from puking, but a few people gag—myself included—and the others just moan at the imagery James provided.

A part of this discussion feels…familiar. Like we're back in class trying to delegate roles for a group project, but none of us wants to take the lead.

None of us except for one, anyway.

"Let's put him in the garage for now," James decides, wincing. "We'll bury him when the storm settles."

Nobody likes it, but it's our only option. Joe helps Aaron, Brett, and James carry Zeke into the garage, the rest of us remaining frozen and silent. The puking has stopped, for the most part, and even Erin has managed to stop hyperventilating. Half of us are standing and staring at the spot where Zeke's body was, and the other half are still kneeling on the floor, staring at the wet towel between them with the shape of Zeke's body imprinted on the terrycloth.

I spot Magnus standing by the fireplace, his hand on his abdomen. I assume he's just trying to keep himself from vomiting, but his white shirt is covered in blood, so I don't hesitate to ask if he's hurt.

"No. I'm okay." He gestures down to the crimson staining his shirt, wincing, as tears well in his pale eyes. "It's not mine."

Ava wipes her cheeks. “W-What happened?”

“I was sleeping with Danica in her room after we...you know. Then the storm hit, and the next thing I know, I'm covered in debris after the ceiling caved in. A few trees fell down on top of the house and absolutely leveled it. I'm a little scraped and bruised, but I'm not hurt, by some miracle. And Danica...I looked for her so I could pull her out, and I saw her in bed with a big iron rod sticking out of her stomach. Her eyes were still open and everything.”

That makes me want to throw up, too, but I hold it in. “What about her sisters?”

“I saw a leg sticking out of the debris when I left,” he says, his skin turning green. “I'm not sure what happened, but I called out for them, and nobody answered. I tried to search the house, but it was impossible. I just hid myself under the couch cushions in the living room and waited until things calmed down.”

“We found him when we were running here from the Airbnb. Danica's house is on the way. Heard him yelling from the wreckage, so we found a way inside and got him out,” Reid adds, rubbing his glassy eyes with his knuckles. “He wanted to head back to our place. Not a good idea.”

“What happened with you guys?” Henry asks.

Joe winces. “The house flooded right away. It's not on a hill like this one. And it's only one floor, so we had to find shelter in the attic. We were hiding under mattresses and couch cushions. It sounded a lot worse than it was up there, though. I still can't believe a tree didn't come down and wipe us all out.”

“We had to break a high window downstairs to get out,” Reid concludes. “The front door and lower windows were completely inaccessible. Tons of debris and water blocking them. We made it out just in time—I bet the attic's starting to flood now, too. The house on the other side of us...They had worse luck. As soon as the break in the storm came, and we started running here, we saw our neighbor's house sliding down a little hill it was built on. Completely flooded. I think the residents left yesterday, though.”

“There's no way to get here from the front, either, by the way,” Nick says as the guys return from the garage. “The road is totally blocked, and so is the driveway. We had to take the stairs on the beach.”

“We didn't even see you while we were out there,” Erin murmurs.

"We couldn't see you, either." Nick's face crumples. "Dani...God, she's probably so scared right now. Do you...Do you think she and Eli might've found each other somehow? Do you think they're together, and they're okay?"

Nobody answers. If it was almost impossible for two groups of us to see one another on the beach, then it'd definitely be impossible for two drunk, stoned people to run into each other, especially during the heart of the storm.

Nobody will say this, either, but we're all thinking it, even if we don't want to accept it: Eli and Dani have probably been dead since the storm started.

3:12 P.M.

"When I asked him why he left an Ivy League school for Saint Maren, he was like, 'Dude, I'm smart as fuck, but I'm an idiot.'" Reid laughs. "He partied a little too hard one too many times, and they kicked him out. I still can't believe campo only got him once. He should've been kicked out, like, ten times over by now."

"Remember when he sprayed cooking spray all over the windows at the admin building?" Joe says, grinning. "Never got caught, that sneaky motherfucker. Beach privileges were threatened for the whole school while they were trying to find the culprit, but they eventually just gave up."

"Or the time he got way too fucked up at that party we threw for Aaron's birthday," Zayn adds, "and me and Sadie had to drag him out of the bathroom when he locked himself in there. Someone called campo because we couldn't get the door open, then Magnus and Nick took it off the hinges, and we dragged him outside right as campo showed up to unlock the door. He had to get his stomach pumped after that."

I crack a smile. "For such a skinny kid, he was heavy as fuck."

"I don't know why we had Zayn and Sadie do it," James says, mirroring my smile. "They're tiny, and they were struggling like hell. Remember when Zayn slipped, and Duke's head hit the wall? He woke up enough to say, 'Ouch, man.' Then he knocked out again. Didn't even wake up when Sadie tripped outside and almost fell on top of him. I remember thinking, *if her tits in his face didn't wake him up, I'm not sure anything will.* He scared the shit out of me that night."

"That's what molly and Jack Daniels will do to you," Leah says, stifling laughter.

"Eli's the same way," Sydney adds. "He's scared me once or twice with that shit, too."

Brett winces. "He's still scaring me."

The mood sobers now. We've spent the last few hours trying to come to terms with what happened by celebrating Zeke's life—trading stories, cracking jokes, and passing around a few bottles, exactly as he would've wanted. For a little while, it was starting to feel like his drowned corpse isn't sitting in the cold, dark garage a few yards away from us. The reminder that Eli is still out there somewhere brings us back to that, too.

"I hope he's okay," Ava murmurs.

James sighs. "We all do."

"Dani, too," Nick chimes in, like we've all forgotten she's still missing. "Even if the storm doesn't calm down by morning, I'm going after them."

"Nick, man—" Joe starts.

"No." Nick shakes his head frantically. "I shouldn't have left her here. I should've known she'd follow us back. She's lost out there because of me. She could be dead because of me. I have to at least try to find her, even if I get myself killed."

"Do you hear yourself?" Reid snaps at him. "Duke's already gone. Eli might be dead, too. And if Dani's gone...We're not losing you just so you can find her body. I'm sorry, dude. I know it's hard to hear, but it's the truth. We need to wait for our opening before we risk ourselves."

Nick opens his mouth like he wants to argue, but when he sees the looks on our faces, he presses his lips together and clenches his jaw, choosing silence instead. He knows as well as we do that while we may not all love Dani, we want her found safe and sound, too—just not at the expense of his life or anyone else's.

From my left, Sydney hands me a bag of pretzels, but other than crumbs, there's only a few left. We've been trying to save our snacks, but there's a lot of us, and the food's running out faster than we expected. There are plenty of things to cook if we get power back, and even if we don't, we can wait for the rain and wind to stop and build a fire. We'll need boiling water, anyway, and I'm sure we can figure out how to build a spit or something so we can cook.

At least we have liquor. It's not the best time to get drunk, but it's keeping us warm and feeling full. That, and it's making the pain of losing Zeke—and the stress over Eli and Dani—a little bit better.

"When do you think help will come?" Zayn asks.

It's the third time he's asked—not only since the storm started, but since we got back from searching earlier.

Henry sighs. "A search and rescue team will come after the storm ends. It's just a matter of how bad the weather is after the hurricane passes us completely. They won't risk the rescue team if the ocean's still too rough for a boat, or if the wind's still too strong for a helicopter. And our families know exactly where we are, so the rescue team won't have a problem finding us as long as we stay put. But..."

"But what, man?" Zayn presses.

When Henry doesn't reply, I take over for him. "But the hurricane hit Florida, too, remember? U.S. search and rescue will be focused on Florida first. It's possible they won't come here for a while, because this isn't U.S. soil, even if U.S. citizens are trapped here. Bahamian search and rescue will probably get to us first, but there are much bigger and more populated islands in the Bahamas that probably got hit a lot worse than we did."

"So, you're saying it might be a while before anyone comes to help us," Brett finishes. All I can do is grimace in response. "Great."

"We'll be okay," James says in that authoritative, matter-of-fact way of his. "Everything will be fine after another few days."

Zayn nods, chewing on the mouthpiece of his Juul. "For sure."

"Tell that to Duke," Magnus mutters.

"And Dani and Eli," Sydney adds.

James only sighs.

8:45 P.M.

Everyone decides to go to bed early tonight. We ate the last real meal we'd prepped before we got here—buffalo chicken subs—for dinner, and nobody wanted to acknowledge the fact that everything else we have is either perishable or unable to be cooked without power.

Oh, well. We'll cross that bridge when we come to it.

Henry, Zayn, Madison, and Leah had their rooms ruined enough that they can't stay in there anymore, so the guys sleep on the floor in the room Aaron shares with Eli, and the girls sleep on the floor in Ava and Erin's room. I offer to share my room, since I have it completely to myself, but Leah politely declines for both herself and Madison.

I don't mind. They'd just end up whispering and laughing with each other like I wasn't in the room, anyway.

The Airbnb group decides to sleep in the living room. We all offer to let them bunk with us, but Reid, Joe, and Magnus claim they want to be with Nick, who's opting to stay by the door in case Dani or Eli arrive. Nobody has the heart to tell him that neither Dani nor Eli will be coming to the house tonight—or ever, if I'm being rational.

I'm the last in line as we trudge up to the third floor. We all choose to ignore the damage at the other end of the hallway—the rain seeping in from a hole in the wall, the pile of debris on the floor, the wind rattling whatever's still hanging on the walls. Someone threw towels down to soak up the water, and somehow, they're doing a pretty good job of preventing the water from flooding the whole floor.

After Aaron disappears into his room with Zayn and Henry, I linger close to James, wondering if he still wants to finish what we started earlier. But he slips into his room and closes the door without looking back, and a guilty pit forms in my stomach. We just lost one of our friends, and two more are missing, and I'm here selfishly thinking about when I can try making another move on James.

I blame it on the liquor. I shouldn't have had as much as I did earlier, but it's the only reason I'm not panicking now.

I crawl into bed and check my phone, even though I already know it won't work. Part of me still hopes it might, because I told Taylor I'd check in every day. She's probably worried, because she's the only person I actually planned on staying in touch with this week. I don't talk to most of my other friends as much when we're apart.

My family probably hasn't even noticed I haven't called.

I did tell my parents I was going on the trip. My mom wasn't happy about it. One of her friends has a son my age—clean-cut, ambitious, the kind of boy she thinks I should want—and she'd been trying to arrange a dinner for this week. When I said no, she sighed the way she does when she's already decided I'm being difficult. She told me he was going to do great things, that he'd take care of me if I ever needed it.

I told her I didn't need anyone to take care of me.

That led her to tell me she wasn't going to pay for the trip, and I told her I'd saved enough myself. There was a pause, the kind that meant she was recalculating. When she hung up, she said, "Have fun with your little friends" in that tone that sounds like a joke but isn't.

My dad didn't say much. He was watching football in the background—I could hear the announcers through the phone. Later, he texted me and told me to enjoy myself and bring him back a sombrero. I don't know why he thought I was going to Mexico. I guess that told me everything I needed to know about how closely he was listening.

Thunder cracks outside, loud enough to make the windows shake. I think about when I was younger and how I never ran to my parents during storms; even when they were home, and even when my siblings were there, too. I learned early on how to sit still and wait things out on my own.

It's strange. I'm not particularly close to anyone here, and yet, I trust them more than I would trust my family to show up for me now. Maybe because they don't pretend to be something they aren't.

If I wanted to, I could find someone in the house right now. Anyone. I know they'd let me sit with them.

And that, somehow, feels safer than calling home.

DAY FOUR

7:21 A.M.

The next morning, Brett wakes everyone up by knocking on our doors and telling us to get downstairs for a team meeting. I don't bother changing out of my pajamas—I just run a comb through my hair and slip on a pair of shoes in case there's any water or glass on the floor.

As soon as I get downstairs, Sydney hands me a bowl of cereal topped with blueberries, muttering something about how the fruit and the milk are going to go bad today, so we have to eat it all up as soon as possible. Everyone else is eating the same thing, and we're passing around a jug of warm orange juice that didn't fit in the coolers.

The storm's still raging, but it's definitely starting to calm down. The wind isn't as loud and the house isn't shaking as much. I can still hear the rain pattering, but it's less intense than it has been. There's even some sunlight breaking through the gaps in the windows that the mattresses can't reach. If I'm right, the hurricane is pretty close to passing us completely, and we'll be in the clear by the end of the day.

James stands in front of the fireplace, demanding our attention while we're gathered around the living room and the kitchen, filling our growling stomachs with extremely warm orange juice, soggy blueberries or pineapple, cereal, and lukewarm milk. It's not very appetizing, but we're all too hungry to say anything about it.

"All right. We need to make a plan," James says. "Sadie and Henry know what they're talking about, and neither of them thinks search and rescue will be here in a timely fashion. Other than finding Eli and Dani, our biggest concern is power. We need running water and electricity. We still won't be able to use our phones fully without service, but we need light, and we need the stove and the microwave if we're gonna eat something other than snacks and cereal. There's still time to save the perishables, too, so we need the fridges and the freezers working again. We'll get to the backup generator as soon as we can, but it's still too rough out there."

Ava smacks her long-dead phone on the armrest of the couch. "I *need* service back. I bet I have, like, a thousand texts asking where I've been. My socials are the only way I communicate with anyone. People all around the world, no matter where I am. And my fashion account—"

“Will survive,” James interrupts. “You aren’t gonna lose a thousand followers because you didn’t post for a few days. Don’t worry about it.”

Ava’s face darkens. “It’s literally the best point of communication I have, and I need it to build my brand. You don’t know what it’s like. I spent the last two years building that account. Employers consider it like a resume in my industry. If I start losing engagement and followers, they’re gonna think—”

“What? That you suddenly don’t know what you’re doing because you were stuck on an island with no service?” James snorts. “Priorities, Ava.”

“She’s not exactly wrong,” Brett says. “I mean, yeah, losing followers isn’t the main issue, but she’s got a point about social media. Some apps still work without service. We might not be able to call or text, but we could get a message out if we had power.”

James considers that. “Yeah. That’s fair.”

I watch Ava deflate as the conversation moves on. She mutters something to Erin, frustrated, while James is already moving on to the next problem.

I’ve seen this before. James doesn’t ignore ideas; he ignores where they come from. On the plane a few days ago, Magnus suggested something James brushed off, only for Aaron to say the same thing minutes later and be taken seriously. The same thing happened with Ava and the rain.

I bite my lip and store that thought in the back of my mind.

Aaron sighs. “We need to try making some repairs, too. It's getting chilly upstairs with all the holes in the walls. The downstairs bathroom is totally fucked, too. We need to fix it up so we can at least piss in the bathtub if we can't use the toilet. We're running out of clean bathrooms.”

That makes me grimace. We've all been peeing in the tubs, showers, or sinks and rinsing them out with bottled water, but when it comes to number two...I don't know where the others have been going, but I haven't even let myself think about it since the power went out. My gut won't be happy with me if we don't figure this out soon.

“We all need to pool our supplies,” Brett adds. “Anything we think might be useful, we have to share. We'll break off into groups and scavenge when the storm ends, too. I'm betting we'll find a ton of materials around the beach. We'll have to send some of us to the other side of the island, too. It's busier over there, and more touristy, so I'm sure they're better off than we are, and they can help us.”

“Finish eating, and let's all get to work,” James tells us. “Hopefully, by the time we figure some things out, the storm ends enough for us to go looking for the others and turn on the backup generator.”

We do as we're told, despite everyone appearing to feel the same irritation at James's authoritative voice—mainly because we have nothing else to do but wait. I bring my bags downstairs from my room like the others are doing, and we each claim a spot on the floor while we dump out our things and start sorting through the mess.

All I have that might be useful are wet wipes, painkillers, tissues, and a travel-size disinfectant spray. I didn't bring any pads or tampons, but the other girls did, and they put everything in a pile, saying we'll have to share what they brought if we're stuck here for longer than expected. I'm glad I have another two weeks to go, because the stash doesn't look like it'll last the six of us very long.

Ava holds up a mini sewing kit. “I have this if we need to—”

“Don't even finish that sentence,” Sydney snaps. She hides her bandaged arm—which Madison has had to clean and rewrap twice already, since the wound keeps bleeding—behind her back. “Mads isn't stitching my arm with a fucking sewing kit.”

Ava glowers. “I'm just saying, it's here if we need it.”

Other than clothing, sunscreen, tanning oil, liquor, and drugs, there isn't much. A few of us have snacks that we bought for the plane and the boat, but they're small bags and won't last very long. We have enough toiletries to last a little while, but without running water, the only way we can bathe is by using bottled water. Nobody's bathed since the storm, and we've all been brushing our teeth with bottled water, but we know we have to save the water for as long as we can. It won't be pleasant, but it's better to smell a little than to go thirsty.

“Seriously, dude?” James, fuming, snatches something from Aaron. “You've had this the whole time, and you didn't say anything?”

“I didn't know it was in there,” Aaron fires back. “My mom must've put it in my suitcase. She packed my shit when I stopped home before the flight.”

“What is it?” Zayn asks.

James shows the crowd, making a few of my friends mutter in annoyance. It's a solar-powered portable battery—not large enough or with compatible charging ports to fix our power problem, but I guess we can still use it for other things.

"You're fucking unbelievable," James snaps at Aaron. "We may not have service, but there's a satellite feature on all of our phones—we probably could've sent an SOS message by now, or at least tried to. Everyone woke up yesterday with dead or almost dead phones, and you've had a solar-powered charger in your suitcase this entire fucking time?"

"Oh, give me a break." Aaron stands and seizes the battery, his pale cheeks flushed with anger. "In case you haven't noticed, we haven't seen the sun since the storm started."

"No, but we could've charged the battery before the hurricane, and we might've had time to send a message before our phones died again."

"Come on, man."

"Do you have any idea what we could've done with this?" James's eyes are wild now, and the look on his face...It's like he's a different person. "We have battery-powered speakers everywhere. They use both Bluetooth and cords. We could've hooked up someone's phone to a speaker using a cord, and blasted a song or an alarm or something so the others could've followed the sound back to the house. They probably tried getting back here when the storm got bad, and they had no idea where they were going."

Erin winces. "Christ, James."

"You're pissed at me because of hypotheticals," Aaron shoots back. "We don't know if any of that would've worked, and even if it did, I'll repeat myself: I didn't fucking know I had this."

"You haven't gone through your luggage since we got here?" James demands.

"It was literally buried under piles of clothes I haven't touched yet."

"You really expect me to believe that your mom buried a charger at the bottom of your suitcase?"

"I didn't fucking know, James!" Aaron shouts, his free hand balling into a fist. "Do you want me to apologize for being a twenty-one-year-old dude whose mom still packs his bags? Hmm? Look, I'm sorry I didn't know it was in there, but seriously—you're being ridiculous."

James's eyes only grow wilder. *"I'm* being ridiculous? Really?"

"Kind of," Joe mutters.

"Just a little," Sydney adds.

"We know you're stressed out, dude," Brett says calmly, "and rightfully so—it's your house, so you're kind of responsible for us. We get that. It's been rough on all of us, but it's worse for you, and nobody's gonna argue that. But you can't lose your shit like this over something so dumb. It's not like he was hiding it on purpose."

James grits his teeth. "I need some air."

Nobody says anything when he heads for the garage. Nobody says anything when he returns in seconds, only to trudge upstairs instead, either—likely because he forgot Zeke's body is festering out there.

"I'm going after him," Madison declares, standing up from the floor.

"No." Leah shakes her head and pulls Madison back down. "He needs to cool off. Give him a minute."

Madison reluctantly agrees, and we spend the next three-and-a-half hours waiting here—both for James and for the storm to calm down enough for us to leave this God-forsaken house.

11:53 A.M.

It's almost noon now, and by some miracle, the hurricane breaks.

It's still raining, but not nearly as hard as it has been, and the wind has calmed down a lot, too. Even the dark clouds are starting to roll away, but the sun isn't as bright as it was the first two days since we arrived. It's still pretty foggy, but it's safe enough for us to leave.

Nick doesn't waste a second getting the hell out of here to find Dani. We're still worried this is only a temporary break, but he's taking the chance, just like we did when we went looking for Eli and Zeke. Reid, Joe, and Aaron volunteer to go with him, too.

"Let's figure out a plan of attack," Aaron says before they leave. He's calmed down since his fight with James, but he's still tense, and he seems annoyed that James still hasn't returned—despite Brett heading upstairs about an hour ago to talk to him. "The four of us will look for Dani and Eli. We'll shoot to be back here at three o'clock, by the latest. If we're not back by then, the rest of you can start panicking. If we don't find them, we'll try again until it gets dark, but we'll be sure to check in first so you guys don't worry."

Madison nods. "Good plan. The rest of us should split up, too. I think half of us should poke around the beach to look for supplies and figure out the generator, and the other half should try checking out the other side of the island. I'll stay here and look around the property. Henry and Sydney should stay in the house—I don't want them getting hurt again."

"I'm fine," Henry insists. "It was a small cut, and no offense, but my experience is most valuable here. Me and Sadie should check out the other side of the island."

"I agree," I chime in. "Who wants to come with us?"

"I'm staying," Magnus mutters, hands on his abdomen. "My stomach is killing me."

Zayn snorts. "It's because you normally eat for five grown ass men, and you've been eating for one toddler these last few days. But stay if you want to stay. I'll go with Sadie and Henry."

"Me, too," Ava offers.

“Okay. That leaves me, Leah, Erin, Brett, and James to scavenge around the property,” Madison concludes. “Sydney and Magnus will hold down the fort. If you two are up for it, maybe you can find a way to organize our supplies. The perishables are pretty close to going bad, so we should figure out what's gonna last us.”

Nick grits his teeth, his patience visibly wearing thin. “Can we go now?”

Madison waves her hand like a princess dismissing her court jesters. Nick's group disappears through the back door right away, and my group isn't far behind. As we're walking out, I hear Madison say something to Sydney and Magnus about telling James and Brett the plan whenever they leave James's room. She sounds annoyed, and we all are, a little bit; as much as I like James, this isn't the time or the place for tantrums. We need him to get it together.

Despite myself, I shudder when we get down to the beach. This isn’t the first time I’ve stepped out into the world after a hurricane, but even so, the aftermath never fails to chill me to my bones. The darkness makes it feel like the beach we stepped onto on our first day here was an alternate reality. Everything is muted and gray, like this once vibrant tropical scene had every bit of its color sucked out.

Nick's group takes a sharp left turn toward the other houses on the strip, believing Dani and Eli would've tried to find shelter over there if they couldn't make it back to us. My group follows them for a bit, then turns to cut through the sparse forest dividing the beach from the road, leading to the front of James's house.

My friends were right—there are a few massive trees blocking the road leading up to the driveway, and from what I can see from the bottom of the hill, there's even more debris in the driveway. I doubt we can get James's grandfather's car a foot out of the garage, let alone down the driveway and onto the road.

It doesn't matter if we can get the car out, though. The more we walk, the clearer it becomes that no vehicles will be traveling here for a long time. The road, which extends from James's property at the edge of the island all the way to the other end, is almost completely blocked off by debris and fallen trees. It's manageable by foot, but even a bike wouldn't work here.

“Down the road a little bit, there's a fork,” Zayn explains as we trample vines, palm leaves, and miscellaneous debris beneath our shoes. “Another road will take us to a bridge, and that leads through the forest to the other side of the island. The bridge is only wide enough for one car, so it's kind of a one-way street. There's another bridge further down the road that lets cars go the other way, but it's a hike from here."

"Based on what the others said, the damage is a lot worse down the road," Henry adds. "We probably won't make it to the other bridge. Our path will have way too many obstacles."

Zayn nods. "Yeah. I don't even want to try it."

Ava raises an amused eyebrow. "How do you know so much about the island, Zayn? You've never been here before."

"I looked at a few maps before we left home. Wanted to see what I'd be dealing with here."

I don't know Zayn very well. He's one of those people who I always see at parties, no matter where they are or who's hosting, but I've barely ever spoken to him. It always feels like he just appears out of thin air. I've never seen him come or go—he's just there one second and gone the next. He has a lot of friends on campus, arguably more than any of us, but he's gotten pretty close to James and Aaron over the years. I've seen a lot more of him this past year, but I wasn't really expecting him to come here. There's just nowhere for him to go to escape, like he always seems to do.

I guess Zayn is one of those people who brings everyone together. It's almost a given at any event that you'll meet someone for the first time and find out your only mutual friend is Zayn. Maybe that's partly why he always gets the invite from this group, even from individuals he isn't very close with—because he brings more attention, more bodies, more fun.

When his instructions lead us directly to the river—after tripping over planks of wood, street signs, pieces of furniture, and broken chunks of beach equipment—I realize I need to give him more credit. He may be something of an enigma, but he's a lot more aware than I thought he was, given how he only ever seems to appear or care about something when alcohol is involved. I'm not sure if James could've even gotten us here so quickly and directly, what with all the debris making our surroundings nearly unrecognizable.

There's nothing to be excited about, though. The bridge is gone. If I didn't know any better, I wouldn't think it was here to begin with. There isn't so much as a plank of wood left behind. It must've fallen apart during the storm, and the wind and the current carried the pieces away.

"The current's too strong for us to swim across," Ava mutters, chewing on her lower lip. "Look at it. We'll be swept away as soon as we dip a toe in."

“She's right.” Henry grimaces as he swats an insect away from his face. “The forest is too thick to see anything beyond the river, too. I know there's a little outdoor marketplace on the other side of the forest, but we're too far away to get a look at it.”

“Doesn't matter.” A hot, thick lump forms in my throat. “Look.”

On the other side of the river, evidence of the hurricane's warpath is almost impossible to miss. Not only are there fallen trees and debris from destroyed structures, but it's clear the wind carried a lot more from the other side of the island, too. I can see deflated pool floats, children's toys, strips of clothing, tires, roof paneling—even the faded, painted store sign from that little restaurant Nick's group stopped at for breakfast on our second day here. Even if we managed to cross, I don't think we'd make it very far. The debris is piled up, blended in with the fallen trees and palm leaves, and it's clear the more populated side of the island is worse off now than we are, if there’s anything left of it.

It's amazing, the kind of damage a hurricane can do. Tragic, but amazing. Shorelines change and create new boundaries between land and sea. Roads families have traveled on for generations are wiped away like they were never there at all. Trees we remember climbing as children aren’t only knocked down, but sometimes blown into pieces and swept away, too.

There’s nothing we can do to stop it or control it, either. The only thing we *can* do is endure—endure, and adapt to the new reality nature has created for us.

Ava sighs. “We have to go back.”

“Yeah.” Zayn winces and turns away from the river. “Let's see what we can take back with us. Hopefully, whatever we find will last us another day or two before search and rescue comes.”

Another day or two. His optimism is admirable, but he’s in for a rude awakening when that time comes and goes, and we’re all still here.

2:39 P.M.

We return to the house with disappointing news about the other side of the island, but a decent haul from a few hours of scavenging around the river.

We managed to gather a few coconuts, guavas, and mangoes, which Zayn carried back after taking off his shirt to use as a makeshift basket. Henry brought back two large pieces of metal roof paneling, both painted turquoise, so we can use them to patch the holes in the walls upstairs. I brought the driest pieces of wood I could find for a fire, and Ava, by some miracle, managed to find a vacuum-sealed bag of scallops, which we assume blew away from a nearby general store or something.

Madison's group, plus Sydney, is gathered on the beach when we return. Magnus is apparently inside taking a nap, but Sydney got antsy, so she decided to help them search the property. James and Brett were trying to figure out the generator while we were gone, but they're here on the beach with the others now, having tried and failed. Apparently, the generator let off a few sparks and zapped Brett's hand, and they decided to try again later to avoid burning the house down.

Apparently, despite everything being soaking wet and there being no electricity, the house somehow became extremely flammable the moment Brett was zapped.

Everyone's damp and covered in muck, but luckily, the rain seems to be slowing down. It should stop soon enough, and then we can build a fire in the pit on the deck to cook something and dry our clothing. It's eerie enough with the darkness, so I'm curious if the glow of a fire will make that better or worse.

"It's not great," Leah says when we arrive. "We found a few tattered sheets and curtains, rope, some canned food, and a few plastic containers. It's mostly just a lot of wood, though."

"That helps," I tell her. "We can make a water filter if we burn the wood. Charred wood plus sand and cloth usually does the trick, if Professor Wilson was telling the truth."

Henry smiles a little. "She's right."

“That's good.” James nods, but he won't meet our eyes. I assume he's still embarrassed by his outburst earlier. “We found a pole from an umbrella, too. I was thinking we can try to make a fishing rod out of it. There's fishing line in the house, and we found a can of sardines, so we can try fishing.”

“Good idea,” Zayn replies. “I'm sure we can figure out how to make a net of some sort so we can try snagging some shellfish, too.”

“Let's get everything up to the house,” Brett says. “We can start trying to fix the damage while it's still somewhat light out. We'll figure out how to make the nets and the fishing rod, too.”

Madison snorts. “We'll see how that goes. Not like we can pull up a YouTube tutorial for a DIY fishing rod.”

“Your pessimism,” James says with a smile, poking her stomach, “isn't helping.”

Everyone chuckles a bit. It seems like we've all chosen to ignore what happened earlier between him and Aaron, and I'm glad for it. Miserable James—and, by default, a ticked off group—isn't what we need today.

We're almost at the stairs when we hear yelling behind us. I recognize Nick's voice right away, and the urgency in his tone frightens me enough that I drop the wood in my arms. The others drop their things, too, and run toward the beach again when we get a good look at the group. The four of them—Nick, Joe, Reid, and Aaron—are running toward us, albeit stumbling, but they're not alone. They're carrying someone.

My feet are pounding against the sand before I can fully comprehend what's happening. In the blink of an eye, we're all either standing or kneeling while Nick's group carefully lays a body on the sand. It's Eli, covered in blood. He's gasping for air, his eyes wide open, but he's gray and sweating, and there's a piece of wood lodged in his lower abdomen.

“Oh my God.” Leah lifts Eli's head so she can set it down in her lap. Every breath he expels is a wheeze, and my heart shatters when I see how violently his chest is heaving. “Jesus Christ. Eli...”

“We found him on the other side of the Airbnb,” Joe explains, panting for air. “Saw his legs sticking out from under this overturned boat. W-We think he must've fallen overboard, and the waves dragged him down the beach, and he washed up during the storm. Must've crawled his way over to the houses somehow.”

Eli doesn't react at all. He's staring up at the sky, wheezing and trembling, blood staining his mouth, chin, and hands. Leah tries to hold his hand, but it falls out of her grasp. Moving him must've dislodged the wood, because it's bleeding heavily, mixing with the dried blood on his shirt.

I don't know how he's survived this long, but he doesn't have much longer. I don't think he knows where he is or what's happening. His eyes are just...blank.

Madison's hands hover over the wood impaling him. "This is the only reason he's still alive. If he pulled it out, he would've bled to death already."

"What can we do?" James whispers. He and Henry both take off their hoodies and drape them over Eli's trembling, freezing body, careful not to go near the injury. "W-We can use the sewing kit to—"

Tears stream down Madison's cheeks as she shakes her head. She doesn't say anything, but we all know what she's thinking: he'll die in minutes when the wood is removed and there's no longer any pressure keeping him from bleeding out. Madison can't stitch him up that quickly, and even if she could, there's no telling what kind of internal injuries he's sustained. She's no surgeon. That, and he's visibly hypothermic. It's clear he's gone into shock already. Even if she could fix him up, his body has been through enough.

"Eli. Can you hear me?" Brett puts his hands on either side of Eli's face, but our friend only stares beyond him, not blinking. "Y-You're gonna be okay, man. We're gonna get you fixed up, and you'll be good as new. Just keep your eyes open for us, okay? Help is on the way."

Eli's breath catches—a horrible, guttural, choking sound—and his body trembles even more, like he's seizing. Then he freezes, his dark eyes still open and facing the sky, and one last breath of air escapes his lips.

I can't tell who's sobbing and screaming, or who's simply staring at him, dumbfounded by the loss of yet another friend—not only the loss, but the fact that he practically died in our arms after he was missing for two days. He's been alive all this time, only to die as soon as we found him.

I'm the one who reaches over to close his eyes. I shiver when my fingers graze his cold skin, and it takes me a moment to fully realize that he'll never open his eyes again. It doesn't feel real, yet I'm staring at his corpse while my friends wail around me, begging him to open his eyes again.

Eli is gone. Zeke is gone. Dani's probably gone, too. I never thought I'd have to bury a friend, let alone two or three of them.

And I never thought I'd find myself doing it on spring break, either.

3:04 P.M.

We bring Eli back to the house and put him in the garage with Zeke. I'm glad I'm not the one doing it, especially when the guys—Aaron, Nick, Joe, and Reid—return from the garage, covering their noses with their hands. It's hot and humid out there, which probably isn't helping the decomposition process.

It's one thing to see your friend's corpse laying on a cold stone floor, but it's something else to smell him rotting away.

"We can't leave them out there," Leah whispers, wiping her cheeks. "We need to bury them."

Zayn nods in agreement. "Search and rescue can dig them up when they come for us."

"Don't say it like that." Madison sounds like she meant to snap at him, but her voice is too hoarse from crying, so it comes out more like a sharp croak. "They aren't toys a dog buried in the backyard."

"I didn't mean it that way."

James sighs, ignoring them, and runs a hand through his hair. "There are shovels in the garage. W-We'll bury them at the bottom of the hill. There's plenty of flat land over there."

"He doesn't know about Eli yet." Nick blinks the tears from his eyes as he gestures toward a sleeping Magnus on the couch. "We have to wake him up and tell him before we go out there."

I'm closest to Magnus, so I reach over and set a hand on his shoulder. "Hey, sleepwalker," I murmur, trying to wake him up gently. "Time to get up."

He doesn't stir, so I pull away the pillow propping up his head like I usually do when I have to wake him—somehow, I've always been the one tasked with getting him up after parties. I expect him to grunt and open his eyes when I take the pillow away, but instead, his head slams against the couch cushion, and he doesn't budge. A nervous jolt courses through me as I set my hands over his on his abdomen and shake, only for the motion to knock his arms to the side.

A gasp escapes me as I shake his shoulder. "Magnus. Get up."

Everyone's watching, wide-eyed and silent, as I slowly bring my ear to his chest. I know he's fine, but after what's happened these past few days, I can't help but think the worst.

And I'm right to think that way—he's not fine. I can't hear his heartbeat, there's no heat radiating from his body, and he's not breathing.

Instinctively, I cry out and back away, speaking so incoherently that even I don't know what I'm trying to say. Joe takes my place and grabs Magnus by the shoulders, shaking him, but he still doesn't budge.

"What the fuck is going on?" James clings to the back of the couch, staring down at Magnus with unblinking eyes, as Joe, Reid, and Brett take turns trying to find a pulse. "He's not...He can't be..."

Reid chokes on a sob. "He's not breathing. He's not breathing, guys."

"Try CPR!" James yells at Madison, grabbing her by the elbow.

She shrugs him off and orders the guys to set Magnus on the floor. They do so as gently as they can as she kneels at his side and starts compressions. I've been stepping away slowly, and I only stop when my back hits the wall beside the fireplace, when I have nowhere else to go. My breathing has hitched, and all I can do is stare at Magnus's pale face, hoping and praying that Madison gets his heart going again.

"H-He said he had a stomachache," Sydney manages as she cries, leaning against Leah for support. "He said..."

While Madison keeps trying CPR, Joe raises Magnus's t-shirt as far as he can without getting in her way. I can barely see from here, but a few of them gasp and back away, visibly startled. As soon as Joe moves, I see vibrant purple and red splotches across Magnus's stomach. The sight makes Madison stop instantly and turn five shades paler.

"Oh, God." Her fingers on her left hand hover over the bruises, while her right hand is hovering over his heart. "T-That looks like an internal hematoma."

Erin clears her throat. "Translation?"

"He-He's bleeding out from the inside," Madison says, her voice filled with defeat. "He probably had organ damage from whatever happened at Danica's house, and he didn't think anything of it because there were no external injuries. I bet he was sore, but he wouldn't have thought..."

Everyone quiets for a moment. Then James snaps, "What the hell are you doing? Keep going!"

“I can't,” she whispers, her eyes welling with tears. “It won't help. Even if I got his heart beating again...He's bleeding internally, James. He'd need surgery. Without proper treatment, a patient can die in hours. I-I'm surprised he survived as long as he did.”

“He's not a patient, Madison!”

“I know, but—”

“What the fuck do we do?” James looks around at each of us, his eyes wild and frenzied. “We can't just let him die! We can't—”

“He's already gone,” Sydney says, hiccupping into a sob. “He's gone, James.”

For a second, James doesn't react. Then he grabs the nearest object—a lamp—and hurls it against the wall. It shatters onto the floor, but nobody winces at the sound. We're all too shocked, unable to do anything but stare at Magnus's pale, limp body on the floor as Madison kneels beside him, her hands still hovering over his torso.

I don't want to believe it. All this time, we thought Magnus was safe with the others, but he wasn't, was he? He was bleeding out while he—and the rest of us—thought he just had a stomachache. We'd even teased him about it, saying his stomach was bothering him because he hadn't eaten enough to appease his massive appetite. And the whole time, he was slowly dying, and nobody knew.

We left him inside to go scavenge and look for Dani and Eli. We thought he'd feel better after a nap. We left him, and he died alone in his sleep.

Zeke, Eli, probably Dani, and now Magnus...That's four. Four of our friends have died in the four days we've been on the island. There's still hope for Dani, but that hope is dangling by a thread now. It's only rational to assume she's been dead since she set out on her own.

I thought the worst of it was over. I thought the hardest part moving forward would be burying our friends. No, the hardest part will be telling four sets of parents—three while looking them in the eye, and one over the phone while they hear the news from the other side of the world—that their children are dead.

Even worse? We could've prevented this. We could've tried to stop Magnus from spending the night with Danica. We could've dragged Eli and Zeke back into the house. We could've tied Dani to a chair, if necessary, to keep her from leaving on her own. But we didn't—we seemed to favor convenience more than the risk of death.

5:19 P.M.

Imagine watching your friend's body being lowered into the ground.

Now imagine being the one who digs the hole.

If someone asked me to consider this hypothetical two days ago, I would've told them imagining such a thing was impossible. It's an unfathomable thought; and yet, here we are.

The guys carried the bodies down to the beach, and us girls carried the shovels, flashlights, and trinkets to bury our friends with. Now, we all take turns digging, because even though sand is easier to carve out than soil, it's still exhausting to dig three six-foot-deep holes. I don't think any of us even know what six feet really looks like, either.

The only person not digging is James. He's kneeling beside the bodies, where they're resting side by side on the sand, just staring at them. I can't imagine what he's thinking. He brought almost twenty of his friends to his Caribbean paradise for spring break, and now at least three of them are dead, and the survivors are digging their graves.

I climb out of the hole I've been digging with Zayn and hand the shovel to Aaron. The two of them finish up as I wipe sweat from my brow, trying my hardest to avert my gaze from the bodies. One drowned, one impaled, one bleeding internally...and we only managed to be with one of them while he took his last breath.

Brett and Joe, the strongest of us, volunteer to place the bodies in the graves. They do it as respectfully as possible, but the bodies are heavy and stiff. It's still damp out, so everything's slippery. I try not to wince when Eli slides out of their grip and slams against the bottom of the hole, but the others aren't able to mask their horror. Some of them turn and gag, and the others just yelp like they've been stabbed.

After Magnus, the last one, has been placed in his grave, Brett and Joe join us again. By now, we're all holding a can of beer that Erin passed around for a toast. Nobody so much as cracks the cans as we stare at our friends in the ground, covered in dirt and blood, unable to fully process the sight before us.

Finally, Leah clears her throat and steps forward. She's holding her beer in one hand and what looks like a Polaroid photo in the other. She looks down at Eli as tears fall from her eyes, and she's trembling so much that her nails rattle against the can.

"The first time I met Eli," she begins, her voice cracking, "he was dancing on a table at one of the hockey parties, and I was right beneath him. He spilled an entire cup of jungle juice on my head. I was pissed. I yelled at him for God knows how long, then went back to my dorm to shower and change. When I headed back to the party, Eli was sitting in the hallway outside of my room. He brought a bottle of Tito's as a peace offering, then apologized and offered to walk me back. We talked a lot on that walk, and by the time we made it back to the hockey house, I knew I'd made a friend for life."

Sniffling, she fiddles with the Polaroid before tossing it into the grave. I catch a glimpse of it for a split second before it falls. It's a photo she took on our first day here of Eli holding up two six-packs on either side of his head, mid-laugh, looking the happiest he'd ever been.

"Bye, Eli," she chokes out. "I-I wasn't super close to Zeke or Magnus, but they were always so nice to me, and I knew I was safe when they were around. They didn't owe me anything, but they protected me like brothers would. I'll never forget that."

Her breath catches on the last word, and soon enough, she's bawling. She turns to the side as she crumples, but everyone else is too distracted by our own grief to even realize that she's in need of comfort—everyone except for James, who pulls her into his arms while she melts against him. He holds her tightly with his arms around her back as her face is lost in his chest, then presses his cheek to the top of her head as he closes his eyes. His eyes are bloodshot and glassy, but by some miracle, he's not crying like the rest of us.

One by one, each of us follows Leah's lead, taking some time to say a few words for our friends. Excluding me and Henry, everyone drops something in at least one of the graves—things that belonged to the boys, things they liked, things that remind us of them, whatever it may be. Photos, drinks, articles of clothing, knickknacks. Nothing we might need while we're stuck here, but anything we can sacrifice.

I take my turn after Sydney, who collapses into Brett's arms and sobs after finishing her speech for Eli. I'm not sure where to start, and I have no gifts to leave, but this is goodbye—I know I have to say something, even if the lump in my throat makes it hard to form words.

"Zeke taught me how to have fun." I keep my voice as steady as possible, trying to ignore the way everyone watches me as I avoid looking into the graves. "I had a hard time enjoying myself at parties when we started school. I never wanted to do anything. Then I met Zeke, and he showed me how to make the most out of my college experience. He helped me figure out which drinks I like, how to be confident using my fake, and where to hide my alcohol at parties so nobody would find it and steal it." I chuckle a little. "We used to take a shot together after hiding our stuff. It was like our little ritual."

"I remember that," Nick says softly, a smile tugging at the corners of his lips.

"Magnus would join us once in a while, too," I continue. "He'd always give me something of his because he felt bad for waking me up so often when he was sleepwalking. He tried to teach me Swedish once, and it ended up being one of the best nights of my life. I-I'm gonna miss being silly with him. And Eli...We weren't super close, but he was always nice to me, and he always knew how to make me laugh. He brought everything to life without even knowing it."

It's all true. I may not have known what was going to come out of my mouth when I started talking, but it's all true. And the more I talk, the more I realize I'm going to miss the three of them more than I thought. I may not have been as close to them as I am with others, but it's the small moments that mean the most, and we have plenty of those. I'll never get them again. All I have left are those little memories, and one day, I may not even remember those moments.

When I step back so Zayn can take my place, Henry inches over to my side, forcing a smile even as the glow from the flashlights reflects the tears on his cheeks. I don't pay much attention to him until I feel his fingers grazing mine. He doesn't reach for my hand or pull away when I look up at him. He's just smiling—that sad, understanding, I-know-how-you-feel type of smile.

That's when I realize that he's probably the only person here who *does* know exactly how I feel. Neither of us were particularly close to Zeke, Eli, or Magnus. Our relationships with each of them were pretty much the same. Everyone else here was ridiculously close with at least one of the three, but not us. We're still the outliers, even after everything that's happened these past few days, and even as badly as we—or I, at least—wish that was different.

It makes me wonder how many of these people would mourn either of us like they're mourning the three guys. How many of them would crumple into each other's arms while standing over our graves. How many of them would leave something for us before they covered our bodies with sand. How many of them would cry until they lost their voices at the idea of never seeing us again.

Not many, if any at all, would be my guess.

But if I was the one lying in a grave, I think Henry would mourn for me. I would mourn for him, too, if the roles were reversed. We may not be particularly close, either, but at the very least, I'd grieve for the boy in nearly each of my classes who sat in the back with his head down. The boy I never made any effort to become friends with until tragedy brought us closer.

When Aaron, the last of us to say a few words, finishes his speech for the fallen, we take turns with the shovels to fill the graves. Each person drops a pile of sand into the three holes before passing their shovel to someone else. We repeat the process until the graves turn into large mounds of sand, and our friends disappear from view.

Only now, as I watch James toss one last shovelful of sand onto Magnus's grave, do I realize James didn't say anything for any of them. Nobody else seems to have noticed, though; or maybe they just don't care.

We linger for a moment longer before wordlessly agreeing to return to the house. Erin mutters something about carving letters into rocks to use as headstones, so we can easily identify which grave belongs to which friend. For now, though, we have to rely on memory to tell them apart. I find myself repeating the arrangement in my head so I don't forget: *Eli on the left, Magnus in the middle, Zeke on the right.* I don't want to disrespect them while visiting Magnus's grave, only to find myself talking to the sand mound where Zeke is buried.

Eli on the left, Magnus in the middle, Zeke on the right.

9:59 P.M.

We were outside for a lot longer than we realized. By the time we made it back inside, it was almost nine at night, and nobody was in the mood for dinner.

Everyone with a room went straight to bed—everyone except for me and James. We've been downstairs with our friends who are crashing in the living room now. I'm just not ready to be alone after what we did tonight, and James seems to be distracting himself by making a list of repairs we need to focus on. The others downstairs with us went to sleep on the couches or the floor, but I can still hear a few sniffles here and there, so I know not everyone has found sleep easy to come by tonight.

I've been sitting at the island in the kitchen with James while he writes, keeping quiet while I replay the burial over and over in my head. There's nothing to talk about, and even if there was, I don't think either of us is in the mood for it.

After a while, James straightens up from where he's been slouched over the island, then slides his notepad over to me. "Am I forgetting anything?" he asks quietly.

I scan the list before sliding it back. "I think that's everything important. There's a hole in my window, too, but it's not a big deal."

"What?" His eyes widen as his lips part. "Why didn't you say anything?"

I shrug. "Didn't seem important in the grand scheme of things."

"Christ, Sadie. You've been sleeping in a room with a broken window?"

"I plugged the hole. It's fine."

"You're not sleeping there tonight," he insists, ignoring my protests. "Even if the storm's over, it gets cold, and I wouldn't be a good host if I let you stay there. We'll switch rooms tonight, and I'll get the window fixed tomorrow. Don't worry—nobody's sharing my room. You'll have privacy."

I smile. "You don't have to do that."

“I want to. I know things haven't gone according to plan, but I'm still your host, so I have to take care of you.” He mirrors my expression, but his smile looks more forced, like he doesn't actually want to switch rooms. “I'll go inspect the damage. Be right back.”

I nod and thank him politely as he leaves. As soon as he disappears upstairs, I regret not saying something about the two of us sharing his room instead. I mean, after what happened between us yesterday, I think it's safe to assume that the two of us sharing a room wouldn't be the craziest idea in the world. But then again, I don't want to overstep or suggest something like that after what happened today.

He's gone for so long that my lack of patience—and the way Nick is softly crying into his pillow in the living room—finally gets to me. I feel bad for him, I really do, but I can't keep listening to this; especially when he's the only person who still thinks Dani is alive. It's nice that he has hope, but the more I listen to him crying about it, the more I dread the moment he realizes she's gone for good.

It's like cranking a Jack-in-the-box: you know the jump scare is coming eventually, but still, the more you crank it, the more your dread at experiencing that *pop* grows until it makes your heart drop.

I head upstairs, and right as I'm approaching my door, James emerges out of his room, all dressed in his pajamas. “It's all yours,” he says with a smile. “That window shouldn't be too hard to board up tomorrow. I'll take care of it first thing when I wake up.”

“Thank you, James.”

“Of course. Go ahead and get what you need for the night, but I'm gonna head to bed when you're finished.”

I nod and slip into my room, but there's really no point in grabbing anything other than my pajamas. I used up all of my bottled water, and I don't feel like going downstairs for more, so I skip brushing my teeth for tonight. I leave my dead phone and everything else behind, then meet James in the hallway once more.

“Thank you again for doing this,” I murmur. “It's really nice of you.”

He smiles through his yawn. “Of course. I'm happy to do it.”

He reaches up to tuck a lock of my hair behind my ear, his knuckles brushing against my cheek—too slowly—in the process. I try to ignore the butterflies in my stomach when his hand drops to my shoulder, and he traces his knuckle down my arm to my wrist. He opens my clenched fist with his fingers, and while he doesn't hold my hand, he uses that same knuckle to draw circles on my palm.

"Today was a hard day for everyone." His voice is quieter when he speaks again, but there's little emotion in his tone. "If you need anything, I'm here for you."

I nod. "Thanks. The same to you."

"Appreciate it." He drops his hand from mine and smiles again. "Night, Sadie. I'll see you in a bit."

My lips part like there's something I want to say, but no words come out. I loiter here for a moment longer as he disappears into my room, and the last thing I see before the door closes is James's smile and wink.

A shiver courses through me as I turn toward his room. I can tell he tried to make the bed for me: the olive sheets and comforter are pulled up, and the pillows have been straightened out, but everything is still a bit crumpled. Other than that and his open suitcase on the floor, the room is basically a replica of his dorm: lots of green and brown with rustic, beachy decor, and perfectly organized.

I run my fingers along his record player on the dresser before inspecting the bin of vinyl records on the floor. He has good music taste, albeit somewhat outdated. It's mostly classic rock and surf rock with some current indie thrown in the mix. It's a stark contrast from what the other guys listen to, which is mainly just hip-hop and rap. The sight makes me smile when I realize how many similar records we own.

I know I shouldn't be snooping, but I can't help it. His room looks exactly like him—unchanged by context. The same records stacked against the wall, the same half-empty water glass on the bedside table, the same careful order to everything that doesn't feel careful at all.

It's unsettling, realizing how little he seems to need to adjust whether he's here or at school. Like he's never had to split himself into versions that make sense in different places.

I try to get comfortable in his bed, surrounded by the faint, familiar smell of him, and immediately feel wrong here. Not because it's his—but because I'm here without him.

For months, I let myself imagine this differently. Him here with me, or me here with him. Some quiet, mutual shift I mistook for possibility. I never pictured being alone in his space, wearing the shape of something that almost happened.

This isn't how it was supposed to feel.

That's why I decide to spring up from the bed, despite my conscience telling me this is a detrimentally bad idea, given the day's events. I feel like an asshole, but at the same time, I know my three friends probably would've wanted the rest of us to end the day of their burial with a bang. That's the only way I can rationalize what I'm about to do—that, and the way James looked at me while he grazed my skin when we said goodnight.

I linger by the door for a few minutes, bringing my hand to the knob before dropping it, pacing, and running through the whole process over and over again. I tell myself I'm being crazy, but I can't decide what's bringing out the insanity: is it because I'm an idiot for thinking James wants to hook up after we buried three of our friends today, or is it because I'm an idiot for debating this while he's probably waiting in bed for me?

He said we'd finish what we started yesterday. That has to be what he meant by *I'll see you in a bit,* right?

I'm opening the door before I realize what I'm doing. I then quietly tiptoe down the hallway until I find myself outside of the room I've been staying in. I'm lifting my hand to knock, nervous jitters making my insides feel like TV static, but I freeze when I hear what sounds like a conversation on the other side of the door.

As I lean in closer to the wood to listen, I quickly realize it's not a conversation at all.

It's no wonder James wanted to switch rooms instead of asking me to stay with him. He wasn't trying to tell me that he wanted to hook up tonight—he was just doing me a kindness, and he used that kindness to mask what he's doing with someone else.

"Oh, *fuck,* James!" If the squeaking bed and James's grunts don't give it away, the female voice certainly does. "Oh, fuck. Mmm. God, that feels so fucking good. Don't stop!"

James's reply is muffled, but I get some of it: "You're so fucking hot." There's a slapping sound, followed by a squeal, making me scowl. "You like that?"

"Fuck, yes. Do it the fuck again—and pull my hair! Harder! God, yes!"

I rush back to my room—James's room—and close the door, leaning my back against it while I try to calm my racing heart. Black splotches cloud my vision, and for a second, all I want is to curl up in a ball and cry.

To have a moment with me and plan to do it again, only to fuck Madison instead? It has to be her with that annoying, bratty voice. Even if he's been flirting with Erin, I don't think she reciprocates, and she's not the type to hook up with someone, anyway—she's a relationship girl. I guess Madison just got over her frustration, and James was more than happy to oblige.

I think this is the answer I was circling without wanting to name. With James, it's never been about pursuit. Things would happen around him, and he let them. If someone made a move, he didn't stop it—not because it meant something, but because it didn't have to.

I don't know if Madison sought him out or if he went looking for her. The difference barely matters. He had options, and he chose what fit.

That's the part that sticks. Not that he picked her—but how easily she slid into place.

For a moment, I feel something familiar pressing at the edges of my thoughts—not words, exactly, but just the sense that there's a right way to move through the world, and that some people understand it instinctively. I push the feeling aside before it can take shape.

The ache in my chest sharpens, then shifts. Anger, first, and then something that feels like relief—because whatever *this* was, it was never solid enough to hold me. I've liked James—for longer than I want to admit, really—but liking him was never the point. It didn't stop me from living my life, from wanting other people, from moving on when I chose to. It was quieter than that. An idea I kept turning over: would someone like him ever notice me in a way that matters? Not casually. Not kindly. *Deliberately.*

I can see now that it was never about feelings for James. It was about visibility, about whether I could be chosen in a room where *he* never had to try.

Madison didn't take that from me. How could she take something from me that was never actually mine?

James has been difficult all day, sharp in a way that feels practiced, and I find myself wondering how much of it is stress, grief, or fear—and how much of it is just *him.* Is this the mask slipping, or the truth finally getting tired of hiding?

Maybe I'm not the only one in this house who has mistaken charm for care, either.

I don't reach for excuses anymore. I don't replay the last few years, looking for ways I might have misunderstood what was right in front of me. I just let the realization sit where it's landed.

Knowing it doesn't make things easier. But it does make things clearer.

And that, I think, is enough to change what comes next.

DAY FIVE

8:58 A.M.

My room is empty when I return to it after a restless night in James's bed. The window still hasn't been fixed, but the bed's made, and my things haven't been touched. Everything's the same as I left it—except for the condom wrapper in the bathroom trashcan, naturally.

My hands clench into fists as I stare down at the trash. There's a slightly damp, balled-up wad of toilet paper sitting beside the wrapper, and I don't have to use my imagination to figure out what's inside of it.

God. Is he really so dense that he didn't think about me seeing it? Or does he just not care? Either way, the sight of it sharpens everything I spent the entire night trying to keep contained. I should've known better, but I won't make that mistake again.

I strip the sheets off the bed and ball them up before throwing them in the corner of the room. It's not like I can wash them, but I'm sure there are extra sheets in this house—and if not, I'd rather sleep on the naked mattress using my own clothing as blankets and pillows than sleep on these sheets. I don't need to spend my nights rolling around in James and Madison's sex sweat.

After getting dressed in a pair of denim shorts and a cropped tank top, I run a brush through my hair and take a long, deep breath before making my way downstairs. The last thing I want to do is face James after last night, so I'll have to do my best to avoid him; that, or I'll have to find a way to make sure he doesn't have that kind of power again.

I think I like the second option better.

Downstairs, it looks like everyone's up except for Aaron and Leah. I spot James rationing food at the kitchen island with Brett and Sydney, so I make a beeline to the living room in hopes of ignoring him for the time being. Nearby, some of the guys—Zayn, Nick, Joe, and Reid—are walking back and forth from the kitchen to the bathroom, all carrying tools and bickering about methods as they try to repair some of the damage.

I collapse on the couch beside Henry, who greets me with a warm smile, and try not to glare as I watch the girls on the floor in front of us. Madison is braiding Erin's hair while explaining the technique to Ava. The sound of Madison's voice makes that anger in my gut bubble up again, but

I'm quickly distracted when Aaron comes downstairs, letting everyone know he's headed outside for his "morning evacuation" in the woods.

I never thought me and my friends would be choosing designated bathroom spots in the woods, but here we are.

"I wonder why Leah's sleeping in so late," Madison remarks as she continues to work on Erin's French braid. "She's usually up pretty early."

"Maybe she heard the same things I did until one in the morning," I say coolly. "Kind of hard to get a good night's sleep when beds won't stop squeaking."

She looks over her shoulder at me, matching my stony expression, but nothing—not an ounce of knowing, shame, or even surprise—shimmers in her eyes. She's just looking at me like she always does—like I'm a bot she forgets has the ability to speak. She doesn't seem to care that I overheard her with James, or about the fact that she fucked him *in my bed.*

Henry lightly pokes my arm, drawing my attention away from Madison. When I look at him, his lips form the word *who*, but no sound comes out of his mouth. I nonchalantly tilt my head in Madison's direction, then briefly flicker my gaze toward the kitchen. He presses his lips in a thin line and offers me a slight nod. There are a dozen other people in the room with us, yet I know he knows exactly who I'm talking about. I'm sure everyone would make the same guess if they heard what I did last night, too.

Leah comes down not long after, and her arrival seems to set the morning in motion. James, Brett, and Sydney start delivering breakfast to each of us: perfectly portioned servings of dry cereal topped with dried apricots and raisins from the pantry. We have nothing left to drink other than alcohol and water, but even that's running low, so we aren't given bottled water. Instead, they deliver cups containing about two inches of water to each of us.

Joe frowns at his meal. "This is sad."

"It's the best we can do," James replies, sitting on the floor beside Aaron and Leah. "We need to try scavenging for supplies again today. Everything's running low. We need fresh water bad, too."

"Sadie knows how to make a filter," Ava pipes up. "Someone can help her with that today, and we can try making a fishing rod or something."

"It still won't be enough. We don't know how long we'll be here for, so we need to think long term." James picks out the apricots from his bowl to eat them first before his eyes land on me. "I'll get to the hole in your window soon, I promise. I got distracted this morning when I realized we barely have enough for breakfast. I'll see what I can do about it if I have time after scavenging. If not, you're welcome to stay in my room, and I'll stick to yours. How's that sound?"

I don't bat an eye. "Fine."

I hold his gaze for a moment longer. I want him to know that I know what happened last night, but I'm not about to make a scene in front of everyone. I'll find a better way to shame him later on.

"We need to split up." It's Nick who speaks next as he holds his untouched cereal bowl on his lap. "I'm gonna look for Dani again. Anybody want to come with?"

"I will," Joe replies, squeezing Nick's shoulder. "I don't think we're gonna find much else over here, though. A few people should try to cross the river."

"It's practically impossible." Zayn pauses to try puffing on his Juul, but it's clearly dead. He runs a frustrated hand through his hair before stuffing it in his pocket. "We'd have to find a way around it, and that could take a while."

"We should at least give it a go," James adds. "Let's draw straws to see who gets to go. The rest of us will work on things here. If we're lucky, we might find some supplies we missed yesterday in the wreckage."

When Madison finishes her hair, Erin leaves for the kitchen, then returns a moment later after looking through a few drawers. She's holding a bunch of plastic straws when she sits on the floor again and asks Aaron for his pocketknife. She cuts most of the straws in half so there's nine of equal length, then cuts one into thirds.

"It should be at least three of us who try to cross the river," she says as she looks around at each of us. "I think one person should stay on this side in case something happens. They'd need to let the rest of us know there's an issue so we can help."

"Smart." Reid nods in agreement while she arranges the cut straws in her grasp. He's the first person Erin approaches, which makes him shudder and take a deep breath as he reaches for a straw. "No offense, guys, but I really hope it's not me."

It's not. He pulls a longer straw and immediately exhales, relieved, as Erin moves on to Leah. Another long straw. She skips over Nick and Joe since they're headed out to find Dani, and the next person up—Aaron—

picks a short straw. Brett, Sydney, and Madison draw long straws, leading Erin to Henry next.

"If I pick a long one," he says to the group, "I'll switch with someone. My area of expertise makes me most useful out there."

"Can't argue with that," Brett mutters.

By some miracle, Henry draws a short straw—and I do, too, when my turn comes up next. Erin doesn't bother having anyone else choose since the short straws are gone now, but before anyone can speak, James shakes his head and turns his eyes to me.

"I'm switching with you," he decides. "We need you here making the water filter, and it's too dangerous out there, anyway. The girls should stay here where it's safer."

Madison sniffs and folds her arms over her chest. "We don't need you to treat us like porcelain dolls. We're all adults here."

"For once, I agree with Madison." The cool edge to my voice prevails as I meet James's emerald gaze once more. "Thanks for the offer, but I don't need you to protect me."

He blinks, visibly startled by my change in attitude, and purses his lips. "That may be true, but I still need you here to make the filter."

"She's not staying if she doesn't want to," Henry retorts. My lips part at the bitterness in his voice, and from the corner of my eye, I see the others exchanging surprised looks. Nobody would expect Henry to talk to anyone like this, let alone James. "It's easy to make the filter—we can do it right now. It's not worth keeping her here when we all know her skills are more useful out there."

"You can handle everything out there," James fires back. "She's safer here."

"She already made her choice, man."

He and James maintain eye contact for a moment, neither so much as blinking, before Zayn breaks the awkward silence by asking what materials we need. James finally looks away—his eyes burning with aggravation—when he hears Zayn, and I don't miss the way his gaze flickers over to me for a split second before he stares at the floor, his jaw clenched and his eyes still blazing.

Henry tells Zayn to fetch two of the six empty plastic buckets in the garage—apparently belonging to the home's gardeners—then gives Ava and Erin the task of ripping a white cotton bedsheet into smaller pieces while the rest of us grab the other materials. Joe and Aaron take a stock pot down to the beach to collect sand, while Brett and Sydney follow them with an identical pot to fill with rocks and leaves. Nick and Reid, on the other hand, each grab an empty serving pitcher to fill with seawater. Henry and I take a large serving bowl to collect charred wood from the firepit, leaving Madison and Leah taskless alongside a cranky James.

On the deck, Henry removes the protective cover from the firepit and comments, “Thank God someone remembered to tie down the cover before the storm.”

“I'm surprised the whole thing wasn't blown away.” I kneel beside him and watch his brows furrow as he carefully removes larger pieces of charred wood from the pit. “Thanks for speaking up for me back there. I-I appreciate it.”

“Don't mention it. I just don't like the way he talks to you sometimes.” He pauses, still not looking at me as he pokes at the charred wood at the bottom of the pit, dropping a piece into the bowl. “He’s not like that with everyone. With most people, he’s easy. He tells them what to do and they don’t mind, because he’s usually right, or because he’s already done them a favor.” He exhales. “But with you—with me—it’s different.”

I wait, not wanting to contribute to the conversation so I can see where he goes with this on his own.

“He starts out nice. Really nice. Covers things without being asked. Makes it feel like you don’t have to worry about anything—and at first, you don’t.” His jaw tightens slightly. “Then, at some point, it stops feeling generous, and the spell fades. It starts feeling…monitored.”

Monitored. It’s the perfect word to describe this sensation I chose not to notice until I was given reason to.

“There’s no way he didn’t pick up on the tension between us today,” Henry continues. “The way he kept inserting himself. Framing it like he was just trying to help, trying to keep you safe. Or keep things smooth.” He lets out a quiet, humorless laugh. “It’s a good trick. You can’t call it out without sounding like an ass.”

“I didn’t realize you felt that way about him,” I say finally.

He shrugs. “I didn’t, either. Not until recently.” There’s a pause, and then he adds, “We lived together first semester sophomore year. He asked for a room transfer in the spring. Said he needed a change of pace.” His mouth twists. “At the time, I thought he was just sick of me pushing back. Wanted to live with someone who didn’t.”

"Aaron," I mutter.

"Yeah." He nods. "He never cut me off, though. Still invited me to things. Still wanted to hang out. Just…not like before." He finally glances my way. "Moving out was probably the only reason we stayed friends."

My heart gives a sharp, uncomfortable beat. "Why?"

"Because distance made it easier not to notice," he explains. "And because I never let myself get that close to him again. It's not worth it. And I definitely don't want to see him trying that shit with you—more than he already has."

My heart hammers. "Why not?"

He opens his mouth to respond, but he doesn't get the chance. The other three pairs trudge up the stairs to the deck, each carrying one handle of their respective pots or pitchers, complaining about the heavy lifting as they reenter the house.

"We have plenty," Henry decides, peering into the charcoal bucket. "Let's head back in."

I follow him as he lifts the bowl from the ground, but stop him by setting my hand on his forearm. "Can we finish this conversation later?" I ask. "If it comes up again, anyway."

A full, genuine smile forms on his lips. "I'd like that."

My stomach does a somersault as I let him lead me back into the house. I don't miss the way he shoots a bitter look in James's direction before he sets the bowl on the kitchen floor beside the other materials. Everyone gathers around us as soon as we're situated, all curious to see how we're going to make freshwater out of burnt wood, cloth, rocks, and stones.

"You want to start by poking holes." I borrow Aaron's pocketknife as I demonstrate. "The bucket with holes on the bottom will sit on top of the bucket with holes in the lid. The bottom bucket will catch the filtered water."

"Normally, we'd rinse the sand and rocks a few times until the water runs clear to get rid of any impurities," Henry adds, "but this is a test run to make sure it works. We can do that next time. We'll still need to boil the filtered water after, too. Better to be safe."

Practically quoting the video tutorial our professor had us watch during our lesson on creating a water filter, Henry and I take turns explaining the process to our friends. I can't help but notice how in sync we are—it's so seamless, like this isn't the first time we've given a lesson on the subject.

"Layer rocks on the bottom, and cover them tightly with cloth. Put some rocks around the edges of the cloth to weigh it down." Henry finishes the first step, then lets me take over. "Sand goes next, then another layer of cloth and a rock border, and then the charcoal. Charcoal gets covered by more cloth, and at the very top, we have more rocks, plus the leaves."

"Now, for the fun part," I say. He lifts the filled bucket atop the empty one, then grabs one of the pitchers of seawater from the counter and slowly begins to pour it over the rocks and leaves. "It's a slow process because the bucket is so densely filled. We can't add the water all at once, or it'll overflow."

"As long as this works," Henry adds, "we can use the other empty buckets in the garage to make multiple filters. We can never have too much drinking water. But someone has to keep an eye on them, and we need to make sure we're keeping the freshwater separate from the seawater."

"I'll be in charge of the filters," Madison declares, tossing a length of dark hair over her shoulder. "I can't go back out there right now. It's too soon for me to be that close to...you know."

I do. And for once, I don't blame her for picking the easy job.

"Okay. Now that we have this sorted, let's get back to our tasks," James says, arms folded over his chest. "Nick and Joe are going out looking for Dani. Sadie, Henry, and Aaron are gonna attempt crossing the river. Someone should stay with Mads to help with the filters. Any takers?"

"I'll do it," Leah volunteers.

"Cool. Who wants to try making a few fishing rods? We had a few, but they were destroyed in the shed, so we'll have to get creative."

After some back-and-forth, the last teams have been established—like this disaster might behave and work in our favor now that we've formed neat little groups. Zayn, Ava, and Erin claim fishing duties, leaving James and Reid to work on repairs around the house. We go our separate ways when we've figured out our duties, but to my surprise, Madison stops me as I'm about to follow Henry and Aaron out of the house.

"Here." She sniffs as she hands me her backpack, making me frown. "I put a few things in here while you were outside; some of the last few water bottles, snacks, the first aid kit, a flashlight. Just in case something happens."

All I can do is stare at the backpack. "I, um—thank you?"

It comes out sounding more like a question, but she doesn't seem to notice. "Good luck," she says, then turns on her heel and crouches down in front of the filter as the first droplets of freshwater seep into the bottom bucket.

Somehow, her act of kindness only makes me angrier. Clearly, she feels guilty about what she did last night, but not guilty enough to address it or apologize. I know she doesn't feel guilty about fucking James, but rather about doing it in my bed, surrounded by my things.

At least she has *some* decency.

10:00 A.M.

There's still no way to cross the river from our end of the island—other than chopping down a tree and laying it over the water, which is physically impossible for us—so we don't bother dallying around the area where the bridge used to be. Instead, we remember what Zayn said about another bridge further down the island, so we make our way there.

"I have a bad feeling about this," Aaron mutters.

Henry snorts. "Can you be more specific?"

Aaron adjusts his glasses as he shoots Henry a glare. "I don't think anything's gonna happen to us, if that's what you mean, but...but I think we'll run into things we won't be able to unsee."

A shudder wracks my body, but I don't say anything. He's right, and I wasn't even thinking about that until now. Not only were there at least a dozen other vacation homes built along the coast on this side of the island, but James had mentioned there being other residences and stores belonging to the locals around here, too. That, and we already know the storm carried debris from the other side of the island to our area—we've just been lucky enough that we haven't stumbled across any bodies yet.

Who knows what we'll find the further we trek into the destruction? I've lived through events like these, and I've heard all the stories: the ones about the elderly couples found in their beds, having chosen to die in each other's arms while the floodwaters swallowed their homes; the ones about rescue teams finding bodies caught in treetops, miles and miles away from where they went missing; and even the ones about entire families being swept away while trying to flee in cars, only to be found separated and dead weeks after the storm's end.

My heart can take a lot, but what it can't take is stumbling across the body of a kid who died alone in the wilderness after the hurricane pulled them out of their mother's arms.

After walking for a bit, Aaron asks, "Did Zayn mention how far the other bridge is from the first?"

"No. Just said it's a hike," Henry replies. "If it's still there, we'll see it from a ways away. But even if we can't find it—and we can't cross the river—I'm sure we'll still find supplies out here. We haven't been over here yet."

"Might even find some survivors," Aaron adds with a shrug.

Henry meets my eyes as we walk side-by-side, Aaron a few paces ahead of us, but neither of us says what we're both thinking: we're more than likely the only people left alive on this side of the island, judging by the wreckage. We haven't passed even one other house that's even remotely intact, because only James's was built on a hill, and there was never anywhere else for people to take shelter other than their homes.

That's how I know Nick and Joe won't find Dani alive. She had nowhere to go other than James's or the Airbnb, and clearly, she didn't make it back to either location.

We stop every now and then to collect anything that might be valuable, but it's not much. Aaron manages to find a half-full jar of peanut butter sitting on a pile of palm leaves, and I spot some fallen mangoes that are probably a day or two away from rotting. Henry strikes gold, though, when he sees something partially submerged in a muddy puddle. After digging it out and wiping the sludge away, it's revealed to be a plastic toiletry bag.

We crouch down on the ground as he inspects the contents, and to my surprise, it's perfectly intact. No rips or holes, no broken zipper, and nothing appears to be missing—in fact, it's so full that I know whomever it belonged to likely spent a long time organizing the contents so everything fit properly.

"Damn." Henry pulls out a prescription pill bottle and squints to read the label. "Sleeping meds. Looks like a full stash."

Aaron sighs as he, too, reads the label. "Anne McFarley, wherever you are, I hope you're okay and thanks for the goods."

It really is a decent haul: antiseptic wipes, bandages, soaps, individual cloths for using the bathroom on the go, a week's worth of vitamins, hairspray, the sleeping pills, moisturizer, and those little, disposable toothbrushes you can use without water.

We put the toiletry bag into Madison's backpack alongside the peanut butter and the mangoes, which Henry has been carrying for me, and keep hiking toward where we think the bridge is. I don't know how long we've been walking for, but there's still no sign of a bridge, and I'm starting to think this one doesn't exist anymore, either.

Fortunately, we come across a shallower part of the river where the current isn't very strong, so we should be able to cross without issue. It'll flood and become dangerous if it rains again, but I'm not too worried about that possibility.

"I'm only saying this because I don't know what I'm doing out here." Aaron holds up his hands like he's pleading for his life as he looks between us. "I think I should stay on this side and scavenge, and you two go on ahead. Just in case something happens, so one of us can get the others together for a search party, you know?"

"Fine by us," Henry responds for the both of us as he points to Aaron's watch, then to his own. "If we're not back in two hours, go find the others and come looking for us. Do you remember how to get back?"

"I think so."

"Okay. We'll see how far we can get in two hours. If we think it looks promising over there, we'll come back and get the others. I'm betting we'll need more hands if we find anything valuable."

Aaron nods and smiles at us. "Good luck. I'll be here."

I squeeze his arm for encouragement. "Don't attract any wild dogs."

He narrows his eyes, but he's still smiling. "Not funny, Sadie."

I chuckle a little as we say our final goodbyes. He watches from behind as Henry steps into the river first, the water barely lapping over his sneakers, then offers me a hand. I hold onto him tightly, because even if the current isn't dangerous here, it's still possible that we'd run into some trouble if one of us happens to trip and fall. As long as one of us remains steady while holding onto the other, we'll both be okay.

The water's colder than expected, and we have to navigate around both floating debris and the current—weak, but still there—with every step. We reach the deepest point when we're halfway across, and it comes up to a few inches above my navel. It's only hip-deep for Henry, who has some height on me, but it'd definitely be a lot worse if we attempted this near the first bridge.

We make it across in one piece, but disappointment settles in when I get a better look at this side of the river. The scale of the hurricane's destruction is much easier to see up close, and it's clear that this half of the island sustained far worse damages than the other. I can see yellow paint on the ground where a road used to be, but that patch of asphalt is only about as large as my foot. The rest of the road is completely hidden by debris, so there's no way of knowing where it might've led to, or where it once began and ended.

We were taught that heavily wooded areas are usually somewhat safe—and protect whatever's on the other side of them—during a storm like this one. But it's clear to see that the palm trees and pineyard forest did very little to curb the damage.

Mother Nature turns on herself sometimes. That was one of the first things I learned as a kid when I was old enough to understand hurricanes and what they did to our community. It's always proven true.

"Can I tell you something?" Henry mutters as he helps me over a fallen tree.

"Of course."

He swallows. "I don't think we're gonna find anything other than corpses and debris."

"I don't think we'll find anything else, either, but it's worth a shot."

He nods, but his face is twisted with something indecipherable. "Do you think the resort—?"

"How many stories was it?"

"Eight, I think. It was right on the beach at sea-level, though. Not on a hill like James's house."

A grimace forms on my lips. "Maybe the top floors were okay, and most of the guests and employees managed to get up there in time, but..."

"But the hurricane hit in the middle of the night when everyone was asleep." Henry sighs as his eyes land on a deflated, filthy beach ball to our left. "I know there have to be survivors. We can't be the only ones left alive on this entire island. But we haven't seen any flares, or heard any sirens, or anything like that. Not even a whistle. You'd think we'd be made aware of *some* sign of life by now."

"I don't know. It-It's impossible to say anything for certain anymore."

"Yeah." His lips curl into a weak smile as he gazes at me. "I'm glad it's you and me out here. I don't know what I'd talk about with anyone else."

I chuckle. "The same things you talk about with me."

"No. Since we started talking a few days ago, I realized how much easier it is to carry on a conversation with you than with the others. There aren't as many awkward pauses."

I know the feeling. I've experienced it with almost all of the others, too. "Well, no matter what, I'm glad it's us out here, too. And even though it didn't happen under the best circumstances, I'm glad we've gotten closer on this trip."

"So am I. Here, I'll give you a boost."

He crouches down and cups his hands when we approach an enormous hill of debris, our paths around it blocked by muddy puddles. I mutter apologies as I step onto his hands and let him give me a push so I can get to the top of the hill. I carefully climb down the other side as he makes his own way up, giggling when he accepts my hand to help him hop down.

"My hero," he teases.

My giggle morphs into full-fledged laughter. "Don't say I've never done nothin' for ya."

"I'd never dream of it," he replies, making me laugh harder. His eyes twinkle like the sound excites him. As if he can read my thoughts, he softens his voice and adds, "I like it when you laugh."

Butterflies erupt in my stomach. "Yeah?"

"Yeah. It's cute. I'm surprised you don't snort, though. You look like someone who'd snort when you laugh."

"Fuck off," I retort, making him guffaw. "I absolutely *do not.*"

"Oh, you *so* do."

"You're full of it."

"Maybe."

I nudge him with my elbow as he keeps laughing, and for a second, I almost laugh, too. *Almost.*

Instead, I catch myself wondering why it took so long to get here—why it took me this long to notice the boy in the back of the classroom. The one who didn't try to be louder or funnier or more impressive than anyone else.

There's a brief, uncomfortable flicker of embarrassment when I realize I didn't really look at him until he looked at me first.

I've seen that pattern before in the way attention circulates through certain people, the way you're pulled toward whoever seems already chosen. As much as I've always wanted to belong, to fall into that gravity, I've never liked what it turns people into.

The thought settles heavier than I expect.

I don't say anything. I just keep walking.

After a beat, I'm about to hit him with some sort of comeback when he stops dead in his tracks, holding out his arm to prevent me from taking another step. I'm still looking at him, so the way his face drains of color—paired with the sudden tension practically radiating off of him—is what makes me turn to face the path ahead.

A gasp catches in my throat. We've reached the far end of the forest, where I assume this section of woodlands was cut down to make room for something enormous, since the forest continues on the other side of this mess. I can see chunks of concrete and asphalt scattered around, so I know there were roads and crosswalks here once.

There's a massive building—likely a warehouse or factory—blocking our path forward, and we can't go around it or through it: it's sitting on a low point of elevation, surrounded by several feet of water that gathered here during the storm. Telephone poles came crashing down on top of it, leveling whatever remained of the top floor, and now the wires are dangling in the water.

"Jesus." Henry doesn't look away from the scene as he reaches for my hand. "You think—?"

I swallow the lump in my throat and shake my head. "We have to assume they're still live. It's possible to have live wires even after a power outage, remember? That's, like, one of the first things Professor Marks said about safety precautions during natural disaster aftermath efforts."

"That's not what I was gonna say," he murmurs. I furrow my eyebrows as he lifts a shaking arm and points. "I was gonna ask if you think it hurt before..."

"If what hurt—?"

The last syllable dies on my lips as I follow his eyes, and by some miracle, I don't cry out when I finally spot what he's referencing. I'm left numb and voiceless, too horrified by the sight to so much as gasp.

A male body is just barely visible from one of the windows on the top floor. He's pinned to the opposite wall by a metal beam impaling him through the gut. If we were standing at any other angle, we wouldn't be able to see him, but from here, we have a perfect view of his remains from the waist up.

"No." My voice is barely a whisper. "I don't think he had the chance to feel anything at all."

Henry turns me around and clears his throat. "L-Let's head back to the river. We can't go any further here. James's house is on the very edge of the beach on his side of the island, but nobody's checked out the other end. We'll follow the river down that way, and then we can cross and make our way back to the house—if there's a good place to cross, anyway. We'll have to come back the way we came from if there isn't."

"Should we let Aaron know first?"

He checks his watch. "We have time before he's expecting us. Plus, I'm enjoying it being just the two of us for now."

That makes me smile. "Me too."

Only now do I realize he's still holding my hand. He hasn't tried to let go. Neither have I.

His thumb brushes my knuckle, absentminded, grounding. The kind of touch you don't notice until it's gone. It steadies me in a way I don't have words for yet.

I stop walking. "Henry?"

He turns, concern flickering across his face. "What's wrong?"

"Nothing," I say, much too quickly. My throat tightens, heat creeping up my neck. "I just—"

He's close. Closer than I realized. I can feel his breath when he exhales—the faint hitch in it, like he's bracing for something.

He studies my face like he's checking for permission. When he leans in, it's slow enough that I can pull away if I want to.

I don't.

His mouth meets mine, tentative at first, like he's asking a question instead of making a move. The answer slips out of me, anyway. I kiss him back, my hands curling into his shirt as my body catches up to the decision.

For a second, the world narrows to this. To the way he holds my face like I might break. To the steadiness of him; even here, even now.

When he pulls back, his forehead rests against mine. "I'm sorry," he murmurs.

"For what?" My voice barely works.

He huffs a breath. "The timing."

I glance past him at the wreckage, the silence pressing in around us. "Yeah. Me too."

He kisses me again, anyway—deeper this time—and whatever guilt I was holding onto loosens its grip. Not because it disappears, but because it can't compete with the fact that this feels *real.*

He breaks the kiss for good after a moment, leaving me feeling empty, and wipes my saliva from the corner of his mouth with the pad of his thumb. The way he's looking at me with such hunger and desire in his eyes makes my entire body hot, yet covered in goosebumps at the same time.

I think back to what Taylor told me about judging a kiss, and this one is the kind every woman wants to experience, even if we don't always realize it—the kind of kiss that means we're wanted for something more than the primal need for sex.

"Sorry," he says again.

I frown. "For what?"

"Until this trip, we spoke all of, like, two words to each other, and suddenly I'm kissing you next to a demolished warehouse with a body impaled to the wall."

I let out a shaky laugh. "I guess it's still better than fucking someone you met at the bar an hour earlier. We've all been there."

"Fair point." He grins, running a hand through his hair. "Plus, at the rate things are going, there's a decent chance we're all gonna die here, so I figured I should finally make a move while we're both still breathing."

It should scare me—the way he says it so lightly, so casually. But it doesn't.

Maybe it's the exhaustion. Or the shock. Or the fact that standing next to him, the world feels contained—like if I don't look too far ahead, nothing else can touch us.

I don't say that out loud, though.

"It should worry me that you're joking about this," I say instead.

He shrugs. "If I don't laugh, I think I might lose it."

"Fair enough." After a beat, I add, "There's no good time to make a move when everything feels like it could end. No point in waiting in that case, you know?"

Henry laughs softly. "Couldn't have said it better myself." He nods toward the trees. "We should get moving again."

I nod. "Yeah. We still have time before we're supposed to meet Aaron."

His fingers thread through mine as we start walking. "We'll find time to sneak away later," he says. "I promise."

Something tight in my chest loosens. "Good."

I don't question it. I just let myself believe it, because right now, believing him feels easier than not.

We fall back into easy conversation as we walk—about school, about nothing, about the next thing we need to do—like we didn't just have our lips on each other a minute ago.

And for a few moments—just a few—I forget. I forget the tight, unresolved anger sitting just under my ribs; the way certain thoughts keep circling, sharp and unfinished; and the things I don't want to look at yet, the questions I'm deliberately not answering.

For a moment, it's just me and Henry, suspended in something that feels almost gentle. Like time has narrowed down to this exact space, this exact breath.

Then I see the sun catch on something bright and orange poking out from within the swampy, colorless brush nearby.

Something that appears to be attached to human feet.

That's when I remember.

12:20 P.M.

It's Dani.

I know it the moment I see the shoes—her telltale, fluorescent orange running sneakers—but it's confirmed when I spot her hand within the debris. The ring on her right ring finger, a thick silver band with a ruby for Dani's birthstone, and an amethyst for Nick's. It was a gift from Nick to Dani on their first anniversary. She showed it off like an engagement ring for weeks after he gave it to her, like she hadn't sent it to him beforehand and practically forced him to buy it.

I don't say anything yet, though. I'm more than certain it's her, but until we see her face, there's still a possibility it's someone else.

Henry and I crouch down by her hand while we start brushing away the mud, leaves, and debris. Soon enough, her forearm is visible, and then her bicep—complete with a pawprint tattoo in remembrance of her dog—and then her shoulder and part of her chest. We're as careful and respectful as possible while we clear away the grime around her neck and face, and by now, there's no denying it's Dani.

Until I get a good look at her face, I don't process the signs of decay on her arm and chest. A quiet dread settles over me when I see that her eyes and lips have begun to rot away, and part of her cheek is missing, revealing teeth on one side of her mouth. Most of her hair is still buried, but what I can see is matted down with mud and twigs. I debate suggesting that we uncover the rest of her body, but I really don't want to see more evidence of what her body has been through these last few days.

Decomposition is to be expected. She's been out here in the elements for days, after all. It's disturbing, but not a shock. What I don't think I'd be able to handle is realizing that wild animals ran off with one of her arms or feasted on her internal organs.

We haven't said a word since we started uncovering her, but Henry breaks the silence as we stare at her, both kneeling in the dirt with our hands on our knees: "What do we do?"

I can barely get the words out when I reply, "I don't know."

"What the fuck do we do, Sadie?"

The panic in his voice grows with each syllable, and I force myself to look at him instead of Dani. Neither of us was close with her—or even particularly liked her—but seeing anyone you once knew like this...It's indescribable.

Dozens of thoughts play on a loop in my head as I weigh our options. Somewhere in the forest, Nick and Joe are searching desperately for her. They haven't been this far from James's, though. She's out here in a swampy part of the forest where the mud reaches past my ankles, and if it hadn't been for her fluorescent orange shoes, I wouldn't have seen her. I doubt they would've seen her if they'd made it this far, too.

"We can't carry her back," I whisper. "She's all muscle, and I'm not strong enough to help you. Either way, our routes back to the house are too unstable. We'll have a really hard time keeping our grips, and I don't want her to go through more than she already has. We'd need help."

Henry's green-tinted skin starts to perspire, both from the heat and the panic. "I don't know if I can find my way back here. You?"

I shake my head. "I tried keeping track of land markers since we've been outside, but it's so dark that everything started blending together. I barely remember how to get back to Aaron by going the way we came."

"Agreed." His dark eyes gleam with uncertainty as he stares at me. "We still don't have a plan."

I look back at Dani's decaying face and swallow back bile. I'm just glad her eyes are closed—I couldn't manage to look at her again if her eyes were open, staring aimlessly into a strange, empty forest while desperately awaiting someone who cares about her; and instead, she's been found by two people who barely gave her the time of day while she was alive.

The others were never her biggest fans, either. We all put up with her because she was dating Nick, and he loved her—*loves* her. Now isn't the time to feel guilty about any of that, though. I'm just thinking about poor Nick, and the way he's going to crumble into a million pieces when he sees what's happened to her.

She set off on her own because they fought, and he went back to the Airbnb without her. He's been drowning in guilt enough as it is since the storm. When he learns that she was swept away into a swamp while trying to find her way back to him, only to be buried in a thick layer of muck as her body began to rot away...It'll break him.

"I don't know, but..." I swallow once more and close my eyes. "But I don't think Nick can handle seeing her like this."

I open them to see Henry raising an eyebrow. “What are you saying?”

He knows exactly what I'm saying, but neither of us wants to utter it aloud. He doesn't understand it to the extent I do, either, but I won't tell him what I know about Nick and his past struggles with depression and suicidal thoughts. That's a secret Nick told me in confidence, and I won't betray his trust.

“We have to leave her.” My voice barely sounds like my own as I stare down at my hands in my lap. “We can't say anything to the others, either.”

His lips part. “Sadie...”

“Look at her, Henry.” He doesn't—he only burns holes through my skull, his eyes wild and unsure, as I meet his gaze again. “Nick won't be okay if he sees her, and I can't risk something happening to another friend. Hope is keeping him going, but the second he sees her for himself, he'll start to wear down. W-We can tell search and rescue that she's out here when they come—when there are more people around to make sure Nick doesn't do anything stupid.”

“You really think he'd—?”

I just give him a look that tells him I'm sure of what I'm saying, and that's enough. He takes a moment to decide before nodding slowly, making me sigh, and suggesting we recover her body in hopes of diverting wild animals. Once more, we're as respectful as possible while we bring handfuls of mud and leaves to the exposed parts of her body, and Henry mutters something about forgiveness as he covers her face. There's a large, rounded gray rock nearby, so he rolls that over to a spot above the top of her head, marking the location.

“This is fucked,” he says when we stand, both wiping muck from our hands onto our equally-as-dirty legs. “So beyond fucked.”

“If it means Nick doesn't give up,” I remind him, “then I'm okay with it. We'll think of a better plan later on.”

He nods. “Okay.”

I take his hand for reassurance. “Come on. Aaron's waiting for us.”

2:33 P.M.

Cutting through the wreckage of the homes on the coast isn't easy. I almost wish we tried going back the way we came from when we find ourselves tripping and falling while climbing over mountains of debris. It's impossible to navigate without holding onto something, but every time we reach out to grab anything that looks sturdy, it ends up collapsing. We have to be quick to help each other, before one of us falls. It's the best way to go because we know we're headed in the right direction, but it's definitely not the easiest path to take.

At least we don't find anymore bodies. I've had enough of that for one day.

We follow the trees separating the remains of the coastal homes from the denser woodlands, calling out for Aaron as we inch toward the spot where we separated. Henry happens to recognize something—a red pair of running shorts dangling from a palm tree—and claims he's sure that spot by the river is just up ahead. We leave the wreckage behind to slip into the woods again, where we find Aaron exactly where we left him.

He's sitting on a rock while using his pocketknife to fashion a spear out of a long, thick branch. I see a few others resting on the ground beside him, so he's definitely been at this for a while. Other than that, I notice he ripped off a strip of his navy shirt and tied it around the tree trunk behind him, likely to mark this spot so we know it's safe to cross here.

He jumps to his feet as soon as he sees us, his eyes wide behind his glasses. "Jesus. Were you two mud wrestling out there or something?"

"You wish," I reply, making him snort. "We didn't find much. There's a spot not far from where we crossed that's surrounded by electrified water. We'd have to get around it somehow, but I'm not sure how far it goes, and I don't know where else we'd cross."

His shoulders slump as he exhales. "At least we tried. I poked around a little bit more over here, but I didn't find anything, either. I doubt the others are having success with making fishing rods, so I thought I'd pass the time by making spears."

Henry nods. "Smart. Let's head back before they start to worry."

We exchange a brief glance before following Aaron back toward James's house. I can tell it's killing him to keep quiet about Dani—he's still pale and a little green, and there's a new, distant look in his eyes. I don't like it, either, but I trust my instincts, and my instincts are telling me that Nick would do something detrimentally stupid if he finds out what happened to Dani.

Nick was one of my first friends at Saint Maren. He and Aaron are the closest friends I have on this trip—other than Henry now—and even if things have been different since the storm, that much hasn't changed. I just don't want to lose him to his own guilt, especially after accepting the fact that four of my friends have already died.

He'll find out eventually. I won't let us leave the island without telling the rescue team that Dani's out there somewhere. She'll come home with us one way or another, and Nick will have closure; but for now, I don't think he's in the right headspace to see what became of his decision to leave without her.

To my surprise, everyone's on the beach when we get back—even Nick and Joe. Nick's sitting on the sand with his head between his knees while Joe sits beside him, muttering things I can't hear and rubbing Nick's back in circles.

It kills me inside to see Nick like this, but I'd rather him be agonizing out of hope than falling to pieces out of grief.

I spot Madison and Leah filling pots with sand or seawater while Erin and Reid do the same with rocks and leaves around the property. Nearby, Brett and Sydney are seemingly rinsing other containers of the same things, so I assume they listened to Henry and are attempting to clean the materials before returning to the filters. I guess the filters are working like we hoped, then.

The other three—James, Ava, and Zayn—are in the water. I can't tell what Ava's doing because she's crouched down and submerged up to her collarbone, but the guys seem to be trying to fish with spears they must've fashioned while we were gone. Their spears aren't long enough to do much good, though, so Aaron doesn't hesitate to kick off his shoes and run into the water to join them, waving his own spears and hollering to catch their attention.

"Find anything?" It's Madison who speaks first when we approach everyone huddled on the beach, but she doesn't look up at us as she pours sand into a bucket with a small gardening shovel.

"A little bit." Henry shows them the haul—the peanut butter, toiletry bag, and mangoes—but they don't seem very impressed, as they only glance at the items before returning to their tasks. "How have you all been doing?"

"Oh, just great," she grumbles. "The filters are working fine, but we decided we should clean the materials to be safe, like you said. We've been at it this whole time, making trips back and forth. We're exhausted."

I ignore her. "The other side of the island is blocked by a big pool of electrified water. We didn't see a clear way around it from where we were."

Leah only sighs. "We'll figure something out. James reminded us that Zayn used to work on boats with his grandpa, so Zayn's gonna try to fix it tomorrow. If he can fix it, then a few of us can take it out to the other side and see what's going on over there."

"That's a good plan." Henry clears his throat as he looks over his shoulder at Nick and Joe. "Any...Any luck finding Dani?"

"None."

"Oh. That's...That's too bad."

"We'll just have to keep trying." I raise an eyebrow when I see Joe look down at his lap and tap something—his phone. "Is Joe trying to get his phone to work or something?"

Leah sighs. "Yeah. He tried using Aaron's solar charger, but it's still a little too dark for that to work. He's all torn up about not being able to get in touch with Cait and let her know what's going on. It's not like he'd have service even if he got the thing charged, though."

"Wishful thinking, I guess." I jab my finger over my shoulder toward our friends in the water. "I see the fishing rods didn't work out."

"Not at all," Leah replies, chuckling a little. "Ava had a good idea, though. She brought this net beach bag, so she's trying to catch fish and shellfish with it. Actually already got a few crabs after she held it down buried in the sand for a little bit. They're in a bucket of water in the house."

Madison wipes sweaty hair from her face and looks up at us. "Speaking of, we need people digging for clams and stuff. The two of you should be doing that."

I shrug. "Maybe you could do that while Henry and I finish working on the filters. We know the most about the filters, plus—didn't you say on our way to the island that you used to dig for clams with your grandpa when you'd visit him in Cape Cod? You'd be better at that than us."

We hold each other's stares as her lips part—I can tell she didn't expect me to remember that, or maybe she just didn't think I was in the room when she said it. I can see in her eyes that the last thing she wants right now is to get elbow deep in the wet sand, but I can also see that she knows I have her.

"Whatever. Just do something," she snips, her cheeks slightly pink. "There are a lot of mouths to feed. We need to work twice as hard."

She says it like the rest of us shouldn't be here, and everything would be easier if it'd been just the best friends—herself, Leah, James, Aaron, Brett, and Eli—from the start of this trip.

I frown. *"Twice as hard?* What does that mean?"

That's when an ear-piercing, painful shriek echoes throughout the beach, pulling all attention away from me and Madison. I'm not sure where to look until I see Ava slip beneath the surface of the water. Everyone's screaming in a matter of seconds, with those of us on the sand and the guys in the water rushing toward her as quickly as we can.

Aaron and James manage to get hold of her and pull her up. She's still screaming, but she's choking on all the water she inhaled while she was under, too. Her face is beet-red, and she's thrashing around, making it hard for the guys to drag her out. Henry and I step forward to help as they wade toward the beach, their faces revealing their panic as they try to calm her down. But we back away when we see the cause of her distress: clear, blue-tinted tentacles wrapped around her left leg, attached to a big sac of goo.

With the jellyfish still latched onto her, nobody can sweep her into their arms and carry her to the beach. She's a bigger girl, too, and slippery, so it takes both Aaron and James holding her by the underarms to drag her onto the sand while she wails and thrashes.

As soon as she's lying down, everyone's gathered around her, trying this and that, but not really doing anything useful. Madison keeps lurching forward like she wants to touch Ava, maybe set a comforting hand on her shoulder, but pulls back before she gets too close. Reid and Brett have both stepped back and turned away—I see them looking around, maybe like they're searching for something they can use to help, but the color draining from their faces and the hollow looks in their eyes tell me they're just trying to find something else to focus on, something to take their minds anywhere but here.

I can see the jellyfish's warpath when Sydney steps aside, covering her eyes: its incredibly long tentacles have wrapped around her entire leg, with the ends lapping over her hips and pelvis. The coiling is thickest around her foot, which I can barely see. I can already spot the severe, reddish-purple marks left behind on her skin. But there's no helping her until the jellyfish is gone.

"Get me a spear!" Aaron screams as he stands above her. "Someone get me a fucking spear!"

"Are you nuts?" Joe demands as Aaron starts running around in search of said spear. "Don't fucking touch it!"

Aaron comes to a halt, eyes widening, before someone else—I'm not sure who—says something along the lines of, "For fuck's sake! We have to try!"

Henry's the only person to join Aaron when the latter rushes into the water, likely to dive for the spears that were lost in the panic when Ava first went under.

Leah puts a shrieking Ava's head on her lap and tries to calm her, and Erin's holding her hand, trembling worse than Ava is and doing very little to actually calm Ava down. Everyone else, myself included, is standing in a semicircle behind Ava and Leah, too mortified to do anything other than stare in horror—some of us staying close, and others slowly creating distance between themselves and Ava.

Aaron manages to find a spear and brings it out, Henry not far behind him. The two of them either kneel or stand by Ava's feet—a safe distance from the jellyfish—while Aaron spears the creature. It has to be dead now, but its tentacles are still tightly wrapped around Ava, so Aaron carefully uses the spear to pull them away.

"We have to turn her!" he yells over Ava's cries. "I-I can't get them all—"

"Stop it!" Ava's pleading makes Sydney move her hands from her eyes so she can cover her ears instead. It's a horrible sound—crying mixed with moaning and choking from the remains of seawater she hasn't coughed up yet. "Please! It hurts! *Stop it!"*

"We have—We have to move you," Erin says gently, squeezing her hand. "We have to get the tentacles off you, Ava. It'll be quick, I promise."

"I don't want to!" She's bawling and gasping at the same time, flailing her arms and trying to grasp anything or anyone she can in her fists. "I-I want my mom! Someone get my mom!"

Leah turns and chokes out a sob. I almost do, too. It's one thing to want your mom when you're in pain, but to be so out of it that you forget you're trapped on an island, thousands of miles away from her...It's heartbreaking.

For a split second, I look away from Ava and at James, who's standing the furthest away in the water as it laps up to his calves. He's only staring, wide-eyed and silent, with his hands clasped together over his mouth and nose.

And for the first time all day, I don't feel the urge to hurt him. I just feel pity for him, because he's the one who invited all of us here in the first place.

"It's gonna be okay, Ava," Zayn says through gritted teeth while he tries to get a good grip on her slippery body. "Help is coming really soon. They should be here any time now, okay? Just a little bit longer. They'll be taking good care of you by the time the sun comes up tomorrow. I know they will. Just trust us to help you until then, and everything will be okay."

Erin nods. "He's right. Help will be here by sunrise, but we'll take care of you until then, okay?"

"Just hang tight, Ava," Nick adds, his face tinged with green. "We'll get you to a doctor soon."

I wince. These promises are hollow—it won't help anyone by saying that out loud, but I know it's true. What I don't know, however, is whether they're saying all of this because they're trying to calm Ava down, or because they're trying to convince themselves that this won't be another problem for us to worry about if we wait just a little bit longer.

Fortunately, Zayn and Erin manage to turn Ava enough for Aaron to unlatch the remaining tentacles. It's a messy process: the homemade spear is jagged from being shaved down with a knife, and while it's not sharp enough to puncture Ava's flesh, it's scratching her skin, making her wail when it scrapes against the stings.

"I'm sorry," Aaron cries out over her screams. "I'm so sorry."

He repeats this like a mantra, over and over again, while Ava shrieks and begs him to stop.

As soon as Ava's free, he nudges the jellyfish away with the spear, ensuring it's a safe distance from the group, before stabbing it again and again; it's likely dead by now, but that doesn't seem to make a difference to him.

That's when we all take a moment—just a moment—to look at the stings while Ava keeps whimpering and sobbing. It's almost unfathomable that she hasn't passed out.

It looks like she's been whipped. That's the best way I can describe it. Her flesh is throbbing, and certain sting marks are so severe that they almost look black. I've never seen a sting or burn so purple that it could be mistaken for black. I've never seen raw skin start to melt away and turn white within seconds, either.

"Madison!" When Brett's voice rings out, I realize he's been calling her name, and both she and I—and probably most of the others, too—have been too dazed to hear. "What do we do? How do we help her?"

She snaps out of it when he grabs her by the shoulders. "I-um—" she starts. She pauses to glance at Ava again, then clears her throat and slithers out of his grasp. "W-We need to rinse the stings with saltwater. We can't touch them or put any sort of pressure on them, because that'll make the venom worse. And we need vinegar. A-A lot of it."

"No!" Ava hollers. "D-Don't touch me!"

"What kind of vinegar?" Nick asks, ignoring her. "I'll see if there's any in the pantry."

"White."

"I'll be right back."

While he rushes off, Reid swallows and says, "I'm not trying to be a smartass, but should someone pee on her?"

"No—" Madison barely gets the word out over Ava screams as some of our friends pour seawater over the stings from buckets they've just filled. "We just have to clean it and monitor her. There's nothing we can do except give her something for the pain."

"Like what?" Joe demands. "It's not like any of us have opioids, and if there were any in the house, Zeke would've found them when he raided all the medicine cabinets on day one."

"Guys. She's passing out." Leah's voice wobbles as she gives Ava's cheek a gentle pat. When Ava doesn't react, Leah looks up at Madison. "Is this okay? Is she supposed to stay awake?"

Madison's eyes are still wider than I've ever seen them. "I…uh…I don't know. I only have basic knowledge of how to treat jellyfish stings, and I don't know what kind this one was, so I'm not sure." She crouches down and presses her fingers to Ava's neck. "Her heartrate is a little fast, but not concerning. Probably just from the pain. But we should probably try waking her up."

"She's in so much pain," Sydney whispers, peeking her head out from where she's been cowering against Brett's chest. "Do we really want to wake her up and make her suffer more?"

“We need to know if she's feeling any other symptoms,” Madison insists. “Chest pains, cramping, anything like that. We won't know if she can't tell us, and if she's feeling any of that...”

Finally, James speaks from behind us: “Then what?”

“I'm not totally sure,” she admits, chewing on her lower lip, “but I know it's not good.”

5:04 P.M.

Ava woke up the instant Nick and Madison started pouring a gallon of white vinegar over her stings. I don't think I'll ever forget the sound of her screams.

She passed out once more, but Leah got her awake again with a firm slap to the cheek. We rolled her onto a sheet Reid grabbed from the house, and the guys carried her inside while us girls directed them and tried to keep her calm. We put her on the couch and made sure she was comfortable. Between whimpers and moans, she was able to confirm that she didn't feel any other symptoms.

It's been a little over two hours since then. Madison's been at her side monitoring her pulse and her breathing patterns, but she still won't let Ava sleep. She wants Ava awake until dark, just to be extra sure that the jellyfish venom isn't causing internal damage. We haven't been able to find anything other than over-the-counter painkillers, either, and they don't seem to be making much of a difference.

Nobody has left the house since we brought her back. Joe spotted a framed map of the island hanging in the upstairs hallway a little while ago and thought it'd be a good idea to mark the spots we've already searched for Dani. He and Nick have been trying to make sense of it, even going as far as to think of potential routes Dani might've taken the night of the storm, and where she could've ended up in search of shelter.

Others—Reid, Erin, Leah, and Sydney—have been working on rationing supplies so we can better keep track of how long our haul will last, and how much more we'll need each day. They've been arguing about it nonstop—almost as badly as the four of them, strangely enough, did last semester when they were divvying up Leah's baggie of cocaine.

James, Brett, Zayn, and Aaron, on the other hand, have been keeping themselves busy trying to make a few small repairs. They claim my bedroom window and the downstairs bathroom will be fine by the end of the night, but judging by the bickering I've overheard, it may be longer than that.

Henry and I, of course, are in charge of water. We've been doing little other than filling used, empty bottles with our new freshwater, and refilling the filters as needed. There are so many things I wish we could talk about while we've been sitting here for hours, but we haven't had a private moment. Everyone wants to stay close to the living room to make sure Ava's okay, despite nothing having changed.

This side of the house is pretty much silent, other than Ava's sounds of pain, until the guys come back from making repairs near the foyer. Aaron's carrying a heavy book, and the other three are following him as he flips through the pages.

"We found this in James's grandpa's office," Brett says to nobody in particular. Everyone except for Ava and Madison gathers around the kitchen table as Aaron plops down with the book. "It's about marine life native to the Caribbean. Aaron thinks we might be able to identify the type of jellyfish that stung Ava. Knowing more about it might help us treat her better."

"They all look the same," Leah states, arms crossed over her chest. "I doubt we'll actually find—oh. I stand corrected."

Lo and behold, after flipping through the jellyfish chapter for a moment, there's a page featuring a photo of the exact species that attacked Ava: a box jellyfish.

"This is it," Reid insists, jabbing his finger at the photo. "It has the same cube shape as the one from the beach."

"Jesus." The tip of Aaron's pointer finger runs along a paragraph of text as he reads. "They're one of the most venomous sea creatures out there. Stings can lead to paralysis and cardiac arrest. There have been a ton of...a ton of fatalities."

Erin shivers and wraps her arms around herself. "But Ava's gonna be okay, right? Does it say anything about treatment? What about recovery time?"

"It basically just says to do the same things Madison already did," Aaron replies. "Clean the stings with saltwater and vinegar, don't apply pressure, and administer painkillers. Nothing about recovery time, as far as I can tell. And she's still moving and talking, so that's good. I don't think we need to worry about the venom poisoning her. We acted quickly enough."

James squints and gestures when Aaron turns the page, revealing the last section about box jellyfish. "What's this say about other symptoms?"

Aaron clears his throat before reading aloud: "'Individuals who have been stung by a box jellyfish have mixed reports on the way it feels, as the experience is dependent on the location and severity of the injury. Some say they imagine it as comparable to being branded with a hot iron, electrocution, or repeatedly scratching a severe sunburn. A sting can also result in headache, nausea, or uncontrollable muscle spasms, which often accentuates the burning sensation caused by the venom.'"

For a moment when he finishes reading, nobody utters a word. Instead, we all just shudder as we imagine what Ava felt when she was stung—and what she's still feeling now. A few of us look over our shoulders at where a shaking, whimpering Ava lies on the couch while staring at the ceiling, her eyes distant and glossed over. It's like she can't look anywhere but up out of fear of seeing the state of her leg. I don't blame her; from her hip to her toes, her entire left leg is swollen and purple.

"Those white spots on her stings." It's Sydney who speaks next, her face tinged green as she looks away from Ava and back to us. "T-That's what happens when someone has a third-degree burn, isn't it?"

Nick shivers. "Yeah."

"She must be in so much pain," Erin whispers, her eyes filling with tears. "At least she's gonna be okay. I-It could've been worse."

"We still have to keep a close eye on her," Brett mutters, eyes scanning the text on the page. "If she gets any other symptoms..."

He doesn't finish, but he doesn't have to. The sting caused venom to seep into her flesh, and everyone knows that venom doesn't always have an immediate effect on the human body. Nobody wants to say it, but we're all aware that Ava may not be in the clear just yet.

For some reason, this brings me back to what Henry asked me in the woods when we found the body in the building: *I was gonna ask if you think it hurt.* If that poor man felt himself being impaled before he died, or if his death was instant. It makes me wonder what kind of end I'd want for myself: a quick, painless death; or a death I'd have to fight through, but one that'd give me more time with the people I care about.

I look back at Ava once more, and I really hope her condition changes for the better; not only because I don't want to lose another friend, but also because I don't want to think about what her last moments might feel like.

9:50 P.M.

We ended up eating dinner late tonight at around eight, and it wasn't a very impressive meal. Ava's the only one who didn't eat, and that was only because she's been in too much pain to speak coherently, let alone sit up and try to keep food down.

Joe suggested that James and Brett prepare the crabs that were caught today since they've both done it before, which achieved nothing except for starting an argument. James dismissed the idea, saying food preparation wasn't his job or his responsibility, and declared that he and Brett would focus their attention on something more important: taking care of the house and the repairs.

After that fiasco, Reid and Zayn boiled the four crabs they caught over the firepit, but when split up between twelve of us, it didn't amount to much per person. We divvyed up the mangoes we found in the forest, too, and spread the peanut butter over some saltines in the pantry. There's no denying that we're all still hungry after such a meager meal, but our stash is going fast, so we have to make do with what we have.

At least we have alcohol. We found an unopened twenty-four pack of beer that Eli left in the garage, so we cracked that open to fill us up with some extra calories. Unfortunately, with our drinking records, two beers a person didn't last very long, nor did it make much of a difference in filling our bellies.

Joe got so desperate about trying to make contact with the outside world that he tried charging Aaron's battery with a flashlight. He ignored everyone who told him that solar light isn't the same as artificial light. I think he was at it for a solid twenty minutes before he gave up.

Ava's asleep now, and while we're all exhausted from today's events, nobody has made a move to go to bed. We're all gathered around the living room and kitchen, doing the same things we've been doing for the last few hours: keeping the water filters running, rationing and preparing meals, checking on our supply inventory, and trying to formulate plans for the next few days.

James let me know that he fixed my window when dinner was served—he took my dinnerplate from Reid and delivered it himself along with the update. I responded with a simple *thank you,* and I didn't miss the way his eyes lingered on me for a moment, like he couldn't for the life of him determine why I've been giving him the cold shoulder today.

What Henry said earlier popped back into my head when James served me. I noticed immediately how I was the only person he served. When Reid and Zayn announced that the crab was done, James and Brett emerged from the office—James's only contribution to dinner being peering over their shoulders to make sure everyone had equal portions. James didn't hesitate to grab a plate and bring it to me, but nobody else. It filled my chest with discomfort and just a twinge of embarrassment; especially when I caught him watching me for a split second, like he was analyzing how I responded to the gesture.

I see it now—the way things work around here. The things Henry said when we were gathering charcoal are becoming more obvious to me. This wasn't a generous move on James's part, but rather a reaction he wanted to monitor. He doesn't have to do that with the others because they've all been there already. Their initiation ended long before mine began.

My thoughts have been circling back to that every so often since dinner. Now, as I bottle up the last of the freshwater before giving the filters a break for the night, I find myself watching Henry as he washes his hair over the sink, wondering what more he has to say about James's odd behavior.

"Look what I found!" Erin arrives in the living room after being gone for a few minutes, attracting everyone's attention as she holds up a bottle of wine in either hand. "Totally forgot about the wine cellar."

"What do you think you're doing?" James marches up to her and snatches the bottles away, making her shrink back as her face falls. "We're not supposed to go down there. My grandparents have been collecting that wine for decades. It's probably worth more than our tuition."

Her lower lip wobbles. "I-I just thought—"

"Wine is one of the best things to have when food is hard to come by," I say, drawing James's furious eyes away from Erin. "It has a ton of calories. It doesn't help hunger, but it keeps you going."

"That's why I had the idea," Erin says softly. "I saw it in a movie once. I'm sorry, James. I should've asked."

"You didn't do anything wrong," Joe assures her.

James glowers at him. "No, she was right—she should've asked."

"The island is destroyed, parts of the house are in pieces, and you're worried about your grandparents' wine collection?" Joe folds his arms over his chest. "Put things into perspective, would you?"

His lips part in shock and just a touch of anger, but before he can reply, Leah intervenes: "All right, all right. Both sides are in the wrong here. Yes, it would've been nice to ask first. But really, James, I don't think your grandparents would care, seeing as though it could help keep fourteen people alive. Let's all just relax and be grateful that we're still finding supplies."

James runs a hand through his sandy hair, his ears reddening, and mutters, "Whatever. Sadie made a good point about it, though—it doesn't help with hunger. We still need to find real food. A few of us have to try fishing again first thing in the morning."

For a minute, nobody replies. Then Zayn asks, "Do you really think that's the best idea?"

"Why wouldn't it be?"

"Are you really that dense?" Madison gestures to Ava, who's still whimpering in her sleep. "Our friend just got stung by an insane fucking jellyfish, and that's not all that's out there. We didn't think about the dangers, and look what happened. Somebody else is gonna get hurt if we don't think things through."

"Think what through, Madison?" he snaps. "There's twelve of us and not enough food to go around. If help doesn't come tomorrow—and I sincerely doubt it will—we're gonna start to feel the effects. We've tried scavenging, and we barely found anything. Our best bet is out in the water. We can't let fear of a God-forsaken jellyfish stop us from eating."

"Christ Almighty," Joe remarks, his eyes hard and narrow. "Have some empathy."

"I have plenty of empathy." James's gaze is wild and unrelenting, but I can't tell if it's because his authority is being questioned, or because he can't handle being in the wrong. Probably a mix of both. "I'm just trying to be practical. There's *fourteen of us."*

Sydney sighs. "We understand where you're coming from, but Madison's right. We need to be more careful. Spear fishing and wading through the water with a net has already proven to be risky. Let's calm down and think of other options. Maybe we can try making a real trap for lobsters and crabs, or we can try making fishing rods again. Something that doesn't require us to be waist-deep in the water."

"We don't have time for that."

"We're fine, James." Henry stands beside me by the water filters as he dries his hair with a towel. "Just relax a little. We'll figure something out. Let's just try not to be insensitive to Ava."

"She can't even hear us," James mutters under his breath. It's loud enough for me—just two or three feet away from him—to hear, but the others don't catch it. Louder, he adds, "I'm gonna go think of ideas in the office."

As soon as he's gone, Leah sighs and says, "Maybe he's just hangry."

"We're all hangry," Aaron grumbles, only half-jokingly.

"We'll see where his head's at when he comes back." Madison's dark blue eyes are focused only on Ava, but they're swimming with uncertainty. "If he still hasn't budged...Maybe he's right. He usually is."

Some of the others mutter in agreement, leading me and Henry to lock eyes immediately. We don't have to say a word to know what the other person is thinking: most of this group, if not all of them, can disagree with James until they're blue in the face, but when push comes to shove, they always let up. That's how it's always been: they argue, he doesn't budge, and they end up agreeing with him.

As I watch the last drops of freshwater drip from the filter, with Ava's sleep-whimpering serving as the only sound in the room, everything clicks into place.

They all push back. Every last one of them. They argue, and protest, and insist they know better until James decides otherwise. After that, it's like the disagreement never happened. Even worse—sometimes, they almost seem to be relieved when a decision is made for them, even if it's not the right decision.

This isn't the first time I've noticed this, either. I guess I didn't notice it before because I wasn't looking for it.

There was the night last year at one of James's parties when a kid passed out drunk, and we didn't notice him slumped in the bathroom until the other guests had already left. We were all talking over each other and trying to come up with a game plan—call campo, call an ambulance, call someone's parents to come and help us. James shut it down; not because the kid was fine, but because it'd be a problem for us if we got anyone else involved.

He reminded us of everything we could lose. Scholarships, visas, futures. Somehow, that was enough.

The next morning, hours after a few of the guys dropped the kid off outside of his dorm room, we found out the kid ended up in the hospital, anyway. He needed his stomach pumped. Everyone felt bad; for a little while.

I remember what happened after, too. James smiling, bagels appearing from his favorite shop off campus, and the night getting folded away in the backs of our memories like it never happened.

What I don't remember is anyone mentioning the Good Samaritan law; or maybe we did, and we decided it was easier not to test it.

Looking back, I now know that if someone had called for help like we wanted to—protection under the Good Samaritan law or not—that person wouldn't be here on the island with us.

Obedience is access. I recognize that now; just as I recognize how quickly we learned to obey.

11:35 P.M.

Everyone's still awake. A part of me is surprised, given that we haven't had a late night since the storm hit, but I get it—we're all too worried about Ava to separate. We all want to see for ourselves that her condition isn't changing for the worst. She's been okay so far, but nobody knows what might happen.

James hasn't come back from the office, either. Brett went to check on him a few minutes ago; he's the only person brave enough to deal with James right now, and he's probably the only person James might listen to at this point. Everyone else is just hoping James comes back in a better mood, and with a plan we can all agree on.

I take a sip from one of the refilled water bottles as I play a round of checkers with Henry at the kitchen table. It definitely doesn't taste the same as bottled water, but it's close enough. I'm glad we boiled it over the firepit about an hour ago—if not, it'd probably taste a bit saltier.

"I'm glad I can brush my teeth again," Henry says, gesturing to my water bottle. "I've had the worst breath of my life these past two days."

"Mine's always bad." Sydney, filing her nails in the seat to my left, cracks a smile. "Brett used to offer me breath strips after our dates when we first started seeing each other. I thought he just liked them, 'cause he always popped one, too. After enough time went by, he came clean and told me my breath always stinks, and he used them just so I wouldn't feel bad." She laughs. "He's not wrong. I think there's something wrong with my mouth."

"I heard something crawled in there and died," Aaron jokes as he brushes past the table to toss something in the trash. Sydney socks him in the bicep, but her hiss of pain is louder than his as she immediately clutches her own arm. Aaron forgets about her punch and sets a worried hand on her shoulder. "You okay?"

"Yeah." She grimaces as she glances at her bandage. "It's not bleeding again, so I think it's okay."

"I can't believe that closed up without stitches," I remark. "It's really lucky."

Sydney forces a smile. "Yeah. No infection, either, thanks to Madison."

The girl in question doesn't hear us. She's still sitting beside Ava, but she's entertaining herself by spinning one of her rings, her eyes glazed over like she's deep in thought. I wonder if she'll sleep tonight, or if she'll be up until sunrise keeping an eye on Ava. Maybe she'll task someone else with taking her place so she can sleep—or meet James later on, for that matter.

"Do we have anything to snack on?" Joe joins us in the kitchen while the rest of the group remains in the living room, either playing board games or staring outside at the darkness. "I'm starving."

"Not really," Aaron replies. "We've pretty much rationed everything out. We'll have two good meals tomorrow, though, now that we have plenty of freshwater. We can make the instant oatmeal for breakfast and the pasta for dinner. Not enough for another day, though. I'm not sure what we'll do if we're still here after tomorrow."

"We won't be," Zayn says confidently.

"Maybe James was right," Sydney says lowly, gnawing on her lower lip. "We have to get back into the water. Something like that can't happen twice, right? Besides, we were out there swimming and paddleboarding before the storm, and we didn't run into any jellyfish, or sharks, or piranhas then."

"There were also a shit ton more people in the water before the storm. All the vacationers," Joe reminds her. "I bet most of the marine life got spooked and kept their distance. It's too calm out there now."

She shrugs. "Maybe."

"We'll have to take a group vote tomorrow," Joe continues. "I don't wanna see anyone else get hurt like Ava, but if we're really gonna be stuck here for a few more days...I don't know. But I still think James was wrong for mentioning it so soon. Anyone else?"

For a split second, my eyes find Henry's. It's good to know that Joe hasn't fallen under James's spell, too. I have faith that Nick and Reid are in the same boat—and even Aaron, at times—but not so much when it comes to the others.

"He was just trying to help." It's Leah's voice that rings out next as she strolls over to grab a bottle of water from the kitchen island. "He didn't mean for it to come off as insensitive. I'm sure anyone else would've said the same thing if this was their house."

"He's been insensitive for half the trip," Joe bites back. "It's not right."

I get up to grab another water bottle when I finish mine, and just as I'm returning to my seat, Sydney holds something out in my direction while blinking her large, pleading brown eyes up at me.

"Can you bring this to Brett for me?" she asks. When I accept it, I realize it's her nail file. "I don't wanna get up."

I chuckle a little. "Yeah, sure."

Aaron guffaws. "Bretty Boo needs a *manicure."*

When he finishes singing the last word, Sydney rolls her eyes and says, "He has these two jagged nails he broke when he was doing repairs earlier. He keeps scratching the fuck out of me whenever he touches me."

"Do you give him pedis, too?"

While Aaron continues to be a menace, I head toward the foyer to bring Brett the file in the office. The door's partially open, and I can hear him and James talking. Curiosity compels me to lean against the wall and listen in for a moment. I know it's wrong, but I can't help myself.

"...not your fault, man." It's Brett I hear first. "We've been through this, like, ten times already."

"Still. I should've been more prepared." I can tell from James's voice that he's gotten into some of his grandfather's liquor—maybe a little more than *some*. "Could've gotten enough groceries for the whole week if I wanted to on day one. But I was dumb, and—"

"You weren't dumb. Nobody could've known this would happen."

"Yeah, you're right. Dumb isn't the right word. I guess I was trying to be cautious, but I still should've done things differently. I could've—"

"Stop saying that," Brett interrupts. "Look, dude, there are a lot of things we *all* could've done differently. But guess what? I bet most of it wouldn't have made a big difference in the grand scheme of things. Perishables still would've gone bad in a day or two. Water still would've run out. Snacks still would've gotten demolished. Nobody thinks about conserving shit when they have no reason to. Stop beating yourself up over it."

"You don't get it," James argues. "It's not like we didn't do a big shopping trip that first day because of money. I have Dad's card, remember? He said no limit as long as everyone's happy and fed. He wanted to take care of everyone on this trip. I just didn't—"

"You had no reason to think we'd have to make one huge trip on day one to last us the whole week. Nobody does that on vacation, man. People always buy what they need when they need it. It's not a big deal."

I bite the insides of my cheeks to keep from audibly reacting. *James's dad gave him his credit card to buy us groceries on the island?* That can't be right. James asked all of us to cough up two hundred bucks to put toward groceries before the trip.

I feel like I've just figured out the trick to winning a card game. People who already know the trick might be accused of cheating, but they're not—they've just played the game enough to know the key to winning, each and every time.

For a moment, my anger at James remerges. My hands clench at my sides, my left hand nails digging into the file. I think about how James's dad gave him a credit card with no limit, and then about how I had to pick up extra shifts before we booked the plane tickets, triple-checking that I could afford it.

Something settles in my chest, heavy and final.

"I've said it a thousand times now, and I'll say it again: you couldn't have known this would happen. You've been doing your best since we got here," Brett assures him. "We'll figure something out, man. Don't worry. There are a bunch of us here—we can put our heads together and think of something to get us by."

"We only have one option, and everyone jumped down my throat when I brought it up."

"Bad timing. Everyone's still shaken up after what happened to Ava. Just let them sleep on it." He pauses. "Ready to head back out?"

James mutters an affirmative response. The instant I hear the desk chair squeaking, I take a few soft, quiet steps back and make it seem like I'm approaching from the other side of the house. I make it three steps toward the office when the two of them walk out, Brett nearly crashing into me.

"Sadie." He takes a step back and smiles. "You okay?"

"Yeah." I return his smile and hand him the nail file. "Sydney wanted me to give this to you."

He snorts into a laugh. "Great, thanks."

He walks off to rejoin the others, but just as I'm starting to follow him, James's hand wraps around my wrist. I sigh and slither out of his grasp as I turn back to face him. His eyes are bloodshot and his hair's a mess, like he's been nervously tousling it since the second he left us.

I raise an eyebrow. “Yes?”

“Sadie...” He coughs awkwardly and mimics my expression. “Are we okay?”

I bat my eyes and offer him a sweet smile—a harmless one, a smile I know he’ll recognize. “Why wouldn't we be, James?”

His lips part, but when he doesn't immediately reply, I turn on my heel and walk away.

A real smile forms on my lips when a few seconds pass before I hear his footsteps behind me. I register the satisfaction, file it away, and move on before it can evolve into something messier.

I'm still not totally sure if he knows that I know about him fucking Madison last night. I hope he does, and not because I still care about him leading me on only to screw me over. Kissing Henry today made me realize that James isn't worth being upset over—but at the same time, he's certainly worth keeping off-balance.

Everyone's gathered in the kitchen when I make it there, excluding Ava. It's the first time we've all been together in the same room, laughing and joking around, in what feels like forever. Someone opened those expensive bottles of wine from the cellar, and they're all holding plastic cups while claiming various spots around the kitchen.

Henry appears beside me with a cup before I realize I need one. His gaze flicks over to James—assessing, not reacting—then settles back into the room. I reach out for his hand and give it a gentle squeeze before dropping it. Something lights up in his eyes, making me smile, before we both sip from our cups and turn our attention back to our friends.

All I can think about is how excited I am for everyone to go to sleep so I can tell Henry about what I overheard. I know I can trust him to read that situation correctly.

I barely notice James as he mopes his way over to the other side of the kitchen, where he sits alone at the table while everyone else stands. He doesn't touch the wine, despite there being about a third of a bottle left right in front of him. He just stares at it as if waiting for permission from people who aren’t here.

Brett and Sydney stand on my other side—closer to me and Henry than anyone else—and though I don't mean to eavesdrop, I catch most of what they're whispering to each other.

"...camera?" Brett murmurs. "If it's charged, I mean. I doubt it, but I'll check later. Even if things haven't gone as planned, we'll have a few good memories to look back on from this trip."

"If you want to take pictures, then do it, babe," she replies. "Not sure if anyone else will be interested, but do what you want."

"How does it work? Like, what are the settings and shit?"

Sydney shrugs. "I don't know. Ask Spencer. It's his camera."

What follows seems to happen in slow motion. I watch as Brett lifts his chin a bit to scan the room, looking for his brother. Then his face goes slack and white in a split second—so fast that I'd miss it if I blinked. His lips part as his eyes bug out of his skull, and with just five words, he brings an end to the first semi-normal night we've had since the storm:

"Where the fuck is Spencer?"

DAY SIX

12:00 A.M.

Brett's probably one of the most in control, level-headed people I've ever met. I've heard him raise his voice, but I've never seen him lose his shit. Until now, I didn't think it was even possible for him to lose his shit.

In all honesty, I've never seen anyone snap like this. One minute, he's casually chatting with Sydney about a camera, and the next, he's screaming bloody murder, rushing around the house, slamming doors, and shoving people out of his way like we're nothing to him. His eyes are already bloodshot, and his face went from white, to green, to red in a matter of seconds.

I don't blame him. It took him almost four full days to realize his little brother hasn't been seen since the storm hit. Of course, the rest of us didn't notice Spencer's absence, either, but we're not related to him. That doesn't make it any better—I barely know Spencer, but I still feel shitty for forgetting him—but it's no wonder Brett's transformed into a different person.

"He has to fucking be here!" Brett throws the pantry door open to check, like we all haven't been in there a hundred times already. "He's here somewhere! He didn't just fucking disappear!"

"Try to calm down." It's James who finally stops Brett's warpath by grabbing his shoulders. Brett tries to squirm out of James's grasp, to no avail. "L-Let's take a minute and think about this. When's the last time anyone saw him?"

Brett shrugs him off and runs a hand through his messy hair. "I-I don't know. I could've sworn—"

"I remember he went to do a line with Zeke and Eli the night of the storm, but he didn't follow them outside," Erin says, wiping tears from her cheeks. "I-I heard him say something about the library after Sydney got here, though. He was gonna sleep in there so Sydney could have his spot in Brett's room."

"Library? What library?" Henry frowns. "You mean the office?"

James sighs. "It's locked. He wouldn't have gone in there."

With some help from James and Sydney, Brett sinks into a chair at the island and scrubs a hand down his face. “I-I forgot he came with us. I forgot I brought him here. I forgot my little brother during a fucking hurricane.”

“It's okay,” Leah consoles, though the bewilderment in her eyes betrays her. “H-He doesn't always come with us, and he usually does his own thing, anyway. You're not the only one who forgot he was here, either.”

“He's *my* brother, Leah!”

“You know what? You're right.” Madison faces him with her arms crossed over her chest and her eyebrows set in a thin, unrelenting line. “You brought him here. You should've noticed that your own brother wasn't with us after the storm. You've had days to realize he was missing, Brett. That’s all on you.”

Aaron opens his mouth like he wants to say something—agree with her or tell her to cool it, I’m not really sure—but he doesn’t speak.

Sydney rubs Brett’s back in circles and glares at Madison. “You’re not helping. None of us noticed, either. We've all been responsible for each other since the second the storm hit, and we all let Spencer down.”

Brett just shakes his head. “I should've paid more attention to him. I thought he'd be fine on his own because he always is, but I was stupid. I should've involved him more. Should've let him take the floor in the room instead of thanking him for giving us privacy. Should've looked for him the second the storm started getting bad.”

“We all should've been better,” Sydney murmurs. “We didn't even think to do a headcount.”

“It’s worth noting that his things aren’t here,” Reid says. “He must've taken them with him.”

I furrow my brows. “Why would he take his things out of the house with him?”

Aaron shrugs. “He was high and drunk out of his mind. We all were. Maybe he wanted to stay at the Airbnb after he gave up his spot in the room, and he forgot to tell us.”

“We would've found him already if he was headed that way,” Erin says.

“We haven't found Dani, and she was headed in that direction, too,” Joe reminds her. “If we're thinking optimistically, then they both found shelter somewhere when the storm started, and they've been trapped there ever since. The other possibility is that—”

"We know what the other possibility is, man," Nick snaps. "We don't need to say it out loud. We just need to keep thinking positive—that they found shelter, they're stuck or lost somewhere, and they're waiting for us to find them."

Suddenly, Brett picks up his head, his eyes wide and rimmed with red. "Hey. Do we have any fireworks left?"

"A few," James confirms. "I brought the rest into the garage after you hooligans set them off before the storm. Why? What are you thinking?"

"If we set them off, they'd be like flares." Brett's talking so frantically that his words are blending together. "If there are any boats in the distance, they'll see us. And if anyone's out there trying to find their way back here—"

"—the sound could lure them in the right direction. That's like what James was saying the other day about the speakers," Leah recalls, nodding thoughtfully. "I mean, it wouldn't help if they're stuck, but still. If they think they're alone out there, the fireworks will let them know they're not, and they can find a way to attract us to their location. I'm not sure if it would work, but it's definitely worth trying. It's the only option we have left."

"James?" Madison raises an eyebrow at him. "What do you think?"

He hesitates for just a beat too long. I can see the frenzy in Brett's eyes—he's opening his mouth, ready to bark at James to make a decision, when James finally answers.

"Leah's right. I had a good idea with the speaker thing the other day. This could be the next best thing. Might even work better."

"I don't know," Erin mutters, chewing on her lower lip. "It could be a hazard. What would we do if the fireworks hit the house and set it on fire?"

James ignores her. "I'll set them off. I have the steadiest hands."

"We should set them off on the deck instead of the beach," Zayn suggests as James leaves to grab the fireworks from the garage. "They'll be higher and easier to see from a distance since we're on a hill."

Everyone mutters in agreement and starts flooding out the back door, leaving only Ava inside. Somehow, the commotion over Spencer hasn't woken her; we'll see if the fireworks get her stirring, but I have a feeling she'll be sleeping for a while.

James arrives as we're all settling on the deck in optimum viewing spots. Most of us try to stay close to the house to avoid getting hit with any stray sparks. James takes the first set of fireworks out of the box and positions them across from us—right at the top of the stairs at the edge of the deck—before accepting the lighter from Aaron, who snagged it out of a kitchen drawer on his way out.

As soon as he lights it, it sizzles and crackles while he scurries away, and a flicker of hope stirs in my chest. I watch it shoot straight up toward the sky before it curves, then falls down over the stairs and lands on the beach, where it's extinguished by the sand.

There are a few sighs and mutters of disappointment, but Brett silences them by barking, "Try another one!"

James shoots him a dirty look, but does as he's told. Unfortunately, this one only hisses and sparks for a few seconds before it dies. James tries lighting it once more, but nothing happens.

"Are they wet?" Reid asks as he lifts up the box and inspects it with a frown. "Not anymore, but they might've gotten damaged. There were a few small leaks in the garage, plus we weren't really taking great care of them when we used them the other night."

"We have to keep trying," Brett insists, peering into the box. "There's two more."

The third one ignites more than the second, but it's basically just a sparkler. James curses when some of the sparks land on his bare feet—a dumb move for someone setting off fireworks—but by the time he blows them away, the firework has died, leaving nothing but a few tiny embers on the deck.

James takes a deep breath as he puts the last one in position. "Here we go. Fingers crossed."

My eyes flick over to Brett a few paces ahead of me. His hands are balled into fists at his sides as he watches James, and though I can't see his face, I picture the combination of hope, dread, and guilt he's probably wearing like a mask.

Then I glance at Nick to my left, separated from me by Joe and Henry, and I notice he's adopted the same expression I imagine Brett has. His hands aren't balled into fists, though, but rather clutched to his chest.

They're in the same boat, Brett and Nick. They both know in their hearts that Spencer and Dani are gone, and they're partially responsible for it. But this slim-to-nothing chance gives them hope that their efforts will make everything better—and make their guilt a little less. All they need is to see this last firework explode in the sky, to hope that Spencer and Dani see it and find their way back to us; and if it doesn't, they're right back where they started.

I keep staring at Nick, and I don't realize that James has lit the last firework until I see the reflection of the sparks in Nick's eyes. I watch the light in his eyes swell, only to disappear with a hiss and a squeal in seconds. If I blinked, I would've missed that small, brief flash of light.

That last glimmer of hope in my friend's eyes.

Brett lets out a howl of frustration, pulling everyone's attention away from the failed firework, and kicks the firepit over with the strength of a thousand men. He's storming off into the house before anyone can react, Sydney hot on his heels, screaming something about *what the fuck are we supposed to do now?*

I walk over to the toppled firepit and look at the flecks of charred wood scattered on the deck. For a split second as everyone slowly trickles inside, I hear a soft mumble, mostly drowned out by the sound of the wood crunching under sandals and sneakers. I don't know who the voice belongs to while I'm distracted by my thoughts, but I do know exactly what they're saying:

"I just assumed he'd turn up."

4:08 A.M.

I wake up to the feeling of a light weight settling on my back. It takes me a minute to get my eyes open, and when I do, I find myself staring at the legs of the couch. I spot Ava's burned foot from the corner of my eye, too, and someone's arm dangling over the edge of the couch. When I lift my head up and look around, I see everyone except for Brett and Sydney snoozing in random spots across the living room.

I vaguely remember coming back inside after the fireworks failed us, and everyone collectively—and silently—agreeing it was time to sleep. The disappointment that followed our signal attempt exhausted all of us. That, and I think it's safe to say all of us falling asleep was the best reprieve from listening to Brett's yelling.

The stages of grief are hitting him fast—faster than they've hit Nick, at least. Denial? He tried insisting that Spencer was just in the house somewhere, doing his own thing apart from the rest of us, despite knowing that was vastly unlikely. Anger? Yeah, there's been plenty of that. Bargaining? We all heard his *I should've done this* and *I should've done that* rant before we set off the fireworks. The depression will hit as soon as he loses hope in finding Spencer out there, dead or alive. After that...Well, the only way he's ever going to reach the acceptance stage is if Spencer is found, and for all we know, Spencer was swept out to sea and has been drifting across the ocean this entire time.

Nick's been stuck in the depression phase for days now. I think Brett will recover when he has closure, because even if he didn't notice his brother was missing, he didn't leave Spencer or let him wander off. But Nick? I'm not sure he'll ever reach the point of acceptance. That's when the boat he and Brett are in together throws him overboard, and leaves him to drown.

When the weight slides from my back, pulling me from my thoughts, I glance down and see Henry below me. I've been sleeping with my cheek pressed against his chest, and just my luck, there's a little puddle of drool on his gray t-shirt. His hand is on his stomach now rather than my back, and when he feels me sit up, he cracks an eye open.

"You drool," he whispers, smirking.

My cheeks burn. “Sorry.”

“It's okay.” He yawns and looks around for the analog clock on the wall nearby, but it's too dark to see the time. “Must be late.”

“Early,” I correct. “We came back in around one, I think.”

“Shut up,” Aaron's voice snaps. “I'm tired.”

Someone mutters in agreement, but I can't tell who it is. I meet Henry's eyes and tilt my head toward the staircase, and he simply nods in response. We both stand and try to avoid the others sleeping on the floor next to us—Joe, Leah, Reid, and Nick—as we navigate our way out of the room. Only now do I realize that James isn't here, either.

As we quietly ascend the stairs, we pass by a window, and I see a flash of light outside. I don't have to investigate closer to know it's Brett and Sydney. They probably went back out there as soon as the rest of us called it quits for the night. I bet they'll be out there until sunrise, too.

We tiptoe toward my bedroom, and as we do so, I see a faint light peeking out from beneath James's door. I don't give it a second thought as I lead Henry into my room, which is darker than usual thanks to the wooden planks on the window concealing the starlight.

At least the hole's gone, and James keeps his word on *some* things.

I brought us up here so we can talk without disturbing the others, but I'm also aware that we need to sleep eventually, and I'm not letting him take the floor again. I've shared a bed with my guy friends before—you tend to sleep wherever you land after eight hours of drinking at a party, regardless of who's next to you—but never one I've kissed, and never one I'm currently thinking about seeing without pants on.

I refuse to make the first move, though. I already did that with James, and while I know Henry won't go back on his word like James did, I also don't want to risk the repercussions if James happens to tell anyone about what happened with us. Sure, I might get judged for having sex with Henry three days after playing around with James, but at least I won't be initiating this time.

I let myself believe the difference matters.

“Ahh. Free of the volume police,” Henry teases as we perch on my bed. I laugh while he stretches out his muscular shoulders. “Damn. It sucks sleeping on the floor. Didn't even get a pillow.”

“I had a nice one.”

He grins. “You can use me as a pillow and drool on me any time you want.”

“Gee, thanks.” I smile when he laughs, but something pops into my head and sobers me up. “Hey...I know it's the middle of the night and we need to get back to sleep, but there's something I want to ask you.”

“Shoot.”

I clear my throat, look down at my fiddling hands in my lap, then meet his curious eyes once more. He's sitting diagonal from where I'm positioned against the headboard, leaning his hands back on the mattress while his legs dangle over the edge. He's so casual, so comfortable, like we've been doing this forever. I'm not as relaxed, but somehow, seeing him like this starts to ease my tension.

“Right after the storm,” I begin, “I was talking to James, and he...he mentioned thinking you've had a thing for me for a while. I-I know things have happened these last few days, but everything's been different since the storm, so I guess I'm just wondering if there's always been something here that I was too stupid to notice, or if…”

I trail off when I catch him studying me—long enough that I wonder if I’ve said the wrong thing. After a beat, he leaves the bottom corner of the bed behind to position himself directly beside me. One of his hands is cupping my cheek, his fingers digging into my scalp, as he brings my face to his and strips me of air with a firm, deep kiss.

Huh. Maybe I *did* initiate. The realization lands too late to matter, though.

My body melts into his instinctively, but as he presses himself against me, the sudden shift makes me teeter toward the edge of the bed. He grabs my hip with his free hand and tugs me over, breaking the kiss just long enough to look into my eyes and smile.

“I've got you,” he whispers.

Then I'm gone, worlds away from this stupid little island, as I climb onto his lap and kiss him so deeply that it makes my lips ache. The force of it makes him fall back onto the mattress—his head now at the foot of the bed—and he lets out a little *oomph* sound, breaking us apart again.

I smile sheepishly. “Sorry.”

He just keeps looking into my eyes as he brushes hair from my face. “You don’t have to hold back with me, Sadie.”

The way he says my name sends shivers up my spine. He leans up to kiss me again, a jolt coursing through me when he grabs my hips at the same moment I feel a hardness between my legs. He flips us over in the time it takes me to blink, pinning our now-conjoined hands above my head. I feel our hands starting to slip over the edge of the bed, and when he notices it, too, he releases me just long enough to grab my hips again and pull us back toward the headboard.

I let out a little squeal of surprise, making him grin, as he dips down to kiss me again. Our hands are pinned together once more, and his hips are forcing my legs apart. A moan escapes me when his lips find my jaw and my neck, but that doesn't satisfy him for very long. Before I know it, my shirt and bra are on the floor, and I'm wrestling his drool-stained t-shirt off of him.

The only thing that stalls the moment is our search for a condom. Luckily, I have some in my carry-on bag—a gift from Taylor, who sent me away with them in hopes that this trip would satisfy my little crush on James.

She's not going to believe me when I tell her about this.

After grabbing the condom and throwing it onto the mattress beside us, Henry positions himself between my legs again, both of us still wearing our bottoms. Every inch of me is hot and throbbing, demanding more, but I can see in his eyes that he's enjoying the pace. The way he's studying me...It's like he's taking a mental photograph of the way I look beneath him, his hips spreading mine apart, and our centers perfectly aligned.

He leans back on his knees, admiring me while he towers above me, and strokes his palms up and down my legs. Shivers attack my body like electric shocks, but it's not just from the way he's touching me—it's the way he's looking at me, too. Like I'm the most perfect thing he's ever laid eyes on.

I can almost see the flash of that mental camera, only this time, it's not in his head—it's in mine.

"Yes," he says.

I raise an eyebrow, panting for air. "Yes?"

Henry smiles. "Yes."

"What are you talking about?"

"You wanted to know if I've had a thing for you." He leans down and cups my face, spreading kisses along my neck and down to my breasts. "The answer is yes."

I shiver again when his tongue traces my nipple. “C-Can you tell me more?”

“Eventually.”

I giggle. “You're an ass.”

He grins. “We'll see.”

He slides my shorts and underwear off after kissing his way down to my navel, and as much as I want to do the same to him, I lose all control of my thoughts and senses when I feel his tongue between my legs. I'm arching off the bed before I know what I'm doing, and as the pressure builds within me, I hear myself—sounding worlds away—begging him to take off his pants and fuck me.

I've never begged like this before. Never thought I would, either.

His mouth is on mine again after he takes off his pants and puts on the condom, the length of him nudging me exactly where I need it to, but remaining still. I grab the back of his neck while my tongue explores the hollows of his mouth. One of his hands is beside my head holding him upright, and the other is firmly wrapped around my tit, squeezing and kneading like his life depends on it.

“Sadie,” he whispers into my mouth.

All I can do is moan in response, clenching my thighs around him.

“Are you sure you want this?”

The throbbing between my legs stills for just a second. “Yes.”

He smiles and kisses me at the same moment his hips surge forward, making me cry out and squirm. He doesn’t even give me the chance to get used to him, which I know he did on purpose once I feel him grinning against my mouth.

As soon as I feel him moving inside of me, I'm lost again. The way he fits so perfectly, the way he moans my name into my ear with each thrust, the way he kisses me like it's second nature...It's like we were made to be here, locked together as one being—like we should've been doing this all along.

Everything comes to a peak for the both of us at the same moment, and I don't bother trying to keep quiet. I just sink into the explosion of pleasure and completion, relishing the feel of his release against mine, and dig my nails into the taut muscles of his back while he groans into my neck before his body relaxes on top of mine.

He rolls over onto the mattress beside me, but he only takes a few seconds to catch his breath and throw the condom onto the floor before he sweeps me into his arms again. He buries his face into the crook of my neck again, kissing me softly, as he splays his palm over my throbbing abdomen.

“Henry?” I manage.

“Hmm?”

“Thank you.”

I feel him frown against me. “For having sex with you?”

I laugh a little. “No, no. Just...Just for being on my team.”

He doesn't say anything in response. It's quiet for so long that I think he's fallen asleep, so I close my eyes and try to do the same. After a few minutes, though, his breath tickles my ear as his soft voice carries me away to a dream:

“I've been on your team from the moment I saw you.”

Smiling to myself, I grab onto his hand over my abdomen with both of mine, smiling when I feel his racing pulse against my fingers on his wrist.

The beat matches mine.

9:29 A.M.

I wish I was woken up to the sound of Henry's breathing, or his heart beating against mine, or him brushing hair from my face to wake me slowly. Instead, I'm woken by the sound of commotion downstairs—banging, thumping, and a whole lot of yelling.

Henry and I both jump awake at the same time. We're exactly as we were when we fell asleep: naked and using only each other's body heat for warmth. I just now remember that I stripped the bed so I wouldn't have to sleep in James and Madison's sex sweat-stained sheets.

We meet eyes when another bang makes us flinch. “The fuck's going on down there?” he asks groggily, rubbing his eyes.

“I guess we should go find out.”

I start to climb out of bed, but he stops me by grabbing my wrist and pulling me in for a kiss. I smile a little as he circles his arms around my waist and presses his lips to mine, and for once, I'm not worried about my morning breath. I'm just glad to have someone who wants to kiss me first thing in the morning.

“Mhm.” He licks his lips when we separate and tucks a lock of hair behind my ear. “Good morning.”

I smile. “Good morning.”

He kisses the corner of my mouth before swinging his legs out of bed. I expect him to get a new change of clothes out of his room, but instead, he just cleans his dick off with a wet wipe and throws on exactly what he was wearing yesterday—despite his clothes being stained with muck from the woods.

He sees me smirking as he pulls on his shirt and says, “Checking me out, or making fun of my clothes?”

“A little bit of both.”

That makes him laugh. “I'll change later. We better get the hell out of here soon, though, or we'll all have to start doing laundry. I don't want to see how that goes.”

I picture the arguments that would ensue over soap, and techniques, and the littlest, stupid things that everyone would find reason to fight about. Our friends' bodies are laying in the ground a few yards away from the house, but that wouldn't matter so much if the time came to argue about who got to use the good detergent for their delicates.

After dressing and quickly running a comb through my tangled hair, we head downstairs to join the others. We come to a halt at the bottom of the stairs when we see that two of the water filters have been knocked over. Reid and Erin are on their hands and knees trying to clean up the mess and put the filters back together. They don't look very happy as they get elbow deep in water, sand, leaves, and wet charcoal while nobody else offers to help.

Around the kitchen island, a group is yelling over one another about something I can't decipher: James, Brett, Aaron, Madison, and Leah. Joe, Zayn, and Nick are sitting on a mattress by the fireplace, trying their best to ignore the others as they study the map of the island again. We've been keeping the mattresses propped up against the broken windows for the most part, especially at night, to help keep the humidity and the insects from getting inside.

Sydney—with incredibly dark circles under her eyes—is sitting with Ava on the couch, helping her find a comfortable position for her leg and foot. At least Ava seems to be okay today. Her eyes are swollen, and her puffy cheeks are painted with pink squiggles from the paths of her relentless tears. She's not crying or whimpering anymore, but she hasn't moved much since I last saw her.

"What's going on?" Henry asks as we approach the island.

"Brett had a meltdown," Reid grumbles from the floor.

Brett ignores him as everyone quiets. "We're trying to figure out a plan, and nobody can agree on a fucking thing. Two of us are missing—that needs to be our top priority. I can't believe we're even talking about it."

"We've looked as much as we can," James insists. "Nick's been all over this side of the island looking for Dani. Sadie and Henry got as far as they could on the other side. We need a better plan before we just head out there again. We'll end up wasting time searching the same spots we've already looked at."

"That's why they're playing with the map," Madison explains, jabbing her finger over her shoulder at the trio on the mattress. "They're trying to cross off the places we've already searched. We'll wait for them to finish up, and then we can make a plan. For now, though—"

"For now *what,* Madison?" Brett snaps, his eyes blazing with fury. "Twiddle our thumbs and play board games? Hmm? The fuck do you want us to do?"

She narrows her eyes. "Watch your mouth, you prick. We're all worried about Dani and Spencer, and we all feel guilty as fuck about everything. But we need to think about everyone in this house, too. Like, how we're going to eat if we're still here tomorrow, which we probably will be."

Zayn looks up from the map to glare at her. "Don't be so pessimistic. Help could be here any minute."

"That's not rational, Zayn, even—"

"All right, all right." Aaron massages his temples, his complexion slowly returning to its normal shade of umber from pissed-off scarlet, as his eyes find me and Henry. "The spot where you crossed the river. You must've gone straight—let's call it north, even though I'm sure that's not right—and then turned eastward. You followed the river east for a little bit until you crossed over to this side again, where you found yourselves hiking through the neighbors' wreckage. You set out west from there and found me where you left me."

It doesn't occur to me until he lays it all out that we didn't cross the river to get back onto this side of the island. The spot where we found Dani was swampy, but the river was on either side of it, which means that spot is a point of higher elevation than the rest of the river. Not high enough that it creates two separate bodies of water, but just elevated enough for the river water to keep flowing, even if it spit out mostly mud from one end to the other.

I didn't even think of it. I'm sure Henry didn't, either. We were both so shocked at finding Dani that we didn't even consider how we were on one side of the river one second, and marching through wreckage on the other the next.

I raise an eyebrow. "And?"

He rolls his eyes. *"And,* you never went west toward the house when you were on the other side of the river. You didn't go all the way to the eastern end, either. That could mean there's a way around the electrified water. It'd just take a hell of a long time."

Erin pauses her cleaning efforts and chews on her lower lip. "Do we really think they'd be carried that far away?"

“For sure,” Zayn replies. “People end up miles and miles away from where they went missing during natural disasters. Recovery teams are always finding bodies up in trees and—”

“Stop it,” Nick snaps at him. “We're not looking for bodies.”

Ahh. We're back to denial, I see.

“I'm just sayin', man—”

“Let's say the flooding carried them away, but they survived,” Ava says weakly, wincing when she attempts turning to look at everyone. “They'd look for shelter immediately, right? There were plenty of homes and buildings on the other side before the storm. If any survived, that's where they'd be.”

“And if we can get around the electrified water, we might be able to check out the other side in more depth. You know, the resort and shit,” Joe adds. “Could find more supplies or even other survivors.”

“So, you want me and Sadie out there again,” Henry summarizes.

“I think we should all go and split up into groups,” Leah suggests. “Two of us should stay here with Ava. That pair can take care of anything that needs to be done here, like keeping the filters running and stuff. Everyone else goes to that spot where Sadie and Henry crossed the river. Divide and conquer from there.”

“I don't know what you were all fighting about,” I tease. “That was easy.”

Soon enough, we have our groups. Sydney and Madison are staying to keep an eye on Ava, make more freshwater, and see what more they can do about preparing food from whatever random, sparse ingredients we still have. Zayn, Erin, and Leah will search the other end of this side of the island, all the way to the coast where the last of the neighboring homes once stood opposite of James's.

Brett, Aaron, and James will cross the river and head west back toward James’s house—again, all the way to the coast, just across the water from the house. Meanwhile, Nick, Joe, and Reid are going to attempt going around the electrified water from the east, while Henry and I will attempt it from the west.

I'm not happy about it, given that Nick's route increases his chances of finding Dani, but I'm just glad he suggested that Henry and I search in the opposite direction. I don't want to be there if he finds her.

Nobody's in the mood to eat right now, but we all take the rationed baggies of trail mix and dried fruit that were prepared yesterday to hold us over. We were supposed to boil water and make some instant oatmeal for breakfast this morning, but I guess that just means we have at least one meal set for tomorrow.

We trade our sandals for sneakers, fill our beach bags or backpacks with any supplies we can spare in case we need them, and promise the girls staying at the house that we'll be back by noon. There are only two watches among us, though, which means the groups without one will just have to hope they make it back before they scare the shit out of us.

Me, Henry, and Aaron lead them to the same route we took yesterday. Not everyone has been out this far since the storm, so they're all looking around for supplies or fallen fruit with every step, like we haven't already searched this area extensively.

“Okay.” Everyone stops when Henry, leading the pack, halts by the shallow part of the river. “This is where we split up. Look—there’s a pair of shorts stuck in that tree, and Aaron’s shirt tied to that one. Keep an eye out for them.”

“What if we get lost?” Erin asks, hugging herself. “How do we find our way back?”

James shrugs. “You just do.”

She glowers, but doesn't say anything. I wish she would.

“Good luck, guys,” Aaron mutters, adjusting his backpack strap. “Holler if you run into any venomous snakes.”

“Don't even fucking go there,” Leah warns.

With that, the groups go their separate ways, with Henry and I lagging behind under the guise of needing to discuss our route before we go.

Henry clears his throat when they're out of earshot. “They're gonna find her, you know.”

“I don't know. She's pretty well hidden.”

“Our fault,” he reminds me.

I sigh. “Henry, if he sees her like that—”

“I know.” He exhales once. “We just don’t go that way.”

I nod, prompting him to continue. “I glanced at the map earlier. That building we found yesterday? It's a distillery. Been here long enough that it made it onto a map from the 60s. You know what's right on the other side of it, the side we're supposed to be searching? An old toxic waste dump. The GEF didn't do much about waste disposal in the Caribbean until fairly recently. I'm betting they demolished the dump, but the groundwater is still all sorts of fucked over there."

"How bad could it be?"

"We don't know what they dumped there. Could be anything, you know?" He takes a few steps toward our path, one hand gently pressed against my lower back. "I'm not letting you get elbow-deep in toxic waste sludge."

I smile a little. "Worried about me, Henry?"

"Can't help it, Sadie."

I punch his arm lightly, still smiling, and say, "Okay, then. What's our Plan B?"

"What do you think?"

I consider that for a moment. "I think we should check it out, anyway. Try going around the dump site. It can't be that big—it's in the center of a forest on a small island, and it's too far inland to be anywhere near the coast."

He takes a deep breath in and reaches for my hand. "Okay. If you insist."

I thread my fingers through his. "It'll be fine."

We cross the shallow part of the river like we did yesterday, following the path northbound, hoping we find the edge of the distillery. While we walk, I take the opportunity to tell him what I overheard James telling Brett about the money, and his reaction is everything I hoped it would be.

"You're fucking with me," he says, wide-eyed. I just shake my head in response. "So, you're telling me I gave him three hundred bucks for food and drinks, and he—"

"Three hundred?" My lips part in shock. "He only asked me for two."

"Asshole." A bitter laugh escapes him. "I bet his folks cut his allowance or something. I know he's been traveling a lot when we're not in school—I heard him talking to Brett about girls he's been visiting around the country. His folks probably don't know that's the reason he's been traveling a lot, but still. I'd bet anything he's using the extra cash to make a few visits before his parents expect him to settle down with a new job."

"Makes sense," I mutter. "I wouldn't be surprised, either. We've all seen the things he'll do for sex."

"Tell me about it. Remember sophomore year when he drove six hours to Maine to fuck Erin's cousin? She visited Saint Maren for one night, and he was following her home the next day."

"Oh, I remember. Then there's Madison, too," I add. "Did you know they've been fucking? Have we talked about that?"

"Everyone knows they've been fucking," he says with a snort. "They try to hide it, but everyone knows. It's the worst-kept secret since Aaron's crush on Erin." He raises an eyebrow as he offers me a hand to climb over a fallen tree. "You heard them the other night, right? James and Madison?"

I nod.

"How do you know it was them?"

"James was in my room, remember? I went back and heard them through the door."

"Oh. Why'd you go back?"

I don't answer as I look away at the path ahead, well aware that my cheeks are turning scarlet. I feel him watching me, but after a moment, he just sighs and looks away. He knows, and I hate that he does.

"It's okay, you know," he murmurs. My head whips in his direction, and a combination of guilt and adoration flows through me when I see the kindness in his eyes, the understanding on his face, and the smile on his lips. "I get it. I just wish I was brave enough to tell you how I felt and to warn you about him before it got to that point. Would've saved you a whole lot of heartbreak."

"My heart's not broken." The sentence comes out sounding firmer and slightly more aggressive than I intend it to, so I soften and try again: "My heart's not broken. I was pissed at him for leading me on, but now I'm just pissed off in general. It was stupid of me to think that anything would happen with him, and it was stupid to want that to begin with. I guess I wish you were braver before, too."

That makes him chuckle, but before he can reply, I quickly ask, "Have you, uh, been with anyone else in the group?"

"Depends on what you mean by that."

A flare of envy gurgles in my gut. "Been with anyone else...in any way, I guess."

Henry just shrugs. “I kissed Ava once. New Year's Eve party. She came at me when the ball dropped, then invited me back to her room—a guest room at James’s place back home—but she started puking before I could even get her shirt off. Never spoke of it again. I'm not sure she even remembers it.” He raises an amused eyebrow as he studies me. “Jealous?”

My cheeks burn hotter. “No. Are you?”

“It's eating me alive.”

“Don't let it.”

“Why not? You crushing on me, Sadie?”

“Something like that.”

“My prayers have been answered.”

I smile, but the way he says it so sincerely makes my stomach flutter. “I'm glad you put in a good word with the big guy upstairs. And I'm glad we've both been brave these last few days.” I take his hand again as we keep hiking through the debris. “I'm sorry it took me so long to notice.”

He waves his free hand dismissively. “It's okay. The spell—it got you. But it's broken now, and that's what matters.”

I crinkle my brows. “The spell?”

He gives me a pointed look, reminding me of our conversation at the firepit about James and the so-called “spell” he casts over his friends. That's what made me want to ask more before we were interrupted, and he doesn't hesitate to share the stories with me now. The more he shares, the more I realize just how calculating James really is.

When we first started hanging out, James would offer to pay for things for me, even though he knew I had money. He'd ask what I wanted from the liquor store, and if we went out for food, he'd usher me up to order with him and shoo me when I reached for my wallet. After a while, he'd keep paying for me, but he'd ask me for money afterward. I didn't think anything of it; I was just thankful that he'd taken care of me for as long as he did. He did the same exact thing to Henry—even going as far as to ask for *one dollar* after buying Henry a water at the gas station.

James used to reach for the check without thinking twice about it. Then, after a time, there were days when he’d hesitate, like he was waiting to see if anyone else would offer. He’s stopped offering entirely more recently, for the most part.

I didn't notice the moment all of that changed; only that it had. My perspective was clouded by rose-colored glasses—a tint I brought upon myself through my desperation to have a secure place in the group.

I should've been smarter. I grew up with that behavior, after all. I just couldn't comprehend that everything I'd left behind had found me again in something I actually *wanted.* I may not have noticed the exact moment it all changed, but I knew it did, and still, I'd tell myself it'd be different this time because I was choosing it. Wanting something, as I've learned, doesn't make it any less of a trap when you have to rely on someone else to give it to you.

"The last straw for me wasn't even something James did to *me,"* Henry continues, wiping sweat from his forehead with the back of his hand. "It was Magnus, actually."

"What happened?"

He sighs. "Magnus didn't wanna go back to Sweden after graduation. He was hoping to find a job in Connecticut. James offered him a position at his dad's company in Hartford."

"I remember that," I murmur. "Magnus interned there last summer, didn't he?"

"Yeah. This story happened before that," he continues. "So, James told Magnus that he could set him up with a great job at his dad's company, straight out of college. No need to apply, no strings attached, and an internship beforehand to make sure he was a good fit. Magnus accepted, of course, because who wouldn't? Then—this was right before winter break last year—they got into a fight about something dumb. James got on the phone with his dad and told him to give the internship to someone else."

My stomach drops. "What?"

"Yeah. That's why Magnus didn't come around a lot when we got back from break. They weren't on the best terms. They figured it out, obviously. James got his dad to offer Magnus the job again, and Magnus just pretended like the whole thing never happened."

I swallow the lump in my throat. "Did James ever try anything like that with you?"

Henry just stares at me. "Remember the concert you all went to last year? April, I think?"

"Yeah. You weren't there."

He hesitates for a moment. “I was supposed to be. James got me a ticket. But something happened—nothing bad, either, just something that inconvenienced him—and he gave my ticket to Brian Harpman. That kid who always smells like cheese.”

I shudder. “Yeah, I remember.”

“You know how James made it up to me?” he asks. I shake my head, making him sigh and hold up his arms to gesture toward our surroundings. “He paid for my flights to and from Miami for this trip. Didn't even ask if I wanted to come—just bought the tickets and said, ‘I hope you're not still upset about the concert.’ He wanted to make things right, I guess.”

“I can't believe you didn't throw them back in his face,” I admit. “Why didn't you?”

Henry’s face is twisted with something I can’t put my finger on—not quite shame, but something close to it.

“I heard you were gonna be here. I wouldn’t have come otherwise.” He sighs. “I guess it was just easier to accept the gesture than to ask why I was accepting it.”

I chew on my lower lip, soaking up his words. It’s dangerous, this confession—that he didn’t exactly choose me or this trip, but that someone else chose for him.

11:18 A.M.

"Henry, I—"

"Look," he interrupts me as I'm still reeling over what he just said, pointing at something through the trees. "That's the distillery."

I swallow my questions and follow his eyes. We have, in fact, reached the building we found yesterday. I can still see the body impaled to the wall inside. Instead of getting any closer, though, we turn left from our position atop a mound of debris, keeping an eye on the pool of electrified water as we wait for it to thin out.

We're walking for a while from here, and neither of us reignites our previous conversation. I know he's probably a bit embarrassed after admitting that he came on this trip for me—partly, anyway—when I barely even knew what the color of his eyes was until we got here. I mean, he already told me he's been crushing on me for a while now—since the first time he saw me, if he wasn't exaggerating—but after everything he just shared about James, it's still baffling that he let James treat him like that solely because he wanted to vacation with me.

Luckily, we're not walking in silence. He strikes up a conversation about the rest of our friends—mainly about the things he's observed about them since we got here, like the roles they've all sunk into since the storm—but leaves James out of it.

I'm glad for the change of pace. It was starting to scare me, the way Henry's demeanor changed when he talked about James. It didn't scare me because he was genuinely frightening me, though. It scared me because the way he looked is exactly how I feel when I think about everything I've always noticed about James—things I just didn't care enough about to stop wanting him or wanting to be close to him.

I'm in the middle of talking about Brett and Spencer when Henry stops in front of me, and I nearly crash into his back. He reaches his arms behind him to steady me, but he's silent, just staring at whatever's in front of him. I walk around him to get a better look, and what I see renders me silent, too.

The toxic waste dump is long gone, and it's clear to anyone with eyes that it wasn't just demolished—it was blown up. From where we're standing—the same elevation as nearly the rest of the island—there's about a twenty-foot drop down to a crater in the earth. It must not have been a very large dump, though, because the space is smaller than the length and width of James's house. Directly across from us, the elevation continues as normal.

Henry was definitely right about there being remains of toxic waste in the groundwater. This space flooded during the storm, and I can't tell how deep the water is. Of course, it's collected a ton of debris, but that's not what makes it murky. The water has a rust-colored tinge to it, and there are plenty of tiny corpses—birds, lizards, and fish brought in during the flooding—floating at the surface.

On the far end of the crater, there's a slope that leads back up to ground-level. I spot the remains of a few charred, gray barrels propped up against the slope, just high enough that they aren't touching the water. The ground surrounding the barrels is gray, too, like something spilled and rotted.

Henry clears his throat. “How deep do you think it is?”

I think on that for a moment. “I don't know. Maybe six feet.”

“No telling what's under the water, either.”

“Probably a lot of rubble infected with toxins. I'm surprised the groundwater didn't spread further throughout the island and contaminate natural sources.” That makes me widen my eyes as I set a hand on his arm. “Do you think there are freshwater sources on this side of the island? A waterfall and a stream, maybe? Or wells?”

He sighs. “If there are, I wouldn't trust them. They've been contaminated by whatever the storm dragged through them. It's worth looking, though. That's why we're out here.”

We carefully navigate through the debris surrounding the side of the crater, hoping to make our way around it to the other side. We're closer to the resort and the unknown than anyone has gotten since the storm struck. If we find a clear path onward from here, we'll have the most success out of anyone else in the group—if we're being optimistic, anyway.

“Look.” Henry stops us when we're standing by the crater's slope. I see what he's talking about: carved out chunks of earth along the side of the slope, where some sort of structure used to be. “They probably had a ladder hooked up here. I bet they tried to clean the waste, but someone got sick, so they just left it.”

“It can't be radioactive, though. Just a lot of chemicals, like lead and mercury. I'm betting it's still water.”

"That kills just as well as radiation," he reminds me. "You can see where it's starting to erode at the earth. The flooding won't help with that, either. It could be flammable, too, for all we know."

"Don't light a cigarette," I tease.

He snorts. "Not my thing. James is the one who loves a drunk cig."

I know he does; he gave me my first one. It's not my thing, either.

After reaching the other side of the crater, we keep moving straight toward where we hope civilization is—or used to be, anyway. The debris is thicker over here, as expected, yet we soon come across a house that's partially standing. We don't see anyone inside or nearby, though, so we keep moving. It's pretty obvious that we could blow on this house, and whatever's still holding it together would fracture and take the whole thing down.

Then, by some miracle, we find something else in the remains of another demolished house: a refrigerator laying on its side, surrounded by coconuts from a nearby tree that fell down.

I start loading coconuts into my bag while Henry opens the refrigerator. A rancid smell leaves it as soon as he opens it, making us both gag and plug our noses, but we do manage to find a few things that haven't gone bad—things that most people probably wouldn't keep chilled.

Thank God this homeowner decided to keep everything in one place.

A loaf of sliced bread, a bag of russet potatoes, an onion, half-a-dozen oranges, and two jars of pickles—one hot, one dill.

We're practically giddy with excitement as we fill our bags, even going as far as to take things that look questionable, but may still be good, like condiments and leftover meals in plastic containers.

"Imagine what we'll find if we keep moving," Henry says with a grin. "This still isn't a very populated side of the island. Everything gets thicker the closer you get to the resort. I'm betting—"

Then, somewhere in the distance, something that sounds like a howl renders him silent. We exchange nervous glances before examining our surroundings, hoping we didn't attract any unwanted attention. That's when we hear it again, and this time, it's clear the sound isn't the howl of a hungry wild animal.

It's a human howl, cutting through the eerie silence and gloom of the forest, and one of excruciating pain.

2:12 P.M.

I knew it was a bad idea for Nick's group to head in the direction they did. I told myself they wouldn't see her in the muck—that she was too well-concealed for them to spot her like we did, if they even found the swamp.

Apparently, I underestimated Nick's determination.

Henry and I found ourselves torn between moving forward to the other side of the island and meeting our friends. We decided to keep going—it's not like we'd contribute anything to the group by watching Nick sob over Dani's corpse—but karma struck not long after we made our choice.

We made it to the edge of the forest, where we immediately knew we'd found the more populated side of the island when we spotted traffic lights atop the mounds of debris. The difference between this side and ours was catastrophic: not only was the wreckage worse, but the area we came to—which we assumed was once a busy street with a massive intersection, based on what we observed—had sunken into the ground. It was just as low, if not lower, as the pit at the old dump site filled with still water, and extended for as far as we could see in either direction.

We knew the road had to end at some point in both directions, but it'd take too long to go around either way, and we didn't want to risk treading on unstable ground. There was nothing of value that we could see, so it wasn't worth exploring further and potentially getting hurt so far from the others.

That's when we decided to turn back. By the time we made it to the tree with the red shorts, Henry's watch told us that we were only minutes away from going over the allotted timeframe agreed upon by the entire group. We figured everyone else was already at the house after the screams sent them rushing back, so we didn't bother waiting around for anyone else before finishing our hike to James's.

We crossed the beach just in time to see an expressionless Joe and Reid piling sand onto a freshly dug grave while the others—save Nick, Ava, Brett, and Sydney—watched from a few feet away.

“They found Dani,” Erin told us when we approached. Her eyes were misty and her voice was hoarse, but her face was completely blank. “Sorry we didn't wait for you before we buried her. She, uh...The smell...”

We assured them that it was all right, that we understood what the state of her body must've been, and that we were glad to at least have some closure on what happened to Dani.

According to our friends, it was Zayn, Leah, and Erin who responded to Nick's screams and met his group in the swamp. His horror quickly transformed into hyperventilation as they pulled her out of the muck to carry her back, revealing the extent of her injuries—I was right about her having been attacked by an animal; she's missing her other arm, chewed off all the way to her shoulder. While Reid and Joe carried Dani back, the others had to prop Nick up between them to keep him from falling, as his knees buckled with every step.

By the time they made it out of the woods, Nick was catatonic, refusing to speak or to look anyone in the eye. He managed to regain some control, though: instead of staying for the burial and saying a few words in remembrance of his dead girlfriend, he walked wordlessly into the house and locked himself in an upstairs bedroom. They tried to coax him out, to no avail.

It's been a little over half an hour since then. Joe and Reid have just finished filling the grave—on the end beside Eli—and are now sitting on the sand with the rest of us, wiping sweat from their faces while their shovels lay beside them.

"I should go check on Nick," Joe murmurs.

"Nah, man." Aaron shakes his head as he stares at the newest sand mound. "He needs more time, and we all smell like..."

He trails off, but he doesn't need to finish for us to know what he means: *We all smell like Dani's rotting corpse.*

"We'll check on him when we figure out dinner," Leah decides. "He'll be hungry. We still have some pasta, plus whatever we can make with what Sadie and Henry found."

"It's a lot of miscellaneous ingredients, but we can think of something," Henry says, nodding. "Hey—where are Brett and Sydney?"

"We went back to the meeting spot at the river early. Didn't find anything in our search area." James, sitting with his knees drawn up across from me, picks up fistfuls of sand and watches as the granules slither through his fingers. "Brett saw them walking back with Dani, and I think it really hit him that he could find Spencer like that, too. Me and Aaron thought it best to stay here to bury Dani and be there for Nick, but Brett wasn't having it. Wanted to go out searching again. Sydney went with him."

I look at Madison to his right. “Who's with Ava?”

“Nobody,” she replies. “She's napping. She's been fine, though. If anything was gonna happen, it would've happened by now.”

Fair enough.

“She'll be mobile again soon. At least, I hope she will be—we need all hands on deck,” James says with a grimace. He looks around at each of us, one by one. “Anyone find anything promising?”

Of course, the only thing Reid and Joe found with Nick was Dani, and as James just said, his group didn't have any luck. Erin's trio actually managed to recover a few items from the wreckage of the coastal homes along the same strip of the island as James's house: a carry-on suitcase filled with a large man's clothing and shoes, but no toiletries; a box of stale yet undamaged crackers; and, best of all, a reusable water bottle with a built-in filter.

Henry and I reveal our haul, delighting our friends, before disappointing them with our findings about the other side of the island.

“We could see a clear way to get across,” Henry explains as we tell them about the collapsed intersection. “It looked pretty sketchy. Like, lots of unstable mountains of debris that would collapse underneath us if we tried climbing. I mean, the road has to end somewhere, so we might be able to get around from there, but I don't know. We would've missed the return time if we tried that, and I have a feeling the other side isn't any better than what we saw.”

“We have to try,” James insists, his eyes hard with authority. “We still have another four hours of sunlight today. A few of us will hang back with Nick and Ava, and the rest of us will head out to find a way around the intersection. It's our best bet if we want to find more supplies, and potentially other survivors, too.”

Henry shakes his head. “I don't think that's a good idea. It may take a lot longer than that to get to where we want to go. And what if we do manage to get across? Are we just gonna celebrate that we found the route and head back here before it gets dark? I don't think so. We'll want to keep moving, and it could take us hours to navigate through everything over there. If we're gonna go back there, it should be first thing tomorrow morning when we have plenty of time to spare.”

“What's the point?” James's octave is increasing to a dangerously loud level, making me scowl at him. “We have nothing better to do today than sit here and wallow. That's not gonna bring Dani or Spencer back. It's not gonna keep us alive. We're not on vacation anymore, guys. We can't just do nothing when we have four hours of daylight left."

Reid's staring at him like he just grew nine heads. "Come on, man. We just buried Dani. Nick's in shambles, and so is Brett. And four hours really isn't that long when you think about how much time it takes to get around this mess on foot. We're all tired, too. Let's try to have some empathy for our friends, and let's give ourselves a little break for now. We're not going anywhere."

"That's what I'm saying!" James snaps. He's finally stopped playing with the sand, and now, his fists are clenched at his sides, his knuckles sinking into the granules. "Just because we managed to find some supplies doesn't mean they'll last us very long. We could be here for another week, for all we know, and being tired, and sad, and *empathetic* won't do us much good. Sure, we won't starve to death in another week, but it'll start to make us miserable and angry. More than we already are, anyway. It's better to keep going at it for the chance that we find stuff out there that'll keep us alive. I don't wanna start eating bugs to keep myself going."

"I'm with James on this one," Madison pipes up. "I know what I said before about needing to be sensitive to Ava and what she went through, and that should apply to the others now, too, but...but James is right. We can't prioritize empathy or rest when we're running out of food, and we don't know how much longer we'll be stuck here. Even if it gets dark on us, we need to try."

"We're all forgetting something," Zayn adds, scowling. "I think it's safe to assume there are at least a few survivors on the other side. I can't imagine the entire resort coming down, or even every single other structure over there. What happens if we make it there, and we find a few dozen—or even hundred—survivors holed up somewhere? They probably won't welcome us with open arms. They have their supplies, and they'll keep them for themselves instead of sharing with strangers. I'm not trying to pick a fight with a ton of angry parents trying to save what little food they have to feed their terrified kids."

Madison rolls her eyes. "Don't think so lowly of people, Zayn."

"I'm just being realistic. It's been days—if they're out there, then they have a plan for rationing, and scavenging, and keeping everyone alive just like we do. They won't be happy when a dozen people show up begging for scraps." He runs a hand through his hair and nibbles on his already-cut and bleeding lips. "Man, I need a rip. Even a cig would work. I need something to help me deal with this shit."

"If we have a feeling there are survivors nearby, we'll just keep our distance," James decides, stretching his legs out. "Stick to scavenging around an area that's far enough away for us to go unnoticed. I think it'd be worthwhile to at least talk to someone, though. We don't have to ask them for anything. It'd just suck if they have power or a way to contact help or even a way to get out of here, and we're too afraid of being shooed away with pitchforks and torches to let them know that we're here, too."

"He's right." Madison doesn't bother looking up as she picks at her nails. "It's worth trying."

"It's really impressive how aligned the two of you are all the time." The words come out of my mouth before I can stop them. "I bet it makes things really easy."

She finally looks up, glowering. "What's that supposed to mean?"

Even though the two of us are staring each other down, I feel everyone's eyes on me, flicking back and forth between us. I feel James's eyes more than anyone else's, and I clock this shimmer within them that tells me I've hit my mark.

I know I have to be clever about this. The rumor has already spread through the group that James and Madison have been hooking up in secret for a while now, even if they try to hide it by seeing other people. Outing them in front of our friends won't surprise anyone, and it probably won't make them sweat like I want them to.

I smile. "I just didn't realize favors still count when we're trying to plan for our survival."

"Excuse me?" Madison's cheeks pinken, her doll-like eyes widening just a fraction of an inch before narrowing, posed for defense. "What are you trying to say?"

Aaron cackles before I can respond. "She's got a point. You kinda have to agree with the person you're getting special treat—"

"Fuck off," James snaps, throwing a fistful of sand at Aaron. He drags his gaze back to me, and I refuse to break eye contact when I see the aggravation in his eyes. "I'm not sure what you think you're talking about—both of you," he adds, glaring between me and Aaron, "but you're wrong."

"Hmm." I shrug my shoulders. "I guess it was just a rumor, then. Sorry."

"Wait. What am I missing here?" Zayn asks, looking between me, James, and Madison. "Is something going on that I don't know about?"

Nobody replies. After a few seconds, a red-faced Madison stands abruptly and storms off toward the house, but not before shooting a scathing look in my direction. Leah rushes to follow her, and James watches them go until they're out of sight. He doesn't look at me when he's facing our group again, though. He just stares at the sand, jaw clenched, before sighing, standing, and muttering something about fishing.

Erin decides to help him, leaving me sitting on the beach triumphantly with Henry, Aaron, Joe, Reid, and Zayn. They're all still smirking and chuckling after what just happened, and I can't help but take pride in it when I see the way they grin at me.

"I'm sure anyone else would blindly agree with him, too, if we had an arrangement like theirs." It's Henry who breaks the silence, smiling a bit. "He's not my type, though."

That's when the dam breaks, and everyone left on the beach with us starts laughing until they're scarlet and breathless.

While they're containing themselves, Henry reaches over to give my hand a squeeze. When our eyes meet, I see the same satisfied glint in them that I feel stirring within me.

He likes the way this feels, too.

5:38 P.M.

None of us left the beach after Madison, Leah, James, and Erin went back to the house. The latter two returned a few minutes later with our makeshift fishing gear, but Erin got nervous about getting into the water after checking on Ava and seeing her injuries, so Aaron and Joe volunteered to help James in her place.

Reid went inside to check on Nick and figure out what we're doing for dinner. An increasingly irritable and anxious Zayn, on the other hand, decided to start trying to repair the motorboat as per James's suggestion the other day. Reid came out briefly to let us know that dinner tonight is potatoes, oranges, and half a slice of bread each. Henry and I gave him the oranges and the bread so the girls could start dividing them up, and then we took charge of boiling water over the firepit to cook the potatoes.

Someone threw a bunch of scrap wood into the firepit at some point, thankfully, and we have just enough freshwater to spare for boiling. We don't bother bringing the pot of cooked potatoes inside when they're finished; Henry just pokes his head into the doorway to tell our friends so we can continue keeping our distance from Madison, who's still upset that I brought up the rumor about her and James in front of everyone.

We go back to the beach to let everyone know that dinner's almost ready, just as Brett and Sydney return from their search for Spencer. They're defeated and exhausted, naturally, and Brett looks worse than he did last night when he realized Spencer is missing. He doesn't even want anything to eat, despite Sydney reminding him that he needs to keep his strength up for the searches.

Leah and Reid come down to the beach, each holding a plate in either hand. They deliver the meals to the guys first—James, Aaron, and Joe in the water, and Zayn tinkering beneath the boat—then head back to the house to grab the rest. We offer to grab our plates ourselves, to which Leah—with surprising politeness while directing her words at me—states there's a mess in the house from Madison kicking over a water filter, so it's best to have as little foot traffic as possible inside right now while she cleans it up.

In other words: Madison's still furious, and the less people she interacts with, the better.

Erin decides to follow them, anyway. The three of them come back a few minutes later with plates for the rest of us and themselves, and they make no effort to join Madison, Ava, and Nick, who are eating inside.

We devour our dinners quickly, not bothering to speak for a few minutes, as we're all huddled around in a circle; everyone except for Zayn and James. Zayn's picking at his plate as it rests beside him while he works—a lit cigarette balancing on the plate, dangerously close to his food, despite his complaints about how much he hates cigarettes—and James's plate is still sitting a few feet from shore, narrowly missing the tide as it awaits him while he continues to fish.

I can tell he's pissed. He keeps stabbing at nothing in the water with his spear, using more force than necessary, and soaking his entire body in the process. I wonder if he knows he's making a fool out of himself by splashing like a kid throwing a tantrum. Probably not.

“I left Nick's plate outside his door. Still won't open up, but I got a *thank you* out of him,” Reid tells us. “I'm just hoping the smell of potatoes gets him to eat something. I can handle him not talking if it means he's not starving himself.”

“He won't be able to resist,” Aaron says, orange juice dribbling down his chin. “He wouldn't let it go bad, either.”

I hope not. This may be the last decent meal we have. The loaf of bread came with twenty-four slices, so when cut in half and split between fourteen of us, that means we have thirty-four half-slices left. That's enough for each of us to have another half-slice for breakfast and dinner tomorrow, but it won't be enough for everyone after that. There were only six oranges, too, and we saved four of them, cutting the other two into eight wedges each. We gave the extra two wedges to Ava and Nick, but with the rest of the oranges, we'll only have another two servings at one wedge per person, plus four leftover.

It'll probably turn into a battle over which four people get an extra wedge when we run out.

Luckily, the potatoes will last a little longer. I knew they were heavy when I hoisted the bag into Henry's backpack—and when I saw him teeter a little while carrying it—but I didn't realize how many were in there until we opened the bag. There were twenty-two of them, so we saved the majority and cooked seven, splitting each one in half. Leah even sprinkled them with some salt and pepper to help the bland starch go down easier, but that was never going to be a problem, given how ravenous we all are.

“This was a great find,” Leah says to me. “Madison was so happy when she smelled the potatoes that I think she may forgive you for earlier.” I don’t answer. Her eyes flick down to my neck as she adds, “I know you're not a malicious person, so I'm assuming you had a reason for bringing that up. Not my business. I know how Mads can be, too. She's my best friend, but she's hard to be around sometimes. She makes herself an easy target. But I don't think it was right to shame her for something you did, too.”

I freeze just as I'm clearing my plate. “What?”

“You have a nice bruise on your neck, and I know it didn't come from a curling iron.” Her tone is more playful now, but there's still a seriousness behind her eyes. She jerks her chin toward where Henry sits across from us, talking about something with Joe and Reid. “I've seen how you two have been together lately. I'm not an idiot. I think it's sweet, actually. You're cute together. But still—don't come after Madison for getting some since we've been trapped here while you did the same thing.”

“It's different,” I say, setting my plate down on the sand. I focus my gaze on Zayn as he pops the cigarette in his mouth and crawls under the boat. “Like you said, it's not your business, so I won't get into it. But it's different.”

“If you say so.” She swallows a mouthful of dry bread, finishing her meal, before mimicking my position by drawing her knees up to her chest. Her eyes are still locked on Henry. “Soooo...How was it?”

I turn to stare at her. “You just gave me shit for embarrassing your best friend, and now you want to know how sex with Henry was?”

Leah shrugs, a ghost of a smile on her lips. “I told you—I know how Madison can be, and I know how you are, so whatever your reason was for bringing that up, I'm sure it was justified. I love her to death, but I won't sit here and pretend like she doesn't need a reality check once in a while. I don't love how she kisses James's ass all the time, either. So, I get it, and now, I want to talk about something else so it doesn't seem like I'm shit-talking my best friend.” She raises an amused, curious eyebrow. “So?”

I can't help it—I crack a smile. “It was great. Really great.”

“Oh, come on.” She rolls her eyes and wiggles her brows. “Give me more than that.”

“He's right there, Leah.”

“And he's yapping with Joe. He's not paying attention. Just give me the details before I have to beg.”

That makes me laugh, and I reluctantly share a few details from last night's adventure with Henry. I don't tell her much—privacy still exists, even here, after everything—but I give her just enough to get her giggling and squirming with excitement.

It's moments like this when I wonder if Leah and I could've been good friends this entire time, had we given it a shot; or, rather, had she given me more of a shot. She's a sweetheart, and she makes it easy to talk about girl things I wouldn't normally tell any of the other women in the group. If things had gone differently in the past, I have a feeling Leah would've been the easiest way for me to access the group a long time ago.

She lowers her voice as her nails dig into my forearm. "Is he...? You know."

I frown. "I really don't."

"Does he have any...preferences?"

"Is he kinky? Is that what you mean?" I ask. She only grins in response. "I mean, we didn't really get the chance to explore that. I'm not sure."

"Well, you'll have to let me know next time. He looks like someone who'd be kinky behind closed doors. You know, appearances-can-be-deceiving and all of that. I think you're the same way."

My cheeks burn. "Not true. I like bland, vanilla sex."

She cackles and nudges me with her elbow. "Very funny. No, you're like me. I know it. I like my hair pulled until it feels like it's gonna come out. Madison hates it, though. She spends too much money getting her hair colored to risk it being torn out."

She's still talking a mile a minute about kinks—not only hers or what she thinks mine are, but about what she's learned from others in the group, too—but I'm barely listening anymore. I'm stuck in my head, replaying what I overheard from Madison while she and James were fucking in my bed: *Do it the fuck again—and pull my hair!*

According to Leah, Madison hates getting her hair pulled during sex. Leah, on the other hand, seems to crave it.

As I listen to her talk, staring right through her and not hearing a word she's saying, everything starts to come together. On our first day here, Madison was torn up about James potentially hooking up with someone else in the group, and Leah talked her out of it. The morning after I overheard them in my room, Leah was the very last person to wake up. I expected her to defend Madison more than she did today, too, yet she's been unnaturally—and suspiciously—relaxed about it, like I didn't humiliate her best friend in front of everyone.

That's when it clicks. I didn't overhear Madison and James at all. I overheard *Leah* with James—not only an even juicier pairing to expose, but a damning, backstabbing secret that could tear a close-knit group of friends to shreds.

I'm not even upset that it was Leah or that I was wrong about Madison. In fact, I want to laugh. I was embarrassed before, even if my reason for feeling that way was kind of dumb. But now, I'm just *so fucking happy* to know that James is an even bigger piece of shit than I gave him credit for.

I don't want to hurt Leah. She's always been kind to me, even if it was messed up of her to fuck James in my bed. But James handed me a weapon, and though I started learning how to use it earlier today, I can practically feel it in my hand now, pulling me toward its next purpose—away from Madison, and closer to the person who gave it to me.

Leah will just have to be collateral damage.

I open my mouth to reply, but I don't get the chance. The moment my lips part, a chain reaction of events follows: a deafening bang blows through my eardrums; a wave of foul-smelling, unfathomably hot air lifts my hair from my shoulders; small pieces of debris fly through the air, miraculously missing me; and a burst of incredible orange light illuminates the sky, nearly blinding me.

The motorboat is ablaze and blown into pieces, and Zayn is nowhere to be seen.

6:10 P.M.

I never realized flames could climb so high, even when they have nothing but oxygen to cling to. I guess it's the best signal flare we're going to get out here.

It's hot. Really hot. I'm yards and yards away, and I can still feel my skin burning. It's brighter than any fire I've ever seen, too, which is surprising, given that it's accompanied by enormous plumes of black smoke. I crane my head back while I watch the smoke fade into the air, far beyond where the tallest flames lap against the sky, just as the smell hits me.

Gasoline. Burnt rubber. A rotten egg-like smell from byproduct gases. Sulfur from burnt hair. It's a disgusting combination, but for some reason, I can't bring myself to cover my nose.

I look to either side at my friends. Nobody's moving a muscle. We're like those ancient warrior statues you see in museums: faces and bodies frozen in time, forever trapped in our formations, our autonomy governed by the battles we never stood a chance at winning.

Only we're not statues. We're flesh and bone, and the battles we'll never win are against foes we can't defeat: Mother Nature, ourselves, and each other. Our general didn't prepare us for this—only for the press release that may come later, if we make it there.

Nobody has a reaction. Nobody runs in a frenzied perimeter around the flaming remains of the boat, screaming for Zayn. Nobody looks around for any trace of him—even a shoe. Nobody cries, mourns, or utters a single syllable. We all just stare at the inferno, shellshocked and desensitized to the death of another friend.

Movement to my right catches my eye. I watch as Aaron lowers himself onto the sand, sniffing, with his legs drawn up and his arms dangling over his knees. The break in the stillness of our formation makes others look in his direction, too. That's when Joe mimics him, and then Erin, and then myself.

When I look over my shoulder at the house, I see Madison and Ava on the deck, clinging to the railing keeping them from tumbling down the hill and onto the beach. Ava's leaning against Madison for support because of her leg, but neither of them appear to be breaking down. They're just watching the inferno, still and silent, like the rest of us.

I barely acknowledge Henry sinking down beside me until his knee bumps mine. I'm sitting cross-legged, but he has one leg bent against mine, and the other stretched out straight in front of him. Our hands sit firmly in our laps rather than intertwined, as the need for comfort is now long gone.

It died with Zayn, and so did the last shreds of our ability to mourn.

I didn't think we'd lose anyone else after Ava pulled through, and even if we did, I thought we'd grieve like we grieved the others. That's the appropriate response, isn't it? Not anymore. Finding Dani, then watching Zayn disappear in the blink of an eye...I'm realizing now that it's stupid to keep going with the mindset that we're all going to leave this island alive.

I thought we were done burying friends after Zeke, Eli, and Magnus. I was wrong. I thought we were done grieving after we found Dani, too. I was wrong. Spencer's presumed dead, and now Zayn has joined them, too. The list just keeps growing, and I'm kidding myself if I believe that all thirteen of us are going to make it through unscathed.

Unless help comes tomorrow, we'll find ourselves exactly where we are now, yet again: sitting on the beach in silence, watching the sun set on the horizon line as we fail to shed a single tear for the one we've just lost.

DAY SEVEN

6:52 A.M.

For the second day in a row, I'm woken by the sound of screaming downstairs. Today, however, I'm not given the luxury of sleeping in. I can't be sure of the exact time, but the sun's just starting to come up, so it can't be later than seven.

When I roll over and try to cover my ears with a pillow, my leg bumps into something firm and warm. I open my eyes to find Henry beside me. He, too, is trying to muffle the yelling by folding a pillow over his head. It's only when I see the soot still staining his hands that I remember what happened last night, and how we ended up here.

Zayn's dead. Nobody knows for sure how it happened, but Henry and I imagine it had something to do with the cigarette between his lips and the traces of gasoline he probably got a little too close to. One second, he's underneath the thing, and the next, we're all watching the boat go up in flames, and he's nowhere to be found. I'm not sure how long we stayed sitting on the beach, watching the blazing boat, but we didn't go back inside until it was nearly pitch-black outside. I don't think we even said anything the entire time we watched that stupid boat burn, either.

The next thing I remember is following my friends inside when the flames started to die down. A few of them were hit with some debris when the boat exploded, so I'm pretty sure they stayed up to have Madison clean and bandage their minor wounds while the rest of us went to bed. Henry followed me to my room when I started for the stairs, and we didn't so much as cuddle up together before we went to sleep.

The rest of the night following the explosion was tainted by a dark, unbeatable silence that took mercy on nobody. It's like everything that's happened on this trip caught up to us all at once, leaving us incapable of feeling anything other than numbness. I guess it just doesn't make sense to talk at all if the one thing you should be talking about—the loss of a friend—leaves you mute.

When the yelling doesn't cease, I sigh and swing my legs out of bed. Henry follows my lead after he feels the mattress shift, and we both wordlessly get dressed. Until this moment, I didn't realize he brought his belongings into my room. He must've done it at some point last night when I was too discombobulated to notice.

As I take out my contacts and put in a new pair, his hoarse voice asks, "Why do you sleep in your contacts?"

"Just in case something happens, and I need to move quickly in the middle of the night." I shrug and blink a few times as the saline coats my dry eyes. "Takes too long to put them in when I'm rushing."

"You don't have glasses?"

"I don't have the face for glasses."

"I beg to differ. You'd look cute in glasses."

Another boom of escalating voices has us both flinching. "We can talk about how cute I'd look later on," I say. "Let's go see what they're bitching about now."

Even today, the fifth day since the storm, it feels weird to just get dressed and start the day. We don't have enough freshwater for brushing our teeth after we used most of it for the potatoes, rinsing off our filter supplies, and cleaning some of the food we've found. A good amount of it was spilled by both Brett and Madison during their tantrums yesterday, and the rest has to be reserved for drinking water. I haven't even bathed properly since the storm, either. Taking soap into the ocean to wash my body and my hair doesn't leave me feeling as clean as I'd like.

No brushing our teeth, washing our faces, showering, or using the bathroom in actual toilets...It feels wrong because it is, but at the same time, it's starting to feel routine, too. The habits we all arrived here with are long gone, and I can't say for certain when it happened.

I'm not sure what day of the week it is, either. The dark haze that's come to characterize the island has infiltrated its way into my head, making it impossible for me to keep track when I attempt to count the number of sunrises I've seen since we got here.

When we reach the bottom of the stairs, Joe is leaning against the banister with his arms folded over his chest, watching a large group of our friends argue in the kitchen exactly as they did yesterday. In the living room, Ava's back on her spot on the couch, elevating her foot while Madison inspects the purple, still-swollen sting marks. The mattresses are leaned up against the windows again, and Reid sits with his back to one of them, looking exhausted as he observes the fighting.

Nick's nowhere to be seen, so I imagine he hasn't yet come out of whatever room he's been holed up in. The only other person not contributing to the arguing is Erin, who's sitting at the kitchen table while draining coconut water into a clear pitcher.

My eyes find Leah sitting on the countertop beside James, who's standing in front of the sink. I finally remember what Zayn's death led me to forget: it was Leah, not Madison, who I overheard with James in my room the other night.

I don't get the chance to think on it any further. Henry mutters something to Joe that I can't hear, but I figure it out when Joe turns to face us, keeping his voice low so only we can hear him:

“Most of us slept down here last night. Woke up half an hour ago when Brett started getting noisy. He was, like, dragging Sydney to the door so she could help him look for Spencer again. She was barely awake. James and Aaron stepped in to cool him off, and he just lost it on them.”

I frown. “I know he's freaked out by the whole situation, but we have an entire day to look for him. Nobody's stopping him from going out there whenever he wants. I don't get why he's making such a big deal out of it first thing in the morning.”

“He's insisting he needs help, but we all have other things to prioritize, too, and he's mad that not everyone is on the same page as him,” Joe continues, scoffing a little. “Doesn't know how to do shit on his own. Needs his hand held.”

I could say the same about most of the people in this house, I want to say, but I don't.

“He said something about wanting to get Nick out of the room, too, because we need all hands on deck,” he adds. “Doesn't seem to care that Dani and Zayn just died.”

“He's worried about his brother,” I murmur. “I get that. I just don't think he's going about it the right way.”

“We're all in agreement, then,” he says with a snort. “You should've heard what he—”

“Oh, for fuck's sake!” Aaron's booming voice interrupts Joe, dragging our attention back to the kitchen island. He's standing across from Brett at the island, his hands curled into fists at his sides. “Not one person here doesn't want Spencer found alive and safe, dude. That's not the issue. You just can't expect every single one of us to put everything else aside to look for him all day, every day. You can't be dragging Nick and Ava into this, either. They're not a part of this right now.”

Ava sniffs from the couch. “I wish I could help, but my leg—”

“We know,” Brett snaps, not bothering to look over his shoulder at her. I can't see his face, but his body is so rigid that it looks like he'd shatter into pieces like a statue if he fell down. "None of you are fucking listening. We had two people missing, and one's been found. We can't be wasting time on other things when we're still missing someone. Spencer needs to be everyone's top priority."

"Everyone's top priority is staying alive," Leah reminds him.

"Not working out so well, is it? None of us know what the fuck we're doing!" he shouts. *No kidding,* I think. "We thought everyone was gonna be okay after the storm. Then Magnus bleeds out internally, Ava almost dies from a jellyfish sting, and Zayn blows himself up. It doesn't matter what the fuck we try to do, guys. We're not in control here. The only thing we can control is being here for each other, and we're not doing that if we're leaving one of us stranded out there."

"Do you hear yourself?" Joe steps forward, making Brett and Sydney turn to face us as the others turn their gazes to him. "Zayn didn't blow himself up 'cause he wanted to, man. He was trying to get us out of here. All you've done is yell at us and kick things. Nick was missing someone close to him, too, and he wasn't doing that bullshit. You can't expect us to listen to you when you're treating us like shit."

Brett just rolls his eyes. "Oh, please. We're all adults, and this isn't the time or the place to be worried about hurting feelings. I bet any one of you would be saying the same shit if it was your brother or sister."

"Of course we would," Henry chimes in. "We get what you're going through. It's just not as simple as you're making it out to be. Sure, we're at a disadvantage, and there are things we can't control. But you're right—we can control taking care of each other, and the way we do that isn't forcing a dozen people to go out looking for one person. It's dividing and conquering to make sure that everyone's staying healthy, that we have enough food and water, and that our shelter holds up."

Brett throws his hands up in the air, fury illuminating his dark eyes. "Why am I the only person who feels guilty that we have the supplies we do or that we still have a roof over our heads? Spencer doesn't, wherever he is. He's starving, dehydrated, sunburnt, freezing at night, and scared as fuck every second of every day. Why doesn't anyone else feel guilty? Why doesn't anyone else want to try harder to free him from that?"

Because he's dead, I want to say. I know it, everyone else knows it, and deep down, Brett knows it, too. It's pointless to keep wasting time searching for a dead man when we need to be doing other things, but we can't say that to Brett. He can't handle it.

Apparently, James disagrees.

"Look, man..." James steps away from the sink to lean his hands on the island, making Brett and Sydney turn again. "I speak for everyone when I say we knew what we'd find if we came across Dani or Spencer out there yesterday. We've known all along. Finding Dani was proof that we were right to think that way. If he's not in this house, he's gone. I'm sorry, but it's the truth. We can dedicate some time to finding him so we can lay him to rest and gain some closure, but we can't have every single one of us spending all day looking for a corpse. We have better things to do."

Ouch.

A dark crimson flush rises up on the back of Brett's neck as he starts to shake. "You piece of fucking shit. The fuck's wrong with you? Huh? That's my baby brother you're talking about. You've known him for half your life. He thought of you like a brother, and now you're saying we have better things to do than search for him? And you don't even have the decency to pretend he might still be alive?" He laughs humorlessly and shakes his head. "Man, I've always known you're an insensitive prick, but I never thought you'd stoop so low, especially when it comes to Spence. He was your family, too, and you didn't even know he—your guest—was missing."

James's eyes harden. "You were taking the blame for yourself yesterday because he's your brother, not ours. Everyone disagreeing with you for perfectly logical reasons doesn't give you the right to blame anyone for this shit."

"James," Leah says quietly, warning him as the rest of us watch the showdown in silence.

He ignores her. "Nobody's agreed on anything these past few days, but right now, it's all of us against you. It's the first time we've agreed on anything. You need to calm down, help us come up with a better plan, and stop being an asshole to your friends because *you* lost *your* little brother during *a fucking hurricane!"*

That's what does it. In the blink of an eye, Brett's rounding the side of the island with his arm raised, headed straight for James. Sydney inserts herself between them, holding her hands up in an attempt to keep Brett at bay, but he doesn't seem to notice her. Between the yelling, the screeching of Erin's chair when she jumps to her feet, and the flash of people moving too slowly toward the warring friends as they try to intervene, I almost miss the moment Brett swings at James.

Only he doesn't hit James. His fist grazes the side of Sydney's jaw as she tries pushing him away from James, sending her crumpling to the ground. Luckily, her head was moving, so she didn't get the full force of

Brett's sucker punch. Even so, she's on the ground weeping and holding her face, her other arm still outstretched to keep Brett away from James.

I watch, paralyzed by the unfolding scene, as Leah hops down from the counter and rushes to Sydney's aid. James is just looking between Brett and Sydney, wild-eyed, though he seems more surprised that Brett actually tried to hit him than concerned about Sydney—and for a split second, I swear I see him smirk.

At the same time, Aaron and Joe rush forward to grab Brett's arms and pull him back. Despite Brett lowering his fist now that he's realized he punched his girlfriend in the jaw, he's still surging toward James, and it's hard to tell if what he did to Sydney is enough to distract him from his mission.

Brett calms down for a split second when his eyes land on Sydney. "Baby, I'm—"

"What's wrong with you?" Aaron demands as he and Joe keep an iron grip on Brett's arms. "Are you fucking insane?"

"I didn't mean—"

"I-It's okay," Sydney manages, but she's still crying in Leah's arms on the floor. There's already a blossoming red splotch on her jaw. "It was an accident."

"The fuck it was," Madison snarls from behind me.

"You need to get out of here and cool off." It's James who speaks next, and while there's a bitter edge to his voice, he's surprisingly calm. "Go look for Spencer on your own, since that's the only thing that matters to you. I bet you this wouldn't have happened if you'd cared more about what your brother was doing when the storm hit."

Just when I thought James couldn't make this any worse.

Brett lets out an enraged growl and surges forward, forcing Aaron and Joe to tighten their grips, yank him backward, and attempt pinning his arms behind his back. He's screaming at them to get off of him while he thrashes and struggles, which leads Henry to attempt helping them restrain him further. Aaron loses his grip, making Brett's elbow fly backward and nearly come into contact with Henry's temple, as he tries to fight his way toward James. James, on the other hand, doesn't move a muscle as he watches—this time, I'm absolutely sure he's smirking.

In seconds, Brett's on his stomach on the ground, with the three guys bent around him like they're playing Twister as they try to keep him down.

It'd be hilarious if Sydney wasn't still crying and holding her throbbing jaw on the floor.

"Stop!"

Speak of the devil.

Everyone—even Brett—stops when Sydney's voice rings out, silencing the room. Leah helps her to her feet as she wipes her wet cheeks and reluctantly removes her hand from her jaw. Even from my poor angle, I can see Brett's eyes shift when he catches sight of what will soon be a nasty bruise.

"It's okay," Leah assures her, setting a comforting hand on her shoulder. "Let's go in the other room and calm down for a minute. Let the guys handle—"

"No!" Sydney's still sobbing, but somehow, they seem to be tears of shame rather than pain, judging by the way she stares at her feet. "I-I have something I need to say."

Nobody answers for a moment. It's Madison who finally says, "Go ahead. It's okay."

Sydney takes a long, shaky breath in as she tries to calm herself. "I-I noticed Spencer wasn't with us after the storm."

"What?" So many people say it at the same time that I have no idea who's spoken and who hasn't.

"I-I..." She trails off as the tears keep coming. At this point, the guys have relaxed their grips on Brett out of sheer curiosity, and he's stopped fighting for the same reason. They're all just staring at her, waiting for more. "I didn't want to say anything 'cause I didn't want to upset you, babe. B-But the night of the storm..." She hiccups through a sob and hugs herself. "The night of the storm, I was getting ready for bed, and Spencer came in to get his stuff out of the room. H-He said I looked really good at the beach, and then he said some other stuff, and...and it started getting weird."

Erin stares at her in disbelief. "He hit on you?"

Sydney nods and sniffles. "He said he's had feelings for me since we met, and he thought Brett wasn't treating me like he should, so he asked if I wanted to go on a walk with him and 'see where it goes.' I didn't know how else to respond, so I asked him to go. He said he'd be waiting for me if I changed my mind and wanted to meet him later. I thought he just hid out in the basement or something. I didn't think he'd take it *literally* and actually leave the house."

I sigh. “He thought you’d change your mind about meeting him, so he went out to wait for you someplace where you wouldn’t be seen together.” I don’t know if that’s the whole truth or even close to it, but it’s a truth we can all live with. “It makes sense, given how fucked up he was that night.”

I don't miss the way Brett turns just enough to glower at me, like me stating facts is somehow an insult to Spencer's memory.

“That's not possible,” Brett argues. “Spencer would never make a move on my girlfriend. He wouldn't. He thinks of you like a sister.”

“Of course that's what he'd tell you,” Madison says sharply. “Do you really think he'd admit to having a crush on his brother's girlfriend?”

No reply. It's Aaron who says, “Either way, this information doesn't help us. Knowing Spencer's motive for leaving doesn't take away from what just happened and what we were talking about.”

“Maybe it does,” Ava offers. “If he was still hoping she'd meet him, he wouldn't stay on the property. He'd be worried about someone catching them. He might've found somewhere else nearby, like a neighbor's shed or something.”

“But we've been all around that entire area,” Henry adds, loosening his grip on Brett. “Wherever he went, it came down during the storm, and he's probably buried so deep that we won't be able to find him without proper equipment. There's too much rubble to sort through with our hands.”

Brett's eyes lock on Sydney's trembling, flushed form. “Why didn't you tell me?”

“I didn't want to cause problems…” she whispers.

“You should've told me. I could've—”

“Nothing you could've said or done would've changed anything,” James insists. “He'd still be embarrassed or pissed off, and he'd still want to get as far away from you as possible.”

Brett's body appears to deflate. “What are you saying? That Spencer would've left anyway because of *me?”*

“Well, he wouldn't have left if you didn't invite Sydney at the last minute.”

“Christ, James,” Joe mutters.

“Uh, guys?” Reid says from behind us. Nobody acknowledges him.

Brett's struggling against the guys again now, but still flailing on the floor. “Fuck you, man. I could say the same to you. None of us would be in this mess if you didn't feel like showing off your fancy house in the Caribbean one last time before we graduate. You were the one who insisted it was safe to stay while everyone else was leaving, too, remember?"

"That's not fair," James hisses.

"Doesn't feel so good, does it, motherfucker?"

"Stop it," Sydney pleads. "I-I already feel bad enough. I can't keep listening to you fighting over this."

"Guys," Reid says again.

"What?" Madison snaps, turning to face him from her kneeling position on the couch. "What could possibly be so important, Reid?"

Only now do I notice he took down the mattress he's been leaning against. He's standing in front of the exposed window, his face gray and slack, but he's positioned sideways so he can see both us and the beach.

I recognize the look in his eyes immediately. It's the same look he had when we realized Magnus was dead.

Without a word, he just turns so he's fully facing the window. A few of us exchange glances as we walk over to see what he's looking at, but Henry and Aaron remain on the floor with Brett. Sydney stays back, too, profusely apologizing to Brett like all of this is her fault.

A knot forms in my chest when I see what Reid's spotted outside: a body floating face-down in the ocean, just yards away from the still-smoking remains of both Zayn and the motorboat.

8:00 A.M.

I don't know how long we've been out here on the beach, silently standing as we stare down at Nick's blue, puffy body resting on the sand.

The darkness is starting to clear up just the tiniest bit, so visibility is better than it has been—the sky is brighter and the ocean is clearer. That tells me only one thing: it wasn't the gloom and the darkness that hid Nick from us, but rather our own lack of attention.

Nobody even knew he left his room. He must've come out here in the middle of the night when he was sure we were all asleep. The worst part isn't even that he managed to get out here undetected—it's that we were all too busy to realize he needed help, to step in and prevent this before he committed to it.

Erin just asked how long we think he's been out here, and nobody has been able to answer. The last time anyone so much as heard his voice was last night when Reid brought him dinner, so for all we know, he came out here after the rest of us went to sleep last night, and we've lived half a day without knowing he was dead.

Aaron, Joe, and Henry didn't come out with us right away after Reid identified Nick's AC/DC t-shirt and khakis from the living room window. They locked Brett in a room on the third floor, claiming he needs to be alone to keep us all safe if he lashes out again. While the rest of us—excluding Ava—went out to pull Nick's body to shore, they stopped to check the room Nick locked himself in, hoping to find a note of some sort.

They're coming out now. As I watch them stroll toward us, I spot Ava standing on the deck by the railing, tilted to one side as she puts her weight on her good foot. I'm not close enough to see her face, but I know she's not crying. None of us are.

We should be, though.

Joe and Reid are Nick's closest friends in the world—and Aaron, too, when he's not distracted by James's core group. I'm only friends with these people because I was close to Nick and Aaron first. The four of us should be feeling the pain of this loss more than anyone else, and yet, two of them didn't even feel the urge to come straight out here. That, or they used the time spent on locking Brett up and searching Nick's room to process the loss. That possibility doesn't feel right to me, though.

I've already made peace with the fact that I'll never dance on tables with Nick again, or rub his back and clean him up when he pukes all over himself, or absolutely demolish him while playing Flip Cup. I don't need to cry over the fact that I'll never hear his laugh again, or make fun of him when his glasses fog up, or throw spitballs at him while he's trying to study.

I know all of this. His death may have been unexpected, but it's not shocking, given everything else that's happened. It's just easier to accept that he's gone when he's the seventh friend I've said goodbye to in as many days; and if the others don't feel the same way, then they'd be shedding at least one tear over Nick's body.

"Found these in his room," Joe says hoarsely, holding up an item in either hand. "Looks like he stole Anne McFarley's sleeping meds from our stash of supplies. They're half gone."

Reid just sighs. "He couldn't swim. If the pills didn't do it...He wanted to make sure the job got done."

The job. What a way to talk about your best friend's suicide.

I clear my throat and nod my head toward Joe's left hand. "What's that?"

He grimaces. "He left a note."

He passes it around rather than reading it aloud. When it gets into Erin's hands, I look over her shoulder while Madison does the same on her other side. There's only one sentence written in Nick's handwriting, smudged across the small piece of notebook paper. His writing has always been messy like this—a result of him being lefthanded, and always choosing easily-smudged gel pens because he preferred the way they wrote.

Tell our parents I'm sorry.

"He must mean his and Dani's parents," Erin murmurs.

"It's not like we're gonna tell Dani's parents why she was outside during the hurricane," James states. "We'll have to think of something else to tell them about how she died, but either way, they're gonna blame someone."

I scowl at him. "They won't be blaming anyone. They'll be mourning their child."

He mirrors my expression. "They'll want answers, too. All of our families will want answers."

“A fucking hurricane hit the island, and people died. That's enough,” Madison retorts. “They don't need to know anything more than that. It's not like we killed her, either.”

“Might as well have,” he snaps back. “We all let her go.”

“Jesus fuck,” Aaron says through gritted teeth. “We don't need to be having this conversation right now. Let's just show him one last ounce of respect before we move on.”

Before we move on. It comes out as smoothly as it would coming from a professor when it’s time to wrap up one lesson and start the next—procedural, habitual.

The guys carry Nick's sopping body toward the gravesite while us girls hike over there to fetch the shovels, which haven't moved since we buried Dani—and if I'm being honest, we left them here after burying the guys, too, like some distant part of us knew we'd need them again.

We start digging a hole right beside the mound where Dani lies six feet beneath the sand. We take turns every now and then to catch our breath, and soon enough, there's a fifth grave at our makeshift cemetery.

As Joe and Henry carefully lower Nick into the grave, they disrupt some of the sand on the side, and Dani's hand pops out. Nobody reacts to it—not a gag, not a gasp, not a shriek of horror. It's almost like we all expected it; like we all knew Dani would find a way to be latched onto Nick, even as a corpse.

We don't bother saying a few words or leaving treasures with his body, whether it be his own belongings or our own, like we did for the first three to leave us. Nobody thought about it with Dani because of the smell and the state of her body, and it's not like we were able to bury Zayn. We have every opportunity to have a small memorial for Nick, but nobody seems to be thinking about it—and if anyone is, they make no move to act on it.

While I watch Leah and Aaron toss shovelfuls of sand atop Nick's body, I think about the way today started. I didn't hear how the argument began, but clearly, Brett wanted everyone to go out searching for Spencer, while the others thought our daylight hours would be better spent on scavenging, fishing, and other tasks. Either option would've amounted to something, but instead, we're out here burying another friend.

Brett was right. We're not in control here. It doesn't matter how many plans we come up with, how viciously we fight about them, or what we end up doing with our time here. Nothing will ever go as planned while we're stuck on this island.

Nick's suicide should make what happened earlier feel unimportant, but it doesn't. It just makes me realize that we're going to walk away when we're finished here, only to resume our previous discussion about our efforts for the rest of the day like this never happened.

When they finish, there's a tall mound of sand beside the others. They drop the shovels on the flat side of Nick's grave and take a few steps back to stand with the rest of us. We stay like this for a few minutes, staring at the grave, using this moment of silence as a supplement for the memorial we're incapable of giving him.

James walks away first. Leah and Joe follow, and then Aaron and Erin, with Madison, Sydney, and Reid at the rear. I don't move a muscle yet, but Henry starts to follow them, pausing a few feet away from the graves to wait for me.

I don't bother acknowledging him. I'm too lost in my own head as I stare at the graves, trying my hardest to remember the new arrangement so I don't disrespect the dead more than I already have.

Nick and Dani on the left, Eli and Magnus in the middle, Zeke on the right, and Zayn is gone.

11:19 A.M.

It's been a few hours since we left Nick. It's a good thing Brett's still confined to a room upstairs, because if he was out here with us, he'd be furious that we're not jumping into action like everyone wanted to this morning while fighting with him about searching for Spencer.

We took turns bathing not long after we came back inside. Madison and Erin had to give Ava what was basically a shitty saltwater sponge bath while the guys were outside washing off in the ocean. She panicked over the thought of us being chest-deep in the water with predators surrounding us, and we weren't thrilled by the idea, either, so we came up with a plan: everyone bathes in pairs from now on, with one person keeping an eye out for approaching marine life while the other cleans up.

I know a lot of girls have no problem being naked around their girl friends, but I've never been like that. It's humiliating enough to bathe in the ocean with four other girls, but it's even worse when one of them—or two, in my case, since there's an uneven number while Ava is incapacitated—is literally looking straight down at your vagina while ensuring no barracudas arrive to gnaw at your legs.

Thanks to the fire we built to boil the potatoes, we were able to collect more charred wood from the pit, so we've gotten some of the filters going again. There's a big plastic tub with rope handles—once used for James's little cousins' beach toys—sitting on the deck that Aaron and Joe filled with seawater, which we've been treating like a stream as we walk back and forth to pour pitchers of it into the filters. We have the filtered water bottle, too, but it still tastes like salt and seaweed unless we boil the water first.

The water filtration process is slow, and though we're a long ways away from dehydration—especially compared to the state we'd be in without the filters—that doesn't stop some of us from acting like it's the absolute end of the world. Joe keeps shaking the filters in hopes of making the water move faster, but all that does is disrupt the layers of the filter and force us to start over. He seems to forget that every time he stalks over the filters and rattles them.

Most of us are suffering from dry lips, so we've been passing around the same two lip balms, with Reid and Ava slathering so much over their mouths that soon enough, we'll have to start using the Crisco in the pantry to avoid cracked and bleeding lips.

I swear, I caught Madison crying a few minutes ago when she looked in the mirror and started toying with her hair. She's probably never let it get this oily before. My hair is short, but I can still tie it into Dutch braids, and that's the closest I can get to masking the greasy look of it. The other girls are dealing with it by tying their hair up in buns or slicked back ponytails, but Madison just shivers whenever she touches her hair, like there's no option good enough other than washing it—and not with saltwater.

Not to mention, the fights that have ensued over bad breath and body odor—despite heavy layers of deodorant, perfume, and cologne—have led to a significant number of slamming doors and high-pitched screaming.

As for food…we ate the rest of the bread, oranges, and a can of lentils from the pantry after we got back from burying Nick. Now, all we have left is a few more slices of bread, coconut water and flesh, a sleeve of crackers, an onion, the two pickle jars, and whatever's left from the pantry: a little bit of pasta, trail mix, about half a cup of granola, and one more can of lentils. With twelve of us left, that's enough for dinner tonight, and possibly tiny portions for everyone for breakfast tomorrow, but it's not like we'll be able to make anything appetizing out of an onion, crackers, coconut, and lentils.

I have to remind myself that it's not about our food being appetizing. We said goodbye to that days ago—I'm not even sure when, to be honest. The only thing we have the luxury of caring about now is keeping our bodies from shutting down, even if it means surviving on onion scales.

As we're figuring out our rations with the new supplies, Erin volunteers to try fishing again, and a visibly irritated Reid goes with her when nobody else steps up.

Bathing, organizing our food supply, refilling the filters, and now three of us heading out to fish...It's all we've done over the last three hours. Nobody's made an effort to keep working at the repairs around the house, or giving the backup generator another shot, or anything else. We're just bumming around and trying to entertain ourselves like there's nothing more to worry about.

I've been sitting on the floor studying the map of the island with Henry. We're using a permanent marker to identify the locations we've explored, the spots where we found our dead friends, and any potential danger zones we came across. Nick and Joe left some markings already, but only regarding the places they'd searched for Dani.

"Do you two wanna play with us?" Ava offers from the kitchen. We look up to see her sitting at the table with Madison, Leah, Sydney, Joe, and Aaron, playing Uno in pairs. "We can make room."

"Might as well take some time to chill before Sarge starts handing out assignments," Joe adds.

I know he's referring to James, who went straight to the office when we came in from burying Nick. He didn't say a word before he disappeared, and nobody's made any effort to check on him. It's the first day he hasn't been up our asses about gathering supplies, and we're all so burnt out that we're taking advantage of every second of his silence.

Before we can reply, Ava frowns and asks, "What are you doing, anyway?"

"We're trying to figure out if we missed any spots while we've all been out searching," Henry replies, turning the map to reveal the colored markings. "I guess I'm starting to see why Brett got so frustrated. Doesn't excuse his behavior, and even though he didn't say it, I think he knows it's pointless to keep scavenging. We've found as much as we can."

"Unless we go around whatever hazard you two ran into," Leah says. "But that raises the point we were arguing about yesterday. I still think it's worth looking, but I can admit that Zayn had a point. We might put ourselves in a bad position if we find survivors."

"I wasn't even thinking about that," Ava admits, frowning.

Joe just shrugs. "I think he was right. It's pretty safe to assume that any survivors won't want to share what little they have with us, even if they think help's coming tomorrow. They won't risk running out of food because they want to show kindness to strangers, and they won't let us stay with them—not like we need to, anyway—because they'll be afraid of us stealing from them. Think about it: if other survivors made it over here and asked for help, what would we do?"

Nobody answers, and I know it's because none of us wants to be the person to say what we're all thinking: we'd tell those people to go back to their side of the island, and that there isn't enough food or space for us to spare for them.

"Then there's the possibility of invasion," Aaron says as he slaps a card down. "What if we find survivors, and they follow us back because they think we're better off than they are? If there's enough of them, they could force us out of the house and steal our shit. I'm not willing to risk that, personally."

"There's already so many of us." Sydney chews on her lower lip. "Someone gets hungry enough…The odds of that are a lot higher."

She doesn't have to elaborate for us to understand. It's more likely that someone in this house will panic over starvation enough to steal the remaining rations for themselves than it is for survivors to find us and steal our things.

Soon enough, we'll start guarding our food like it's under siege, despite the fact that the siege will be coming from inside the house.

I see the genuine worry—and fear—in our friends' eyes as they process that. I don't miss the way Leah and Madison quickly glance at Ava and Joe, either. We've all heard the two of them complain about hunger and ask if there's any extra food more than anyone else has. The two of them don't seem to notice the looks they've gotten, though. They have no idea their friends think they'll be the first to betray us when food truly gets scarce.

The best part? Nobody argues with Sydney or tries to insist that none of us would do something like that. The lack of trust here is astounding, but I guess we would've found ourselves in this position sooner or later.

"What do you suggest we do about food, then?" Madison asks. "The resort area might be our only hope. If we don't have enough success fishing, then what do we do?"

Joe shrugs. "Try to make some traps. I mean, I haven't seen a ton of wildlife recently, but I've heard things, so I know they're out there. What kind of animals are native to the Bahamas?"

"Mostly tropical birds and reptiles, but there are a few mammals, too," Henry answers. "Wild cats and dogs, peccaries, mice, flying squirrels, monkeys. Plenty of common woodland creatures. My only concern is that anything we hunt or catch could carry diseases we're not equipped to treat. Zika virus, ciguatera, leptospirosis. They might also carry bacteria that wouldn't harm natives to the Caribbean, but they could be lethal for us because our bodies aren't familiar with that bacteria."

"So, even if we're desperate enough that we start eating bugs, we could still die because they carry diseases?" Sydney summarizes. Henry and I nod in unison as she shivers and hugs herself. "We're so fucked."

"I think it's something we should seriously be considering," Madison presses. "It's a risk we have to take if we don't want to starve. We'll just steer clear of animals that are commonly associated with carrying diseases, like bats. But we can't just take our fishing spears into the woods. We need to find traps."

She says it like traps are something we'll just miraculously stumble upon in the debris instead of something we have to work for.

A lightbulb appears to go off behind Leah's eyes as she turns to Madison. "Hey. Remember the first time we came here? James's grandparents were leaving the day we arrived. They wanted to give us a tour of the house before they left. It was the one and only time we ever got to see their bedroom."

Madison's eyes widen. "I remember that. Their room is, like, totally nautical. They converted old lobster traps and stuff into furniture."

"We can try modifying them, too," Joe suggests. "If they're lobster traps, they might not work for land animals, so we can tweak them to get the job done."

"They'd be perfect for catching actual lobsters—probably other crustaceans, too—if we had buoys to attach them to," I add. "We'll lose them if we just drop them out there. I didn't see any floatation devices in the garage, but maybe there's something of the sort in the basement."

Sydney moves to face me fully, excited by something I said, and I finally get a good glimpse of her face after she's been turned away these last few hours. The bruise has already started forming on her jaw, and it's a lot bigger than I expected. It's a good thing Brett didn't get a direct hit, because if he did, he probably would've broken her jaw. The bruise won't feel any better, though. After the painkillers Madison gave her from the first aid kit wear off, it'll start getting difficult for her to talk and eat without feeling excruciating pain.

"The wine cellar," she says, practically bouncing in her chair. "You said the wine has enough calories to keep us going. We can take more of it."

"If James doesn't throw a fit about it, then yeah," Joe mutters with a roll of his eyes. "We need his permission before we take any more, and before we steal his nana's pretty nightstands."

"I'll go ask him." As I'm standing, I don't miss the odd looks tossed my way by both Henry and Madison. "Be right back."

Do I want to interact with James alone right now? No. But do I think I can get through to him? Absolutely. I have leverage over him, and only he knows it.

Well, Leah does, too, but she won't use it against him. That wouldn't look good for her.

I don't bother knocking before I open the office door. James is partially slouched over the desk as he scribbles something in a black, leatherbound journal. He doesn't lift his head up when he hears my footsteps, but I see his eyes flicker upward at the same moment he releases a frustrated exhale.

"We came up with some ideas," I say dully. "It seems like everyone's pretty set on not scavenging further. We've found all we can, and moving any further toward the other side could land us in hot water. We're gonna need some of that wine in the cellar, plus your grandparents' bedroom furniture. We think we can make traps to help us hunt."

He looks up from the journal with hollow eyes. "We're not destroying more of the house. This entire island is gonna be rebuilt eventually—I don't wanna make more work for my grandparents."

"Restocking their fancy wine collection isn't making more work for them. It's keeping us alive," I retort, arms folded over my chest. "And I don't think they'd mind sacrificing a couple of end tables if it means we're not starving to death. Nobody here has ever gone more than half a day without food, so it won't be a pretty scene when our rations run out."

"It won't work, anyway. I know what you're talking about, and it won't work like you think it will. We just have to keep thinking."

"It's worth a shot, James."

"I said no, Sadie."

I take a few steps forward, narrowing my eyes. "All you've been talking about is us joining forces to find food in any way we can. Well, that's exactly what we've done, and you're saying no. I guess I should've known you'd react like this, though. You say a lot of things and make a lot of promises, and yet you don't keep them."

That makes him drop the pen and scowl at me. "What the fuck's that supposed to mean?"

"You know exactly what I mean."

"I don't know what you're talking about, but whatever it is, I'm sure it's all a big misunderstanding."

"Telling me we'd finish what we started later, only to fuck someone else in my bed? *That* was a misunderstanding?"

"You don't seem to be losing any sleep over it," he says coolly, leaning back in his chair. He juts his chin forward, and I know he's referencing the fading hickey on my neck. "You moved on quickly enough."

As I stare at him—his eyes dead and blank, his nostrils flaring like a bull ready to charge—I realize the James I was blushing at a few days ago is long gone, and in his place is someone I barely recognize.

"That doesn't mean what you did wasn't fucked up, and you know it," I seethe. He releases a huff of frustration and runs a hand through his hair. I can tell it's taking everything within him to refrain from yelling at me. "Listen, James...You're right. I've moved on. But you still did what you did, and I'm pretty sure everyone would have words for you if they knew what I do."

Again, the faintest glimmer of some sort of emotion appears in his eyes, but it's gone as quickly as it came. It's like when your Alexa tells you she loves you back, but you're fully aware it's just an automated response to the silly thing you said to a talking machine.

"Go ahead," he says after a moment of silence. "I think everyone knows I wouldn't do something like that."

I bristle at him, somehow shocked by his arrogance. "Maybe not at first, but I'd be curious to see how they feel when they find out you've been hooking up with your fuck buddy's best friend behind her back."

Finally, a clear emotion fills his gaze and stays there:

Dread.

"Sadie—"

"Have you changed your mind about what I said, then?"

He grits his teeth as his knuckles turn white from his grip on the armrests. "You know what? Sure. Fine. Whatever the fuck you guys want to do, do it."

I beam at him. "Thanks. I had a feeling you'd see things our way." I start to turn toward the door when he grumbles something under his breath, but I think better of it and stop. "Aren't you coming? We need all the help we can get."

"I'm busy."

"Doing what?"

"None of your business."

I narrow my eyes at him. "People notice patterns, you know."

"Not when they're too busy making sure nobody's sticky fingers touch the rations," he retorts, making me roll my eyes. "And if you really need to know, I'm trying to keep track of how and when everyone died."

I soften a little. "Why? We can just tell everyone what happened when we get out of here."

"None of it looks good for us," he says sharply, picking up the pen again. "We should've stopped Zeke and Eli from getting onto the boat. Should've stopped Dani from leaving. Should've told Zayn not to mess with the boat. Should've kept a closer eye on Nick and fatal dosages of medication. We have to bend the truth a little unless we want a ton of angry parents blaming us for their kids' deaths."

We already went through this yesterday, but clearly, it didn't stick. "I don't think anyone would blame us. It's not like we knew anything like this was gonna happen."

"Still." He runs a hand through his hair again and clenches his jaw. "I need everyone to know that the blame isn't on us—or on my family. I can't have investigators thinking we're liable for all of this because they think my grandpa left bottles of pills laying around or left us access to a shitty boat."

I shake my head at him. "Jesus. You're already planning how this is gonna look. Thinking about the fallout, not the people."

"Wouldn't you do the same?"

"No." My answer is immediate. "If this was my house, I wouldn't be giving a second thought to anyone faulting my family for what happened. I'd be thinking of ways to tell my friends' parents that their kids are dead in a way that isn't so heartless." A humorless laugh escapes me. "They're gonna be looking to you to find out what their kids' last moments were like, and you're gonna look them in the eye and tell them their kids died because of dumb choices that had nothing to do with you or your family, when you know that isn't totally true."

He just stares at me. "Was it smart to leave the house during a storm, then?"

I hardly liked Dani, but still, the statement irritates me. "It's true—they might blame someone. But instead of caring that Dani's gone and that we all let her go, you're just hoping the blame doesn't land on you."

"What's going on?" Henry and Aaron both pop their heads into the doorway. It's Henry who adds, "Everything okay?"

"Depends what you mean by that," I reply. "James is trying to keep track of how everyone died. I think he's worried about getting the details right for search and rescue when we're questioned."

"What?" Aaron frowns as he looks between me and James, whose face has turned red. "Seriously, dude? That's what you're worried about right now?"

"It's not like that!" For a split second, I see panic brewing in James's eyes at the way Aaron is looking at him. "I just want to make sure we have everything documented so we're not grappling for answers. It'd be fucked up of us if we can't remember details when someone's parent asks us how their kid died."

"I don't think any of us will be forgetting a single detail of anything that went down any time soon," Henry cuts in. "We'll probably never forget any of it, honestly."

"That's not what I meant."

"That's what you said," Aaron shoots back.

When James says nothing, Aaron scoffs, shakes his head, and mutters, "Unbelievable," as he turns on his heel and leaves. I follow him after tossing one last disappointed look in James's direction, with Henry right behind me. I'm not surprised when I hear the journal slam shut and James's heavy footsteps trailing behind us.

He's not following to fight about it. He's following because he knows he'll need to do some damage control in a minute or two.

Someone must've asked why Aaron looks so pissed off, because we join him and the others right as he's telling them what I just relayed to he and Henry. It's not long before everyone's bickering, choosing sides as we always do: Madison, Leah, and Sydney agree with James that it's smart to have a plan so the blame doesn't fall on us, though they don't say anything about James wanting to protect his family more than us or our friends' memories; but Aaron, Joe, Ava, and Henry agree with me that James's insensitivity has gone too far.

For a minute, it seems like we might lose Ava and even Aaron, thanks to James's persuasiveness. He's insisting it's not about his family's reputation, but ours. Thankfully, Joe and Henry aren't fooled by that. Even Sydney's face falters a bit when James argues it, like she knows he wouldn't be so worked up about this if it wasn't true.

Then James delivers the kicker, ruining his argument for all:

"My family will be dealing with enough after search and rescue comes," James says, his chest rising and falling rapidly as he chooses self-defense over breathing properly. "We don't need a ton of bereaved parents accusing them of not providing a safe environment for their kids. I don't know what's so hard to understand about that."

James—and so many of the others, too—talks about his parents like people talk about foreign embassies.

Madison's eyes grow a fraction of an inch. “James...”

I cast a sidelong glance at Henry. He’s still and silent, his eyes trained solely on James, and the only sign of his aggravation is a slight twitching in his jaw. I’m waiting for him to say something, but he doesn’t. He’s locked in, watching as everything unravels.

“I really don’t think that’s something to be concerned with right now,” Joe states.

I nod. “Yeah. A family with money like yours wouldn’t own a property that’s unsafe. They’d be on top of everything, and everyone knows that. Plus, didn’t you say your dad gave you his card so we wouldn’t have to worry about food? Nobody would think to accuse your family of not taking care of us if that’s true, too.”

James's face goes white as his jaw slacks. Aaron furrows his eyebrows and says, "What are you talking about?”

“Nothing,” James says quickly.

“Your dad gave you his card?” Madison demands, hands on her hips.

“That’s not what happened.”

“I must’ve heard you wrong, then,” I say.

I can practically see the gears turning behind Leah’s eyes. “Wait a sec. Why did you ask us for grocery money if your dad gave you his card for us to use?”

“Maybe he needed it for something else,” I mutter, “or someone else.”

None of them except for James appears to hear me. When I meet his wide, furious eyes, I can't tell if his rage is stemming from the realization that I'm blackmailing him, or the fact that I'm the reason his friends are looking at him like he's the scum of the earth.

I used to think he was one of the greatest people I've ever met. Now, I’m realizing who he’s been all along, and how blind I’ve been to all of it.

1:46 P.M.

James and Madison have fully given up on hiding their 'secret' hook-ups. They've been outside screaming at each other for the last hour since Madison put the pieces together and realized James more than likely wanted the money to visit a past hookup or two. Apparently, Madison has been under the impression that their casual sex is a little more than that, whereas James has been taking full advantage of the lack of a label on whatever the fuck they are.

That makes me think they've hooked up at some point on this trip. If they've been sleeping together for as long and as often as it appears, I can't imagine they wouldn't want to keep it up while being here, especially while James has his own room. So, if I'm right, then he's slept with both Madison and Leah on this trip, and he implied that he wanted to sleep with me, too.

Unbelievable.

Henry raises an eyebrow. “Hmm?”

“Nothing.” I didn't realize I spoke the thought out loud. “Just thinking.”

He nods and darts his eyes around the room. “We all are.”

I look, too. Reid and Erin are still outside, and Brett's still confined to an upstairs room, but everyone else is scattered around. Nobody got the chance to demand answers from James or yell at him or anything before Madison grabbed him and dragged him outside. He'll be getting one earful after another unless he thinks of a good cover story, which I don't see happening.

After they went outside, the others asked me to recall exactly what I overheard between James and Brett. I obliged, of course, and it's pretty safe to say they're taking my word over James's. It's not like I could make any of that up. Why? Because it sounds exactly like something he'd do, and everyone knows it. Even if they don't want to accept it.

Madison opens the door and slips inside, still fuming. She doesn't say a word as she plops down on the mattress by the window, hugging her knees to her chest and staring out at the beach. I'm across the room at the island with Henry, scraping the flesh of the coconuts into bowls, but even from a distance, I can see the tears staining her cheeks and glistening in her eyes.

A part of me feels bad for her, but not bad enough.

My eyes find Leah at the table with the others. She's looking between Madison and James outside, who's sitting on the deck with his back to us. She mutters something to our friends at the table, and just when I think she's going to comfort Madison, she turns and walks out the back door to sit beside James.

I almost want to laugh. Yesterday, I felt bad about hurting her if I let everyone know about her and James. Today, not so much.

Sensing an opportunity, I place the coconut on the counter and tell Henry, "Be right back."

He nods, silent, and I can feel his eyes on the back of my head as I stroll over to Madison. She looks away from the window long enough to see me, scoff, and turn back as she wipes her cheeks. I sink down onto the other end of the mattress, a good amount of space between us, and mimic her by drawing my knees to my chest.

"You okay?" I ask.

"Why do you care?"

"I don't, but I figured I'd be nice today."

She snorts. "I bet. You've been nothing but nice."

"You're no ray of sunshine, either," I retort. She doesn't answer, but I see her rolling her eyes. "I just wanted to say sorry. I'm sure it hurt to hear what I told everyone. I'm sure it didn't feel great when I jumped down your throat yesterday, either. I was wrong."

"Yeah, you were. I don't know you very well, but I know you had a thing for James, even if it's over now. Most girls do. Just because you wanted to fuck him while he's been with me...That doesn't give you the right to bring that up in front of everyone, even if you didn't say it explicitly. It's a sign of a sore loser."

I brush off the insult. "Everyone knows you two have been fucking. Not a big deal. I was just upset because James wanted to see me that night, and instead, I heard him with you in *my* bed. But I was wrong, and for that, I'm sorry."

She finally meets my gaze. Her eyebrows are furrowed, and her lips are turned in a puzzled frown.

"I still don't know what you're talking about," she says. "We haven't touched each other this whole trip. Too drunk before the storm, and after...I thought it was insensitive when he wanted to hook up. Didn't feel right to do that after we buried our friends."

I nod, feigning understanding. "I get that. I guess that's partly why I was so mad when I thought it was you."

Madison releases a frustrated exhale and tosses hair over her shoulder. "Sadie, for the tenth time, I have no idea what you're talking about."

"I thought I heard the two of you in my room after he switched with me, but I was wrong. Leah said in passing you don't like having your hair pulled, and I heard whoever it was with him asking him to pull her hair." I shrug. "Could've been any of the other girls. I just thought it was you because...well, you know. Anyway, I'm sorry I came at you like that, and I'm sorry you're hurting. It must feel really shitty."

With that, I offer her a kind smile as I stand, inwardly relishing the way her lips part and her eyes widen. I can see the exact moment she puts the pieces together: the moment her gaze flicks toward the clear deck door at where Leah and James sit outside—at where Madison's best friend chose to comfort James instead of her.

When I sit beside Henry at the island again, he raises an eyebrow and asks, "What was that all about?"

I just smile.

A few minutes later, James and Leah return. "Hey, guys," Leah says with a small smile. Everyone immediately glowers at James with their arms crossed. "We talked about what happened, and James—"

"You fucking *bitch!*" Madison storms up to Leah and shoves her so hard that she stumbles into the wall, prompting James to step between them as Leah stares at her, wide-eyed and shocked. "Get out of my face, James! You're no fucking better. I can't believe I fell for—"

"What are you talking about?" Leah's keeping her voice calm and steady, but I can see it in her eyes: she knows exactly what's happening. "What's going on, jellybean?"

Jellybean. Smart move. That's been Leah's nickname for Madison for as long as they've been friends. They met at a party the week before Easter break while Madison was throwing up jellybean-flavored liqueur, and Leah heroically held her hair back. She knows it's sentimental to their friendship—it's no wonder she's whipping it out now.

"Don't you talk to me," Madison seethes, pointing a finger at Leah. "You have no fucking right to look at me like that and talk to me like everything's normal. You know exactly what the fuck you've done." She pauses to take a breath and look between Leah and James. “How long has it been going on? Hmm?”

When they both choose silence, bowing their heads and exchanging brief glances, Joe pipes up from the other side of the room, asking, “How long has *what* been going on?”

“They've been fucking,” Madison says, folding her arms over her chest without looking away from Leah. “Is that what you were doing the other night when you couldn't sleep, and you left our room to get some air on the deck? Were you with him?”

Leah's eyes are filled with tears, her face pink with shame, as she whispers, “Yes,” at the same moment James sputters, “What? No!”

“You gotta give it up, man,” Henry says. “It's not like you were quiet.”

I silently remind myself to thank him later for lying for me. He didn't hear shit that night—nobody did except for me, as far as I'm aware—but how's anyone supposed to know that?

“I'll ask again: how long has it been going on?” Madison drags her eyes away from Leah to direct the question at James, too. “I'm waiting.”

“Jesus, Maddie,” James mutters.

She pokes his chest with her bony finger. “Don't call me that.”

James took a page from Leah's book, apparently. He's the only person other than Madison's family who's ever called her *Maddie*.

“Well?” When he stays silent, she shoves him, making him stumble back into the island. “You've been doing nothing but running your damn mouth since everything happened, and *now* you're choosing to be quiet? What's that all about? Huh? Say something, you fucking coward!”

“Stop it!” Leah, crying in earnest now, steps to the side to stand between Madison and James. She tries to reach for Madison, who yanks her arms away and steps backward. “I-It's been a few months, okay? Since— Since Savannah Leper's party after Thanksgiving break. You were still at home 'cause you had the stomach flu.”

Madison's eyes widen. “Five months? You've been hooking up for *five months?*”

“Give or take…” James says lowly.

Leah shoots him a nasty look. “Seriously?”

“Shut the fuck up. Both of you,” Madison hisses. When she faces Leah again, her eyes are misty, but her fists are trembling at her sides. “I came to you for advice about him. I thought you really wanted to help me, but you were just trying to push me away. Why? Because you wanted him to yourself, or because you wanted to keep fucking him without taking him away from me?"

Leah shakes her head rapidly. "I-I just—"

"Can't really come back from this," Aaron says. When all eyes shoot him scathing glares, he just shrugs. "It's true."

"He's right," Madison says, "but I still want to hear it." She raises a brow, tears beginning to fall from her own eyes, and crosses her arms. "Well?"

"It was my fault," James tells her, mimicking her as he folds his arms over his chest. "I was all over her at the party, and I invited her back to my room after we left. She felt like shit about it the next day, and I—"

"She didn't feel shitty in the moment, and clearly, she didn't feel shitty enough to stop doing it," she interrupts. "That's not a good enough reason."

"There is no good reason," Leah admits, her chin trembling. She tries reaching for Madison again, but she's rebuffed. "It was stupid, Mads. So fucking stupid. I was horny, and dumb, and selfish, and I wasn't thinking about you. I know nothing I say will make it better, but I'm sorry. I'm so sorry."

Madison ignores her and turns to James. "And you?"

"We were never exclusive," he reminds her, and for a second, I think she might actually growl and lunge at him—but she doesn't. "You know by now I've been seeing other people, and honestly, I thought you were, too. But I know it was wrong to go after your best friend. I shouldn't have even thought about it."

I almost pity Madison when I see the heartbreak in her eyes. "I've always known you're not a relationship guy. You're a serial cheater when you're in one, and everyone acts like you're not because you're our friend. I never wanted to put myself in a position to get cheated on. The sex was good enough for a while, and then I wanted more, but I should've known better. Doesn't matter if we were just fucking or dating—you would've started sleeping with my best friend, anyway."

"Mads, I swear—" Leah starts.

"I know it's not because the sex is phenomenal or because you have feelings for her. Everyone on campus has heard the rumors that she's annoying and needy in bed," she continues, talking about Leah like she's not here. Leah's lips part as her eyes fill with tears all over again. "It was because you were doing something that made you feel powerful—because you knew, and I didn't. It was fun for you, thinking I'd never find out. And you'd never break things off with me, either, because the secret and the control wouldn't be as fun if you weren't doing something fucked up."

James's eyes harden. "That's not fair. You're hurt and angry, so you're saying shit you don't mean that you know isn't true."

"Everyone knows it's true," she snaps back. "You're just too high-and-mighty to pay attention to the way everyone sees you."

For a split second, I see his gaze flicker over to everyone else in the room. Only the most self-centered person in the world could see the looks on our faces and disagree with what she's saying. It's clear as day that he's sickened us, and not just because of what he did with Madison and Leah.

He opens his mouth to respond just as the deck door opens. Erin and Reid bound inside, grinning from ear to ear, each holding the reusable shopping bags we found in the pantry. The bags are dripping, like the duo, and the smell of ocean immediately smacks me in the face.

Erin proudly holds up her bag, oblivious to what she just interrupted. "Dinner's on us tonight!"

3:23 P.M.

Erin and Reid's interruption seemed to set something off in Madison. She pushed James so hard that he fell to the ground, and when Leah tried to intervene, Madison gave her a good shove, too. Aaron and Joe pulled her back when she geared up to swing—though I still don't know who she was aiming for—while Sydney grabbed Leah and brought her outside, insisting it was best to give Madison some space for now.

Naturally, as everyone ganged up on James for his behavior—about various topics, for that matter—he hollered at us to mind our own business, then stormed off and locked himself in the office. The instant he realized that nobody was on his side anymore, he fled the scene like a hit-and-run, incapable of taking accountability or offering a genuine apology.

I know everyone was hoping to tear him a new one about the journal and the money thing—more than we already have, anyway—but I also know that his absence is only going to make our friends angrier at him, too.

The explosion will come in due time, and I'll be ready for it.

As soon as James and Leah were gone, Erin and Ava tried to console Madison, who immediately ran upstairs as she began to sob. We heard the door slam shut, and we haven't seen her since. Leah's still outside, too, but Sydney came in to check on Brett. It's been over an hour, and we haven't seen anyone who left after the fight.

“I'm gonna start cooking these,” Erin announces, gesturing to the bags of fish on the floor. She and Reid caught four, which is better than nothing, but still not much. “Better to eat them when they're as fresh as possible. Anyone wanna help with the fire?”

It's barely four o'clock, but nobody says a word about it not being dinnertime yet. We've been trying to schedule our meals within twelve hours of one another to make sure we have enough sustenance to get us through each half of the day, and it's way too early now. I mean, we’re used to eating whenever we’re hungry—it’s kind of part of the college experience—but we originally wanted structure to keep us all going strong. Not anymore. I don’t think any of us know what we want anymore.

We’re just a few steps away from that concern Sydney mentioned. I can tell everyone’s thinking about it, too: whoever’s in charge of rationing each meal being watched extra closely, like we're expecting them to sneak bites from someone else's plate. People constantly checking the rations we've already divided to make sure everything's still even. It's not a matter of who might be the first to break, but of *when* it'll happen. Soon, would be my guess.

It's not really a matter of trust anymore either—it's a matter of scheduling.

Aaron goes outside with Erin, taking the bags while she grabs a skillet and a spatula from the kitchen. Within minutes of them arriving at the firepit, a glum, puffy-eyed Leah reenters the house. Nobody says a word to her as she claims Madison's earlier spot on the mattress by the window. She practically curls up in a ball as she leans against the window, and only when she curls an arm around her legs do I see the strip of bloody cloth around her hand, and the missing piece of fabric from her white shirt.

I approach her with a bottle of water. "What did you do?"

She sniffs but doesn't bother looking at me or accepting the peace offering. "Cut myself on a nail on the railing."

"Do you want help cleaning it?"

"No," she says, sharper than necessary. "I rinsed it in some of the saltwater from the bucket."

I want to ask if she scooped the water out somehow or if she just dunked her bloody hand directly into the water we're using for the filters, but I really don't want to stick around for longer than necessary. As soon as her emotions die down and she starts thinking clearly, she might figure out that I was the one who told Madison about her and James.

I return to the kitchen to help Henry, Joe, and Reid prep for dinner. Henry's spreading out the plates and cutlery on the counters while the others add the food to the plates. Joe's adding about a tablespoon of trail mix to each plate—which we rationed out in Dixie cups earlier—and it almost looks like he's counting each piece that lands on the plates. Reid follows with a spoonful of lentils per person, but he runs out before the last two plates are given any, so he has to take small amounts from the other plates to make them all even. For a split second, I catch him look up as his eyes dart around the room, like he's expecting someone to jump down his throat for taking from another plate to give to another.

I set a bottle of filtered water by each plate, but I, too, run out with three people to go. We seem to have lost the rest of the plastic bottles we've been refilling, so I use one of the full bottles as a measuring cup as I fill cups from what's left in the filters.

I didn't realize until now just how much water we've all been drinking today while we've been sitting around the house. I guess it's easy to fall back into normal habits when we're inside playing games and bickering rather than trekking through the debris outside, far away from the eerie silence of the once-noisy beach and the reminder that we're on our own here.

Even then, our *normal habits* aren't quite normal. The bickering isn't the same as it used to be. It isn't about stupid debates over which cartoon characters are the sexiest or which professors we think are the kinkiest behind closed doors anymore. It's about little things now: like why the water isn't lasting as long and pointing fingers at Aaron because his bottle is always on his lips, even though he's taking tiny sips and not refilling it; Joe talking about the dead as *they* instead of using their names, making Leah snap at him for being disrespectful, even though *they* makes more sense when referring to so many people; and even Ava gently requesting more rations than the rest of us because she's healing, and everyone indirectly telling her to stop being selfish as their octaves raise.

After Reid and Erin return with the cooked fish—and I don't even like fish, but it smells so good that my mouth starts watering—Ava hobbles over to the stairs to call for Madison, Brett, and Sydney. James comes out when he hears the commotion, peering over Erin's shoulder as she proudly reveals the haul, and I can see the calculation in his eyes, like he's counting each lentil and each piece of trail mix.

The two cooks start cutting the four fish into three even pieces so there's enough for all of us. Erin lifts one of the heads, wrinkling her nose, and goes to drop it in the trash, but James stops her by grabbing her wrist, his grip tighter than necessary.

"Don't waste it," he tells her. "That's where all the meat is."

She frowns. "Nobody's gonna wanna eat the heads. It's nasty."

"They will," he insists. "You should keep one for yourself. You'll feel fuller than everyone else."

Her frown morphs into an expression of utter disgust. "I don't want to."

He shrugs. "Suit yourself."

Then he retreats back to the office without another word, like he just came out here to monitor our dinner preparation and make sure we're not hiding any secret stashes of food from him. At the same time, Erin places one of the fish heads on her plate, puffing her cheeks like she's trying not to gag.

When the plates have been filled, Joe takes one to the office and drops it outside of the door, muttering something that I'm not sure James can even hear. He'll smell it soon enough, though. I hope he comes out in a hurry and steps on his plate instead of looking down first.

Right as Erin silently brings a plate to Leah, Madison and Sydney come downstairs. Sydney tells us she'll be bringing Brett's dinner to him; she doesn't tell us why he won't come down—or why she thinks he's better off confined to the room—but her eyes are full of worry and guilt. I can only imagine what the two of them talked about.

We all take our plates and find spots to sit after that. Nobody says a word after taking a few seconds to eyeball each other's plates. We just eat in silence, occasionally looking up to see if Madison's shooting any scathing looks at Leah. She isn't. She's sitting at the table with her back to Leah, as silent and calm as the rest of us.

"What kind of fish is this?" Joe asks, breaking the silence. "It's pretty damn good."

"It's good because we're hungry," Sydney replies.

"I think it's grouper," Reid says. "I recognized it when we caught it. My dad had it when we were in Aruba for a wedding a few years ago. I remember 'cause there was a picture of the fish on the menu, and my sister was all bent out of shape 'cause she didn't want to see what it looked like alive."

"How'd you get it descaled and gutted?" Henry asks, shoveling the fish into his mouth.

Erin shivers. "Reid did it."

He just grimaces. "Used a big-ass knife. Wasn't pretty. Don't worry, though—I rinsed all the ickiness off the deck with the seawater bucket. We'll need to get more for the filters before we go to bed tonight."

In minutes, my plate is gone, but my stomach is still growling. "I hope we get lucky like this tomorrow. If not with fishing, then maybe with the traps. We should get started on those soon."

Joe raises an eyebrow. "James gave us permission to use the nightstands?"

"Reluctantly." I want to say more, but I don't.

"Yeah, that's a tomorrow problem," Ava agrees. "We've done all the scavenging we can, anyway. We have to switch gears first thing in the morning. I-I don't know if I can be much help outside, but maybe I can help fiddle with the traps."

"Just worry about taking care of your leg," Madison says. It's the first time she's spoken since she came down.

Leah finally gets up to dispose of her plate. All eyes—except Madison's—turn to her when she moves, but we quickly look away. I'm not sure if everyone else looks away because they don't want to embarrass her, or because they just don't want to look at her after learning about her and James.

To everyone's surprise, Leah walks up to Madison's side. "Mads...I know you're still pissed at me, and you have every right to be, but I need you to look at my hand. I cut it when I was outside."

She unravels the cloth to reveal a still-bleeding, diagonal line across her palm. It's not the nastiest cut I've ever seen—I don't think it needs stitches—but injuries to the hands and face tend to bleed a lot, so I'm not surprised she's getting nervous about it while it continues to ooze.

Madison doesn't even bother looking. "Put a Band-Aid on it."

Leah's face falls. "Madison...Please."

No response. Madison just keeps bringing forkfuls of lentils to her mouth, not so much as darting her gaze in Leah's direction. Leah lingers for a moment, visibly defeated, before sighing and returning to exile at the window.

Sydney excuses herself, then returns a few minutes later as we're all cleaning up. "I let James know that his plate was outside the door," she says. "Just wanted to make sure he knew it was there, 'cause if he wasn't planning on eating, I was gonna divvy it up between us."

"What, a lentil per person?" Aaron teases.

That gets a smile out of her. "Shut up."

"I'm gonna get more water," I announce. "Anyone wanna help?"

Henry opens his mouth as we meet eyes, but before he can say anything, Madison's voice replies, "I will."

I stare at her for a minute, look at Henry, then look back to her as she stands. "Uh, okay…" I say slowly. "Thanks."

She follows me outside without a word, and we each grab one of the bucket's rope handles as we descend the stairs, despite it being empty and light enough for me to carry on my own. An awkward silence falls over us as our feet hit the sand and we start walking toward the water. I glance at her from the corner of my eye, wondering why she volunteered, but I don't say a word.

We're holding the bucket sideways in the ocean when she murmurs, “Thanks.”

I furrow my eyebrows and frown. “For what?”

“Telling me the truth.” She stares out at the turquoise abyss, and the way the sunlight hits her face highlights the puffy tearstains on her cheeks. “I bet you anything that other people knew, and they're just too ashamed to admit it.”

“I'm not sure. They all seemed pretty shocked.”

“Wouldn't you pretend, too?”

Now she's looking at me, and the utter despair in her eyes almost makes me feel bad for everything I've played a hand in. Then again, she's thanking me, so maybe my motives are outweighed by the result.

“I don't know,” I say. “Maybe.”

No reply. I watch her as she stares down at the water lapping into the bucket, her face twisted and her eyes filled with a combination of emotions I can't decipher. When the bucket's filled, we haphazardly carry it back up to the house, sloshing the water over the sides with every step.

After setting it down on the deck, she looks into the bucket and remarks, “Good luck picking out all that seaweed.”

Then she disappears into the house, and that's that.

7:59 P.M.

“What's he doing in there?” Ava asks.

Aaron sighs and collapses on the couch beside me. “Trying to get the radio working again. He's insisting someone fucked with it, and that's why it won't work.”

“It probably never worked,” Henry insists. “It's old as shit.”

“That's what I said,” Aaron replies.

“Someone probably messed with it and broke it,” Reid says lowly. “Wouldn’t be surprised if that happened, and whoever did it won’t come clean, ‘cause they know they’ll be fucked.”

“No shit,” Madison mutters, not looking up from where she’s picking her nails in her lap. They’re bitten down to the skin and bleeding at the cuticles—never thought I’d see the day. “Anyone fucked with it and broke it, they ruined our chances of contacting anyone to help us.”

“Well, whoever did it isn’t stepping forward any time soon,” Joe adds.

I soak it all in as I rebraid my hair in silence. Nobody knows if the radio was tampered with, and confirmation or not, they have no problem letting the culprit know—if they even exist—that they won’t be forgiven if they decide to be honest.

“Doesn’t matter what happened to the radio,” Aaron continues. “James won't listen to anything about it. Barely even touched his dinner, either. I asked if I could have it, and he just told me to get out.”

“Classic,” Henry comments, making me smirk a little.

I'm glad James hasn't come out, and for various reasons—one of them being that Joe and Reid grabbed a few more bottles of wine from the cellar, and we've been slowly getting drunk on James's grandparents' award-winning collection of Bordeaux. I can practically hear his reaction in my head: *That's a quarter-of-a-million bucks you're wasting!*

Aaron turns to Sydney, pulling me from my thoughts. “Did Brett say anything when you took his plate?”

She shrugs. “Not really. He's...He's just kinda laying there and staring out the window. Won't say much. He ate, though.”

I almost feel bad for Brett—then I catch a glimpse of Sydney's jaw, and the pity disappears as quickly as it came.

“Ugh.” Erin, on my other side, leans her neck back against the couch cushion with her hands splayed over her stomach. “I forgot I can't eat seafood. Messes with my stomach.”

“I'm not feeling the best, either, but I'll manage,” Joe says.

“You know where the bathroom is,” Aaron says with a grin. “About ten yards from the house, right under the tallest palm tree on this side of the Caribbean.”

“You're not funny,” Erin retorts, but her cheeks are swelling from trying to hold in her laughter.

“I'm just relieved we don't have to worry about toilet paper or ass wipes for a little while,” he continues, still grinning. “I'm so glad my mommy packed those wipes. She's from Nevada—she knows what it's like driving for hours without seeing civilization, and getting fucked over when you gotta go in the middle of nowhere. That's why my car's always stocked.”

“Ew, dude.” Reid wrinkles his nose in disgust. “Nobody wants to hear about your mom's side-of-the-road shits.”

Aaron scowls, but his eyes are still filled with amusement. “Don't talk about my mom like that, man. Not cool.”

I crack a smile as some of the others laugh. Even Madison's smiling. Leah, on the other hand, is just sitting by her lonesome by the window while clutching her knees to her chest, tracing patterns on the mattress with her finger. She hasn't made a peep since she tried and failed to make amends with Madison by asking for help with her hand.

“Oh, shit,” Erin says as her eyes bug.

She's on the move in the blink of an eye. She just barely gets the door open and makes it outside before loud, guttural retching sounds fill our eardrums. Everyone winces, and not because we're grossed out by her puke—it's because we know she's going to be starving after throwing up what little she's eaten, and we really don't have enough to spare.

She returns a few minutes later, grabs a travel-size bottle of mouthwash from our stash of supplies on the kitchen counter, and gargles for a minute before spitting into the sink. The sound of her spitting is almost more disgusting than the sounds of her vomiting.

“You okay in there?” Ava calls.

Erin just gives a thumbs-up as she gargles another round of mouthwash.

"Reminds me of our last night before break," Joe recalls. He's sitting on the floor across from me, watching the carpet shift from dark to light as he runs his hands over the fabric and back again. "Zeke would puke, brush his teeth, drink more, puke again, and just keep going on a loop for hours. I've never seen anyone else boot and rally like such a champ."

"You didn't catch his puke in your hands before it went down his shirt," I remind him, grimacing at the memory of having Zeke's rancid, chunky vomit sliding between my fingers. "Wasn't fun."

He laughs. "Yeah, you were a hero for that one, Sadie. Couldn't be me."

Henry slides over to take Erin's seat beside me. "I'm surprised it didn't make you puke, too."

"I'm okay with vomit," I admit. "I can't handle boogers, though."

I direct those last words at Aaron, who sheepishly shrugs and says, "I didn't know I was wiping my nose on your shirt. Thought it was one of *my* shirts on the floor, since it was *my* room."

"I got changed in there!" I protest.

"At least he didn't wipe his ass with it," Reid points out. "He did that to me once because we ran out of TP, and that drunk bastard thought my undies were a towel."

Joe snickers. *"'Undies.'"*

As everyone laughs, Erin releases a gasp of alarm before rushing outside again, leaving the door open behind her. Aaron follows her but stops at the door, grimacing, though the worry plastered over his face is as clear as day.

I almost forgot that little thing between them. Aaron might say he's over her, but he clearly isn't.

Reid seems to be thinking the same thing. "Christ, dude, just tell her you wanna suck face with her and get it over with already."

Aaron shoots him a nasty look. "Fuck off, man. It's not like that."

"Anymore," Ava says softly.

He glares at her, too. "I'm just worried. She looked pretty green. Should I go out there and see if she needs anything?"

"Is she on the deck?" Madison asks. He shakes his head and responds that Erin went down to the beach, making Madison roll her eyes. "She's probably at the evacuation hole, then. I don't think you'd be very helpful out there."

The evacuation hole. She says it like we've all been going to the bathroom in the same damn hole. We all have our own spots—just in the same general vicinity.

Aaron reluctantly returns to the couch, and a few minutes later, Erin comes back inside. She definitely doesn't look well. She's kind of swaying to either side as she walks, clutching her stomach, and she's turned from green to white. She reaches out for a chair for support as she makes her way back to us, then slumps onto the couch with a groan while closing her eyes.

Aaron gets right up to grab her a water bottle. We just refilled about six of them after getting the filters going again after dinner, and I know we'll need to get more seawater soon when she downs it in thirty seconds and asks for another. Hydration is the best cure for vomiting and diarrhea, but she'll go through our entire supply in minutes if she keeps going at this rate.

"Maybe try to sleep," Ava tells her. "You'll wake up feeling a lot better."

Erin shivers. "I'm so sore. The fishing must've wiped me out."

"You'll be okay after some rest," Henry says kindly. "Try taking some painkillers in a little bit for the muscle aches."

She just moans in response.

As Madison's getting up to dampen a cloth for the back of Erin's neck, Erin startles all of us by vomiting all over herself. She doesn't move a muscle—vomit just pours out of her mouth, all over her face, chest, and lap. It's coating her hands on her stomach, and she doesn't even twitch.

Everyone springs into action to fetch towels and water and what have you, and she barely reacts. Sydney and Madison wipe down her shirt, hands, and lap before taking her shirt off. Even her nude bra is covered in a mixture of half-digested fish, lentils, nuts, and raisins. When her head drops a bit, the puke gets into her hair, which Aaron tries to pull out of her face while he turns to the side and grimaces.

"Let's get her outside," Madison says. "We need to rinse her off."

"I-I can't," Erin manages.

"It's okay, babe. We got you," Sydney assures her, rubbing her back. "Just put your arms around us."

“I can't.”

Madison and Sydney try throwing Erin's arms around their shoulders, but her limbs just fall. That's when I notice Erin's breathing is rapid and unsteady, like she's having trouble.

Nobody other than Madison, Sydney, and Aaron approach Erin. Leah’s still curled up by the window, looking concerned enough that I think she might try to help, but her eyes shine with something—fear, maybe?—and I wonder if she’s keeping her distance to avoid getting into Madison’s space.

Henry and I are both watching, and I know he’s trying to study Erin’s symptoms like I am, trying to come up with an answer for her sudden illness. Ava and the other guys, though, are pretty much inching away from Erin and the girls more and more by the second, as if they’re worried that whatever’s going on with Erin is contagious.

“Woah, woah, woah. Wait a sec.” Joe rushes over to the window just as a boom of thunder has us all jumping. “It's gonna rain. Look—the clouds are rolling in.”

He's right. The clear blue sky is slowly darkening as dark thunderclouds appear overhead.

Ava turns as pale as Erin. “You don't think—?”

“No way,” I say firmly. “Two hurricanes so close together, especially after the first one was so bad...It's just gonna be a little shower.”

“The rain will help clean her and cool her off. She's overheating,” Sydney says, worriedly biting her lower lip as she and Madison struggle to get Erin to her feet.

“What are the rest of us supposed to do?” Reid asks.

“How should I know?”

“It’s probably better if we stay out of the way,” Joe adds.

Ignoring the boys, Madison and Sydney take Erin by the underarms and gently drag her out the door. The rest of us follow, unsure of what to do but sticking close to the scene, anyhow. The guys walk around in circles, shrugging and holding up their hands like *I don’t know, dude,* as they seemingly try to find something to do. Meanwhile, Ava’s trying to hobble over to Erin, but nobody pays her any heed when she asks for help.

Erin's head rolls as she moans, like something's paralyzing her, and that’s when it hits me.

“Oh, God,” I say.

"What?" It's Leah who speaks from her spot on the other side of the door.

I open my mouth to respond just as the rain comes down, dousing all of us instantly. Erin tries to say something from where they have her propped up in a chair outside, but it's not clear. Madison leans in closer to her and asks her to repeat it while setting a hand on hers. Then Madison jerks back, tightens her grip on Erin's wrist, and widens her eyes.

"Her pulse is crazy!" she calls to us over the downpour. "S-She said she can't feel her toes! Something's not right!"

I stand at the door beside Henry while the others rush to inspect Erin. Aaron has one hand on her shoulder while the other is lightly slapping her cheek in his efforts to rouse her. Madison's keeping her hand firmly wrapped around Erin's wrist to monitor her pulse, and Sydney's trying to pour water into Erin's mouth, despite Aaron shouting that she's swallowing enough rain as it is, and Sydney's probably going to drown her.

Ava, who has somehow made it over to them and is now sitting on the ground at Erin's feet, yells something about how Erin isn't reacting to her digging her nails into the bottom of her feet.

After a few minutes, Madison yells, "Her pulse is slowing down! She's not waking up!"

They keep trying to wake her up and understand what's happening, to no avail. Aaron brings his ear to her chest at the same moment Madison drops Erin's wrist and steps back, her eyes widening in that way they do when she realizes she hasn't succeeded at something.

Ava, holding Erin's feet like stress balls, asks, "W-What happened?"

"She's dead." Aaron lifts his head, and with the water splattered over his glasses, I can't tell if he's crying or not. "I-I can't find a heartbeat."

"She didn't just die!" Reid exclaims, looking as gray as Erin's motionless body on the chair. "What the fuck happened?"

"Ciguatera," I say, but nobody acknowledges me.

"M-Maybe she exerted herself today," Sydney offers, wiping her cheeks like she can feel the difference between tears and rain. "S-She had a heart defect as a kid, remember? Had, like, three surgeries up until she was sixteen. Maybe all the strain and the stress—"

"That wouldn't have made her puke and shit and go numb," Aaron snaps. "S-She had to have ingested something she shouldn't have, or—"

"Ciguatera," I say, louder this time.

All eyes turn to me. I stare back for a minute, watching my drenched friends stand around Erin's lifeless body in the pouring rain, shocked and bewildered.

"It could be ciguatera." Henry hesitates for a minute, glancing around nervously like he's rethinking speaking up. "I'm not sure if that would explain everything, but it's definitely a possibility. It's a toxin that can be found in fish."

"Like grouper," Reid says quietly.

Henry just grimaces in response.

"We all ate the fish, and not that much of it," Aaron argues. "We should all be sick, then, too. At least Joe and Reid—they ate the same one she did."

"I don't feel great, but not sick, either," Joe adds. Reid mumbles in agreement.

"She ate the head." It's all coming back to me now. "'Don't waste it—that's where all the meat is.' That's what he said to Erin when he caught her trying to get rid of the heads. He told her to keep one for herself, too, because she'd feel fuller than the rest of us."

I don't have to specify who *he* is. Everyone already knows.

"Why does that matter?" Aaron demands.

"The toxin's more prominent in the head," Henry explains with a wince. "Plus, neither Reid or Joe have any underlying health conditions that would make them more susceptible to poison."

He's right. Sure, most cases of ciguatera poisoning aren't fatal and don't strike within four hours, but with the right combination of factors...For someone like Erin with cardiovascular issues, I can't say I'm surprised to find us here, standing over her body after being given mere minutes to react to her symptoms.

"No way, man," Aaron argues, shaking his head. "Erin didn't die from eating a goddamn fish. We'd all be dead if it was poisoned. Something else happened."

"Like what?" Reid folds his arms over his chest. "You think someone put antifreeze in her fish? One less mouth to feed?"

Aaron's eyes darken. "That's not what I said."

"I don't know why you'd even suggest something like that," Sydney says to Reid, her eyes wide with horror.

"That's what I'm saying! None of us fucking poisoned her, and she didn't just die for no reason. I'm trusting Henry and Sadie on this one."

Madison sighs. "I'm with Reid. Henry's right—Erin had a weak heart. Joe and Reid ate the same fish, and they don't feel the best, but they're fine. The rest of us ate different fish, and we don't feel weird at all. So, she ate the most toxic part of a poison fish, her heart couldn't take it, and…"

The silence falls heavily when she trails off. I glance around at the group as we stand out here in the pouring rain, all staring at Erin's limp body like she'll come back to life and confirm or deny our theory.

"She didn't want to eat it," I say softly, breaking the silence. "She was gonna throw it away."

Again, silence—but this time, it's because we all know what led her to put it on her plate instead of throwing it away. I know we're all analyzing it differently, though. Some of them view this as a friend trying to give the other a helpful suggestion; others view it as a man wanting to confirm if his word is still being followed.

I know that at least Sydney is thinking about James when she mutters something about letting him know what happened. She rushes inside to get him, but doesn't say a word about getting Brett.

"We all ate it." Aaron's voice is barely a whisper as he holds Erin's hand. "We all ate the fish."

Again, not the same one, I think.

"This is my fault." Madison gnaws on her fingernails, her soaked hair slathered over her forehead and falling over her eyes. "I-I should've done more to help her when she started getting sick. Maybe I could've done something. Flushed it out of her system somehow."

"There's nothing you could've done," Henry assures her, but she just bows her head, nails still in her mouth.

It's quiet again other than the pattering of the rain against the deck and the palm leaves, and the whooshing of the trees as the breeze picks up. It's starting to get chilly, but nobody moves an inch. The night sky makes us all look like shadows gathered around a corpse, unable to move or even speak until we're nudged in one direction or the other.

When Sydney returns with James, he just stares at Erin at first, letting the rain soak him, before his blank expression morphs into demands for an explanation.

After we tell him what we think happened, and he says nothing, Leah pipes up, “We can't leave her out here.”

“It'll be hard to dig in the rain, but she's right,” Joe says, slicking back his wet hair. “We can't leave her.”

Aaron, holding one of Erin's hands, sniffles. “Yeah. Yeah, you're right.”

James is the first to move toward the stairs. Henry and a few of the guys are in front of me with Erin in their arms, but they come to a halt—making me slam into Henry’s back as Madison bumps into mine—as James appears to be looking over the side of the hill at our makeshift gravesite.

“No go.” James’s voice cracks a bit as he turns to face the rest of us. “We have to wait.”

Reid frowns. “Why?”

“The rain's washing the sand away on some of the graves,” James replies. “We can't bury her when it's like that. I think we should just cover her up and leave her on the deck for now.”

“Out in the rain?” Madison demands.

He ignores her. “Is there a tarp out here?”

“We should get out there and cover the graves with palm leaves or something,” Henry says. “It won’t take very long.”

I nod. “If the sand washes away, and the bodies rise up because the graves are filling with water...”

James shakes his head as he and the others set Erin down on the deck. He’s the first to release her, and he doesn’t look down at where he drops her before he does it. He just…lets go.

“No,” he says. “We'll deal with that tomorrow.”

Henry furrows his brows. There's no anger, or frustration, or even bitterness in his warm eyes—just genuine confusion.

“We shouldn't risk it,” Henry insists. We start climbing back up the stairs now, all gathered on the deck again as the rain keeps coming down in buckets. “I don't wanna wake up tomorrow to see our friends' decomposing bodies just laying out there. We'll put more sand on the graves, plus some leaves and rocks, and that should keep them down.”

“No,” James repeats. “That’s not how this works, man. You have to trust me on this. They’re six feet deep, so it’s improbable that anything like what you’re saying would actually happen.”

“But…” Reid starts, his lips turned downward.

“There's a tarp in the garage, I think,” James continues. “Let's grab that. We'll take care of everything else in the morning.”

And, like the sheep we are, we obey our shepherd's command despite the entire flock exchanging the same broken, uncertain look.

10:48 P.M.

All tears for Erin ceased within minutes of covering her up and leaving her outside.

In all honesty, I'm surprised anyone cried at all. After the lack of emotion shown for Dani, Nick, and Zayn, I thought everyone had reached an equal point of desensitization. I guess it's the manner of death that got us, though. The majority of us knew Dani was dead all along—everyone except Nick, really. Half of us knew Nick wouldn't survive losing Dani. Zayn was sudden and unexpected, and yet, everyone saw him with a cigarette next to a ticking time bomb, and nobody thought anything of it. If anyone did, they didn't speak up. *We* didn't speak up.

Even with Erin, everyone except for James and Brett saw her deteriorating in real time. Other than Eli, she's the only one who died practically in someone's arms. Besides Erin, no tears have been shed since Magnus, but I guess it's kind of a given when you're that close to such a tragedy.

I'm not surprised at all that everyone's stopped mourning now, though. They've come back to the same realization we all had after Zayn died: she's certainly not the first to go, and she probably won't be the last.

We'll mourn for her when we get home and find our humanity again. We'll mourn for everyone when that day comes. For now, though, choosing to be numb is the only thing keeping us from losing our minds.

Everyone's slowly falling asleep now. Aaron was the first to retreat to his room, and he offered the bed to Madison while he took the floor, knowing she wouldn't want to be down here with Leah. We had to put the mattress back up against the window to keep the rain from coming in, so now Leah's on the floor, curled up with pillows and blankets on the carpet.

James went to bed, too, and Sydney, though she assured us she's sleeping on the floor in the room Brett's holed up in. It's not that anyone thinks he'd hurt her again—but he's not doing well, according to her, so it's probably best to give him some space.

Ava's snoozing on the couch with Joe and Reid, who are just starting to nod off. I'm on the floor with Henry, resting my head on his chest as I stare at the ceiling, unable to sleep. We could go back to my room—most of us could go back to our rooms now that the repairs have been made—but…I don't know. It feels like we need to be in the same room. I'm not sure if everyone else feels that way because of the reason I do: like maybe the comment James made before he left tonight about nobody going after the rations. It was unnecessary, and he tried to frame it as a joke, but I think everyone heard the element of seriousness in his tone. He wants us all together so we can make sure none of us break the rules, and everyone else is in agreement about it.

Henry shifts a bit and whispers, "Are you awake?"

I nod. "Mhm."

"Wanna go for a walk?"

I hesitate, then nod again and slowly get up as he waits for me to situate myself before following suit. We tiptoe our way around to the door and slip on our shoes, then avoid looking to our left at where Erin's body rests on the deck covered by a blue tarp.

At least it's stopped raining. It slowed down to a trickle about an hour ago, but it's stopped completely now. I just hope the tarp did its job.

Henry holds my hand while we use our free hands to tightly clasp the railing on our way down the stairs. It's still pretty slippery out here, but we make it down to the beach in one piece. When we get to the shore, I let go of his hand to take my shoes off, then sink my toes into the gooey sand as the water laps over my feet.

After a few minutes of walking in silence, I throw my shoes a few feet from the water and take his hand again, smiling as he gently tugs me down to a sitting position. We're close enough to the water that it just barely reaches our toes. It's peaceful here, and a stark contrast to the last few days we've had.

"Before the storm, I thought we'd graduate, lose touch, and I'd never think about most people in this group again." He shakes his head and chuckles humorlessly. "Now, I'm gonna remember everyone until the day I die."

I don't answer for a moment. Then I say, "Can I ask you a question?"

"Sure."

"Did you really come here for me?"

"Yes and no," Henry replies, making me frown. "I wasn't going to because of the shit James did, but I was toying with it for a while. Didn't want to sit at home doing nothing when I could've been having a killer last spring break. You're the reason I ultimately decided to come, though. I was about to take the L and stay home, and then I checked the group chat James made for the trip, and I saw your name." Butterflies erupt in my stomach, but before I can reply, he adds, "My turn to ask you a question."

I laugh a little. "Okay. Go ahead."

"Why are you here?"

I just stare at him. "What do you mean?"

"You're only close with a few people here. Your best friends aren't in this group. So, why did you come?"

"Same reason you did, I guess," I mutter, looking down at our conjoined hands. "This was the only offer I got. I didn't want to be at home with my family."

"What are they like?"

I consider the simple answer, the one that would close the topic neatly. I don't use it, though.

"Functional," I decide.

He nods as he stares out at the sea, but he isn't wearing an expression I can read. He's just…listening. Waiting for more.

"My dad works constantly," I add. "If he's home, he's distracted. If he's not, it's because he decided he shouldn't be."

I wait for the familiar tightening in my chest, but it doesn't come. I've said this part enough times that it feels more like inventory than confession.

"My mom's different. She likes things orderly. Presentable." *Strict,* I think. *Controlled.* "Selective," I say instead. "She's really good at making choices for me and making them sound generous, like I should be grateful no matter what it is."

Henry glances at me, then back at the water. He doesn't comment. Most people do—at the very least, they're curious to know more. I take his silence as being intentional, knowing deep in my gut that he's giving me the space to decide whether I want to continue instead of prying for more.

"I have siblings," I continue. "Emmett's my older brother, and Tessa's my younger sister."

"Are you close?"

The answer depends on how he would define *close.* I think of group texts I read but don't respond to. Holidays I attend and leave early. The way we always fall back into a specific rhythm when we're together, but steer clear of saying or doing anything that really matters.

"We talk." I shrug. "It's easier now that I don't live there."

He pauses for a beat. I notice the space he leaves me, the way he doesn't lean in or pull away, physically or emotionally. It makes me hesitate for a minute, too; I'm not used to being given room without being asked to fill it.

"Emmett's always been good at fitting into what was expected," I tell him. "He likes things to be orderly, too."

I remember sitting at the kitchen table while my dad nodded at something my brother said—plans, numbers, next steps—like the future had already chosen him.

I was right next to them, but no one looked at me. No one needed to.

"Tessa's good with people," I continue. "She has this charm about her that always draws people in. One of those people everyone always wants at the gathering, you know?"

For a moment, as I think about my family, I'm sixteen again, standing in the hallway while my mom smooths my sister's hair—a few locks singed off from using a much-too-hot curling iron—and tells her it's fine, really, as long as she's careful next time. I was in that position once, too, only with a flat iron. My mom wasn't as understanding with me then.

I learned early that forgiveness moves faster for some people than others.

"And you?" He looks at me again, his eyebrows raised in gentle inquisition.

I could say I'm the careful sibling. The one who reads the room and the people within it before I speak. The one who chooses every word carefully. I could say I'm the invisible sibling, too. The one whose events aren't marked on the calendar or whose opinion is never asked for. Both of them would be true, but I pick the option that sounds smallest.

"I learned to stay out of the way."

I watch him, waiting for a reflexive contradiction, but it doesn't come. That unsettles me more than if it had.

"I wasn't difficult," I say quickly, maybe too quickly. "I didn't need much. That worked in my favor for a little while."

I'm aware of how controlled my voice sounds. Of how practiced this version of the story is. I wonder if he's aware of it, too.

"And then?" he asks.

"And then I left."

That finally makes him turn toward me fully, one eyebrow quirked in a combination of confusion and curiosity. The emotions almost look the same, but the difference is there.

"Did you miss them?"

I think about how easy it is to love people at a distance, especially when the version of someone you miss isn't the same version of them you have now.

"I miss what things used to be like," I say. "The history, I guess. I don't miss the rest."

He nods, and he doesn't ask what *the rest* is.

We sit here in silence for a beat, processing. His hand brushes mine, light enough that I can pretend it was an accident if I want to. I don't, though. I hook my fingers around his, and he grips me right back.

"I don't think you stayed out of the way," he says after a moment. "I think you learned how to read a room before it turned on you."

I want to tell him that it wasn't fear of the room or the people in it turning on me—it was just a matter of efficiency. I don't tell him that, though. The distinction won't change anything.

"That's one way to put it," I say lowly.

He tightens his grip on my hand, steady and brief. It's not reassurance. It's not possession, either. It's a marker, a sign that he understands.

"You don't have to explain yourself to me," he murmurs. "I just wanted to know where you came from."

Something in me loosens at that; not because he understands me, but because he isn't trying to finalize me. He's letting everything I didn't say remain unfinished—maybe because he's giving me time and space to tell him the rest when I'm ready, or maybe because he wants to fill in the blanks for himself. Either way, I'm content.

We sit in silence for a moment longer. The sound of the waves lapping over the shore fills the space between us, constant and indifferent. I don't feel the need to say more or to manage any conclusions he might be drawing about what I shared. I just…let it sit.

When I squeeze his hand, he squeezes it back. And that small notion that he's here with me—not just physically, but emotionally, too—lets me release a breath I didn't realize I've been holding.

"What about you?" I ask after a beat. "What's your family like?"

He looks out at the water for a long moment before answering.

"Different, I guess. I have a younger brother, Sam. He's autistic."

The word lands softly, like he's careful not to bruise it.

"I've spent most of my life orbiting around him," he goes on. "Not in a bad way. Just…it's always been the center of things. Doctors. Therapies. Schedules. Making sure he's okay, you know?"

I wait, giving him the same space he gave me.

"My parents are good," he continues. "They really are. They just worry a lot. About him. About everything. If I don't answer my phone right away, they assume something's wrong. If I'm gone too long, they want to know where I am. It's like I disappear if I'm not checking in."

"That sounds exhausting."

He smiles a little, like he wasn't expecting sympathy. "Yeah. Sometimes."

He bends to scoop up a shell and turns it over in his fingers.

"Sam loves the beach. He doesn't do great with being outside for long, but he loves the idea of it. His room's basically a shrine—sand, shells, photos he rips out of magazines. I told him I'd bring something back from the trip. Something real from a new place that he can add to his collection."

"That's sweet," I say, and I mean it.

He shrugs, embarrassed in a way that feels boyish. "It's easy. It makes him happy."

He pauses for a bit, looking down at the shell with a distant look in his brown eyes. The tide creeps closer, cool around our ankles, and the gentle breeze blows sand onto our skin, sticking to the spots where the seafoam touched.

"They didn't want me to come on this trip," he shares, not meeting my eyes. "It was really far for them. Unpredictable, I guess. But I wanted to do something that was mine for once."

I look at him now, really look at him, and realize how rare that probably is for him.

"I'm glad you did," I admit.

He finally meets my gaze, and there's something steady and warm there—something that makes me forget about all of the unsteadiness I just shared.

"I am, too." He nudges my shoulder with his. "And when I get home, I'll give him a whole shitload of shells instead of the one super cool shell I promised. He'll line them up in perfect order. Like they matter."

"They do," I say quietly.

Henry smiles, and when he reaches for my hand, it feels like a choice—not obligation, not responsibility. Just us.

"Of course, that perfect order of his won't happen if the next few days continue like this trip has. I might not make it back."

He sounds like he's holding back a laugh, but I elbow him and shake my head, anyway. "Don't say that."

"Sorry. Bad timing."

"I don't even want to consider that possibility," I tell him, slightly sharper than necessary. "We'll get home. You and me—we'll be okay. I know we will. And even though there's been a lot of bad on this trip, there's been a lot of good, too. You'll bring some of that goodness home to Sam like you promised."

He sets the shell down to brush hair from my face. "Yeah, you're right. There are definitely some good things I don't want to forget about this trip." I blush a little, and the way he's looking at me sends shivers up and down my spine. "Can I ask you another question?"

"Sure."

"Have you ever had sex on the beach?"

"No." My answer is immediate. "Almost did once back in high school, but I was worried about getting sand up *there.*"

He laughs. "Still worried about it?"

Grinning, I grab him by the shirt and pull him close. "No."

Is it a bad idea to have sex on the beach without a blanket to lay on? Absolutely. Is it a bad idea to have sex on the beach when our friends can probably see us from the windows? Of course it is.

Do I care? Not a bit.

I climb onto his lap while he's still sitting up, already feeling his lips bruising mine, and set my palms on either side of his neck while he grabs my hips. I rock against him, instantly giddy when I feel him harden against me, and let my tongue explore the hollows of his mouth—the mouth I've grown so familiar with in just a few short days.

He pulls my shirt over my head and unhooks my bra with surprising skill, tossing both aside as he spreads kisses down to my jaw, my neck, and my breasts. I throw my head back and arch my back at the feel of his hot lips against the goosebumps on my skin. When he comes up for air, I take his shirt off, too, and he flips us over so I'm laying on the sand with him hovering over me—but not before he quickly spreads out our clothing so there's some sort of barrier between me and the sand.

As he spreads kisses down my stomach, he hooks his fingers over the waistband of my shorts and tugs them down. A moan escapes me when his lips jump from my lower abdomen to between my thighs, teasing me while he leaves my underwear in place. I grab fistfuls of his dark hair and squirm when his fingers knead me through the cloth, and before I know it, I'm begging him to take his pants off, too, so I can feel him completely.

He was already wiggling out of them when I started pleading, but he still keeps his distance as he squeezes my breasts and nips at the sensitive skin on my neck, exactly where my hickey is. He uses one finger to move my underwear, finally letting me feel him at my entrance, and slides in slowly, teasing me while moaning against my neck.

We stay like this for a moment or two—moving slowly, his face buried in my neck while I claw at his back, with one of his hands holding him steady by my head while the other clutches my hip. He lifts his head up to look at me, his eyes filled with hunger, and passion, and adoration, and as soon as we lock eyes, the slow, romantic pace ceases to be enough.

I'm on top of him in an instant, grinding my hips against his while he grabs my ass. The sound of his moans only makes me move faster, harder. I lean over to run my hands over his hard chest, and he wraps his arms around my back, pulling me down so my tits are flat against him, and my hands have nowhere to go but up to his hair. I bury my fingers in his scalp while he starts doing the work for me, his groans hot and guttural against my ear.

"Fuck." His warm breath tickles my skin as one of his hands reaches up to grab the back of my neck. "Jesus Christ, you feel so fucking good."

I shove my hair out of my face and lean down to kiss him, parting his lips with my tongue. He gasps into my mouth, then takes my hips so tightly that I can feel his fingers kneading against my bones. I'm as close to him as I can physically get now, and his next few thrusts hit a spot that makes me cry out as pressure builds in my stomach. Air lodges in my throat, and I have to remind myself to breathe.

“Oh my God,” I manage, squeezing my eyes shut. He grabs my hair and pulls my head back a little, his other hand still grasping one of my hips. “Fuck, Henry, I'm gonna—”

The words die on my lips when an ear-piercing howl echoes from the trees. We both still, frozen in place, as our eyes meet. My heart is beating rapidly, and I can't tell if it's because I can feel him in my gut, or because we're out on the beach in the middle of the night, just yards away from where predators lurk in the woods.

They sound just like the howling of wolves I've heard in movies and TV shows, right before a character finds themselves surrounded with nothing but a stick for protection.

“There are no wolves on tropical islands…” I whisper, “right?”

He swallows while trying to catch his breath. “No, but there are stray dogs. Tons of them. We heard them once, remember?” Another howl makes us both jump. He sits up, still inside of me while I straddle him and set my hands on his shoulders. “Sounds like it's coming from the other side of the house.”

My ears prick when barking follows, but it's clearly coming from more than one dog. We stay silent, clutching each other and breathing heavily, as a combination of barking, growling, and whining echoes from straight ahead within the darkness our vision can't penetrate.

“They're fighting over something,” I whisper.

I feel his heart pounding against my flesh. “Do you want to go inside?”

I don't know what it is—the way he's throbbing inside me, the way he rubs my back in comforting circles, or the tender, adoring look in his eyes that matches the tone of his voice—but I don't want to leave. I want to stay here with him, to finish what we started, and to enjoy this moment while it lasts.

“No.” I put my hands on his chest and gently push him down again. His eyebrows furrow, but his eyes shimmer with eagerness. I'm already moving my hips again before his back is fully pressed against the sand. “I don't want to stop.”

That's when he flips us again, rips my underwear until it comes apart on the sand, and finishes the job with an incentive that leaves me whining louder than the dogs in the woods.

11:31 P.M.

By the time Henry and I are finished, the howling has ceased, and the night is as silent as every other.

We're crossing the beach to get to the stairs, believing the dogs have gone, when Henry breaks the silence by releasing a sharp gasp. I'm following his gaze toward the mounds of sand to the side of the house when he grabs me by the shoulders and turns me away, telling me not to look.

I pull away from him, curious to see for myself what has him so shaken up. While my back is facing him, I hear him retch into the shrubs just as my eyes find what his did: Zeke's body, partially risen out of the dirt and sand, with chunks of flesh missing from his limbs, face, and torso. I can see some of his bones, and there's a hole on his cheek that reveals most of his teeth. Partial intestines are hanging out of his gut, and one of his legs has been chewed all the way down to the bone.

I was right. The dogs *were* fighting over something—*Zeke*.

DAY EIGHT

8:39 A.M.

Our breakfast today consists of about a teaspoon of coconut flesh, two crackers, and what looks like a tablespoon or so of granola. It's not enough to feel fulfilled or energized by any means in any scenario, but after how much energy I exerted last night, I'm feeling more famished than ever.

I toss a sidelong glance at Henry, who sits beside me at the kitchen table, frowning at his mouthful of breakfast. He has a nice hickey now, too, right above his collarbone. The sight of it makes me smile.

Most of us are either seated at the table or around the living room, but James and Leah are sitting at the island in exile, their heads down and their mouths zipped shut. A minute ago, I saw James try to say something to her. She just gave him a look that could've made Hell freeze over, and he clamped his jaw shut right away. I have a feeling they talked about what's been going on when we all went our separate ways last night, and it didn't go very well.

"Ava."

It's not just James's sudden speech that catches my attention—it's the darkness in his voice that I never would've known existed if I hadn't come on this trip. Everyone else seems to pick up on it, too, because all eyes have landed on him. He's standing now, his eyes hard and his lips curled in a scowl, with his hands balled into fists at his sides.

"The fuck's that tone for?" Aaron asks him.

James grits his teeth, refusing to blink or look away from his current target. "What the hell do you think you're doing?"

That's when all eyes slowly pan to Ava at the far end of the kitchen. She's standing frozen with one hand in her zip-up pocket, and it looks like she's mid-chew.

"What?" Her voice comes out quiet, sheepish.

James storms over to her in a flash and rips her hand out of her pocket, making her stumble a bit while the rest of us holler at him. Aaron and Joe rush forward to intervene, but James just takes a few large steps away from them, leaving Ava to cower between them.

"I *knew* it." James holds up what he snatched from Ava's hand in her pocket—what looks like half a chocolate bar—and seethes at her. "We agreed to share all of our supplies, especially food, and you've had this the entire time. What's the matter with you?"

"I just found it," she says hurriedly, sniffling. "I-It was hidden in my backpack. I was going to tell everyone, but I was so hungry, and—"

"We're all hungry!" he bellows, practically squishing the chocolate in his fist. "I know you haven't gotten your 5000 calories a day like you're used to, but Christ, would it kill you to share your food for once in your life while we're all fucking starving?"

She jerks back, astounded, as her bottom lip starts to quiver. "I-I—"

"Jesus, dude," Henry remarks. "Give her a break. Hunger makes people do selfish things sometimes. You don't have to insult her like that."

"Look at her." James practically growls the words out as he gestures to his own mouth. There's barely any chocolate on Ava's face, yet he's making it seem like she looks like Augustus freakin' Gloop after he found the chocolate river. "She's pigging out like a fat—"

"You better shut your hole right the fuck now, James," Madison warns, horror and disgust plastered over her porcelain doll features. It's not a good look for her. "It's not like we could've divvyed it up between us now, anyway. You're melting it."

He looks down at the half-eaten chocolate bar in his fist, still in the wrapper, and scoffs when he realizes it's started to melt onto his palm. He drops it onto the floor, mutters something about one of us cleaning it up, and storms off—likely to clean himself up and bitch about Ava in the office, where nobody can tell him to shut up.

"Ignore him," I tell Ava as I offer her a comforting smile. "He's the only one who's upset at you. We all probably would've done the same thing."

I wish I could tell her that he didn't mean the things he said, but I can't. It's pretty easy to tell the difference between someone saying something they don't mean in the heat of the moment, and using the heat of the moment as an excuse to say something they've always thought.

She sniffs, her eyes rimmed with red, as she leans against Joe for support. "I was so hungry..."

"It's okay." Joe rubs her back and tries to force a smile. "We should get to work on those traps soon. Even if he didn't melt the chocolate, we're basically out of rations, and I'm not eating seafood again if I can help it. Not taking the chance."

"We might not have another choice," Reid reminds him.

"What happened to Erin..." I clear my throat. "We can't be totally sure that it was a toxin that killed her. If we manage to catch more fish, we'll avoid eating the heads, just to be safe. But either way, I think we'd be fine. Nobody here has any preexisting health conditions that'd put them at risk."

Sydney nods. "The stress of everything that's happened, plus the strain of scavenging and fishing out in the hot sun all day...Her heart probably started getting weak before she ate the fish."

Madison shrugs as Reid takes her plate to the trash with his. "It makes sense now that I've thought about it a little bit more. She was dehydrated and weak, and there was barely anything in her stomach. Her body digested the fish really fast, and I'm sure the same thing is true for all of us. I saw her puke pile outside—it was all bile, so I know it went right through her. Hence, her sprint to the evacuation hole."

Ava wraps her arms around herself. "We shouldn't have let her do so much these last few days."

"She would've insisted," Aaron says quietly, finishing the last of the water in his bottle. "She'd want to help in any way she could. That's who she is." He winces. "Who she *was.*"

The room falls silent. He's right, of course. Erin's always been the mom of the group. She was the one who'd clean up after parties—even if it wasn't her room—while everyone else sat around talking, too drunk or too lazy to help. She was the one who made drinks for almost twenty of us before the storm—not only serving as our bartender, but as our waitress, too, no matter how fast we drank or how many trips she had to take. And she was the one, plus Reid, who decided to go out fishing yesterday, when everyone else was too nervous after what happened to Ava.

Her selflessness was the death of her, in the end. Her selflessness, and her heart.

"We have to bury her before we figure out the traps," Madison says after a moment of silence. "It's hot as shit in here, so it's probably ten times worse out there. We can't let her fester more than she already has. Let's get going."

We murmur in agreement and finish cleaning up from breakfast. A pale, miserable-looking Leah doesn't move an inch from the island after James returns from the office and takes both of their plates to the trash.

Henry gives James a shove with his shoulder when he throws our plates away, and while James stumbles a bit, he regains his composure enough to shoot Henry an icy glare.

I'm surprised James even came back. He knows we're all a ticking time bomb, ready to explode on him at any moment after everything that came to light yesterday, and everything he continues to say and do. I think the only reason he's out here with us is because he wants to keep an eye on what we're doing. He doesn't trust us in his fancy house, even after everything—nor does he trust us in general, it seems.

Ava hobbles over to a living room window. "Someone help me with this," she says, grabbing ahold of the mattress. "I hope there's a breeze outside. It's getting suffocating in here."

Joe rushes to help her expose the broken window as I glance around at my friends. It's been hard to think about the sweltering heat and humidity in the house when we've had so many things on our minds, but I'm definitely starting to feel it. Most of us have frizzy hair and a perpetual sheen of sweat coating every inch of our bodies. Joe and Henry have both already sweated through their shirts, and Aaron's outgrown hair is glued to the back of his neck. Even Madison, who hates wearing her hair up, now has it tied in a high messy bun, with her baby hairs plastered to her face.

Just as I'm heading toward the deck door to check on our rainwater collection, Ava releases an ear-piercing shriek—reminding me of the moment she was stung—at the same moment Joe lets out a string of horrified curses. Ava immediately covers her eyes and tries to run away, forgetting about her injured leg and foot, and falls onto the mattress she and Joe just dropped onto the floor.

Joe's covering his mouth with his hand when we all join him by the window. Ava's on her side with her bad leg extended, dry heaving onto the floor, and that's enough for me to know exactly what they saw out there. I don't even have to look.

It's the same thing Henry and I saw last night: Zeke's body risen out of the sand, chewed up and torn apart by wild dogs.

"Jesus fuck," James says, turning away from the window and gagging. "That's…That's—"

Aaron pushes him so hard that he falls into the wall. "Happy now, you prick?"

James glares at him. "What's that supposed to mean?"

"Oh, come on," he retorts. "We all heard Henry last night. He said we should cover the graves with leaves and shit, and you wouldn't let us. Now look what happened. Zeke's rotting fucking corpse is sitting out there on the beach with his guts hanging out and his limbs chewed off."

"I don't know why we listened," Sydney mutters, fanning her green-tinted face. "We should've just gone ahead and done it anyway."

James folds his arms over his chest. "It was dark, pouring, slippery, and—surprise, surprise—there were ravenous fucking animals out there who are just as hungry as we are. Excuse me for trying to make sure everyone's staying safe."

"Nobody's safe here anymore, James," Reid snaps. "Everything we do to try and survive ends up with someone hurt or dead. We've been taking risks all day, every day. The least we could've done was take another risk to be decent fucking humans." He laughs humorlessly and shakes his head. "You didn't give a fuck about any of us dying or getting hurt from slipping down the stairs. You just didn't want something to happen that could make it seem like your family doesn't give a shit about a safe staircase, and you didn't want any of us to be able to say we saw something happen because of it."

"It's rotting, anyway. Underneath," Henry adds. "Wouldn't look so good for your family if someone did get hurt on those stairs. I bet you knew, too, and Reid's right—you didn't want us going down there just because you were worried about the stairs fucking us up."

I resist the urge to smile. Of course Henry noticed the stairs to the beach are rotting away, and of course he waited until the most opportune moment to bring it up.

If someone did fall, it'd be because of the rain, the darkness, and the slippery steps—likely not because of any issues with the stairs. But that's not the point. The point is that every single one of us knows that James's only concern was somehow getting blamed for any incidents. Given how fed up everyone is with him, I can see why he's so worried: all it'd take is one person to tell our rescuers that the rotting stairs killed or injured someone before the storm even hit, just to stick it to James without a care for the truth.

He and his family can't be blamed for the storm or what it brought, but we were here for two days before the hurricane. A lot can happen in two days, and there are plenty of things the homeowners would have to answer for—if we play our cards correctly, anyway.

"Let's just go take care of this," is all James says in response.

We start to file out—some of us reluctantly due to the horrific sight, and some of us emotionlessly, since it's not the worst thing we've experienced these last few days. As we're making our way onto the deck, I see James stop Ava from the corner of my eye, and I slow my movements to listen in.

He doesn't apologize for what he said to her. He just tells her to stay on the deck instead of putting stress on her leg by following us down the stairs to the beach, and taps a spot by the railing where she can watch us say a few words for Erin.

A few minutes later, a few of the guys have laid Erin down on the sand, and the rest of us have started gathering leaves and heavy sticks to lay on top of the graves. It doesn't take nearly as long to dig Erin's grave—and dig Zeke's for a second time—as it did the first few times we had to do this. Soon enough, Erin is lowered into the ground, Zeke's rotting corpse is nudged into his grave by Aaron with the shovel, and our friends are covered by sand, leaves, and sticks.

I've lost track of who is buried where. I'm sure that guilt will keep me up at night at some point in my life—if I make it out of here—but not right now.

I spot Ava from the corner of my eye before the eulogies start. She's exactly where James told her to stand on the deck, leaning her folded arms on the railing with her butt jutted out, all her weight on her arms and her one good leg.

Aaron clears his throat as he leans against the shovel, the sharp tip buried in the ground. "Erin...Erin and I had a complicated relationship. Depended on the day, I guess. But I've always loved her as a person, even if there have been times when I wanted more out of our relationship. She did everything for everyone, and she never said a word about it. She was funny, too, and nobody ever really said anything about how funny she was."

A weary, flushed Leah cracks a smile as she clutches her injured hand—wrapped in cloth and probably a few Band-Aids underneath it, too—to her chest. "She had a dry sense of humor, but the good kind, you know?"

"Yeah." A tiny sparkle—the first sign of the Aaron I met so many years ago that I've seen in days—illuminates his eyes. "She never had a bad word to say against anyone, either. People walked all over her, and still, she never once—"

A loud cracking sound, like a tree trunk snapping, echoes in my eardrums before he can finish. The sound is closely followed by a short-lived shriek of terror, and then a crash that makes the ground tremble beneath our feet.

Like the night Zayn died, everything that follows happens in slow motion. We look up from the fresh mounds of sand we're gathered around and turn our attention back to the house. A large chunk of the railing encasing the deck is missing, and so is Ava. The wood and our friend are both on the ground beneath the house—a twenty foot drop, at least.

Nobody says a word. Nobody rushes over to investigate. We can see clearly enough from here to know there's no need to rush.

9:21 A.M.

At least it was a quick death.

Ava's neck is broken. There's no debating it was a lethal break, either. No human or animal could have their neck broken at this angle and survive it.

Half of us—me and Henry included—made our way over to her after a minute of processing. Neck broken, no movement, no heartbeat. She was just laying there on top of wood from the railing and some flattened bushes. It's a miracle the wood didn't impale her when she fell on top of it.

We're on our way to the gravesite, body in tow, when we see James lift the shovel and start digging another hole. The others are just watching us carry her over. James, on the other hand, doesn't waste a second before getting to work.

"Eager, huh?" Aaron says to James as he, Joe, Reid, and Henry carefully place Ava on the sand. The other girls, who stayed at the gravesite with James and Brett, turned away the second we got close enough with Ava, and they still won't look at her. "That's a first."

James stops digging and blows a lock of sweaty, sandy hair from his eyes. "You all gave me plenty of shit for not getting the others buried fast enough. I can't do anything right, can I?"

I roll my eyes. "Oh, *please.*"

"Pity party of one." That, surprisingly, comes from Madison, who mirrors the glare James sends her way.

Henry folds his arms over his chest. "You know, man, it's interesting. You tell her to stay up on the deck, and you specifically point out the best place for her to watch us from up there. Then the railing just so happens to give out, and she falls and breaks her neck. That's one hell of a coincidence."

I remember now—the way James tapped the railing when he told her where to stand, the wood splintering a bit under his hand.

James releases a bitter, almost maniacal laugh. “Jesus. You guys will find any reason to make me look like the scum of the earth, won't you?”

“We don't have to try very hard,” Reid mutters, his eyes narrowing.

“Henry's right.” Joe looks down at Ava, winces, and turns his attention back to James. “It's sus as hell, dude. Don’t pretend you didn’t notice the risk when you told her where to stand.”

“You're all insane,” James snaps. “She leaned her full weight on a rotting railing. It was bound to snap.”

Leah's lips part in horror. “Are you seriously still going on about that?”

Madison sticks her nose up at him. “Henry said literally minutes before we left the house that the wood was starting to rot. Did that give you an idea for some sick and twisted revenge over a fucking chocolate bar?”

James practically growls as he tosses the shovel aside. “You're insane. Every last fucking one of you.”

He storms off into the woods, and it takes only a few seconds before the rest of us are following hot on his heels. Everyone's barking at him—demanding he slow down, asking where he thinks he's going, telling him there are more important things to do than run off and throw a tantrum—but he ignores us like it's an instinct.

“You’re the one who decided where she stood. Did you really think the railing didn’t matter?” I ask as we follow him. “Or did you decide it didn’t matter?”

I don’t raise my voice at him because I don’t need to. I just need him to realize what I’ve said.

He spins back toward me so abruptly that I nearly walk into him. In two hard steps, he closes the distance between us, and suddenly, he’s too close—his chest touching mine, closely followed by his hand wrapping around my throat. I feel my body being shoved backward and pinned against the rough trunk of a tree, all while his hand remains firmly in place.

For just a second as I'm pressed between the tree and James, my feet sliding against the muddy soil beneath me, I see his eyes. They've been different these last few days, anyway—no longer the beautiful, charismatic emeralds I used to dream about—but in this moment, I don't even know what they look like anymore.

There’s nothing human in his eyes now.

“You've been running your mouth all fucking week, and for what?” Spit flies out of his mouth as he tightens his grip on my throat. I lose the fight when I try to withhold my gasp. “Because I didn't fuck you? Is that it? Cry me a river, you little fucking slut. It's not like you didn't get dick in one way or another on this trip.”

Someone—or multiple someones, actually—grab him by the back of the shirt and pull him off of me, right as spots start to cloud my vision. I fall to my knees, gasping, as two people appear on either side of me, holding me upright and murmuring things I can't understand.

That's when I hear the laughing. It's the same maniacal, humorless laugh I've been hearing from James off and on this past week. He's on the ground a few feet away from me, laughing hysterically while Henry’s fist snaps James’s head sideways.

Again.

And again

And again.

Aaron and Joe must've helped Henry pull him off of me, because they're standing nearby, chests heaving and cheeks flushed with shock and disgust. They give Henry a minute—to let him get his anger out or to make sure James won’t be getting up to try anything again, I don’t know—then surge forward to pull him off of James.

Brett steps forward, too, just long enough to grip Henry’s arm—but he lets go. Aaron and Joe take the reins while Brett returns to his starting position with Sydney and Reid by a cluster of trees. He turns his head away from James on the ground, but he doesn’t leave.

I get it, though. I get why Brett tried, even if he didn't try very hard. The minimal effort was his way of showing the group that he’s still loyal to the system they’ve created—that he still understands how this works.

I can see it on Brett's face as Madison and Leah—to my immense surprise—help me stand. Everything James has done these last few days hasn't been good, but to put his hands on a woman like that…Not to mention what happened to Ava…It’s enough to make Brett question this little family of his. And that realization is as clear as can be.

James's crimson-stained teeth demand attention, just like the rest of him while his face is soaked in blood, as a psychotic grin plasters over his face while he passes out.

Nearby, a snarling Henry wipes his hands on his pants, and I can't tell if any of the blood on his knuckles is his. His face softens when he spots me, and he takes a few long strides toward me, prompting Madison and Leah to take steps backward in opposite directions. He checks my throat, fingers light against my skin, before enveloping me in his arms. His hand settles on the back of my neck, masking the dull ache in my throat with something steadying, comforting.

I melt into his embrace, my face pressed against his chest so tightly that I can feel the rapid beating of his heart against my cheek, but he doesn't ask if I'm okay. He doesn't need to: he and I have known the truth about James and this fucked up family of his for a while now—neither of us threatened by that truth, unlike the others, but interested in exposing it.

Nobody says anything. It's quiet in the woods, almost serene, as we just stare at James's unconscious body. I don't feel the pain in my throat anymore, and I hardly remember that Ava's body—her neck bent at a near-ninety-degree angle—is just a few yards away, exposed to the unforgiving sun and whatever birds of prey have been attracted to the gravesite by the smell of Zeke's formerly-exposed corpse.

You'd never expect someone like James to be here, having lost control in front of the people who have always turned to him for guidance, for direction.

I tear my eyes away from James to look between Madison and Leah on either side of me and Henry. They see me looking at them, and a silent understanding passes between the three of us—even those two, who haven't spoken since James's relationship with Leah was exposed.

They don't really seem to care anymore. Not now, at least. I know it's because we're thinking the same thing: all three of us, at one point or another, were all fooled by the same man.

Not anymore.

10:40 A.M.

It's quiet for a bit when we get back to the house. Nobody wants to speak first—that's usually James's job. But he's passed out on the floor in the living room, so we won't be hearing a word out of him any time soon.

"What do we do with him?" It's Aaron who breaks the silence.

"We could bring him to his room—" Sydney starts.

"No," Joe interrupts, shaking his head. "Why should we put him somewhere he feels safe? Comfortable? After what he did, we should be leaving him out on the deck or—"

"We're not leaving him outside," Leah states, folding her arms over her chest. "It smells like death out there."

Madison rolls her eyes. "It doesn't."

"So what do we do?" Reid raises an eyebrow as he glances around the living room at each of us, one by one. His gaze hesitates on Henry for a beat. "Any ideas?"

Henry looks away, jaw clenched, rubbing what I imagine are very sore knuckles.

"I say we put him in the office," Aaron decides. "I don't wanna babysit him upstairs, and the office locks."

Brett scoffs at him. "We don't need to lock him up, man."

"And let him roam around so he can choke out one of the girls again? No, thanks." Aaron shakes his head. "Hard pass."

"That's not what I meant." Brett's voice is low, practically a growl.

Sydney sets a comforting hand on his forearm, but he shrugs her away, making her sigh. "The office is probably the best call. We can take turns checking on him to make sure he's not…concussed?"

She directs that last bit at Madison, who just shrugs. "He's probably fine."

"Probably isn't definitive," Reid points out. "What if he has, like, a blood clot or something?"

“That’s not how it works. Haven’t you ever been hit in the face before?”

“No.”

Another roll of her eyes. “It shows.”

“Okay, okay.” Aaron stands up from one of the kitchen chairs and runs a hand through his hair. “Let’s just move him into the office for now. I don’t want to look at him anymore.”

Leah nods. “I’ll check on him in a few minutes.”

Madison snorts. “Of course you will.”

Leah’s eyes narrow as she snaps, “If you have something to say, just say it.”

“Both of you—” Aaron wags a finger between the two of them, “—shut up. Nobody wants to hear about how pissed you are about fucking the same dude. Get a grip.” They scoff at him in unison, glare at each other, and turn away as Aaron impatiently gestures toward the rest of us while approaching James. “Someone help me with him.”

Hesitantly, Joe and Brett stand to help Aaron lift James from the floor and lug him into the office. I hear James groan when he’s lifted, but he doesn’t stir much more than that. A few minutes after they disappear down the hall, the three of them return, and Aaron throws an old-fashioned key—the kind you can lock from either side—onto the carpet in the living room, making it clear he doesn’t want any responsibility over it.

I toss a glance at Henry sitting by the fireplace to my right. He wiped James's blood from his face and neck with his shirt, so the pale blue tee is mostly red now, but he didn't make any effort to clean up his hands. I still can't tell if any of the blood on his knuckles is his.

After tearing my eyes away from Henry, I study the rest of the group. Brett and Sydney are sitting about a foot apart, not touching, on a mattress on the floor by a window. Every now and then, Sydney touches the bluish bruise on her jaw and averts her gaze from Brett, like what James did to me today reminded her of when Brett accidentally struck her. If Brett notices what she’s doing, he doesn’t show it.

They’re on the same mattress Ava moved before she saw Zeke's body out on the sand. Ava's buried now, too, thanks to Reid taking the time to show her that courtesy while the rest of us opted to leave her there for the comfort of the house.

I'm on the floor with Reid to my left, his legs drawn up to his chest and his arms draped over his knees. He's staring into oblivion, as are the others: Madison, Leah, Joe, and Aaron, all sitting on the couch a distance apart from one another.

Everyone's distant from each other now. You'd think we'd want to be close together, us survivors, but it just doesn't feel right anymore. I guess it's hard to want to find comfort in your friends when you've watched them not so much as bat an eye when another friend falls off a balcony and plummets to her death.

Finally, Aaron breaks the silence: "You okay, Sadie?"

He's not even looking at me when I flick my eyes over to him. His eyes are dark, almost cloudy, and his face is completely blank. He's lost in his own head, and for the life of me, I can't figure out where his thoughts are.

"Yeah, I'm fine."

My neck's a little achy, but nothing worse than a typical sore throat. It's nothing compared to the pain our friends must've felt when they died, or the pain Ava spent the last few days managing after the jellyfish sting.

"I can't believe he did that." It's Madison's voice—softer than usual—that speaks next.

"I can."

Brett's voice is what breaks the spell. Everyone collectively turns our gazes to where he's perched on the mattress, elbows on his knees, staring at the floor. He's the last person any of us would expect to say that, and yet, he's not even fazed by his own words. I know there's something he's hiding, some story he's never shared before, but nobody asks him to elaborate.

Those two words are enough—the silence that follows is proof of that.

"What do we do now?" Joe asks, tipping the last of his water bottle into his mouth.

Reid sighs. "We need to get out of here. No power, radio's fucked, no flares—maybe we go out on the beach and spell out *help* in debris. You know, try to flag down a plane or some shit."

"That only works in movies," I say, trying to cut the tension in the room. Reid smiles a little, but nobody else does.

"It's not worth the effort. Everyone already knows a hurricane struck the island," Madison reminds him. "They're just…delayed. We can't prioritize anything like that right now, so we should be focusing on what each of us can do. I can run a few basic tests to make sure everyone's as healthy as we can be. Organize medicine and stuff if we need it. Sadie and Henry can keep at the water filters, Reid and Joe can try to fish, Brett and Sydney can try the generator again, Aaron can try to fix whatever needs to be fixed, and Leah can do…whatever Leah's good at."

Leah glowers at her, but she doesn't engage. Instead, she says, "The only worthwhile tasks you mentioned are fishing and water filters. The generator's not gonna get us anywhere. Repairs are fine. We need a better system. Better tasks."

"What do you suggest?" Aaron asks, raising an eyebrow in a way that's borderline patronizing. "If you haven't noticed, Leah, we've tried everything, and we're barely scraping by."

"We still have the wine cellar," I offer. "That can sustain us for a while."

"Yeah, because a bunch of drunk starving people is exactly what we need," Madison retorts. I don't engage with her, either, other than to roll my eyes when she turns away to face Joe. "What about those lobster trap things upstairs? The nightstands? Can we use those?" Joe's staring off into space, ignoring her. She sighs exasperatedly and waves a hand in his direction. "Hello? Earth to Joey."

That makes him turn and shoot her a glare. "Don't call me that."

"Can you contribute to the conversation, please? Lobster traps. Nightstands. *Comprendo?"*

"Comprende," Sydney corrects, and immediately appears to shrink in size when Madison's glare lands on her. For once.

"What are you thinking?" Henry asks Joe.

"I wish I could call Cait," he admits. "She'd know what to do. She's super smart about this stuff."

"About ten people surviving on an island where everything was destroyed by a fucking hurricane?" Brett laughs bitterly. "Yeah, sure, man. I bet she's a real fucking genius about that."

"Watch your mouth," Joe threatens, rising from his seat. Brett rolls his eyes and doesn't move a muscle. Joe's a big guy—bigger than Brett—but he's a softie. Wouldn't hurt a fly, and everyone knows it. "We need guidance of some sort, anyway, and the only person who knows jack squat about this island is locked in the office and unconscious. I'm not asking that asshole for help anymore either way, though. I don't want to see his face again unless he's on his knees begging for forgiveness for hurting Sadie and getting Ava killed."

Leah fans her face with a palm leaf she must've snatched from the beach on our way back to the house. "That was an accident."

"Choking Sadie was an accident?"

"*Ava* was an accident."

"Yeah, okay."

"This still doesn't give us a game plan," Aaron argues, raising his voice enough that everyone turns to him. "Someone needs to decide what we're doing before we lose our fucking minds."

"I'm fucking hungry," Reid complains.

"We're all hungry."

"Help has to be coming soon, right?" Reid looks around the room, wild-eyed behind his glasses—and only now do I notice there's a crack down the middle of the left lens. "I know there are, like, a bunch of other more populated islands they're helping first, but they have to be coming to us soon. Our parents are probably eating search and rescue alive right now."

"Joe's right—the only person who knows anything about how shit works on this island is James, so he's the one to ask about that." Madison runs a hand through her hair, then makes a face when she feels how slick it is. "We can't keep him locked up forever, especially when we need him for things. But we can't just let him out and pretend like nothing happened, either."

"I wish there was a way to calm him down," Sydney mutters. "He might be more helpful if he's not…you know…"

"Do we actually want to deal with that?" I ask.

"He could be better when he wakes up. Hopefully he apologies and we can figure some shit out." Leah's fanning her face faster now. "Not to change the subject, but dear God—is anyone else sweltering?"

"We've been sweltering since the power went out and the AC died," Joe says with a grunt.

Her cheeks are way more flushed than they have been, and hair is sticking to her face with sweat, but she doesn't say anything more about it. By the looks of her, though, she'll be stripping down to her bra and panties soon enough.

"He's been like this before." Aaron waves a dismissive hand, piquing my interest. "He loses his cool, takes some time to calm down, and he's back to his usual self. But this is different. He's never laid a hand on anyone before. I'm not sure it's a good idea to ask him for help with anything for a while."

"Someone else needs to figure out how shit works here," Reid agrees. "Maybe there's a book or something about emergencies on the island."

"A hurricane survival manual?" Joe snorts. "Unlikely."

When a brief silence washes over us, I take the opportunity to ask Aaron, "What do you mean? James was always so calm and collected before this trip."

He shrugs. "Remember when he tried to join that frat freshman year? What was it called?"

"I don't remember," Madison mutters, gnawing on her lower lip. "It got shut down that year because of the hazing ritual. Didn't someone die?"

"No, but he was hospitalized for, like, a month," Reid replies. "Chris Eddie. He transferred out after that."

"James didn't make it," Leah recalls. "He didn't even get to the point Chris did before he was booted out."

I remember that—vaguely, but I do. I wasn't really friends with James at that point, but we had mutuals, so I heard the story at some point. James wanted to join that frat since he committed to Saint Maren, and he wasn't able to get through phase three of four of rushing. A little more than halfway through rush week, he stopped showing up, telling everyone he'd simply decided against it. His close friends, however, were told some of the truth: he just didn't make the cut.

Interestingly, nobody else in the friend group has ever really cared about Greek life. I always expected Madison and Leah, at the very least, to be all for that sorority sister life, but it was never really a big deal with anyone other than James. Most of my friends had sororities and fraternities begging them to join, knowing they'd probably contribute a boatload of money and generate lots of attention, but they never wanted to. I think that's probably why they were constantly being approached about joining; being rejected by people like Madison, Leah, Ava, Aaron, Reid—people with the money and influence that practically defines Greek life—made those in charge of it even more desperate to have them. My friends knew it, too. I think some of them might've even stayed away because they knew they were getting more attention from pushing back than they would as one of the sorority sisters or one of the frat brothers.

James, though…I can figure out for myself why he wanted to join so badly.

"The last phase of rush was the one that landed Chris in the hospital. Nobody else made it that far. It was a new thing they were trying that year, and obviously, it was a bad idea," Reid explains. "I don't remember what the other phases were, though."

"The first one was something dumb. I think they all had to go to this party, and they all had to bring handles of liquor, and if anyone asked them for a shot, they had to give out their liquor," Aaron says, deep in thought. "Second phase was...Wasn't that the streaking thing?"

Madison snorts loudly. "Yeah. They had to run around campus for two hours after sunset stark-naked. Half of them got caught by campo. Would've gotten charged for public nudity if it wasn't a first time offense."

"And the third...This was the one James didn't make it through." Aaron thinks for a moment. "Right. You know that forest outside of campus? Way behind the hockey rink? It's not technically campus property. Used to be a park until someone got killed there, and they shut it down. All the kids who made it to that point in the rush were brought there, blindfolded. They were told they were all camping for some team building exercises. Then when they were told they could take the blindfolds off, the seniors were back in the bus and driving away. They left each freshman with a water, a flashlight, and a compass. No phones. There was a note left behind that told them to find their way back to campus."

Sydney makes a face. "That's kinda fucked up."

"Not as fucked up as the last phase," Reid reminds her. "Chris was the first one back to campus after they got left in the woods. They had him chug a handle of vodka and smoke an entire blunt. Timed him, too. He wanted to make good time—thought it would put him in their good graces—and it almost killed him."

"What happened to James that night?" I ask.

Aaron shrugs. "Couldn't find his way back. Nobody was helping each other, either, 'cause they knew there were limited spots in the frat, and not everyone would get one, even if they all made it back. James got lost and ended up at a gas station in the opposite direction. Called me on the cashier's phone to come get him."

"Did everyone else find their way back to campus?"

He smiles a little as he looks at me. "Everyone except two others. There were, like, thirty of them, I think."

"That's why he never told many people what happened," Leah says, still waving that God-forsaken fan. I notice how breathy her voice sounds, like she has to gasp to get out her words, but I don't think much of it, and the others don't seem to, either. "He was too embarrassed he was one of three who didn't make it."

"What was he like after all of that?" I ask, sensing an opening. "With all of you, I mean. I wasn't around very much, but I can see how he might've been acting differently. It probably wasn't easy on any of you."

Henry catches my eye, and I swear, I see the barest hint of a smile on his face, like he knows what I'm thinking.

"He was actually really nice," he says. "I remember. We were living together at the time."

Sydney nods. "I remember, too. He told us his family was renting a massive house in the Outer Banks over spring break, and he invited a bunch of us to stay there. He wanted to it to be memorable, so he paid a driver, and we drove down there in a party bus. He paid for everything we did that trip. It was one of the best vacations I ever had. I just started dating Brett at the time, too, so it was really nice of James to include me when I was so new to the group."

"Yeah, that was a fun trip." Aaron makes a face like he's trying to withhold a smile. "He was really great. Never would've known he went through all of that. He just stepped up to make sure all of us had a great spring break. Took care of us."

I force a smile. "I'll bet it was great to see that energy carried over when we all got back to school. I remember him being really nice when sophomore year started."

Madison's lips turn downward in a reflective, instinctive frown. "Yeah, he was. Nicest he's ever been, honestly. Kinda weird."

"Him not joining the frat worked out," Henry says, briefly sparing me a glance. "He didn't get to be a part of that, so he decided to make something of his own."

"Yeah. We were like a family after that." Her frown stays put as her eyes gloss over—not like she's about to cry, but more like she's locked in her own head. "I hope he hasn't forgotten that."

"Well, someone can be the judge of that when he comes to." Aaron lets out a defeated sigh. "I still don't know what the plan is right now. That dumbass story distracted me."

We didn't need the story to keep us from coming up with a game plan. We were never going to get there.

2:09 P.M.

James woke up about an hour ago. He started slamming on the door, screaming and demanding we let him out, and when nobody answered, he tried a different tactic: using a softer, sad-sounding tone while asking us for water and a towel to clean himself up. Soon after, when nobody responded to that tactic, he let out a frustrated growl and kicked the door, and he's been quiet ever since.

I'm sitting on the kitchen counter with Henry now, gently dabbing at the small cuts on his knuckles with a damp cloth. We haven't spoken directly since before Ava's fall, so I haven't had the chance to say anything about him defending me. I'm still trying to find a way to bring it up, given everything else that's been talked about today.

In the living room, an exhausted Leah is trying to stay awake—and keep her head from falling to the side—on the couch while Sydney tries to cool her down with wet cloths. Of course, the water from our filters is lukewarm at best, nowhere near cold, so it's probably not doing much good. I think all the chaos has finally caught up to her, and it's not helping that it's pushing ninety degrees today, all without AC in the house and no breeze outside.

Meanwhile, Madison's sitting on the mattress with Brett, who hasn't moved an inch since we got back to the house. She's been trying, unsuccessfully, to comfort him about Spencer. He's not yelling or arguing, though. He's just staring off into space, silent, not budging, while she yaps on. It's a kind effort on her part, and even though it's not going anywhere, I'm sure he appreciates it. I think maybe she's trying to make herself feel better about not noticing Spencer was missing by offering some solace to Brett, too.

The rest of the group—Aaron, Reid, and Joe—are outside tinkering with the backup generator after a long discussion summed up as, *it's worth a shot.* We didn't have any luck the first few times we fiddled with it, but they're determined. Leah sweltering like she is made us all aware of how hot we are, too, even if it's not the first thing on our minds, so AC would be nice. We'd be able to charge our phones and potentially make contact with our families and rescue teams, too. Potentially.

There's a bang from the office, pulling me from my thoughts, but nobody else really acknowledges it. James is probably just kicking things over in his frustration. Plus, he's the last person anyone's worried about right now.

"He's gonna be pissed at me when he gets out of there," Henry comments.

I smirk a little. "For what?"

"Ha-ha." He nudges me with his elbow, making me laugh. "Hopefully it's not *too* bad."

"I mean, you hit him pretty hard, but not hard enough to do any real damage. I'm sure you could've done worse." Henry shrugs as I finish cleaning his knuckles and set the cloth aside. I take his hands in mine again, gently running my fingers over the unscathed skin below the cleaned cuts. "Thank you for that, by the way. I've never had anyone do something like that for me before."

"I'd hope you've never been in a position where that's been necessary." His voice is stern, but his gaze is a little amused—just to keep things lighthearted, I assume. Like he's worried I'm traumatized by what James did to me. I'm not. "You're welcome, but in all honesty...I didn't even realize what I was doing. Something just came over me. Instinct, I guess."

"Doesn't matter. Whatever caused it...thank you." I lean up to press a soft kiss to his cheek. "I would've done the same for you if I had any strength in my arms."

That gets a chuckle out of him. "Oh, I believe it." He lowers his voice as he brushes his thumbs over my knuckles. "The other guys would've done the same thing if I didn't beat them to it. Aaron, Joe, Reid...Maybe not Brett, but the other three would've. Everyone we lost would've done it for you, too. You know that, right?"

I shrug. "Maybe some of them. The ones I'm close to."

"No." He smiles a little—sadly, though, like it breaks his heart that I don't agree. "We may be the outsiders in this group, Sadie, but when push comes to shove...They'd all protect you. Even Madison and Leah ran to your side when he attacked you. That means something."

I open my mouth to respond—to say what, I'm not sure—just as muffled hollering from outside breaks the moment, and seconds later, the three guys stumble inside. Joe and Aaron are pulling Reid in from the deck, despite Reid barking at them that he's fine and can walk on his own.

“What the hell happened?” Madison's on her feet, rushing toward them while Reid nurses his hand against his chest.

“Reid got zapped,” Joe says breathlessly as he sits Reid at one of the kitchen chairs. “We were messing with the generator, and we thought we had it—then the next thing we know, it's sparking, and it got his hand.”

“I'm fine,” Reid insists as Madison inspects his hand. “It was a little zap. As long as my eyebrows didn't get singed off, I'm fine.”

She shakes her head. “You all should've been more careful.”

“Mads?” Sydney asks from the couch.

“We were,” Aaron insists, running a hand through his sweaty hair. “I don't know what happened. We're just lucky it didn't catch fire and burn the fucking house down.”

“Something's definitely wrong with it,” Joe adds. “Must be super old or something. I don't know. But we tried everything, and we can't get it going.”

“It was worth trying,” Henry comments.

“Madison.” Sydney again, firmer this time.

“One sec,” Madison calls, not bothering to look over her shoulder. “It's a little red, Reid, but it looks fine. Does it hurt? What about your arm?”

He grits his teeth. “For the tenth time, I'm fine. It was barely a zap. You're all being helicopter moms about a tiny zap.”

“I don't think you're using that term correctly.” That’s from Aaron.

“Does it matter?” Reid, with a bite.

“Give us a break. We've seen half of our friends die already.” Joe.

“He has a point.” Me.

“Madison!”

“What?” Madison snaps, whirling around to face Sydney. “Jesus, Sydney, what's—”

“Something's wrong with her.” Sydney has a hand on Leah's shoulder, shaking gently, but Leah's fast asleep and not budging. “She's been going in and out of sleep, but she won't move.”

Madison joins them on the couch and gives Leah another shake. When Leah just limply moves to the side, her head falling against her shoulder, Madison's lips part, and real anxiety burns in her eyes. She sets her palm against Leah's forehead, grimaces, and wipes what I assume is sweat from

Leah's clammy skin on her shirt. Leah's still flushed, as she has been for the last day or so, but she's also pretty pale. I didn't think much of it until now—we're all kind of pale, given the lack of nutrients we've consumed lately.

"What's going on?" Aaron approaches the back of the couch, as do the rest of us, while Madison presses two fingers to Leah's wrist. "Is she okay?"

"I-I don't think so." Madison releases Leah's wrist as tears well in her eyes. "H-Her heart rate is really slow. She's shivering, too, but she's burning up."

"Fever?" Joe asks.

"She was being weird before she fell asleep," Sydney says, worrying her lower lip. "She kept asking what time the boat was coming."

I frown. "The boat?"

"I thought she meant search and rescue, and she had a dream about it or something. I—"

"Oh God." Madison's face turns as pale as Leah's as she stares at her best friend's graying face. In a flash, she's unraveling the strips of cloth Leah wrapped around her injured hand, along with the Band-Aids she layered over her cut. "Oh *God.*"

Leah's hand looks like every poster I've ever seen in a hospital or doctor's office about the warning signs of one infection in particular. Inflamed, oozing with pus, swollen—there's no doubt it's infected. I guess dunking it in saltwater didn't get it clean enough.

Then I remember what she cut it on: a rusty nail.

Along with that memory comes another: this time, of Leah asking Madison to take a look at it and help her treat it after Leah and James were exposed, and Madison telling her, *Put a Band-Aid on it.*

That's exactly what she did. Now, her breathing is getting shallower and shallower by the second, and we're all just staring at her, knowing the inevitable will arrive soon enough.

2:57 P.M.

It was 2:45 exactly when Madison couldn't find a pulse on Leah. She's been checking constantly since then, and still, there's nothing. No breathing, no rising and falling of her chest. She's gone, but Madison won't stop checking in hopes of a miracle.

"Mads—" Aaron starts.

"Leave her be." I surprise myself when I interrupt him. Madison hasn't addressed any of us since Leah's heart stopped, so it's not worth trying anymore. "Let's give them some space."

Everyone reluctantly agrees and steps away from the couch, all backing away in different directions. I glance back at a teary-eyed, white-faced Madison one last time before turning my back on her. She's exactly where she's been for the last twelve minutes: perched on her knees beside Leah, gripping Leah's forearm in one hand while two fingers on her other hand are pressed to Leah's pulse. She's just staring at her best friend's face with a completely blank expression, leaving only her eyes to reveal her emotions.

It's one thing to lose your best friend. It's something else entirely to know your best friend could've been saved if you'd helped them when they asked.

It's not her fault. I mean, it's *partly* her fault, but not completely. We used up most of the antiseptic for previous injuries. All of our hard liquor is gone, too. Madison could've agreed to help and given it her best effort, and it's still more than likely that Leah's wound would've gotten infected. Would it still have led to septic shock? Maybe. But there's no point in talking about that. Madison will have the rest of her life to think about it.

"I know he has no right to know after everything, especially given what we have planned..." Aaron sighs. "I think we should tell him. He's been close with Leah since orientation freshman year. He deserves to know."

"He doesn't deserve anything after what he did to Sadie," Joe fires back.

"No, he's right." Again, I surprise myself with my response. Everyone looks at me in shock, too, as expected. Reid even starts to argue with me, but I won't have it. “We've been friends since orientation day, too, Reid, and we're still not as close as they are. If you were Leah and I was James, I'd want to know.”

His stony expression softens. “Yeah, I guess you're right. Plus, they've been fucking, so...”

“They were friends first,” Aaron reminds him. “But yeah. That's a good point.”

“I'll tell him.” Once more, everyone looks at me in complete shock, with a few of them immediately starting to protest. “I'm the one he tried choking the life out of, remember? Maybe if he sees me and remembers what he did, it might...give him a wake-up call. Make him apologize. I don't know.”

Sydney shrugs. “Not a bad idea.”

Henry shakes his head rapidly. “I'm coming with you. If he tries to attack you again—”

“You'll hear it,” I interrupt. “Plus, I think he knows what would happen to him if he did. I'll be fine.”

I force a smile, squeeze his arm to reassure him, and snatch the office key off the living room floor. To my left, Madison doesn't spare me a glance, and to my right, neither does Brett. At least he's moved, unlike Madison. He's now practically curled up in fetal position against the wall, ignoring everything around him—even Leah's death.

I swallow the lump in my throat as I walk to the office, well aware of everyone watching me go. Surprisingly, my hands don't shake as I fit the key into the lock. I guess a part of me knows that showing weakness of any kind would only give James reason to think he got to me—that he succeeded in scaring me like he intended to out there in the woods. I won't let him think that.

He's sitting in the office chair, a glass of untouched scotch and an open bottle on the desk in front of him, just staring out the window at the fallen trees outside. He doesn't turn to look at me when I enter. He doesn't seem to care that someone's finally answered his request to open the damn door.

“What is it now?” His gravelly voice makes me wince. “Did I do something else to hurt someone's feelings?”

I don't waste a second. “Leah's dead.”

That makes him look at me. “What?”

There's the slightest note of sadness in his voice—so brief that if I wasn't paying such close attention to him, I would've missed it. His eyes are gleaming with confusion, but somehow, his battered face remains stoic.

"Sepsis. She cut her hand on a rusty nail, and the cut got infected."

He leans forward to grab the glass. It's silent for a moment as he takes a long drink. "I heard the commotion outside at the generator, too, so I'm assuming someone got zapped. Rusty nail, rotted railing, hazardous generator—am I forgetting anything? Are we adding Spencer being a horny idiot and getting himself lost to the list, too? Wouldn't be surprised."

I know what he's getting at. I won't give him the satisfaction of responding, though. I just bite my tongue and file it away.

He eyes me for a beat, waiting for a response that won't come, then scoffs and takes another sip.

"So," he continues, "the generator killed someone, too? Who?"

The callousness in his voice makes me want to hit him over the head with that fancy scotch. "Nobody."

"Oh. That's nice."

My stomach churns at that. "I'm sure Reid will appreciate your concern."

James laughs that maniacal laugh again. "Whatever. At least you guys couldn't blame that one on me and my family if something did happen, like you said."

"Nobody was gonna blame you for anything."

The corner of his swollen mouth twitches, and I can almost feel the dissatisfaction oozing out of him. It's almost like he wants me to tell him the opposite—that we were all planning on pinning everything that's happened on him.

"Not even Ava?" he finally asks. He's quick—almost too quick—to add, "Not like I did anything wrong there, but you all had a great time acting like it was all my fault. Honestly? Something was bound to happen to her after the sting. She was a walking liability, as unfortunate as it was. At this point, you're all liabilities, and I have to be responsible for damage control as owner of this house."

I pause for a moment, soaking that in. "What do you suggest we do, then? Everyone else is trying to figure out a game plan. If you want to claim responsibility, you could start by contributing to that in your own way, like the rest of us."

"I'm not sure what you think I should do. You know I'm basically useless in this situation." He pauses again, waiting for me to give him something—to agree with him, to tell him he's not useless, whatever it may be—but I don't. "There are plenty of you outside of this room who can put your heads together and figure this out if you stop making stupid choices long enough to do it. You'll all get yourselves killed sooner or later. Reid's a liability just like Ava was if he keeps playing with the generator. He thinks he can make everything better whenever anything goes wrong, but that's not true. Same with Brett if he keeps going outside to find Spencer when we all know Spencer's floating a few nautical miles offshore. Always has to act like a hero. Don't even get me started on Joe, either."

I see what he's doing here—he's trying to get me to see his side of things, see how everyone in this house is a liability in one way or another. Baiting me so I ask for more, sowing the seeds of paranoia and distrust deeper into my bones. He's empty without everyone circling around him, and now, the only hand he has left to play is using what he knows about each of us to break us further apart.

He's moved on. Simple as that.

"Okay." That's all I'll give him. "I just wanted to tell you about Leah. I'll leave you to…mourn."

As I'm turning to leave, he calls after me, "Put her out with the others before the house starts to smell."

I pause, gritting my teeth, and take just a second to calm myself before I whip around and do exactly what I've wanted to since walking into this room—break that bottle over his head. I hear him snort and mutter something to himself as I close the door and lock it behind me.

My hand drifts to my throat as I hesitate outside of the door, and not because it aches or because I'm traumatized by what James did to me—rather, because I could physically feel the moment when everything crumbled. The illusion I've wanted so desperately to be a part of for years now shattered the moment he wrapped his hands around my neck; shattered for me, for the others, and for James.

6:12 P.M.

Aaron asked me about my conversation with James, but neither he nor anyone else had anything to say about it. I saw their responses more than I heard them: Madison turning her head and lowering her eyes, more disappointed than surprised; Joe rolling his eyes as if to say, *figures*; both Reid and Sydney sitting stoic and silent, visibly processing; and Aaron's eyebrows knitting together as if contemplating something. Henry just watched me, more focused on the blank look in my eyes than what I said, while Brett—pretty much catatonic by this point—didn't give me anything. If I didn't know any better, I'd think he hadn't heard a word I said.

It's been a little while since then. Nobody's spoken a word. Leah's still slumped over on the couch, but everyone seems to wordlessly agree we'll worry about her later.

I'm sitting at the kitchen table with Henry, silent, and toying with somebody's empty, long-dead Juul when Aaron—who's been standing in front of a living room window and staring out at the beach for the last few minutes—turns to face all of us, the first person to move since I got back from the office.

"I'm letting him out."

"What?" Joe scowls and drops the lighter he's been playing with onto the island counter. "Why?"

"I have a feeling we're missing something, like I said earlier. Something in the house." Aaron gestures around to our once-pristine surroundings with his arms. "James's grandpa knows his shit. He's had coastal homes his entire life. I can't imagine he wouldn't have some sort of emergency protocol. Something we can use to call for help."

Sydney sighs. "No point. We've checked everything, and James would've told us by now if his grandpa had anything like that."

"Maybe he doesn't know."

"I don't get why you'd want to let him out, then," Reid mutters.

Aaron lets out a ragged, frustrated exhale. "Just because he doesn't know it's here doesn't mean he wouldn't know where to look. He's been preoccupied with other shit this whole time. If we can get him to sit down and really focus on this one thing, we could get somewhere."

"It's not the worst idea." Madison, who has moved from her spot on the couch beside Leah—only by a few feet, as she's now sitting on the floor—shrugs as she looks around at us, though she doesn't meet anyone's eyes. "It's the only option we have."

"I think we should give him a little more time," Henry suggests. "Let's get some food in him first so he's less…cranky."

Sydney nods. "I'll do it."

Nobody protests or offers to help. She slowly gets up from where she's been sitting at the island, across the room from Brett on the mattress by the window, and moves to the counter where we've been keeping the rations. Everyone eyes her for a moment as she selects a Solo cup from the nine remaining. I know what's in each of them: a meager helping of lentils and whatever was left of the trail mix. Fragments of nuts and seeds, if I remember correctly.

My stomach rumbles just thinking about it, even though I know it won't do anything to curb my hunger.

"I'll give him some water, too," Sydney says.

Nobody acknowledges her.

I'm looking down at the Juul, studying the star-shaped carving on the backside—and realizing this belonged to Zayn, remembering when he carved it months ago—when something compels me to look up at Sydney. I just barely catch the moment she screws on the lid of a water bottle that we've recently refilled from one of the filters. She then holds the water bottle low, level between her pelvis and the edge of the counter, and carefully tips it from side to side.

I quickly look back down at the Juul when she turns. She doesn't seem to realize I was watching as she walks to the trashcan and slips something inside. After that, she takes the water and the Solo cup of food into the office without another word.

I stand up when she's gone. "I'm gonna put the trash on the deck. It smells like rotting fish carcass."

Again, no acknowledgement.

I take off the lid, remove the trash bag, and take note of what's resting on top—a plastic baggie with remnants of white powder inside. As I'm tying the bag, my eyes find the bottle of sleeping pills on the counter, and that's when it hits me.

I wish there was a way to calm him down. Those were Sydney's exact words just a few hours ago. I didn't see her take anything from the bottle, and I definitely didn't see or hear her grind pills into powder, but I did notice that she was out at the evacuation hole for a while. I just didn't think anything of it because, well…you know.

I don't say anything, though. I just put the trash onto the deck and reclaim my seat at the kitchen table.

Sydney returns after a minute, saying nothing, and goes back to picking at her nails at the island.

At some point, Reid passes out the remaining rations without being asked, and despite our hunger, everyone just…picks. My stomach is churning as much as it's aching for sustenance, so I'm sure the others feel the same way.

About twenty minutes after we get our food, Aaron tells us he's letting James out of the office. Everyone sits up a little straighter, waiting, until a tired, bloodshot-eyed James appears behind Aaron in the hallway.

"I thought something happened," James says, his voice low and a bit hoarse.

"Like what?" Joe questions.

James just shrugs. His eyes land on Leah's rigid body for a millisecond, but he doesn't so much as blink.

"I don't know. Maybe someone else got hurt. Maybe Spencer came back from his midnight stroll."

In the corner of the living room, Brett's head lifts. His expression is dark, daring to be tested, and his eyes are more bloodshot than James's.

"I don't want to hear you talking about him anymore." His words are curt and emotionless, but his eyes maintain the hollowness that's been his constant companion these last few days.

James rolls his eyes and runs a slow hand through his hair. "You gotta come to terms with it, man. I did."

"What's that supposed to mean?" Now Brett's voice is sharper, and like the rest of us, he's sitting up straighter.

"I mean…I felt bad I forgot to say something after the storm, but we all made mistakes. Only thing we can do now is ask for forgiveness, y'know?"

"What?" Brett rises from the mattress and takes a few steps closer. I almost want to lean further back into my seat when I see the wildness in his dark eyes. "What do you mean, *you forgot to say something after the storm?"*

Once more, a casual shrug from James. "He told me he was going out. Didn't say why, though." His head slowly swivels in Sydney's direction, a pointed look on his face, and she shifts uncomfortably on her stool, averting her gaze. "I was pretty fucked up. Totally forgot until the next day when we were all down here during the storm."

All I can do is sigh and wonder if it's the pills and all the fancy liquor he's been drinking while holed up in the office that led to this confession, or if he's just bored of holding onto the secret.

In seconds, Brett closes the space between them and gives James a two-handed shove to the chest. James stumbles back, but he's slow to steady himself and slow to react. When he does, he just scowls, the look on his face telling me he has absolutely no idea why Brett's attacking him.

"What the fuck, man?" Brett's fists are clenched at his sides, but surprisingly, he's refraining. "Are you serious? All this time, you fucking knew he wasn't here and you didn't say anything? We could've started looking for him sooner! We could've—"

"We were out there looking for others, too," James argues. "We didn't find him. We were never gonna find him."

"That's not the point! We could've fucking tried! We could've tried as soon as the storm hit instead of waiting for fucking days—"

"Until you realized he wasn't here?"

Brett's nostrils flare. "How fucking dare you."

James holds his hands up in defense, slow and calm. "Look, maybe it wasn't the right call, but I knew you'd make us all get out there during the storm to find him if I told you, and I couldn't have that."

"We wouldn't have gone." It's Sydney who speaks next, drawing Brett's eyes from James to her. "We didn't go looking for Eli, Zeke, or Dani while the storm was bad. Spencer would've been no different. But at least we would've known he was out there. It wasn't your call to make, James. What you're saying…it doesn't make any sense."

"She's right," Joe says, shaking his head. "Sounds to me like you just didn't want to add another thing to worry about to your list."

James rolls his eyes. "You're all crazy."

"No." Brett shakes his head. "You just can't do us the kindness of admitting the real reason you didn't say anything. I'm not sure I even want to know."

Then, to my surprise, he walks away, returning to his place of solitude on the mattress, but refraining from leaving the group entirely. I wonder why.

James watches him go, lips parted like he wants to say more, but nothing comes out.

"Anyway." James looks around at us, expressionless, and sways a little as he stands in place. "I thought something happened when Aaron came to get me, but it's a good thing he did."

"And why's that?" I ask.

He doesn't look at me as he replies, "I thought I'd keep myself busy by cleaning up some of the glass in the office. Scooped it up in my empty water cup."

"Glass?" Reid questions.

"I…knocked some shit over on the bookshelves." He waves a dismissive hand, swaying again when he does so. "Anyway, when I was down on all fours, I saw this chest on the bottom shelf behind the desk. Never seen it before. Had some label on it, but the writing was rubbed off. Found this inside."

He reaches into the pocket of his shorts and pulls out a handheld blue and yellow device about the size of a larger cellphone. His hand tremors as he holds it out, and I see him run his tongue over his lips a few times, trying to moisten them.

"What is it?" Madison's standing now, leaning against the back of the couch with her arms folded. She's not looking at the device as much as she's studying James, though—almost like she can tell something's off with him. If the others notice anything strange, too, they don't say anything.

"Emergency beacon." It's Sydney who answers, drawing all attention. Her eyes are wide, and she's staring at the device like it's a five-course meal. "My grandparents keep one on their boat in Florida. It has a locator beacon and a satellite distress signal that can get in contact with other boats."

Henry meets my eyes, and I wonder if he's thinking the same thing I am: Aaron told us that he thought James could help us find something useful in the house, and James just so happened to locate that something before anyone had the chance to bring it up to him. Could it be because he was listening to us by the door and started searching, or because he was listening and already knew it was there?

Always has to prove that he's one step ahead, I think.

"So if there are boats nearby, we can send a distress signal?" Joe summarizes. Sydney nods, practically bouncing on the balls of her feet. "What's the range like?"

"I-I don't know. Depends on the brand, maybe. But it should reach pretty far."

"How far is pretty far?" Aaron demands.

"I don't know."

"What do we do with it?"

"It'll have a better signal outside. I remember my grandparents saying that when I was a kid and I found theirs—they said to go above deck and use it if I was ever in a bad situation."

"Does it work?" Aaron directs that question at James, who only shrugs again.

"Only one way to find out." He takes the device in his other hand so he can wipe his palm on his shorts. "I'll do it. I have the steadiest hands."

I'm not sure why steady hands are required to press a button or two, but I don't say anything.

When nobody answers, he smacks his dry lips together and says, "Any water left?"

"All gone for now. We should have more in a few minutes when the filters catch up." Madison nods her head toward the door. "You'll be okay. You want to be in charge, so go be in charge."

He stares at her like a parent would stare at a kid who's misbehaving, waiting for the kid to apologize before an apology has to be requested. When Madison stands her ground, James just exhales and starts walking—somewhat lopsided, his feet dragging on the floor—toward the deck.

Only Aaron and Joe follow him outside. I'm the only other person who moves, curious, but I decide to watch from the glass door instead. I see James make his way over to the side of the deck, directionless—almost like his feet are taking him one way regardless of where his brain is telling him to go, and he's too disoriented to notice or care. He's a few feet away from where two belts are tied together and to wooden beams on either side of the broken railing where Ava fell.

I know Reid had the idea about the belts. I saw him connecting them—one his, one Joe's—a few hours ago. It's not caution tape, but it's something to act as a barrier. A warning.

Out there in the darkness, James holds the device up to his face, squinting to see the buttons. Water splatters on the deck, a slight drizzle just starting out, and he blinks a few times, likely to get the water out of his eyes. He brings his face closer to the device, then pulls back, then repeats the process like an old man trying to read the newspaper without his glasses.

I'm starting to lose interest when a bright white flashing light emits from the device. James lets out a string of curses as he stumbles backward and drops the device onto the ground, rubbing at his eyes while squeezing them shut.

Joe's voice cuts through next after Aaron collects the device from the ground: "Funny place to stand."

The barest hint of a smile forms on my lips as I turn away, ready to rejoin Henry at the kitchen table. I'm barely sitting for two minutes before I hear the door open behind me. Aaron's standing there, his dark hair damp from the drizzle, his hand still clutching the handle.

"I think you guys are gonna want to be outside for this."

I meet eyes with Henry, then flick my gaze over to the others—Sydney, Madison, Reid, and Brett. I hear James's octave increasing as I'm standing and we start flooding out onto the deck. Brett lingers in the doorway, Sydney a few feet away off to the side of him, while I follow Henry a bit closer to James and the railing. I see Henry eyeing the railing while the others fall into place in a semicircle behind Joe, but he doesn't utter a word about it.

I see Reid looking at it, too. He put the belts there, after all—he knows exactly how strong they are. He doesn't say a word, either.

As soon as James realizes we're all out here to witness whatever's going down between him and Joe, he clamps his jaw shut.

"You had plenty to say a minute ago." Joe folds his arms over his chest and raises a brow. "Well?"

James's eyes land on the device in Aaron's grasp. "Give it to me."

"No." Aaron doesn't move an inch. "Joe's right—you were in the middle of something. Just say it to all of us."

"You were telling me how it wasn't your fault," Joe continues. "What happened to Ava."

"None of it was my fault," James shoots back, shifting his weight between his feet like he's struggling to stay balanced.

"None of what?" Joe pushes. "Oh, I know. Like refusing to tell us that Spencer was missing? Or like telling Zayn to fix the boat when you had to have known it wasn't stable?"

"Nobody else noticed Spencer wasn't here. Nobody advised Zayn against working on the boat. It wasn't my fault."

"It's different. We didn't withhold information. We didn't tell Zayn what to do. We didn't tell Ava where to stand. We didn't tell Erin what to eat. That's all on you, man."

James shakes his head as he takes a step backward. "I did what I thought was best for everyone here. Half of you would probably be dead without me. You can't deny that, and if you try, you're lying to yourselves. I was *protecting* you."

Joe won't back down. "What happened to Ava wasn't about protecting us. We all know that. So what was it, then? Hmm?"

"She was a liability!" James shouts back, his fists clenching tighter at his sides. "She was hurt and weak, man! We all would've had to sacrifice something to keep her going!"

I spare a glance at the others. Madison stiffens, her bitten nails digging into her arms as she holds herself. Reid just looks down at his shoes, jaw clenched. Brett and Aaron keep staring at James, expressionless. Sydney turns her head to the side, unable to look on. Henry, like me, is still and silent, eyes trained solely on James.

"Is that what Spencer was, too?" Joe's voice is softer now, hard to hear over the drizzle pattering on the deck. "A liability?"

James squares his shoulders as the dampness flattens his hair over his eyes. "I had to make hard calls. That's it."

"Nobody asked you to," Aaron says.

James ignores him. "You needed me. All of you. None of you can make tough choices without me."

I choose my words carefully: "You don't know who you are without someone beneath you, do you?"

Silence. The breeze picks up again, making the wind whistle through the trees we can barely see in the darkness, and for a moment, the only sounds to be heard come from the island itself: the wind, and the gentle rainfall tapping against the wood beneath our feet.

"That's not how this works," James says, stepping back like he owns the space. "If you think you can just—"

A cracking sound, like a tree trunk snapping in half, interrupts him, closely followed by a sharp gasp. In the time it takes me to blink, James has disappeared, and so have the safety belts behind him.

Henry shifts forward just a touch—enough for me to notice, but not enough for it to make any difference.

Only now do I realize James isn't gone. Not yet. Fingers are latched onto a splintered piece of rotting wooden flooring, and a pair of terrified eyes, colorless beneath the gloomy overcast, briefly meet mine—meet ours. A desperate plea shines within them, something that looks foreign within this particular gaze, but it isn't answered. I can see his eyes raking over each of us, panicked and deliberate, moving onto the next the instant the former refuses to budge.

A new sound joins the chorus of wind and rain, although barely audible. It could be an appeal, a moan, a cry; I'm not sure. The only thing I'm sure about is the moment I see the fingers release the wood.

Nobody speaks. Nobody screams or cries out or rushes over to the broken railing. There's no need to check if he's dead. We all saw Ava fall from the same place. The height was too great, the ground below too unforgiving. There's just no point in checking on a corpse.

If we're wrong, we'll find out in the morning.

8:30 P.M.

The house is colder tonight than it has been.

Maybe it's the emptiness that makes it feel colder. Like the house itself knows someone is missing—the only person it knew before the rest of us were brought here. Or maybe it's just that I've started processing that there are supposed to be nineteen bodies in here, blowing hot air through debates, and nonstop talking, and puffs from a bowl, so packed together that the temperature rises ten degrees.

The stars are the only light source I have as their beams pour in through the windows, casting an eerie glow over the scattered belongings, the water filters, the mattresses by the windows. If I didn't know a bunch of college kids were trapped here after a hurricane, I'd think people were squatting here.

I've been sitting at the kitchen table, listening to nothing but the wind, the *drip, drip, drip* of the water filters, and the rumbling of my own stomach. I'm alone here. Everyone else disappeared as soon as we made it back to the house—to do what, I'm not sure. Nobody bothered to ask.

When a chill travels down my spine, I find myself standing abruptly, needing to get away from the deck door that's led us to so much tragedy, so much uncertainty. I don't think as I walk; I just let my feet travel across the tiled floors, ignoring the trails of mud and sand that've been tracked inside.

I find myself outside of the office. The door is cracked open, and I see starlight cutting through the window inside. I push the door open, unsure of what I'm here for, and quickly realize the light isn't from the moon. It's from a flashlight resting atop the windowsill.

A familiar head of dark hair and a stained, slightly torn blue t-shirt partially block my view of the window. A smile instinctively forms on my lips when I see Henry positioned in front of the radio, staring down at it like it'll magically start working again.

He must hear me, as he turns around within seconds. He smiles, takes the flashlight, and joins me in the doorway.

"What are you doing in here?" I murmur.

"Just thinking." His smile fades only slightly as he gently swipes his thumb over my lower lip. "Your lips are dry."

"So are yours."

"I know. Want some water?"

I nod, squeezing his hand when it slips into mine, and let him guide me back toward the kitchen. Still, nobody's here except for us.

He manages to half-fill a water bottle for the both of us, letting me drink first, then finishing the rest. He barely has the empty bottle down on the table before I'm wrapping my arms around his middle, nuzzling my nose into his neck and holding him close like he'll evaporate before me. My eyes fall shut, and in this moment, I'm more relaxed than I have been since all nineteen of us were goofing off on the beach that second day.

He doesn't speak. He doesn't need to, and neither do I. There's not much to say anymore.

The darkness I see with my eyes closed shifts—now, a dark orange light interferes with the blackness. Slowly, I open my eyes, and that's when I spot the source through the living room window across from me: what looks like a massive fire on the beach, right in front of the house.

Henry's back is facing the window, but he must see it in the reflection of the shiny refrigerator in front of him. We slowly release each other as he turns, both taking a few hesitant steps closer to the window.

There it is—a bonfire. I see a dark, shadowy figure standing nearby, holding what looks like a canister of gasoline.

I meet Henry's eyes, pausing for a beat to study the reflection of the flames in his gaze, then raise a brow. He nods and slips his hand into mine again, and the two of us head toward the deck.

Brett's out here. I didn't see him before, but here he is, sitting in one of the lounge chairs with his elbows on his knees and his head in his hands. His knees are bouncing uncontrollably, and I think I hear him muttering to himself, but neither I nor Henry says a word to him. We just leave him there and make our way down the stairs.

I spot two other figures on the beach as we descend. The moonlight draws attention to hair being lifted by the breeze—Madison and Sydney. Even from afar, I can see they're both wrapped in a blanket or a towel, I can't tell, while they stand at the shore as the foam laps over their feet. One of them is facing the ocean, and the other is turned toward the fire.

It's Aaron—the figure with the gasoline. As we get closer and I can see the front of him, where the firelight hits him, I recognize his dark complexion and the Lil Wayne t-shirt he's worn out so badly, you can hardly make out the text on the front anymore. The gasoline is clutched in one hand by his hip, and he's using the other hand to swig from a bottle of wine he must've pulled from the cellar.

He polishes off the bottle and throws it into the fire, making the flames soar a bit as the bottle and the alcohol residue shriek. I know he can see us standing nearby, but he doesn't acknowledge us. He just stares into the flames, dead-eyed.

I can see what he used to build the fire: splintered deck wood and the broken legs of lounge chairs. I don't know how much of it was already damaged when he collected it and how much he damaged on purpose, though.

It's warm here, of course. Way warmer than back at the house. I don't hesitate to sit down a few feet from the fire, letting the heat wrap around me like a blanket, and Henry does the same after a few seconds pass. Our knees are pressed together, but other than that, we don't touch.

Aaron sits down, too, but it takes him a minute. His knees are drawn up and his arms are draped over them, and his face remains unreadable.

Across the way, I see movement on the deck. I think it's Brett at first, but then I make out two figures, and neither shape looks like him—one is taller and a bit wider, and the other is a tad shorter and much scrawnier. Joe stays there by the railing, clasping the wood but not leaning on it, while Reid descends the staircase and makes his way toward us.

Madison and Sydney beat him here. Madison doesn't hesitate to plop down in front of the fire—the only one of us facing the ocean, and in the only spot the breeze doesn't seem to be hitting—and cross her legs while she leans closer to it, the light bringing attention to her bloodshot eyes. Sydney, on the other hand, spares a glance up at the deck before following suit, leaving a distance between herself, Madison, and Aaron as she wraps her blanket around her shoulders a bit tighter.

Reid doesn't sit when he arrives. I don't look directly at him, but out of my peripheral, I notice he's lost his glasses. I feel his eyes travel over each of us, one by one—like he's waiting for someone to tell him to sit, to join us. Even as the fire cracks and pops in my ears, I hear him sigh, and from the corner of my eye, I see his frame lower to the ground, several feet away from me and Henry.

It takes him a minute, but Joe eventually joins us, too. The cold must've gotten to him up there—that, or Brett's mutterings.

He sits apart from everyone, too. He's technically between Aaron and Reid, but far behind them, his back to the ocean. He's mimicking Madison's position: legs crossed and torso hunched forward.

There's an open space beside Aaron, directly in line with the house and the fire. A fracture in what should be a perfect circle.

We keep leaving space for people who aren't coming back.

Aaron stands suddenly, using the toe of his sneaker to nudge a broken slat of wood into the fire, then another, though there's no space left for it to catch. The flames choke and spit, but he keeps pushing, anyway, until a charred piece collapses inward. The hissing of the fire is the only sound to be heard until a soft voice pierces the silence.

"Do you think—" Sydney starts, but stops herself. Nobody asks what she means, and nobody reacts.

Aaron doesn't sit back down. The flames dance in his eyes as he stares ahead, motionless.

For a moment as I lose myself in the crackling and the sparks fizzling out onto the sand, I forget I'm not alone out here, and that the heavy silence is shared by eight of us. I know it's impossible to say for certain if we'll all make it home. Another accident. Poisoned food. Heatstroke. Dehydration. Or worse—betrayal. Out here, it's anyone's bet who goes next.

The island let the eight of us live this long; maybe it'll let us live long enough to go home, even if we walk out of here like strangers instead of friends.

That's what we are now, though. Not friends. Not survivors together. Just strangers who happened to endure the same place.

A chair leg in the fire finally gives way, collapsing into splinters and ash. Nobody moves to replace it.

DAY NINE

6:32 A.M.

In my dream, I'm back at Saint Maren. It has to be senior year, because I'm in the off-campus townhouse the six of them share—the first year they all lived together.

Most of the furniture has been pushed to the walls to make space. Chairs are stacked against one side so guests can climb up and dance above the crowd. The kitchen table is wedged beside the speaker, bottles lined across it in uneven rows that catch and blur the colored lights.

I'm standing up on one of those chairs, a Solo cup in my left hand and someone's vape in the other, swaying to a song blaring from the massive speaker. The bass is so loud that it feels thick, slowed, like it's moving through water before it reaches my ears. My eyes are closed, heavy from the alcohol and the late hour, but I'm glad to be here; glad I'd been asked to come early to help set up, and glad I was never going to be one of the people waiting outside in the cold for the chance to be let in.

Something cold splashes my ankle. I look down and see bright red liquid splattered across my white shoes. Eli Acosta is standing below me, laughing, already blotting at the stains with the hem of his shirt, his apology swallowed up by the music.

Beside me on another chair, Aaron Kemper scolds Eli with a grin and shrugs at me, but his attention shifts when Erin Matthews is hoisted onto the chair on his other side. She slips a bit, and Aaron steadies her with a careful hand on her back, quick to let her go once she finds her balance. She smiles at him like it matters more than it did.

The vape I've been holding is snatched—either by its owner or someone else, I'm not sure—but my hand isn't empty for long. Someone presses another drink into my grasp without looking up. I take it, and then another. I'm holding three now, dangerously, hoping my precarious grip doesn't end with another mess on my shoes.

I scan the party for the other hosts. Nick O'Brien stands by the coat closet, looking out at the crowd while his girlfriend, Danielle Perry, clings to his shirt. Her mouth is moving at a rapid pace, and he's just nodding along, though I'm not sure if he can hear her.

Nearby, Joe Graham is holding up his phone, a woman's face bright on the screen. He nearly drops it when Swedish exchange student Magnus Svensson stumbles while dancing, barreling right into his side. Even over the music, I hear Joe holler at his roommate.

The last of the two roommates are in the kitchen. Reid Carroll is leaning up against the fridge, laughing, while Zeke Medina stands across from him, puffing on a joint. Zeke passes it to Ava DaSilva, who's sitting on the kitchen counter with a can between her knees and her phone recording. She coughs instantly and waves it toward Reid, abandoning whatever she'd been doing on the screen.

As the song changes, my shoes sticking to the spilled cocktail on the chair, I see two women pushing through the crowd to find space. Madison Wheeler pulls her best friend, Leah Welch, along by the hand, both laughing, Leah chugging from her reusable bottle—blue to Madison's pink.

Sydney Schultz slips past with Brett Powell close behind her, his hand hovering at the small of her back as they move through the crowd. Then the center of the room shifts—not abruptly, just the way people open up around someone moving through them.

I see James Bishop for a beat before he looks up.

He throws his arms around Madison and Leah both, drawing them toward him, shouting something across the room. Brett is already there, arm hooked over James's shoulders with Sydney tucked against Brett's side. Brett's younger brother, Spencer, trails just behind, laughing too loudly, trying to wedge himself into the same circle. For a moment, the space around them seems to draw inward, people turning in their direction without meaning to.

Movement in my peripheral pulls me away. Zayn Bakshi is climbing through the window near the speaker and the kitchen table. Joe hauls him the rest of the way in instead of scolding him for not using the door. A minute later, Zayn is gone, lost within the bodies, swallowed by the party.

I'm about to climb down when the front door opens again and cold air spills in with a handful of new arrivals. I recognize the faces of all five, but only the name of one: Henry Rhodes. We have most of our classes together, but we've never spoken. He hesitates in the small entryway, scanning the room like he's searching for somewhere to land.

For a moment, his gaze lifts over the crowd—past shoulders and raised cups—and catches on the line of chairs against the wall. On me. Just long enough that I know he's clocked who's already above the floor. Then someone calls his name and he turns, pulled into the bodies closing in around him.

I linger on the chair for a moment longer, looking out over everyone: the small clusters scattered through the house, laughter breaking loose in bursts, hands linked so no one gets lost pushing through the crowd. We always end up in the same places at parties like this, even when we scatter.

They know me, I think. Or they know the version that carries their drinks, guards the table, stays late after to help clean up. Sadie Walden, the name on their guest lists, their group chats, their door counts—close enough to be inside, but never quite at the center.

A party horn blasts a few feet away—Magnus, probably, calling everyone to stop and take a shot.

That's when I wake up.

The horn's still blaring. It's loud, but it's distant, too. It almost feels like it's shaking the ground beneath my feet—or, rather, beneath my head.

I peel my cheek from the sand, ignoring the granules making my skin itch, and blink a few times while I recall where I am. Around me, six of the same people I saw in my dream—the seventh I recall as being back at the house—are mirroring my position: lifting themselves up off the sand, sitting up and looking around in confusion for the source of that incessant horn.

The bonfire from last night is still smoking and smoldering in the center of the circle we formed. I can see shards of glass from the wine bottles blackened at the bottom of it. The breeze blew soot from the fire over us, leaving some of our faces, limbs, and clothing splattered with black smudges.

The horn blows again, louder this time, and that's when we all finally find our footing. We're gathered in a straight line in front of the charred wood, facing the expansive Caribbean ocean. The source of the noise is right there in front of us, blocking our view of the rising sun: several large boats, headed right for the island.

7:28 A.M.

"And yesterday?"

"Yesterday...Yesterday, we wanted to have a fire, and then we went inside. That's when we found the emergency beacon by accident. Stroke of luck, I guess. It was really dark by then and starting to rain, so we decided it'd be better if we tried using it in the morning. We all went to bed, and when we woke up, we couldn't…we couldn't find him. That was when we came back down to the beach and…He must've tried to set off the beacon himself after we all went to bed, and he fell."

"Uh-huh. Okay." Sheryl, a search and rescue officer, records my story in her little notepad, nodding. A strange feeling courses through me, like a flare was set off in my chest, as I wonder if I've said too much.

"We have a great team out there searching for Spencer right now," she continues. "We'll do our best to recover him, and I sincerely hope we find him alive. Nothing is assured, though. Do you all understand that?"

I look around at the others. We're on one of the search and rescue boats, all huddled in a room below deck, wrapped up in blankets with bottled water and snacks surrounding us. Everyone briefly glances at me, like it's an instinct, before we collectively nod.

"That being said," Sheryl continues, "we want to get you eight home to your families as soon as we can, and we don't want to add to your trauma. Our teams will recover the remains and search for Spencer for as long as we can. Everyone will follow you home on another boat. Is that okay?"

I sniff. "That's okay. Thank you, ma'am."

She stands with her notebook tucked under her arm. "You've all been through one of the worst things anyone can experience," she says. "You're all adults, of course, but we'll talk to your parents about helping you move forward. You'll hear more about that when we get back to Miami. Just remember that there's no shame in having a tough transition back to normal life. There are specialists at home who will do their absolute best to guide you forward." She clears her throat. "You've been examined by our medical staff already, but is there anything else I can do for you? Anything else I should know about?"

Madison shakes her head. “No.”

“All right.” She forces a pitiful smile. “Try to get some rest. We'll be departing soon.”

She leaves the room—the cabin, really, given that there's two bathrooms in here, plus four cots on either side so we can sleep on the way back to Miami—and nobody says a word. We all just stare at each other, unsure of what to do next.

Sheryl was responsible for finding us specifically. James's family told search and rescue that nineteen kids were staying at their home on this side of the island; and while there were tons of other people who were here during the hurricane, a group of nineteen certainly caused concern. Other officers are still out on the island looking for more survivors, but as we told them when they first picked us up off the beach, we haven't seen or heard anyone since the storm.

Leah had already been pulled from the house by the time they got us aboard the boat—wrapped in foil blankets, eyes open wide but unseeing.

We gathered our things from the house, boarded the boat, and followed Sheryl down here so we could change into clean clothing, eat, drink, and tell our story. We've been here for two hours now, recapping everything that happened from the night the hurricane struck to the last thing we remember last night.

I took the reins. I didn't ask to, nor did I want to, but nobody else would speak. They just looked at me like I'm somehow in charge now. I don't understand it, but at least I was able to be the voice for all of us when nobody else could.

We—*I*—told the truth, for the most part. I didn't lie about James falling or about Ava dying the same way. I didn't lie about all of us letting Zeke and Eli take the boat out at night, or us letting Dani leave alone after dark, or us letting Zayn try to fix the motorboat. I told Sheryl as much of the truth as possible in as much detail as possible. What I didn't tell her, however, was the truth about what happened to James—that we were all there on the deck with him when he took that fateful step backward.

I stand up right as the boat horn blares, making me wince, and look through the window closest to me. Even from a distance, I can see the red-suited search and rescue team digging on the beach by the house. Digging up the graves we dug nearly every day since the storm. Digging up our friends. Digging up the truth.

The others follow my lead to watch, too. After a moment, Joe clears his throat and says, “Do you think they'll question…?”

“It doesn’t matter. He made his choice.” Aaron’s response is curt and final, ending the conversation before it can truly begin.

The boat jerks, making us stumble a bit, and we stand here in silence as we watch the house on the island get smaller and smaller in the distance. Soon enough, it's just a speck against the sea and sand.

We should be glad that we were rescued. That we're safely aboard a boat and headed home to our families. That we won't have to worry about eating or making clean water. But all we can do is stare at that speck in the distance—not even the house by now, but the entire island—and think about what happened to us there: it didn’t turn us into different people, but it certainly forced us to become versions of ourselves we never wanted each other, nor ourselves, to see in the light of day.

10:45 A.M.

Over three hours go by before Sheryl pays us another visit, a radio in hand. I can tell by the look on her face that she's confused by what she's seeing: all eight of us wide awake instead of resting, spread out as to not touch one another instead of seeking comfort from our friends, and staring aimlessly into nothingness.

She clears her throat and holds up the little radio. “I have some news from my team on the island. They've found Spencer.”

Brett lifts his head, but there's no emotion on his face whatsoever. “Where?”

Not *is he alive?* It's clear by Sheryl's pursed lips that she expected that question, not the one Brett asked.

“A few houses down. He was buried in the wreckage and badly decomposed. It's probably a good thing you didn't find him, in all honesty.”

I know what that translates to: *I'm surprised the smell didn't lead you straight to him.*

Brett just sighs, turns to face the window, and presses his forehead against the glass.

Sheryl clears her throat once more. “I have another question about James. We found men’s belts beneath his body when we recovered him. What was that all about?”

“We tried to block off the broken railing,” I reply when nobody else does.

“So he was aware of the damage there?”

“Yes, ma’am. We were all together on the beach when Ava fell from there.”

Her lips turn downward into a frown. “He knew about the hazard, and he still got close enough to it that he fell? Forgive me—I know it was dark and he was under a lot of stress, but I can’t imagine he’d go anywhere near that area. I’m just trying to fill in the blanks here.”

“He’d been drinking, ma'am.” I try to keep my voice steady, and as I’m looking directly into her eyes, I can’t tell if the others are watching me, sweating with nerves like I'm going to say something I shouldn't. "He had a lot to drink, and, um…He was having trouble sleeping—all the stress, you know?—and we found some sleeping pills in the wreckage. I'm not sure if he mixed them."

Her eyebrows crease. "We did find the medication and the alcohol in the office, where you said he'd been spending a lot of his time. You didn't mention the drinking and the medication before, though."

Heat pricks at the back of my neck. "I wasn't sure if it was relevant. The rest of us were drinking, too, for the calories. And I didn't see him take any of the pills, so I didn't want to say anything at first."

"Fair enough." Sheryl sighs and forces another pitiful smile. "Get some rest. We'll be back in Miami around four o'clock tonight."

She leaves, prompting Henry to lean in close to me and whisper in my ear: "You need to be smarter than that."

I wince. I know that, too. It's best not to give anyone reason to think we knew James was impaired, even if I claim we were all under the influence of something, too. Someone might start to wonder why we weren't taking better care of each other.

Joe looks around at each of us hesitantly, like he's making sure Sheryl is out of earshot, before he asks, "Can we all agree on something?"

"What is it?" Sydney mutters.

"We'll never talk about what happened with anyone. Not even each other."

Nobody answers for a moment. Then Madison: "Agreed."

"Agreed," I chime in.

A chorus of affirmative replies follows, and as soon as silence sweeps over us once more, I know we'll be true to this promise. The truth about what happened last night—what we all did and didn't do—dies with us.

Reid breaks the silence by clearing his throat. He's looking right at me. It's odd to see him without his glasses, but they're long gone by now. I saw them snapped in the sand when we left the fire this morning, trampled beneath someone's shoe.

"I heard the team talking while we were getting on the boat. You know how hurricanes have names?"

"Yes, Reid," Madison says exasperatedly.

He ignores her as a distant sort of smile forms on his lips. "This one? They named it *Hurricane Danielle.*"

That makes me smile, too. I'd laugh, given the conversation he and I had on day two of this trip, but it doesn't feel right to laugh when search and rescue is currently uncovering Dani's rotting, mangled corpse from the sand.

4:19 P.M.

We left the cabin behind to stand on the main deck when Sheryl told us we were approaching Miami. We're inching closer to leaving this trip and all its horrors behind us, and none of us want to be holed up in the cabin when this boat finally stops, bringing us one step closer to home.

The dock is still small in the distance, but even so, I can see that it's crowded. I wonder how many people in the crowd are reporters eager to hear our survival story and plaster our faces over every newspaper and magazine in the country. I wonder how many of those faces belong to loved ones—not only ours, but loved ones of those expecting to see their kids waving to them from the deck, only to realize their kids aren't here, and to know exactly what that means.

I just hope search and rescue tells them for us. I'm not sure I can look into the eyes of my dead friends' parents and tell them their kids are buried on the island.

Joe rejoins us on the deck after leaving to use the bathroom. "I just overheard one of the radio guys talking to Sheryl. They only picked up eleven survivors on the other side of the island."

"Eleven? That's it?" Henry's eyes nearly bug out of his head. "I thought..."

"I guess everyone headed to the resort when the storm was incoming. Thought it'd be the safest place to go. Turns out, there were some structural issues, and it collapsed. That whole beach flooded pretty far inland and wiped out the resort. I think if we searched any further than we did, we would've found the flooding and the bodies and the wreckage. The only survivors were a few natives to the island who opted to stay in their homes. Survived by some miracle."

"Didn't we all?" Madison's joking, I know that, but still—she's not wrong.

"There were, like, a hundred people on the island when the storm hit," Joe continues, swallowing and wiping his hands on his pants. "Only nineteen of us made it out."

"We were lucky," Sydney whispers.

“No.” Brett speaks for the first time since Sheryl told him about Spencer, shaking his head and clenching his jaw. “I don't know what we were, but we weren't lucky.”

No, we weren’t. It’s hitting me now, the realization I’ve been fighting deep in my subconscious for a few days now—that whatever version of me walked onto that island isn’t the same one about to step off this boat.

Soon enough, the boat reaches the dock, and we're impatiently waiting for Sheryl to tell us we can get the hell off and step back onto dry land. The eight of us are like elementary school kids at a concert looking for our parents in the crowd—still, silent, and scanning the area in search of familiar faces. For a while, though, all I see is what I expected: cameras, journalists, and people fighting their way to the front of the crowd while police officers and the Coast Guard hold them back.

I'm about to give up when I finally spot them: my parents, Tessa, and Emmett.

I may be the only one of us who isn’t thrilled to be reunited with my family. Seeing them forces me to acknowledge something that hits hard, like a punch to the gut: there were no consequences on the island. No laws to abide by, no punishments to fear. But that isn’t how things work here. It never was.

Island time always comes to an end sooner or later. I knew that when I stood here nine days ago. I just didn’t realize how much would change when the clock stopped ticking—and at the same time, how much would stay exactly the same.

We're pushing our way toward the gangway when I see and recognize a group of people at the very front of the crowd, battling with the Coast Guard to let them pass. A middle-aged couple, an elderly couple, and a young woman in her mid-to-late twenties. They're all wearing fine clothing, jewelry unbefitting of where they are and why they're here, with the men wearing Rolexes worth my entire tuition and the women holding designer purses worth the same.

The young woman and her mother have the same dyed blonde hair and emerald eyes. Her father's hair, though graying at the roots, is a familiar shade of sandy blonde. This is the Bishop family—James's parents, grandparents, and older sister.

His mother realizes what's happened first. She lets out a howl that pierces the air, louder than the cheering and the screaming around her, and falls to her knees. Her husband and her daughter aren't quick enough to catch her, nor do they understand why she's collapsed. Then it hits them—

but James's grandparents still haven't put the pieces together and are staring at the eight of us in confusion while we cross the gangway—and they, too, fall, forcing the Coast Guard officers to catch them before they topple to the ground.

James's father is on his feet again soon enough. *His* father finally realizes what's happened, and as the eight of us are led through the crowd and to our parents, I can already hear the two men demanding answers as to why we made it back and James didn't.

I try to shrink myself, hiding behind Henry and Joe, to avoid potentially making eye contact with any member of the Bishop family. I don't want to be seen by people who loved him.

Epilogue

Two Months Later

I didn't think we'd make it here. I don't think the others did, either.

Here we are, though. Graduation Day.

Tossed caps scattered over the lawn, camera flashes snapping in every direction, families hugging and crying tears of joy. Everything happened so quickly after the last name was called and the closing remarks were delivered. I haven't been able to spot anyone I'm supposed to be with, so I've just been taking it all in and trying my best to move out of the way when people rush past me.

I don't bother trying to find my cap on the ground within the chaos. I stop trying to find my family, too.

Instead, I lock in on the familiar head of brown hair I've grown so familiar with over the last few months, striding toward me from the other end of the aisle between rows of chairs. The mass of people between us makes it feel like he's farther away than he is, but it doesn't matter. Just knowing he's nearby makes all the noise fade into something manageable.

We meet each other halfway. "Hey," I say with a smile.

"Hey." Henry takes off his cap—he didn't throw it like the rest of us—and smooths out his hair. "You didn't fall."

I snort into a chuckle. "Ye of little faith."

"In my defense, you fell twice when we were practicing our walks," he reminds me. I just roll my eyes and mimic his smile. "What are your plans after this? My folks are wondering if you want to come out to lunch with us."

"That sounds great. Where are you thinking?"

He opens his mouth to reply, but pauses when his eyes catch something behind me. The dread on his face tells me we're facing one of two scenarios: either someone—a classmate, a professor, maybe even the dean—approaching to ask how we're holding up, if we need water or a snack, et cetera, as many of them have been since we came back to school; or my family having finally found me within the madness.

When he mutters something about giving me a minute and swivels to the side, I know it's the latter. Sighing, I turn to find all four of them walking toward me. I look back at Henry, but he's already been pulled away, and I don't get the chance to see who's responsible.

"I couldn't find you," I say when they stop in front of me.

Unfazed, my mom gives a curt response: "We weren't sure where to sit. We ended up on the other side of the field, so we couldn't see very much."

"How does it feel to be a college graduate?" Emmett asks before I can answer her.

I shrug. "The same. How did you feel when you got your degree?"

"I was on cloud nine."

"Yeah, well—"

"I hope my school colors are as cute as yours," Tessa cuts in, toying with the sleeve of my gown. "This is a good color on you."

"Thanks. I guess I…lucked out."

My dad checks his watch. "We have reservations at La Forchetta in twenty minutes. Mom let them know it's a special occasion."

"Sounds good." I'm disappointed I won't be able to spend more time with Henry and his family, and I know there's no point in asking if we can invite them. Mom doesn't like being a difficult customer, so she won't want to bother the restaurant with a change of plans. "I'll meet you at the car. I want to say goodbye to someone first."

"Be quick," Mom says, but she's already gesturing for the rest of the family to follow her to the parking lot.

I scan the crowd—still packed, though small groups are starting to break off—and lock in on Henry right away. He's standing off to the side, and I can finally register who pulled him away earlier: two girls, one lacking a cap and gown with faded pink highlights in her hair, and one dressed for graduation with unmistakable doll-like eyes.

Like he can sense me looking at him, Henry's eyes find me. Madison and Sydney follow his gaze, and Madison gives a slight jerk of her head before she starts moving. Sydney lags for a moment before following, but Henry waits for me to catch up. His hand slithers into mine when we unite, and my eyes track where the girls are headed: toward a hill behind the football field where graduation was held. Ahead of them, two men carrying their balled-up gowns are already disappearing over the top of the hill and into the quad that sits between parking lots and academic buildings.

As we walk, I see two more familiar faces nearby, both wearing gowns. They're separated, both with their families, but when they see where the rest of us are headed, they appear to tell their families to wait for a moment, just as I did, before following us.

I take a moment to examine them when we're all here. Henry's at my right, and Madison next to him, unzipping her gown to reveal a pretty white sundress underneath. Her face is void of makeup, and her hair is tied back in a simple ponytail. She hasn't worried about her hair and makeup since we got back. Her nails have been perpetually bitten down to the skin since we got back, too.

On her other side, Aaron is leaning against a tree with a cigarette dangling from his lips, the circles under his eyes darker than the maroon gown draped over one of his shoulders. His hair has gotten shaggier, and he picked up this bad smoking habit in the last few weeks.

Beside him, Joe's laying on the grass while using his gown as a pillow. He's lost a lot of weight since we got back, so his clothes are a bit loose on him, but he doesn't have that look of disarray the others do.

Sydney, across from us, has lost a lot of weight, too, and her hair looks thinner. Her arms are covered in bruises from where she pinches herself, a habit I noticed she started while we were on the plane home from Miami.

Then there's Reid between me and Sydney, still wearing his gown, flicking a lighter open and closed with one hand while fiddling with a pack of cigarettes with the other. His eyes have become vacant, lacking that goofiness that once defined his character.

Brett's not here. He didn't go to Saint Maren, either, but all of his friends did, so you'd expect him to show up today. He won't be showing up anywhere for a long time. He wasn't doing well when we got home, so his parents had to admit him to a psychiatric hospital. He's been there ever since. He and Sydney aren't together anymore, either.

Madison clears her throat. "That was some speech."

We don't have to ask to know which of the many speeches of the day she's talking about. James's parents spoke early on in the ceremony about what happened to us, and to announce the very large donation they were giving to the school. We had a moment of silence for our dead friends after that, and then we moved on like it never happened.

"They're tearing the house down." It's Aaron who speaks next, his voice dull and lackluster compared to what it used to be. "Heard through the grapevine. I guess the family went down a few weekends ago to see the damage and grab some things, and they said it reeked like decaying flesh so bad that it can't be salvaged. Demolition starts in July."

Henry frowns. "I didn't notice a smell."

"We were used to it," Sydney says softly.

No reply. After a few moments of silence, Reid speaks up: "Where's everyone headed after this?"

Not after the ceremony—after this chapter, after college, after everything.

"I'm headed down to South Carolina with Sadie." Henry flashes me a small smile. "We both got internships for fieldwork studying pollution on the coast."

"That's great. I'm happy for you two." Madison's eyes, while sad, are genuine. They have been for a while. "I'm moving home to Manhattan. My parents are letting me take a gap year before I look for a job. Not sure what I'll do."

"Same." Joe sighs. "I think I'm gonna spend a few months in Denver with my aunt. She has a wellness retreat out there. Said I can stay for as long as I want, free of charge, as long as I help out. I'll see what jobs I can find out there if I like it."

Nobody makes a joke about Joe living at a wellness retreat. Nothing about mornings spent in hot yoga or afternoons spent in meditation. We would've joked about that once, but not anymore.

"I'm actually going abroad for grad school," Sydney shares. "London. Figured I'd get as far away from this side of the world as possible."

And Brett, I think.

"My dad set me up with a job in Texas. I leave in three weeks," Aaron says dully. He raises a brow at Reid. "What about you, Reid?"

"Headed to Cali next month, actually. I have an internship. I was on the waitlist until they heard about what happened to me on the news. Pity acceptance, but still acceptance, I guess."

The silence falls heavily; so much so that even the boisterous sounds of laughter and excitable voices in the near distance feel like they're oceans away. With the cool breeze rattling the trees and the faint sound of pebbles under tires—eerily similar to wood crackling within flames—it might feel like we're back on the beach on that last night if I close my eyes and try hard enough to put myself back there.

I don't.

Madison clears her throat again and tucks a stray hair behind her ear. She looks nervous, like she's not sure how to ask the question brewing on her lips. "Have any of you told—?"

"No," everyone answers at once, like an instinct.

"Good. Good." She swallows. "We're all gonna keep that promise we made to each other, right?"

Sydney nods. "Right. Even Brett, the state he's in...I truly believe he'll never say a word about it. It's bad enough to deal with it in his head. I don't think he could handle anyone else knowing about it."

"Agreed," Joe says.

The rest of us mutter in an affirmative response.

It's quiet for a moment. Then Aaron says, "I thought about something during the speech. Didn't remember it until then." He hesitates for a beat. "The journal."

"What journal?" Reid asks. Then his expression tightens, and he turns his gaze down to his shoes. "Oh."

"Nothing to worry about," I say calmly.

Everyone's eyes are on me now, but only for a moment. I simply nod to reassure them, and that's enough to break their gazes.

His journal had made it into my bag and onto the boat somehow. I don't remember picking it up when I was collecting my things from the house before we boarded—only that it was in my hands when the shoreline was already shrinking behind us.

Nobody was looking when it slipped out of my hands. It didn't sink right away, but that was all right; everyone was distracted by the sight of the Miami port inching closer.

Aaron's eyes land on mine. "My folks are probably looking for me."

"Mine too," Reid mutters.

I nod. Only then do the two of them move, the others following close behind. I lace my fingers through Henry's as we leave the quad in silence. Some of them return to the football field while the rest of us head toward the parking lot to find our families, all fanning out in different directions.

I'm not sure where Henry's family is parked, but I see my dad's BMW up ahead, the engine running and the passenger side window down, my mom's loud octave cutting through the voices and the rolling vehicles nearby.

We walk slowly, dragging out the journey. I look up at him and take note of his distance expression while his gaze hones in on absolutely nothing ahead.

"What are you thinking?" I murmur.

He lowers his eyes to meet mine. "I'm wondering what today would look like if I hadn't broken the radio."

I picture it effortlessly—the radio in the office of the house on the island, which James spent countless hours trying to repair in hopes of calling for help. The radio I learned two months ago that Henry had broken our second day on the island to keep James busy and away from everyone else; especially me.

My lips curl into an unwitting smile. "It wouldn't have mattered. The island would've made sure of it, one way or another."

I don't ask him what he thinks might've happened. I already know.

THE END

Acknowledgements

In January of 2025, I hopped on a plane to visit my long-distance best friend. As we often do, we ended up plotting a new book idea: one she'd come up with as a fan of thrillers and disaster fiction, and one I fell in love with the instant I heard it. Over the course of my four-day trip, we spent the vast majority of it compiling pages upon pages of notes, Pinterest boards, and presentations. We were so dedicated to this project that we never realized when the sun set and the only light in the room came from our iPads.

That being said, the first person I'd like to thank is the same ingenious individual who created *Island Time,* and to whom the book is dedicated: my best friend, my platonic soulmate, and for all intents and purposes, my sister—Nina Ritter. *Island Time* wouldn't exist if you hadn't said those four little words last year: "I have an idea." This isn't the first book you've helped me create, and it certainly won't be the last. I'm a published author because of you and your eternal support, love, and encouragement. When I walked into my dormitory freshman year of college and met my roommate for the first time, I knew we'd be fast—and best—friends, but what I didn't know was that we'd end up here, creating stories together and taking the writing industry by storm. We've been a unit ever since, and there's nobody I'd rather embark on this journey with. Thank you for pushing me when I need it, filling in the blanks during my creative lapses, and for always saying the one thing that never fails to make me believe in myself: "I have a book concept that only you can write." You are my hero, and every day, I thank whichever divine force brought us together all those years ago. I love you.

Thank you Hannah, not only for editing this book and bringing it to its fullest potential, but for giving me the opportunity to help other authors do the same thing. When you hired me as a proofreader last year, I never imagined I'd end up working with you behind the scenes as an admin—nor did I imagine my boss would become one of my best friends. Thank you for your incredible work on this book, your endless support, and for helping me make my dreams come true. Everyone who knows you is made better by it!

To my friends—I've never been prouder to say that you had zero influence on my characters this time around! I'm so lucky to have such amazing friends who, thankfully, are nothing like Sadie's toxic group. Growing up with you for my entire life has taught me to know the difference between the for-lifers and the others, like Sadie's friends. We've never had to want or try to be a family or to be a part of each other's families; that, to me, is the best definition of friendship out there.

To Tasha—we're lucky enough to be family *and* second-generation best friends. I couldn't imagine my life without you: wrestling even at 25 years old, sharing our closets, and saying goodbye 15 times every time we're together in typical Italian fashion.

To my family—my sister, Chrissy, and my father, Gary: the love, encouragement, and support you show me is greater than an entire army would be capable of. Since it's been just the three of us, I've learned something that Sadie's friends never did: there's no such thing as leadership in a family. It's a collective effort on each person's part to keep the boat from sinking. I wouldn't be writing this if it weren't for you being there for me every step of the way.

To the love of my life—from the day we've met, you've supported my dreams more than some people I've known for most of my life. My dreams have become yours, and yours have become mine. The life we've built together has given me more confidence and inspiration with each day that passes. I'm becoming a better version of myself every minute I'm with you. I love you endlessly.

Finally, thank you to my readers—those who have been following my author's journey since I released *Forged in Gold* a few years ago, and those who have just found their way to my little corner of the world through *Island Time.* Thank you for taking a chance on me, for supporting me, and for being a big part of the reason authors do what we do. I'm a believer in writing for yourself first, but knowing there are readers out there whose lives might be forever changed by my stories makes all the difference in the world.

About the Author

Noelle is a pseudonym for a writer, beta reader, and editor from Boston who found her passion for writing early on and pursued it wholeheartedly. Although she is a young writer, she has been honing her craft for more than a decade, having written her first story in middle school!

While Noelle enjoys genres like romance, historical fiction, and science fiction, fantasy has always been her favorite. She fell in love with the genre at an early age after reading C.S. Lewis's *Narnia* series and William Goldman's *The Princess Bride*. Since then, her love of fantasy has only grown!

Much of Noelle's early career reflects her lifelong love of children, having worked as a nanny, infant/toddler daycare teacher, and substitute elementary teacher. However, since graduating with her BA in English Literature, she has immersed herself in the exciting realm of freelancing. When away from her writing desk, Noelle can often be found curled up with a novel or avidly working on expanding the world of her creation.

Noelle currently resides with her father, younger sister, and her feisty kitty, Nugget. *Forged in Gold* is her debut fantasy novel and marks the first of an exciting, heart-stopping series. She writes in honor of her beloved mother, who passed away from cancer in 2015.

Also By Noelle Edwards

The Golden One Trilogy:

Forged in Gold, Forged in Ashes, & Forged in Blood

The First Part of the Interconnected Epic Fantasy Saga, *The Song of the Phoenix Series!*

Available Now on Amazon!

www.ingramcontent.com/pod-product-compliance
Lightning Source LLC
LaVergne TN
LVHW100516110826
845146LV00002B/667

* 9 7 9 8 9 9 4 5 3 1 2 2 8 *